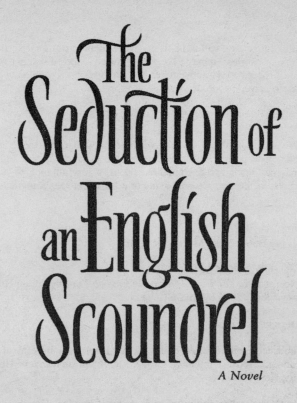

The Seduction of an English Scoundrel

A Novel

Jillian Hunter

BALLANTINE BOOKS • NEW YORK

The Seduction of an English Scoundrel is a work of fiction. Names, characters, places, and incidents are the products of the author's imagination or are used fictitiously. Any resemblance to actual events, locales, or persons, living or dead, is entirely coincidental.

An Ivy Books Mass Market Original

Copyright © 2005 by Maria Hoag
Excerpt from *The Love Affair of an English Lord* by Jillian Hunter copyright © 2005 by Maria Hoag

Published in the United States by Ivy Books, an imprint of The Random House Publishing Group, a division of Random House, Inc., New York.

Ivy Books and colophon are trademarks of Random House, Inc.

This book contains an excerpt from the forthcoming book *The Love Affair of an English Lord* by Jillian Hunter. This excerpt has been set for this edition only and may not reflect the final content of the forthcoming edition.

ISBN 0-345-46121-5

Cover and stepback illustrations: Jon Paul

Printed in the United States of America

Ballantine Books website address: www.ballantinebooks.com

OPM   9   8   7   6   5   4   3   2   1

"*What* do you want?" she whispered, holding her breath.

"To further your education." He bent his head down to hers, his blond hair brushing her cheek. "Since there are obvious deficits, I shall take a moment to provide you with the experience lacking in your background."

"What a gentlemanly thing to do."

"There's no need to thank me," he said, his eyes flickering over her like a spark.

She felt the heat of his gaze burn to her bones. "I'm sure this isn't . . . wise."

He ran his forefinger down the side of her jaw, raising shivers on her skin. "There is a time to be wise and a time to be wicked. Which do you suppose this is?"

His heavy-lidded blue eyes made her feel weak, made her heart quicken. "I think . . . I . . ."

A wanton flame kindled in the depths of his eyes. For the life of her she could not break away from his gaze. His silken voice lulled her. "Be a little wicked just once, Jane. Just for a moment."

For Linda Marrow, with appreciation for her grace, insight, and the support she has given me

Chapter 1

❦

The Boscastle-Welsham marriage would have been the wedding of the year—if the groom had bothered to put in an appearance. Sir Nigel Boscastle was so noticeably absent from his own nuptials that the bride's father had been forced to walk the long-suffering Lady Jane to the altar where, surrounded by a cluster of distraught bridesmaids, the wedding party minus the bridegroom waited. And waited.

"I shall deal with the corkbrain after the ceremony," the distinguished seventh Earl of Belshire muttered as his daughter stood with her back to their bewildered guests. "The idiot will be late to his own funeral."

After several minutes of confusion, the minister and bride's parents decided that perhaps until the bridegroom arrived, Jane's older brother, Simon, Viscount Tarleton, should stand in as temporary proxy. And so brother and abandoned bride stood. And stood.

At first no one doubted that Nigel would eventually show up to rescue Jane from this embarrassment. If, as one guest in the third pew remarked, he remembered what day it was.

After all, Sir Nigel was hardly known about town for his towering intellect, although his generosity had earned him a loyal following of friends.

The bride-to-be had not wished to be married at the popular St. George's Church in Hanover Square. A respectable young lady never previously involved in scandal, she avoided fussy affairs as a rule. Yet today the haut ton were crammed to capacity inside the private chapel of the Marquess of Sedgecroft's Park Lane mansion. To witness a wedding that apparently would not take place.

Lady Jane Welsham, the guests agreed, resembled a royal princess. She positively glowed in an eggshell white satin dress worn over an ivory tissue underbodice. The scalloped hem of the dress foamed daintily around her pearl-seeded slippers. A flowing veil of Honiton lace framed her face, casting in shadow whatever emotion it revealed, to the disappointment of her enrapt audience.

The bouquet of white rosebuds she held glistened from a double-dipping in gilt. White kidskin gloves encased her slender hands, hands that remained remarkably steady considering that their owner was undergoing one of the worst humiliations in a young woman's life. To be abandoned at the altar.

What could have happened?

Everyone in London knew that the parents of both parties had been planning this wedding since Jane and Nigel had toddled about the nursery in nappies. The Society papers had remarked more than once that rarely had a betrothed couple seemed so compatible.

What had gone wrong?

The bride's sister Lady Caroline bitterly remarked,

"Those flowers will have dried into a sachet if Nigel takes any longer. I shall strangle him for this."

Her younger sister, Lady Miranda, shook her head in sympathy. "Poor Nigel. Do you think he might have gotten lost? Jane did say he required a map to find his carriage."

Caroline's golden-brown eyes narrowed in contemplation. "She's holding up well under the humiliation, isn't she?"

"Would you expect less of a Welsham?" Miranda whispered back.

"I don't know," Caroline replied, "but I daresay that such bad behavior is probably typical of the Boscastle male. For all his gentle ways, Nigel did descend from one of the most notorious bloodlines in England. Just look at our host Sedgecroft over there, lounging like the lord of lions in his pew with his ladybirds around him."

"His what?" Miranda asked in a scandalized whisper.

"I can hardly shout out the word, Miranda. That woman in the deep pink dress is Lady Greenhall, his last lover."

"And he brought her here, to Jane's wedding?"

"If there is one."

"Well, his brothers are said to be no better," Miranda added. "The lot of them should have their foreheads branded with an *R* for rogue."

"I wonder what Sedgecroft thinks of all this," Caroline murmured. "He does not look exactly pleased, does he?"

The host in question, the chapel's owner, Grayson Boscastle, the fifth Marquess of Sedgecroft, sat thinking that the bride had the most appealing derriere he had seen in quite a long time. Not that he made a point of lusting after young women in wedding dresses, but he had been staring at the back of her for over two hours now. A normal man's curiosity could not help but be aroused. What else was he to look at? He wondered whether the rest of her was as appealing.

Besides, he was pointedly ignoring the guests in his family's pews: various cousins and dozing uncles; two former mistresses, one of whom had brought along her bumpkin sons; and his three younger brothers, who were sprawled out in irreverent disregard for the holy ceremony.

If the ceremony ever came to its usual unhappy conclusion, that is, the entrapment of another man in wedlock.

His brother, Lieutenant Colonel Lord Heath Boscastle, leaned forward from the pew behind him. "What do you think?" he asked in amusement. "Should we start taking bets on whether he'll show?"

"He'd better show or answer to me," Grayson said darkly. "I've spent half a day already staring at—well, staring at something usually reserved for a husband's eyes, let us say." Nigel happened to be their cousin, a Boscastle whom Grayson actually liked, although at the moment he felt like clobbering him for being such a dolt.

A grin broke across Heath's handsome face. "The last time I saw such a collection of Boscastles in church was at Father's funeral. Who invited the mistresses?"

"I think I did," Grayson said, suppressing a yawn. "God knows I've been sitting here so long my brain's gone stiff."

"You invited them to a wedding?"

"It's not my wedding, thank God."

"Well, it is your chapel."

"Ergo, I invite whom I please."

"Someone might have thought to invite the groom."

Grayson folded his arms across the chest of his charcoal gray long-tailed coat. "This thing has gone on so long I'm tempted to marry the woman myself."

"Say it isn't so."

Grayson gave a deep laugh. "It isn't."

"By the way," Heath said, stifling his own laughter, "I had to refuse a supper invitation for the pair of us at Audrey's last evening. Where the blazes were you when I called?"

Grayson grunted. "Flushing Drake and Devon out of gaming hells so we could put on a pretense of family approval for this wedding."

"I thought nuptials made you nervous."

Grayson's blue eyes glittered with devilish lights. "The avowed bachelor in me is dying by the moment."

Heath's grin faded. "And the soldier in me senses the trouble has only begun. How is the hot-blooded Helene?"

"Considerably cooler the last time I saw her, at least toward me. We did not come to an arrangement."

"Ah. So, anyone new caught your eye?"

"No."

"No, Gray? Not yet?"

Grayson glanced around. Two of his former mistresses appeared to be engaged in a battle of frosty glares. Open hostilities seemed possible.

His younger brothers, Drake and Devon, and one of Drake's disreputable gambling friends had been discussing a certain young demirep they had met last night.

The discussion had escalated to an argument when the trio discovered she had promised herself to them all. A fight seemed inevitable.

Chloe, the younger of Grayson's two sisters, leaned from her pew to whisper to the bridesmaids, all of whom looked more upset than the bride.

Seeded like grenades amid these three dangerous camps sat a small but select group of the beau monde. Politicians, aristocrats, debutantes, and marriage-bent matrons who regarded Grayson much like a fortress to be seized.

He placed his fingers inside his neckcloth as if to ward off the marriage noose. It undid him, the air of holy matrimony, the warring mistresses, the militant bridesmaids, the responsibilities he had inherited almost overnight. No one, least of all him, had expected the sudden death of his father last year when the marquess had learned that his youngest son, Brandon, had been killed in Nepal. Grayson still blamed himself for not being there to deliver the news.

The weight of family obligation had fallen upon his broad shoulders like a shroud. There had been so many questions he longed to ask his father, and now it was too late. The selfish pursuits he had so enjoyed suddenly held no appeal. He could find little pleasure in his previous life.

He did not like the man he had become, and lately had begun to wonder if he could ever change.

And now this, his first public test as patriarch of the Boscastle clan. How to handle the abandonment of the bride by his own cabbage head of a cousin.

"What does one do in such a situation?" he muttered to himself.

Heath shook his head, looking mystified. "It's too bad our Emma is so far away in Scotland. She'd know exactly what to do."

Emma, their older sister, had been recently widowed and was giving etiquette instructions to the elite of Edinburgh to occupy her empty hours.

Grayson returned to his leisurely, more enjoyable inspection of the bride's heart-shaped backside. Very, very nice, he thought. Not a bad choice at all for a bride, if one had to choose one. Of course, Nigel had already claimed her. A pity he hadn't shown to pick up the package. Still, who knew what lurked in the shadows of that veil? A beauty or a beast? A siren or a shrew?

This provocative rake's reverie ended when Heath tapped him on the shoulder to speak again. "The bride is quite lovely, isn't she?"

"Hmm." He steepled his fingers under his clefted chin, his expression neutral. "I haven't made a study of it. I suppose she might be. It is hardly a thing I would notice."

"You great liar, Grayson," Heath said with a subdued laugh. "Those blue eyes of yours are absorbing every detail right down to her garters."

Well, some of his less admirable qualities had not changed. He was still a man even if he wasn't sure of anything else.

"That is a rather crude remark to be making in chapel, Heath," he said with mock piety, as he eyed his once-mistress Mrs. Parks from the other end of the pew, where she sat between her two boisterous offspring from a previous affair. She had been a successful mantua maker when she'd taken up three years ago with Grayson. His generous pension had left her nicely settled for life, and she maintained a friendly relationship with him. "Need I remind you, dear brother, that we are in a holy sanctuary?"

"Is this your first time here, Grayson?" Heath inquired in a droll voice.

"Second," he whispered, clearing his throat.

He took another look around the chapel. One of the bridesmaids had started crying. The bride was comforting her. The guests were definitely becoming restless, squirming in their seats, wondering in whispers what was to happen. He was going to have to take action soon, make up some ludicrous excuse for Nigel's behavior. He began practicing in his mind.

It was highly improbable, but he could not rule out the possibility that his blasted fool of a cousin had fallen down the stairs in one of his satin slippers and knocked himself unconscious. The guests who knew Nigel would not find this difficult to believe.

He turned his attention back to the appealing figure who stood at the altar with her white shoulders held high. A man would have to possess a heart of stone not to feel some empathy, some urge to protect her from the pain his own relative had inflicted.

He spoke quietly to Heath. "One has to admire her for not bursting into hysterical tears or shredding her flowers in a fit as a few other women I know might have done." And with this, he directed a teasing frown at Lady Greenhall and Mrs. Parks, neither of whom were known for their submissiveness.

From one of the pews on the same side of the nave, an elderly MP had just been awakened by his wife. In a befuddled shout, he asked if the accursed wedding was over yet.

"It never began," Mrs. Parks whispered to him in embarrassment. "The groom appears to have gone missing."

The gentleman shook his head, gazing in pity at the abandoned heroine at the altar. "She's bearing up well, I'd say," he said gruffly. "Stoic, like her father. That's the stuff of old stock. Welsham backbone can't be broken."

"The poor innocent must be shattered," Mrs. Parks murmured, sniffing back tears. "To be jilted by the man she has loved her entire life. I wonder what she thinks of this."

What Lady Jane Welsham thought could hardly be repeated in polite company. Her primary concern was to rush home and remove her silk corset and small bustle. The steel buckram underpinnings were squeezing the breath from her like a bellows. Surely she had stood here suffering long enough. Surely by now it was obvious to everyone that she had been jilted.

Her second concern centered around her mother, a delicate flower of femininity who did not hail from Papa's heartier Saxon lineage. Her mama appeared to be quite beside herself. She seemed unable to believe that any young woman, let alone her own daughter, could endure such public shame.

"The only acceptable explanation is that Nigel has been killed," Lady Belshire passionately told anyone who would listen.

To which the earl, with equal passion, replied, "He certainly will be when I get a hold of him."

"But they have been promised to each other forever," his wife said tearfully. "On the day they were born, we all agreed that their future was destined for this—this debacle."

Jane released a deep sigh, burying her nose in her bridal bouquet. The social embarrassment she could withstand, but she did hate to see Mama so distressed that the fairy tale she had plotted would not have the chosen prince at the ending.

The bride's dispirited sigh was interpreted by most of the guests to indicate that she had reached the end of her tether. Her tender maiden's heart was broken. One could almost hear it shattering in her chest. Who could blame her? How could Sir Nigel inflict such indignity upon the young woman who had served as his constant companion and champion since boyhood?

Of course a few malicious opinions did rear their ugly heads here and there, primarily between the debs who had always resented Jane's social standing and bluestocking tendencies, her refusal to follow the herd. And there—

Jane's broken heart leaped into her throat. Her gaze had just connected with a pair of sultry blue eyes that sent the most unsettling shiver of awareness down her back. Struggling to catch her breath, she assessed the rest of this compelling person in a covert glance between the gilt-tipped petals of her bouquet. Oh, goodness, goodness, goodness. So *that* was the scandalous Sedgecroft. That magnificent, menacing specimen of manhood could only be the infamous cousin of whom Nigel had spoken so disparagingly. Jane had always secretly hoped to meet him, but certainly not like this.

"Bear up," her father whispered in her ear. "We shall survive this."

"The Welshams have endured far worse," her brother added, giving her an awkward thump on the shoulder.

Her sister Caroline scowled at him. "Not in this century they haven't."

Jane nodded solemnly, not actually hearing a word. It was the first time she had actually gotten a close look at her host, the notorious Marquess of Sedgecroft, in the flesh. All six feet and several inches of impressive flesh he was, too. She felt a little light-headed at the sight of him, or was her corset obstructing the flow of blood to her brain?

"That is Sedgecroft sitting in the front pew, isn't it?" she whispered behind her bouquet to Caroline.

Caroline's delicate face darkened in distress. "Good gracious, Jane, do not look into his eyes, whatever you do. You might fall under the curse of the Boscastle Blues."

Jane dared another look. "Whatever are you talking about?"

"It is said," Caroline whispered hurriedly, "that whenever a woman looks into those eyes for the first time, she is—oh, what am I saying. You already fell in love with a Boscastle, and your luck couldn't get any worse than it is now. I am heartsick for you, Jane. I must say you are holding up admirably."

"It is a trial, Caroline."

"It must be. My word, three of Sedgecroft's brothers here and a challenge has not been issued. It's a miracle the chapel walls have not fallen down. I don't know where one could find such a collection of imposing, troublemaking entities outside of Mount Olympus."

Jane smiled at that; she and her sisters all tended to wax dramatic under times of duress. Yet it was true. Most of the Boscastle brood did appear to be present for her public shaming. The four handsome men towered head and shoulders above the less physically endowed guests. Chatting and laughing at intervals, the three youngest lounged idly in their pews, while the marquess presided over them in all his leonine glory.

She swallowed, feeling another shiver race down her spine. Sedgecroft's entire demeanor bespoke irritation, and no wonder. He had extended his hospitality to host his cousin's wedding, and by the look on his face, there would be the devil to pay for putting him out. Jane hoped to be hidden away before he lost his temper. She planned to make her escape as soon as possible.

"Do you want me to find a vinaigrette for you?" Miranda asked in concern.

"Whatever for?" Jane tore her gaze away from her intimidating golden-haired host.

"You do look a trifle faint all of a sudden," Caroline said in sympathy.

That would be Sedgecroft's fault, Jane thought with a stab of annoyance. Even halfway across the chapel she could sense he was a man who would not appreciate being inconvenienced. Heaven help her if he took it upon himself to personally investigate Nigel's disappearance, although such a measure did not seem likely.

He appeared to have his hands full enough keeping his own clan under control. Not to mention the two very attractive women who kept whispering to him in a way that suggested a strong personal association.

"Save the vinaigrette for Nigel's mother," she whispered, her cheeks suddenly warm at the thought of Sedgecroft and his lovers witnessing her failed wedding. "I think she's swooned at least five times in the past hour."

"I believe she's taking this whole disaster harder then you are, Jane," Caroline said pensively.

"Jane is merely better at hiding her feelings," Miranda whispered.

A pall of silence fell. Jane stole another peek at Sedgecroft. He looked as restless as she felt. Then Simon asked, "Well, how much longer are we supposed to wait?"

Jane reached down to tug the hem of her gown from beneath her father's shoe. She felt as if she were sinking under the weight of her wedding garments. Socially speaking, of course, she was sunk.

Probably no one who counted would want to wed her after this. Not unless she found a man brave enough to love her beyond reason. Her parents would never dare arrange another marriage. It seemed likely that they might even be afraid to meddle in her sisters' affairs, thereby saving Caroline and Miranda from unhappy unions. The three of them would have to find husbands for themselves.

Jane could barely restrain the impulse to hurl her bouquet in the air and let out a whoop of joy.

The cloud of despair that had darkened the long months of her engagement began to dissipate. Sunshine peeked through. She had done it. She had actually eluded the fate she had dreaded.

"Three hours," her father muttered, staring in disbelief at his golden pocket watch. "That's long enough. Simon, help me escort her to the carriage. One on either side of her in case she collapses from the humiliation."

Lady Belshire gazed around in horror. "Not in public, Howard. Think of all the common people outside, waiting to catch a glimpse of the wedding party. All they shall see is a . . . a collapsed bride."

"I shall walk out on my own," Jane murmured, stung by a prick of guilt at the death of their dreams. Even though it meant the rebirth of her own secret hopes.

This wedding had never been *her* dream. Nor had it been Nigel's.

In fact, at this very moment, Nigel was probably exchanging vows with the woman he had passionately desired for the past four years. The robust Boscastle governess who had dedicated a decade of her young life to supervising the wild clan at their country estate. Jane envied the two of them their future; despite the fact that Nigel's father would surely cut him off without a penny, Nigel would spend his life with the woman he loved.

And that woman had never been Jane. Nor had she loved him, except in the warmest, most affectionate manner. Marrying Nigel would have been tantamount to marrying a brother, a union that neither of them wished, although they had never been able to convince their parents of this.

"What could Nigel be doing as we stand here like a party of proper idiots?" muttered her brother as he grabbed her arm to prop her up for the escape to the carriage.

"Unhand me, Simon," she whispered sharply. "I have never been the fainting sort in my life."

A huge shadow fell across the altar, and a profound silence suddenly engulfed the chapel, stilling whispers. An unnerving chill of foreboding swept through Jane's willowy frame. The shocked expressions on her sisters' faces heightened her presentiment of doom.

"Oh," Caroline whispered, her face as white as her sister's wedding gown. "It's *him*. Dear heaven."

"Him?" Jane whispered, her dark green eyes widening. "Which him?"

Her brother had slipped away, dropping her arm as if it were a loaded pistol. He, too, was staring up at the shadow in a fascinating mix of dread and . . . *respect*.

Her bridal bouquet crushed to her silk-laced décolletage like a shield, she turned to confront her fate. And stared up at the most indecently beautiful face she had ever seen.

Him. The Most Honorable the Marquess of Sedgecroft.

Sedgecroft, who cast a shadow that swallowed her up from her head to the tips of her wedding slippers. Sedgecroft of the stormy blue eyes and steel-muscled body, of a scoundrel's fame and libertine lifestyle, the most charming rascal to entertain the scandal-loving ton. The man in whose chapel she had hoped to pull off her daring scheme. Sedgecroft looking embarrassed and capable and—

What on earth could he be doing at the altar?

She felt the wild palpitations of her heart against the rose petals that she held in a death grip. The strangest thoughts raced inside her mind. She decided a sculptor would have delighted in chiseling Sedgecroft's face, all those proud bones and hard angles, that cleft chin.

Not to mention that sinfully molded mouth, and his manly shoulders. Jane tried to estimate how much broadcloth his tailor would require to stretch across the musculature of his back. And was it true that he and his last mistress had once made love in the Tower?

His deep voice startled her from her embarrassing reverie. "I am profoundly ashamed."

Ashamed? *He* was ashamed? Well, he probably had a hundred good reasons for confessing this, but none unfortunately in which Jane had taken part. She shared a bewildered glance with her sisters. "I beg your pardon. You said you were—"

"Ashamed. On my cousin's behalf. Is there anything I can do?"

"Do?"

"Yes. About this"—he swept his large hand through the air—"this sad affair."

"I think I can manage," Jane replied, then added, "but it is nice of you to offer."

His low pleasant voice sent a peculiar wash of heat swirling through her veins. She had expected a man of his reputation to deny any responsibility in the matter. Not to offer personal assistance. She wondered if he used this endearingly concerned manner with his bevy of love-stricken mistresses and admirers. What an effective way to melt a woman's heart.

Her father bustled between them. "We're facing a tactical problem, Sedgecroft—how to get her to the carriage through the crush outside."

Sedgecroft glanced appraisingly at Jane, an experienced look that seemed to penetrate to her bare bones, to all her wicked secrets, to her most private hopes and fears. "That is not a problem. She may go through the vestry door and use one of my carriages. Unless for some reason you prefer your own vehicle." He paused, studying Jane again. "I could escort her through the gates myself. I could carry her, if it comes to that. That would give the populace a reason to talk."

Caroline drew a breath, and Miranda's eyes widened in amused disbelief. Jane groped for Simon's arm, clasping his wrist in such panic that he turned to frown at her.

"Help," she whispered weakly.

"I thought you had never fainted in your life," he muttered.

She raised her bouquet to whisper back. "This might be the day I make an exception. Could he be serious?"

A glimmer of admiration lit Simon's eyes. "With Sedgecroft, one can never be sure. I've seen him bluff his way at cards to win a fortune."

She stole another glance at that magnificent face and recognized the traces of good humor that the marquess had presumably suppressed, perhaps out of concern for her feelings. She was again pleasantly surprised. Rumors of his family's rash behavior had circulated in the ton's drawing rooms for years.

"I do not think it will be necessary to carry me," she said, although under different circumstances a woman might certainly have been tempted to take him up on the offer.

"No?"

She was horrified at the hot blush that burned her neck as she looked into his blue eyes and found herself captured by a sensual appeal that he seemed to exude almost as second nature. Jane might have been completely overwhelmed by all this blatant male charm if she hadn't been so intent on bringing the situation to an end.

Carry her to the carriage, indeed. Talk about creating a scandal. Although she had to admit those proud shoulders of his looked more then capable of the job— oh, what was she thinking? This was hardly the time or place to go to pieces over a handsome stranger.

"I am prepared to walk to the carriage and face the crowds," she said.

"Of course," he said, his voice polite and deferential.

Lord Belshire gave the marquess an anxious look. "I don't suppose you know anything about where Nigel is."

A cold determination settled on Grayson's face. His reply struck straight to the center of Jane's heart.

"I intend to find out what happened today, believe me." He looked directly at Jane, as if trying to penetrate the shadows of the wedding veil that framed her face. "I know this is a difficult time for you, but please tell me— did you and Nigel have a fight by any chance?" he asked.

She shook her head slowly. She and Nigel had parted the best of friends, in complete agreement that they did not belong together as man and wife. "No. No fights."

Sedgecroft pursed his lips as if he suspected something vital had been omitted from her response. "No little lovers' quarrel that you might have forgotten in all the excitement? No misunderstandings?"

Jane took a moment to answer, murmuring, "Nigel and I understood each other perfectly."

"He must be dead," Lady Belshire said, gazing disconsolately around the chapel. "Jane, I think it would be wise to accept Sedgecroft's kind offer."

Jane looked aghast. "Mama, I am not going to be borne through the crowds like a . . . a football."

Lady Belshire fanned her pink cheeks in embarrassment. "I meant his offer of the carriage, Jane. My goodness, there is no need for the common folk to be gossiping over this."

Lord Belshire gave his wife a grim smile. "Steel yourself, Athena. The story will be printed in all its nasty scandal in the evening papers. There is nothing to do but brazen it out as best we can. Sedgecroft?"

The marquess stirred, as if wondering how he'd managed to become personally involved in this family drama.

"One of my brothers will escort your daughter home while I take care of matters here," he answered. "The guests may as well enjoy the wedding breakfast." He squared his impressive shoulders, his gaze burning with a blue fire that took Jane's breath away. "I will make this right," he added softly, his voice underlaid with all the arrogance of his aristocratic background.

For a dangerous moment Jane almost laughed out loud. Here she stood at the altar with an infamous rogue who had never spoken two words to her in her life, vowing to avenge a wrong that had actually not occurred.

The promise might certainly be meant to reassure her, given by a man who had probably never accepted a rejection in his life. Instead, it had the opposite effect. Rather than feeling comforted, every self-protective instinct that Jane possessed came hurtling forward in warning.

By sabotaging her own marriage, she had thought to make herself safe. Instead, a danger far more insidious than any she could have previously imagined stood before her. Indeed, her scheme today might have brought her to the very gates of hell . . . with the devil himself waiting to claim her deceptive soul.

Chapter 2

Weed, the senior footman in Sedgecroft's London residence, reported to his master less than an hour later in the huge reception hall. Here, beneath a domed ceiling the wedding breakfast had been laid out in a splendor of sparkling crystal, Sèvres china, and polished silverware on crisp white linen tablecloths. After a spell of awkward hesitation, the guests had attacked the lobster salad and champagne as if everything were perfectly normal.

As if the high-backed Chippendale chairs reserved for the bride and bridegroom were not sadly empty.

As if their toplofty host were not presiding over the celebration like a medieval warlord who had ordered his vassals to enjoy themselves while he brooded on plans for his revenge.

"I did as you asked," Weed said in an undertone, bending over Grayson on the pretext of refilling his champagne glass. "Our pigeon has flown the coop."

Grayson's face tightened dangerously. He had little tolerance for a man who lacked the guts to fulfill whatever promises he had been foolish enough to make, especially when that man was a family relation who had used Grayson's chapel to commit his social crime. "Are you certain?"

"His wardrobe and drawers have been emptied, my lord. The servants claimed to have no inkling of his plans—his valet reported the bed unoccupied when he brought up the shaving water earlier this morning. Seeing as Sir Nigel's carriage was still on the premises, everyone assumed he'd gone for an early-morning walk to calm his nerves."

"And never returned," Grayson said in contempt, his opinion of his cousin lowering by the minute. It might have been better all the way around if Nigel had been run over by a hackney or some sort of ridiculous excuse for leaving that young woman at the altar.

"I suppose there is still the possibility of foul play," Weed said doubtfully.

Grayson's brother, Heath, sauntered up to the other side of the chair. "What has happened?" he asked quietly, smiling at the guests who watched him, matrons marking him as a desirable target for their unwed daughters, assuming his elusive heart could be caught. The marquess, of course, would rank first on their list, but no eligible young woman had yet attracted his eye, either, although many had gone to preposterous lengths in this pursuit.

The taming of the Boscastle clan and ensuing matrimonial capture challenged a good many of the ton's wedlock-obsessed mamas. All that wealth, those excessive good looks, their generosity to the few they held dear . . .

"Nigel's gone missing on us," Grayson said, his tapered fingers curled around the scrolled stem of his glass.

"Missing?" Heath gave a cynical laugh. "In the middle of London on his wedding day? I do not think so."

Grayson arched his brow. "Nor do I. The point is, he cannot be found. The question remains, why."

Heath folded his arms across his chest. "We shall need a Bow Street man."

"No," Grayson said quietly, torn between family loyalty and the odd sense of responsibility he felt for the whole unhappy affair. If Belshire's daughter had thrown a tantrum or wept piteously, he might not have been so touched by her abandonment. But her composed acceptance challenged him to defend her. Why? He wasn't sure. Perhaps because no one else appeared likely to assume that role.

He added, "If the rascal has decamped on us and is not lying dead in a gutter, it is and shall remain a family affair."

"Yes," Heath murmured. "And so we keep it quiet. Well, as quiet as possible considering the fact that half of London already knows by now what he did."

Grayson's eyes narrowed. He'd never had any patience with the small-mindedness of society. It brought out a beastly urge in him to act on his most shocking impulses just to show he did not care. The trouble was, he was no longer the prodigal son who could behave however he pleased.

He said, "Gossip is best dealt with by being ignored. His parents are utterly crushed, to say nothing of the bride. I suppose it's up to me to smooth things down for the family."

"You, Gray, a peacemaker? Now there's a lightning bolt from the heavens. I do believe I like it."

None of the six remaining siblings had accustomed themselves to the drastic shift the past year had wrought in the Boscastle hierarchy. Their father had appeared in excellent health until two months before his death. Everyone had expected the old tyrant to go on for decades. And when their youngest brother, Brandon, had been killed while protecting British interests in Nepal, it seemed impossible such a hale young man would not return.

The family had still not recovered from the shock. The reins of responsibility had been tossed into Grayson's lap before he realized quite what had happened. In fact, he had been on his way to China when the news of his father's untimely demise was delivered.

Almost overnight he had been forced to abandon his private pursuits and settle his abundant energy on the management of his vast estates. Boxing, drinking, steeplechasing, traveling to exotic lands in the name of business would have to wait. His time was taken up with finances, family affairs, the pension for his ailing aunts, and the countless charities his parents had supported.

Not to mention the Boscastle clan—three hell-raising brothers; one sister who would dearly love to follow in their path; another in Scotland who had virtually disowned the family; and numerous cousins, including the missing Nigel, most of whom did not appear to have a sensible bone in their collective body. To be a Boscastle meant to ignore boundaries.

Of course if anyone had told Grayson a year ago that he would have been viewing the world from his father's eyes, and not from his usual moment-to-moment hedonism, he would have laughed himself silly.

If this family were to survive, it would clearly be up to him. And in recent weeks, from murky emotional depths he did not care to explore, came the realization that his wretched family meant rather a lot to him. The double loss of his brother and father had brought this startling truth home. Still, responsibility sent a hell of a shock through a rake's system.

"What do we do then?" Heath asked, smiling fleetingly at an attractive young woman across the table.

Grayson sat back in amusement. "Can you tear yourself away from the females long enough to be of service?"

"Me? This from a man who had two past paramours waiting to pounce on him from their pews. But, yes." Heath sobered, his dark blue eyes intent. "I shall help."

Grayson gave a nod. Only a handful of people knew of Heath's involvement with British Intelligence during the war. Grayson himself did not know the details; nor would he pressure his brother to reveal what he had done. The point was that beneath Heath's quiet charm and winning manner lay a quick intellect and almost frightening disregard for danger. Privately he wished to be a little more like his younger brother, calculating his every move instead of acting rashly and regretting it latter.

"Find Nigel for me."

Heath finished his glass of punch. "Consider it done. And then what happens?"

"Then we drag the repentant rat to the altar to finish this business. Take Devon with you if you like. It will keep him out of trouble." Grayson cast a searching glance around the table; he'd just noticed that the two places reserved for his younger brothers were vacant. Drake had not returned after escorting the jilted bride home. "Where *is* Devon?"

Heath adjusted his cuffs. "Gone off with some old friends he met in Covent Garden last week. They've got him looking for pirate treasure off Penzance. A gypsy fortune-teller saw it in her crystal ball."

"God bless us," Grayson said. "This family is going to hell in a handbasket."

"And you our exalted leader," said the raven-haired Lady Chloe Boscastle, who had been sipping champagne the entire time from her nearby chair. "We only follow your example, dear brother."

Grayson released a sigh. The family was doomed if they followed his example. Yet he could not ignore the fact of *his* influence. What was he to do? Repent? Sin in secret? How long could a man pretend his actions did not affect others?

Heaven help him, was he in serious danger of becoming a moral creature?

Grayson glanced over his shoulder at the footman standing against the wall. Suddenly it seemed easier to ponder the sins of others than contemplate his own. Distraction would help deflect him from considering his own murky character. "Has my carriage returned yet, Weed?"

"A few minutes ago, my lord."

"And how did our abandoned bride appear?"

"Eager to be inside the house, I am told, and begging to be left alone."

"She held up remarkably well," Heath said. "I do admire that."

Grayson tried to picture nondescript Nigel with the winsome young woman whose trust he had betrayed. It was difficult to imagine them together, oddly unsettling, in fact.

Chloe shook her dark head in sympathy. "She'll probably never venture from her room again. If I were in her place, I would console myself by roaming the Continent, and taking handsome lovers to heal my heart."

Grayson gave his beautiful blue-eyed sister a reproachful look. "Let us hope that the young lady does not take her revenge to such an absurd degree."

"I mean it, Gray," she said, her voice passionate. "What happened to her today is too horrible to bear by half. I had a friend at school who threw herself into the Thames over a man who left her at the altar. A woman does not ever recover from that deep a betrayal. It has to leave a very painful wound."

In his mind's eye Grayson saw a graceful back, delicate hands hidden in pearl-buttoned gloves, and a face mysteriously half revealed in the shadowy folds of a wedding veil. A composed face of classical features, a refined nose and full tempting mouth. Dark green eyes thankfully not overflowing with dramatic tears, but gazing up at him with an acceptance that almost challenged him to atone for a wrong he had never even committed.

His heavy eyebrows drew into a frown. "The lady did not strike me as the type to do anything quite so desperate as to take her own life." Especially over a nitwit like Nigel, he added silently.

"But it is the death of her in polite society," Chloe insisted, with a shrug of her bare shoulders. "You must do something to make this right, being the head of the family. If you don't, Jane will never be able to show her face in public again."

Grayson thought of the enticing honey-haired maiden sitting alone in stoic misery for the rest of her life. What a deplorable waste of womanhood. "I intend to do something." But *what* he could not say. God forbid that his interference should make the matter worse. He wasn't particularly known for his eagerness to do good deeds. Yet Grayson had always felt a curious compulsion to defend the downtrodden, presumably out of guilt over his own undeserved good fortune.

He glanced up. "Heath?"

"I'll be gone in an hour."

"Thrash the bachelor out of him, but leave no visible marks."

"Why not?"

Grayson smiled grimly. "I do not want him to look disreputable when he is dragged back to the altar."

Chapter 3

Forty-five minutes later Grayson rode through the ornamental gates of the Earl of Belshire's Grosvenor Square home. As his horse was stabled, he noticed that the drapes at the bow windows of the house had been tightly drawn. A morose-looking footman escorted him into one of five formal reception rooms. His own personal visit to Nigel's town house had yielded no helpful clues as to his disappearance.

He stood for several minutes and watched the servants tiptoeing past the door in painstaking silence. Indeed, a pall of profound gloom enshrouded the mansion as if a family member had died unexpectedly. He wondered how the rather impulsive notion that had brought him here would be received. How the jilted bride would feel about his offer to act as her temporary protector, a social proxy for his stupid cousin. With any luck Nigel would appear before Grayson's scheme could be launched. He had no idea how he would go about implementing it, of course. But someone would have to shield her and her family from the inevitable scandal.

As the highest-ranking member of his own family, he

supposed that dubious honor had fallen to him. After all, he had the power and popularity to help, and it provided a bit of novelty, being the white knight for a change.

The true surprise of the day was that it had not been *he* who had caused a scandal.

His motives were not entirely unselfish. For one thing, he hoped to avoid having the family name dragged into a lawsuit. For another, he intended to put an end to the self-destructive behavior to which he and his siblings seemed so naturally drawn.

Lord and Lady Belshire seemed somewhat bewildered by his appearance in their drawing room. Lady Belshire had in fact just finished half a bottle of sherry; the earl's graying black hair stood in disarrayed tufts, his neck-cloth askew, but other than that he managed to present his usual distinguished self to this unexpected caller.

"Sedgecroft. Have a drink. Have you found the black-guard?"

"Not yet." Grayson glanced over his shoulder at the two comely young ladies who sat on the sofa pretending to work on their embroidery. The chilly frowns they sent him between stitches could have turned his entire body to stone. As if he by familial association was responsible for their sister's abandonment.

"Heath is gone on that quest and will be discreet," he added. "If Nigel is alive, he shall be brought back to perform his duty."

Lady Belshire hiccoughed behind her hand. "I confess I rather hope he's found dead. At least it would be an acceptable excuse for what he did to my daughter today."

"Rake," murmured one of the two daughters on the sofa.

"Rogue," added her sister in a crisp undertone.

Grayson examined them from the corner of his eye. He had the distinct impression they were not referring exclusively to Nigel, although, for God's sake, one could accuse his cousin of many faults, stupidity being foremost. But Nigel had never been known for his womanizing skills.

Which made it all the more disturbing that the nodcock had left a beauty like Lady Jane at the altar. But then perhaps her elegant dignity had frightened off the fool. Perhaps, for all Grayson knew, Nigel had run off with a man. Stranger things had happened. Take him, for example, trying to repair a wrong he hadn't done.

He frowned, glancing back to the earl who had collapsed in an armchair, a fat spaniel positioned on his lap. "I would like to speak to your daughter, Belshire. In private, if you please. Someone has to make amends in the Boscastle name."

Grayson had no intention of asking Belshire's permission for what else he had in mind until he presented his plan to the jilted bride. If Jane objected, well, at least he could say he had tried. There was no point in taking his scheme to her parents. Neither Athena nor Howard looked capable of decision making at the moment, emotionally crushed by the day's unprecedented disaster.

The two young women on the sofa rose in a surge of sisterly support. Grayson studied them. One possessed mahogany-gold hair, the other was a fetching brunette. Good looks certainly seemed to run in the females of this family.

As did a rather disconcerting self-assurance.

"What do you want to see Jane for?" demanded the darker-haired sister.

The other added, "She is hardly in the mood for a social call, considering what your cousin did to her today."

"I understand that," he said smoothly.

"I doubt she will see you," the brunette said.

Grayson shrugged. He had a feeling she was mistaken. "It doesn't hurt to try."

"Your appearance here is bad timing, Sedgecroft," Lord Belshire said irritably. "Perhaps you could make your apologies to her at a later date."

"When one falls off a horse," Grayson said guardedly. "one is best advised to remount immediately."

Lady Belshire plunked her sherry glass down on the side table, her eyes glittering with interest. "What sort of remounting are we discussing, Sedgecroft?"

Grayson hesitated, choosing his words with care lest his offer be misinterpreted. "The worst thing your daughter can do is to remove herself from Society. In the event Nigel is not brought around, she will want to attract another husband." Preferably, he thought, one with half a brain to appreciate what his cousin had so mysteriously discarded.

"Are you offering to marry my sister?" the taller of the two other women asked in a tone halfway between hope and horror.

"No," he said quickly, horrified himself at the thought. "I am not. It is my intention to help relaunch her back into Society as soon as possible. The longer she waits, the harder it will be to make her return."

"He does have a point, Howard," Lady Belshire murmured. "If Jane withdraws indefinitely, she will drift into spinsterhood and eventually cease to exist. And Sedgecroft is well considered in Society."

The earl clapped his vinegar cloth back onto his forehead. "Oh, what the devil, Sedgecroft. Do what you can to help her. Jane hasn't spoken a civil word to me in months. She expressed doubts about marrying Nigel, but did I listen? I thought they secretly adored each other. You young people today are entirely too—oh, blast. What do I know of love?"

"What does anyone know?" Grayson murmured, turning to find the two sisters gazing at him as if he had suddenly sprouted horns and a forked tail.

"How long do you think this . . . relaunching will take?" Lady Belshire asked.

Grayson shrugged his broad shoulders. "Not long. I intend to squire Jane around town only until she begins to attract the serious interest of a few acceptable suitors. In time, I would hope she would recover enough to return to her previous life."

"The fact that a marquess finds her desirable will certainly pique the ton's interest," Athena said with a thoughtful frown. "I do see potential in this, Sedgecroft. It is decent of you to consider her future. Without help, Jane is likely to become a lost cause."

"I mean to set an example for the rest of my family," he replied. Although God knew that such self-sacrifice did not come naturally to him. Nor did the complications of even a superficial courtship. "I might not have ever asked a woman to meet me at the altar," he said, "but I have never left one standing there either. I am not utterly without morals, as a few people seem to believe."

Lord Belshire cracked open one eye. "Setting an example is all well and good, my friend, but I do have one minor reservation. You have a bit of a rake's reputation."

"A bit?" both sisters cried in unison.

"Which could make him all the more attractive a suitor for Jane," Lady Belshire said thoughtfully. "Only a woman of considerable charm can attract the attention of a man like Sedgecroft. It might not hurt your poor sister to be thought of in such terms. Perhaps it would even raise her social value, which has sunk to an appalling low after today."

Lord Belshire pursed his lips. "And how does being squired around by a rake—excuse me again, Sedgecroft—enhance Jane's reputation?"

His wife shook her head in resignation. "I do not know that her reputation can ever be repaired. Our only hope is that in time she will meet a young man to whom her scandal does not matter."

Grayson smiled at her. "Precisely my thought. We cannot undo what has been done."

Athena smiled back at him. "But we can detract from it."

Lord Belshire grunted. "What does my opinion matter? Ask her yourself, Sedgecroft. She's languishing in the Red Gallery with all those hideous Roman statues. But do not be surprised if she refuses your offer. She's a strong-minded minx."

Grayson turned to the door, smiling to himself at the warning. Of course he would be surprised if she refused. No female had ever turned down a Boscastle male when he set his mind on her. After all, he was making a gesture that would benefit both of them. What could be the harm in that?

Chapter 4

❦

The gallery stretched across the second floor, a vast sunlit room decorated with red silk hangings and a collection of priceless Italian statues. An entire wall boasted an ornately carved marble chimneypiece, beneath which sat a fireplace large enough to house a family of four. No fire had been lit within. Several shredded letters had been tossed onto the grate, apparently ready to burn.

Jane reclined on a tufted crimson couch in the corner, a half-eaten hothouse peach in one hand. A portfolio of old letters lay across her lap.

Love letters, Grayson thought as he stood in the doorway, temporarily distracted from his task by the languid sensuality of her pose. She must have been pouring over the insipid poetry of Nigel's that he'd sent her through the years. One pale arm was bent at an angle to support her head, a position that thrust her ripe breasts out into an enticing silhouette. Her bare feet dangled over the opposite arm of the couch. The heartbroken beauty had not changed out of her wedding gown.

He took his time to study her in this unguarded moment. Her eyes were closed, silky black eyelashes casting shadows on her finely boned cheeks; her slender toes flexed and unflexed as if she were striving to relax. Coils of lustrous honey-hued hair tumbled over her shoulders to the floor. Grayson imagined burying his face in that hair, shaping her curves with his hands. The unexpected fantasy warmed his blood.

To think that Nigel could be enjoying all that sensual potential in his bed. What an utter moron. But then Grayson did not know her at all. Perhaps she had some hidden defect—well, it would have to be very well hidden. He felt the dangerous stirrings of desire just standing here.

"May I disturb you for a few moments?"

That deep voice wrenched Jane out of her trance. She sat up so abruptly that the letters fluttered from her lap to the floor. The afternoon sun, the tension of the morning had made her drowsy. She'd been daydreaming, wondering how to implement the next phase of her plan.

She had been contemplating the delicious freedom that Nigel had granted her.

The freedom to choose her own mate. To flirt to her heart's content. To fall deeply in love as dear Nigel had been with his governess. Or to *not* fall in love and marry if the perfect man failed to appear.

She had been daydreaming about what it would be like to experience true passion for herself, the sort of horrible, impulsive, tingle-from-head-to-toe sweeping passion, when that dark voice had disturbed her.

Her heart began to thunder with accountable anticipation. A vaguely familiar shadow fell across the corner where she had reclined in a daze of self-congratulatory contentment.

A shadow she remembered from the chapel with a shiver of foreboding. No! It couldn't possibly be. Not here, in her home, her haven—

"Lord Sedgecroft, this is an . . . an unexpected pleasure."

"Unexpected pleasure" did not even begin to describe the unsettling sensations that his appearance evoked. The sunlight played across the chiseled planes of his face and caught the burnished wheat gold glints in his hair like an artist's brush.

And his physique—well, that broad-shouldered torso and lean body so superbly displayed in a charcoal jacket and snug black pantaloons put the statues of the Roman gods that surrounded them to shame.

She slid to her feet, realizing belatedly that she looked nothing like a corresponding goddess. There was a bright spot of peach juice on her skirt. She'd stuffed her stockings under a cushion. And what could he be doing here? Her throat went dry. The devil could not possibly have found out about Nigel's secret marriage already, could he?

"Can I do something to help you, my lord?" she asked quietly, sweeping all her concerns under a demure demeanor.

He took her elbow, guiding her back a step. "It is I who have come to help *you*."

Jane plopped back down onto the couch, too astonished to dissemble. He followed, his movement far more graceful than her shocked *thunk*. His physical presence quite overpowered her, his heavy thigh pressed against her knee, and she could not imagine that her papa had sent him up here to . . . to what?

"I'm not sure I understand."

"This whole affair must be extremely upsetting to you."

"Quite." Although not as upsetting as marrying Nigel would have been.

"I have to admit I admired your composure today."

If he'd had any real understanding of what she was truly composed of, Jane doubted this conversation would be taking place. "Thank you."

"It must have been difficult."

"You have no idea." Intriguing. He seemed quite nice, actually. What could he be trying to say?

"To have everyone staring at you," he said, shaking his head in sympathy.

"I hardly noticed."

"To have everyone whispering while you stood there in utter humiliation."

"It wasn't pleasant, but I am still alive."

He tsked. "To be the object of universal disgrace. Of mockery. Of pity."

Jane stared at him with an admonishing frown. "Is this meant to make me feel better?"

"One must face facts."

Why? she wanted to ask, but she was too drawn into this drama to disagree. It was difficult to deal with him when she had no idea of his intentions. "Yes. One must."

"One must pay a price for humiliating a young woman."

"Yes, one—what sort of price are we talking about?" she asked a trifle impatiently.

"Leave that to me. Know only that Nigel shall answer for what he did to you."

"Perhaps he had an excuse."

"Don't you dare defend the miserable little bugger to me."

Jane coughed. "Language, my lord."

"Excuse me. Sometimes my passions overcome me."

"Of course," she murmured. She had heard more than once about those passions of his, but had certainly never envisioned herself the recipient of them.

He peeled off his gray leather riding gloves. "You are aware that the papers will carry every embarrassing detail of the day's event?"

Jane hesitated, distracted by the sight of his strong elegant hands. This distraction paled, however, compared to the shock she felt when one of those strong hands engulfed hers. "Papers—what—mercy, what are you doing?"

He gave her fingers what she supposed was meant to be a reassuring squeeze. Instead, the most potent flush of pleasure spread in hot rivulets through her body. "The papers will say that another Boscastle rake has broken a lady's heart," he mused. "Much will be made of the fact that my former mistresses flanked me in the chapel."

Jane lifted her brow in delicate reproach, as if to say, Well, no wonder. But in light of the fact she had botched her own marriage, and his thumb was rubbing her knuckles in such a pleasantly disconcerting manner, she decided to hold her tongue.

He sighed. "Right now one of my brothers is resting from the fistfight he instigated during the wedding breakfast over a demirep."

"Oh, dear." Every time his blue eyes looked into hers, the queerest flutters went off in the pit of her belly. She was drifting—into something indefinable, as if magical wings had been attached to her wrists and ankles, lifting her into a dark warm fog.

"My sister Chloe is talking about becoming a Continental courtesan," he added.

"No? Not really?" Jane remembered a gorgeous raven-haired young girl who devoted herself to numerous charities.

No, he thought. Probably not really. But Grayson had a point to make and a little embellishment of the truth would not hurt when he basically had Jane's best interests at heart. To think Nigel could be bedding this interesting beauty at this very moment. Grayson had never met anyone quite like her. She had the softest hands, and that wedding dress, all wrinkled and lacy, should have made her look demure, but it produced the opposite effect on him. The devil in him would have dearly loved to learn what that lace concealed.

"Devon, another brother of mine, has gone off with his useless friends in search of pirate treasure," he said darkly.

"Pirate treasure?" Jane was not quite able to suppress a smile at the charming but frivolous notion; he caught it and smiled back.

"I suppose we've earned our reputation," he admitted, "although for the most part our sins have not been irredeemable. Until what Nigel did today. Never have we humiliated a young lady on purpose."

Jane was drifting higher into that undefinable strato-
sphere, completely spellbound by this devilishly attractive man. What could he possibly be leading to? Rogues
like Sedgecroft lurked beyond the social circle of proper
young women like Jane, even if they did arouse a certain
curiosity.

Nigel had constantly cautioned her to avoid the other
Boscastle boys, and Nigel had been her best friend. Naturally she had not questioned his advice. In fact, she had
always believed herself clever enough to resist seduction.
But then no truly appealing man had ever tried to seduce
her before. Was this . . . an appallingly flattering thought
crossed her mind.

"Do you mean to seduce me?" she asked in a serious
voice.

"Of course not."

"Oh. No. Of course not."

His blue eyes sparkled with wicked amusement.
"Don't look offended. I actually meant to compliment
you. Learning about how cruel the world can be is a lesson that does not come easily to any of us, but you received quite an education today. Darling, if this were a
seduction, we would not be sitting here holding hands."

Exactly what *would* they be doing if a classic Boscastle seduction were under way? Jane wondered. The an-
swers to that intriguing question would certainly keep
her up until the wee small hours. She had quite a fertile
imagination, and Sedgecroft could nourish it for several
months.

"Lord Sedgecroft, if this is not a seduction," she said,
in as polite a tone as possible, "then precisely what is it?
Another personal apology from your family?"

"That. And more." He raised her hands to his chin, his smile warm and more than a little naughty. "It is a proposition."

"A proposition."

"No. Not what you are thinking. I understand how you feel after the humiliation you suffered today. Never have I felt more embarrassed by my family." Never in truth, had he actually paid much notice to the sins the other members of his family were committing. He had heretofore been too busy sinning himself.

"Let me be blunt, Jane."

"I'm afraid I cannot stop you."

"A woman in your unfortunate position is in danger of becoming a pariah. It would take a man of character to marry you today. A man strong enough to ignore the opinions of others. I am not saying that such a man does not exist, but they are few and far between."

Her cheeks flushed pink with annoyance. He had just described the man of her dreams, the man she would probably never find in the shallow waters of Society. She wondered if he even existed, or if she would die of loneliness waiting for him to appear. "Well, it was hardly all my fault."

"Exactly. Which is why *you* should not be punished, and why I intend to court you, ostensibly, that is, to prove to the world you are still a desirable, eligible female."

Jane was rendered speechless. What a cruel, unanticipated coil. Of course, she had foreseen a spell of social ostracism after being jilted today. She had expected to be mocked, to be pitied, to be ignored for quite some time.

But that a notorious scoundrel like Sedgecroft would take up her cause? That this indecently handsome man would sponsor her return to the marriage mart she had schemed to escape? It was the last thing in the world she'd imagined. It was both horribly conceited and endearing of him to suggest such a thing. To offer to protect her from the results of her own machinations. How did one react?

"I realize this is a shock." His blue eyes teased her. "Do you find me too unattractive for our 'courtship'?"

Oh, he had no idea. She found him so devastatingly attractive she could barely think straight. Which in Jane's point of view did present a problem. "Well, you are rather, well—"

"More experienced than you?"

"Among other things," she murmured.

He edged closer to her, squeezing her hands in encouragement. "My experience will only prove to your advantage."

"Why do I doubt that statement?"

"I know all the games of love that are played in our world, Jane," he said, gazing into her eyes.

"I'm sure you do."

"If Nigel does not return to make this situation right, I will help you find another young man who will. I shall investigate him personally before giving him my approval." He winked at her, affecting a friendly tone. "The personal Boscastle seal, hmm?"

The *very* last thing she wanted, another matchmaker to bedevil her life. She cleared her throat, searching for words to thwart this undesirable conspiracy. "This is too kind of you, but—"

His beautifully molded mouth curved into another beguiling smile. "My reasons are not entirely unselfish. I am doing this to set an example for my family. God knows it is time that at least one Boscastle behave in a mature fashion." He paused, mischief twinkling in his eyes. "Of course I never thought it would be me."

Her mind began to reel. What had she gotten herself into? Courted . . . by Sedgecroft. Well, it would be just a game to him, a plan to whip his unruly brood into a semblance of order, but she was not sure her emotions could take . . . this much man. She would perish of heart palpitations after an evening in his presence, and the problems that might arise did not bear predicting.

For a dangerous moment she considered confessing everything to him. But that would mean breaking a Bible vow to Nigel, probably ruining Nigel's life. His parents would try to force him to have his marriage declared invalid. His new wife would be disgraced, as would the child she was carrying. Her own parents would disown her for disgracing them. She, Jane, who had hatched this plot with the best of intentions, would be made to feel very wicked indeed, her sins exposed to a merciless world. Who would understand her desire to carve out her own destiny?

"Lord Sedgecroft—"

"Oh, come now, Jane. Don't frown at me like a governess. This will be fun. Whether you realize it or not, you *are* a very lovely woman."

"Am I?"

"Oh, yes."

She sighed. The man lived and breathed seduction without even being aware of it. He probably flirted in his sleep, and he was good at it, too. Just sitting beside him made her feel shivery and weak in the knees. Weak in the brain, too. Why couldn't she come up with a plausible excuse to refuse his offer? No one would believe that she had attracted a man like the marquess.

"I believe . . . the truth is, I am too shy to pull this sort of thing off in a convincing way."

His eyes locked with hers. "I shall be convincing enough for the two of us."

She held her breath as he lifted his large hands to her shoulders in a powerful but gentle grip. If Nigel had dared to handle her in this fashion, she would have burst into laughter. But when Grayson touched her, the natural instinct came to close her eyes, submit . . . and enjoy.

She shivered as he brushed the back of his knuckles across her cheekbone. He did make a woman feel attractive, which she supposed was part of his appeal. "What are you doing?" she whispered, more curious than put off.

"Convincing you," he answered, in a deep-timbered voice.

Jane hardly knew what to think as he took her face in his hands. But if her mind hung suspended in a sort of frozen curiosity, her physical being was certainly active, a welter of aching needs and fiery blushes. She was practically burned to a crisp by the time his mouth brushed her bottom lip in deliberate sensuality. Her heart thundered in heavy strokes that resounded through her body and faded into painful little throbs.

"Convincing me." Her voice warbled with a faraway

echo quality, a canary being lured from its cage. "Of what?"

"Hmm." Grayson was disconcerted at his own reaction to their kiss. He foundered for several moments, a novelty in his vast realm of experience. The situation had taken an invigorating detour. She seemed quite sharp-witted for a woman in her position. He couldn't decide whether this would prove to her advantage or not. It didn't matter to him one way or another. How others perceived this might be something altogether different.

"Listen to me, Jane. I had not intended to make my point in exactly this way, but a tiger cannot be expected to change its stripes overnight. Something in your nature tempts the primitive male in me. What I mean to say," he went on quietly, "is if your belief in your own desirability has been damaged today, I know several mutually satisfying ways to restore it."

"I—"

"Even if it is only a game."

"A game?" she said shakily.

"A game does not preclude a little pleasure, does it?" he asked softly. "Your future has not ended at an abandoned chapel altar."

Besides, she had a lush body fashioned for lovemaking, for scattering a man's wits, he thought, his pulse quickening with a desire that bordered on dangerous.

She shifted, and he felt his entire body tighten. The sensual brush of her hair against his hand, the pliant softness of her mouth, unleashed a lust in him that obliterated reason. Without even trying, she undid him. A shock of erotic anticipation sent a lightning bolt of en-

ergy down his spine. Every nerve ending in his body reacted, primed for sex.

"Oh," she whispered in astonishment, raising a hand
to push his shoulder, only to drop it limply into her lap.

He flicked his tongue across her full bottom lip. Her
breath came in soft little gasps that aroused him even
more. "Don't you dare move," he warned her gently.
"I'm not finished yet."

He tightened his hold on her, groaning as he felt the
plush contours of her plump breasts press against his
chest. He ran his free hand lightly down her shoulders to
her back, tracing her ribs with his fingers. Of course it
wasn't enough. Every feral male impulse urged him to
ease her deeper into the sofa.

"Lord Sedgecroft—"

"Ssh. It isn't polite to interrupt me when I'm kissing
you."

She gave an uneven laugh. "You dare to speak of
being polite when—"

"You're interrupting again."

"One of us ought to show some self-control."

He smiled at her. "Ah, yes. The wedding guests did remark on the self-control you displayed today."

"I suspect they made a few remarks about you, too.
Self-control was probably not mentioned."

He laughed, delighted by her directness. So the lady
was not all she seemed. A pleasant surprise, and one that
would make this more enjoyable. God forbid he had to
escort a timid miss about town. His lips brushed hers
again, coaxing a soft gasp from her. The tip of his
tongue slid into her mouth, and he felt a flame ignite desire in the deepest recesses of his belly. She wasn't ex-

actly complying, but she didn't resist him either. He liked the taste of her, the faint nectar of peach. He liked the lush contours of her body, too. The warm press of her breasts against his shoulder. Soft, intriguing. He clenched his hand to stop himself from touching her.

"You're not finished yet, are you?" she asked faintly.

"Not quite."

"Very well. Continue."

She leaned back. His blue eyes smoldering, he followed and pinned her to the cushions with his hard-muscled weight. Cool as garden mist, he thought, but the erratic pulse beating in the hollow of her throat did not escape his detection.

He tasted the shape and texture of her moist, pliant lips; absorbed the sighs that escaped her; ate at her mouth with ruthless skill until he could feel her involuntary shivers of excitement.

She excited him, too, more than he'd expected, this fatalistic young woman in her wrinkled wedding dress and naked feet. He liked the fact that she wasn't weeping her head off or screaming for revenge. With a sigh, he summoned what remained of his control; he slid his hand down her shoulder, skimming the curve of her elbow before closing firmly around her waist.

"Well," she said when she had begun to breathe again. "*Well.*"

"There are times in life when one has to forgo a plan in favor of impulse," he said calmly, as he subdued the craving that had gripped him.

Jane gave him a reprimanding look. "Which does not mean one should act aggressively on every impulse that arises."

"We would not be sitting here discussing the matter if that were the case."

"What would . . . no, never mind. I shouldn't ask."

"I don't mind," he said with a smile.

"I'm sure you don't." Jane sighed. His eyes had darkened to midnight blue, the desire in their depths naked and unabashed. The very essence of devilish seduction. "You aren't going to apologize either, are you?"

"For what?" he asked in amusement.

"If I have to explain, then I suppose there is no point in pursuing the subject."

What subject? Grayson almost inquired, not quite sure whether he had offended her or not. Her reaction to the day's events was not exactly what he'd expected. He told himself her acceptance was a relief, no awkward emotions to deal with. But something seemed a little off. Perhaps he had embarrassed her, overwhelmed her. Yes, that must be it. The Boscastle family tended to intimidate the weaker souls in life.

"This is exactly what makes a man like you a perfect rake," she said thoughtfully.

"Excuse me?"

"Your unashamed pursuit of pleasure."

"Oh, *that.*" He stared at her wet, swollen mouth. She was a hard one to read; she did not seem particularly overwhelmed by what had just happened. "Have I offended your sensibilities?"

"Offended? No, my lord. Obliterated, yes. I suspect it will require several days for me to recover. Why did you kiss me anyway?"

He slapped his glove against his kneecap, taken a little aback by the mental acuity behind the question. "For a few reasons, actually. The first is that I could not tolerate watching a lovely woman distress herself over a numbskull like my cousin."

"Yes, but—"

"The second is that I meant to prove how attractive you are." His gaze traveled the length of her body. "Third, I felt like kissing you, and I obeyed the impulse."

She rose unsteadily from the sofa. "I think I shall retire to my room now and drop into a dead faint."

He leaned back, stroking his thumb across his narrow upper lip where the taste of her lingered, a taunt to his senses. She was seeming less like a weaker soul by the moment. "Fair enough. Expect me to call on you when you have recovered."

"This is all very overwhelming, Sedgecroft."

He studied her through half-lidded eyes. Overwhelming a female was something he understood. He felt a vague relief. This he could handle. "My cousin apparently has no idea what a good woman he has lost, but when I'm done, well, he'll eat his heart out for certain."

She turned in consternation to the window as he moved up beside her. "I don't know what came over the pair of us," she murmured. "Behaving like . . . well, I can't compare that kiss to anything I have ever experienced."

"No?" he teased, strangely glad to know he had not lost his capacity to overwhelm.

"The closest memory I can conjure is the time I disobeyed my father and sneaked out to ride his unbroken stallion. The fall knocked the wind out of me. Your kiss has left me in a similar state of breathless agony."

Grayson frowned. There was a vast difference between overwhelming a woman and picturing her gasping in pain on the ground. "I can't say if I should be flattered or not."

She half turned, looking flustered to find he was standing closer than where she had left him. "I do appreciate your intention to help. It's your methods I call into question."

He shrugged. "As I said, helping you is as much for the good of my family as for yours."

"What would you say if I refused to agree?"

"Then I should have to have another go at persuading you. But I think you have already agreed, haven't you?"

"That is an arrogant assumption."

"It is a historical fact, Jane," he said, his voice unapologetic. "No female from feudal times has been able to refuse a Boscastle male once he puts his mark on her."

"His mark?" Her brows lifted. "Oh, lovely. A brand on the proverbial cow's bum."

He reached around her to collect his gloves from the couch, hiding a grin. Weaker soul, had he thought? Well, perhaps she was in shock. Perhaps she wasn't herself. "I shall call on you tomorrow."

"That soon?" she said in alarm, half aware that her question constituted an agreement between them.

"No point in drifting into spinsterhood," he said a little ruthlessly. "Besides, you've wallowed in self-pity long enough. Off with the wedding weeds, please."

"I beg your pardon," Jane said, sputtering at his bluntness.

"Weeds, as in funeral garments," he said more gently. "The day's hopes are dead. Long live tomorrow's foolish whims. Burn his letters, sweetheart. Wear something daring for me when I call."

She stared at him in disdain. "I have nothing daring in my wardrobe, Sedgecroft."

"That will have to be changed," he said, staring right back at her.

She placed her hands on her hips. "What if I don't want it to be changed?"

"Every woman wants to be desirable," he said with another lift of his broad shoulders.

"Perhaps the women *you* associate with. I did notice the harem in the chapel."

"It was only good manners to invite them."

"Was it good manners that brought them to your bed?" she could not stop herself from asking.

His white teeth flashed in a grin. "My manners prevent me from answering that question."

"I can imagine," she said, her mind flooded by images of Sedgecroft at his wicked worst, frolicking in decadence with his mistresses. Suddenly curious, she asked, "Won't your paramours mind you squiring me about?"

"Fortunately for you, Jane, I am free at the moment from romantic entanglements."

"Fortunately for me," she muttered.

A floorboard creaked outside the door. Jane blushed to think someone might be eavesdropping on this encounter. "You are nothing like Nigel," she said in an undertone.

He gave a deep laugh before turning to the door. "I trust that shall prove to your advantage."

Chapter 5

❧❧

·

For a moment Grayson considered acting as if he did not notice the two women caught on their knees outside the door. But when they rose to block his escape, he could hardly ignore them. The pair had to be dealt with if he was to be a frequent visitor to this house.

"Excuse me," he said, clearing his throat to affect a mockingly stern tone. "Do you always eavesdrop on your sister's private conversations, or am I the focus of this prurient interest?"

The mere way he phrased the question, his voice deep with devilish intentions, made the two of them blush to their eyebrows.

Caroline responded first, swooping down to pick up the book she had dropped on the floor. "We, ah, we were chasing a spider—"

"An enormous brown one that ran all the way up the stairs," Miranda added hastily.

Caroline waved the book under his nose for emphasis. "It seemed to be heading straight into the gallery. We hoped to catch it . . . Jane is deathly afraid of spiders."

"And when you caught this creature, you planned to

what"—he arrested the movement of the book with his hand before she could inadvertently swat his chin—"read it a bedtime story?"

"We are simply guarding Jane's best interests," Caroline said, dropping her facade.

Grayson leaned down to look her in the eye. "Is there any particular reason why you think *I* am an obstacle in the path of your noble intentions?"

"Well," Miranda said under her breath, "you are a Boscastle."

Caroline nodded. "A Boscastle broke her heart."

"Which is why," he said, "it is a Boscastle who must restore your sister's spirits."

"How do you intend to do this?" Caroline demanded.

"I don't think that is any of your business," he retorted. "I have the approval of your parents."

"Our parents know absolutely nothing about our best interests," Miranda said in a burst of feeling. "They should have listened to Jane when she expressed her reservations about marrying Nigel."

Grayson hesitated, wondering if there was a weak spirit anywhere in the house. "It would appear that Nigel was the one with the reservations about matrimony."

"Perhaps that is also a Boscastle trait," Caroline said before she could stop herself. "The men of your family are notorious bachelors."

The corners of his mouth curled into a daunting smile. "Perhaps you two lovely young ladies could turn your charms onto remedying that perplexing problem for me. Instead of eavesdropping."

Miranda blushed, contemplating this suggestion until Caroline gave her a poke in the side. "The *problem*,"

Caroline said crisply, "is that Jane is extremely vulnerable. And you are . . ."

He blinked innocently. "Yes?"

"Well," Miranda said, finally taking up the thread, "a little overpowering. For a woman in such a vulnerable state."

They were too precious, he thought in amusement. A pair of self-righteous kittens who had never ventured out into the cruel world. He might have to give them a well-meaning scare back to safety. "I'm not sure I know what you mean."

Caroline clasped her book to her chest. "How can one most delicately phrase this? You see, there is rather a dangerous force about you that attracts young women."

"A dangerous force?" he said with a gasp of modesty. "I never dreamed it possible."

"And our sister," Miranda said uncomfortably, "in her vulnerable state, might not be quite able to resist this force of yours."

Grayson pretended to ponder this preposterous dilemma. Dangerous force? That was at least original. "I understand something of a woman's emotional nature."

"So we've heard," Caroline murmured with an irrepressible trace of sarcasm.

He allowed a look of horror to settle on his face. "Surely you do not think I would *seduce* your sister after the humiliation dealt her today?"

"Of course not!" Miranda exclaimed.

"Good heavens, no!" Caroline said, although that

was exactly what she had thought. "We never meant to imply that."

He leaned one shoulder back against the door, half closing his eyes in contemplation. "Then what exactly did you mean?"

Caroline pursed her lips. "Well. For a start, you might strive to be slightly less . . . appealing to the female senses while in her company."

His thick eyebrows shot up. "And how do I do this?"

"It would help," Miranda said awkwardly, "if you could somehow not seem so manly when you present yourself."

He lowered his voice, assuming a troubled expression. "I had no idea I was so offensive to the opposite sex. This is disturbing."

Caroline glanced at her sister. "You misunderstand."

"Do I?"

"Yes," she continued, "while your masculine qualities are overpowering, they are not necessarily offensive."

"Oh, good," he said, venting a loud sigh of relief.

"In fact," Miranda added, "your qualities are exactly the opposite of offensive."

Caroline nodded vigorously. "Wherein lies the problem."

"I see," he said slowly, wanting nothing more than to burst into laughter. "It seems I shall have to seek a remedy for my appalling . . . 'manliness.'"

"I rather think," said a cool voice through a crack in the door behind him, "that your 'manliness' is not the problem. I believe it is how you use this attribute that puts you to shame."

Grayson shifted his shoulder to allow Jane to squeeze into the hall. Caroline and Miranda stood, frozen in guilt, as she confronted them.

Caroline said hastily, "We were—"

"I heard what you are doing," Jane said, "but hasn't there been enough trouble for one day?"

Grayson nodded in agreement. "For a lifetime, I'd say."

Jane shot him an annoyed look. Unfortunately, her sisters had a good point. The man's virility devastated the ordinary female. Fortunately, Jane wielded tight control over her impulses. At least she had until a few minutes ago.

"If the pair of you are done solving his lordship's problems, I think I shall retire to my room for a nice lie-down."

"Do you require assistance?" Sedgecroft asked blandly.

Jane gave him a look. There he went again! He couldn't help himself. The very air he breathed smoldered with seduction. "I have been jilted, my lord. Not mortally wounded."

"Oh, Jane," Miranda said, tears brimming in her eyes. "How much it must hurt. You are so very brave."

Brave and mysterious, Grayson thought, his body stirring at the memory of their kiss and her disconcertingly enigmatic response. It shouldn't be difficult to help her forget his cad of a cousin in the event Nigel did not return. The sooner, the better. Mourning an unrequited love would only make her less appealing to another prospective husband.

"Jane," he said solemnly, inclining his head. "I shall leave you now to recover from today's ordeal."

She released a sigh. Her debacle of a wedding had not devastated her half as much as he had.

"Thank you," she murmured. "You are far too kind."

And too charming. And too seductive. And too good-looking. And too—

"Rest," he added in a dictatorial voice. "The results of our plan will be worthwhile, but I intend to be a demanding escort."

The thought of what he might demand sent her pulses soaring. "I have not agreed to this yet, my lord," she said a little mutinously as he turned away from her.

He glanced back, his blue eyes twinkling, a man so full of himself it was a feat to offend him. "You strike me as an intelligent woman. You will."

"I might surprise you," she muttered.

"I am always open to a challenge," he replied.

Her eyes widened. "I'm not sure I know what you mean."

He gave a devilish chuckle. "Helping to restore a woman's reputation will be an experience entirely unknown to the Boscastle male."

And with that startling confession, he left Jane and her sisters to wonder exactly what sort of challenge he expected from this courtship. He left them staring after him in a state of horrified admiration, the power of his presence lingering in the silence that had fallen.

It was well into the small hours that same night when Jane dipped her pen into the inkwell, writing furtively at her desk by the light of a single taper.

Dearest N,

I suppose congratulations are in order for you and your new bride. Our "wedding" went off, or did not go off, as anticipated . . . except for one unexpected snag in our scheme.

His name is Sedgecroft—

Need I say more?

Do not worry about me. I shall handle him.

"At least I hope I will," she muttered, dropping her quill in agitation.

She rose from the desk and paced across the Axminster carpet of the candlelit chamber, her linen nightrail rustling in the silence, her green eyes dark with worry.

She wasn't the sort to complain. She had gone into this whole scheme with a willing spirit, but it did seem a little unfair that she was left behind to face the consequences of their thwarted wedding while Nigel was off enjoying matrimonial bliss with his bride.

The consequences, in the form of a breathtaking example of male beauty, the marquess, appeared more dire than the fate she had hoped to avoid.

How did one forestall Sedgecroft?

One didn't, apparently. At least not without a cost. The man's smile alone carried the impact of a shot to a female's sensibilities. Beneath his urbane facade beat the heart of an accomplished conqueror. Of all the damsels in distress he could have chosen to champion, why had he picked her? If the man wanted to atone for his wicked ways, why didn't he rescue orphans or build a village hospital? Because of Nigel, of course.

"Jane?" a voice whispered behind her.

She whirled in the middle of the carpet to discover Caroline standing in the doorway. She'd half expected Sedgecroft to materialize out of her thoughts.

"You gave me a fright," she whispered.

Caroline quietly closed the door behind her. "I knew you wouldn't be able to sleep tonight. I was worried about you."

Jane schooled her features into the mask of lovelorn dejection she had worn all day. "I have a lot on my mind. Nigel and I shared many memories."

"Among other things."

Jane straightened in alarm as her sister veered over to the desk. "Excuse me?"

"The two of you shared secrets, didn't you?"

"Well, a few but—" She darted forward to rescue her revealing note from her sister's hands. "I meant to burn that."

Caroline looked up slowly, realization dawning in her eyes. "It was a letter to Nigel, wasn't it?"

"Yes, but, you mustn't fret over me." She turned and set the letter to the smoldering coals. Was there no privacy to be had in this house anymore? "In due time my heart will heal."

"I'd say it had remarkable powers of restoration," Caroline said wryly.

Jane glanced up from the fireplace as the flames consumed the letter. "You know me. Never one to show my sorrow."

"You cried for a solid month when your spaniel died."

"Well, that was a pet. This is . . . Nigel. A lady doesn't display her personal feelings in public."

Caroline's golden-brown eyes speared her. "This is not public. This is me, Jane."

"I prefer to keep my pain to myself, if you don't mind."

Caroline tapped her fingertips against her arm. "Spill the soup."

"Soup? What—"

"I saw that letter. You mentioned Sedgecroft, whom you had never met before today. Hence, it was a *new* letter."

"Which I never meant to send," Jane said, her voice high and unconvincing.

"Liar."

Caroline sent a suspicious glance around the room. A bowl of fruit sat on Jane's comfortable four-poster, along with a stack of ladies' magazines and a few novels.

"How long do you intend to play the tragic heroine?" she asked in an arch voice.

Jane blinked, aghast and yet a little relieved to have someone to confide in. She had never been able to keep a secret from either of her sisters in her life. They bedeviled her with their incessant curiosity, forever prying where they shouldn't. It was a miracle she had managed to keep the truth from them this long. "I did it for us," she burst out. "I did it so that none of us would have to accept another arranged marriage."

"You did—" Caroline's eyes widened in admiration. "It was a plot! Oh, my heavens. I knew it. I *knew* you and Nigel were planning something during all those private conversations. Miranda thought the pair of you were—well, never mind what she thought. She was wrong, obviously."

Jane sank down onto the bed, emotionally exhausted. "It was a plot, all right, and it might have come off perfectly if not for that scoundrel Sedgecroft suffering a moral sea change and deciding to set an example for his family."

Caroline stared at her in concern, apparently quite willing to be part of the conspiracy. "What are you going to do?"

"What can I do? I can't tell him the truth. He'd be livid. I could never show my face again."

"I suppose the only thing is to play along until he believes his point has been made. It can't last forever. Rumor has it he is going to make a certain Frenchwoman named Helene Renard his next conquest."

"He probably has a collection of conquests," Jane said, shaking her head in chagrin. "I shall not survive."

"Come on, Jane. He isn't that bad."

"No. He's that good. As a scoundrel, I mean."

"You have the strongest will of any woman I know, except perhaps next to me," Caroline said, her forehead wrinkled in a frown. "I have never known you to submit to temptation, not since after the time you rode Papa's stallion."

"Temptation has never, well, it has never tempted me before."

Caroline blinked, finally looking shocked at this revelation. "Does Sedgecroft tempt you?"

"Of course not," she answered quickly, too quickly to convince either one of them. "It wouldn't matter if he did. I have sacrificed my reputation to gain my freedom. I am not about to toss it away for a rogue's kisses." Even if his kisses were unspeakably erotic and would haunt her for the rest of her life.

"He kissed you?"

"Of course he kissed me. He can't help himself."

"What about you?"

"I couldn't help myself either," Jane admitted in misery, covering her face with her hands as if she could erase the memory from her mind.

"Oh, dear. I don't suppose you liked it."

"Yes, I liked it." Jane lowered her hands and released a sigh.

"Well," Caroline said after a long silence. "I suppose you're right. Sedgecroft does not seem the sort to stay interested in a woman forever. I mean, not in a woman who doesn't—"

"Yes, I'm afraid I know what you mean," Jane said. "I am not the sort to hold his interest."

"That doesn't mean that you couldn't become such a woman," Caroline said, striving to be helpful.

"Becoming such a woman was hardly what I had in mind when I plotted this mess," Jane said with another sigh.

"What would Nigel think of all this?" Caroline wondered aloud. "Sedgecroft is his cousin."

Jane's voice was dry. "I doubt Nigel is doing much thinking at this moment. He's happily off on honeymoon."

"On honeymoon?" Caroline gasped in shock.

"With Esther Chasteberry."

"Nigel's governess?" Caroline's voice rose. "The robust, chaste, and chastising Miss Chasteberry? The mean one with the rod?"

"Robust she still is, according to Nigel. Chaste she apparently is no longer."

"Well," Caroline exclaimed, collapsing beside Jane on the bed. "Who would have imagined?"

"They love each other," Jane said with a smile. "It is quite touching, actually, to hear him talk of her."

"Well, that's all very well and good for Nigel, but what about you?" Caroline asked loyally, her eyes brimming with concern. "How will you handle yourself in Society?"

"Never mind Society," Jane said feelingly. "How will I handle Sedgecroft? Did you hear what he said? He promised to be a demanding escort. Do you have any idea what that means?"

Caroline blinked in fascination. "All sorts of indecent ideas are running through my head. What are you going to do with him?"

Jane fell back upon the bed, her face troubled as she whispered, "I haven't plotted that part out yet."

Chapter 6

When Sedgecroft did not call the following morning, Jane dared allow herself to hope that he had reconsidered his rash offer. Perhaps he had forgotten about her, swept back into his own affairs. After all, by his own admission he engaged in impulsive behavior. A night's sleep might have put some sense back into the arrogant man's head.

A good night's sleep might have helped her, too, if she had not been awakened by a vivid dream. In that dream she had been languishing on the gallery couch when one of the statues had come to life, and bent over her, stark naked from head to toe.

Sedgecroft.

"Wear something daring for me," he'd whispered, his firm mouth a breath away from hers.

She struggled to sit up, her face aflame with indignation and curiosity. "You might try wearing something yourself! You're naked!"

"Am I? It's nice of you to notice. . . ."

She had no idea what he said then because she had thrown her arms around his neck and pulled his naked body down on top of her, absorbing his warmth and weight into every fiber of her flesh.

Of course she hadn't gotten another wink of sleep after that. Every time she closed her eyes she saw a bare scoundrel bending over her, his blue eyes seductive, his chest and lower torso corded with muscle. A shadow rogue who taunted her dreams.

She shook off the disturbing image and rose, not bothering to call her maid. After making a leisurely toilette, she took stock of the dresses in her wardrobe, opting for a demure gray silk with onxy-buttoned sleeves and a ruffled bodice. She ought to appear brokenhearted for at least a few weeks. Suddenly a flirty gossamer pink gauze with thin ribbons under the waist caught her attention. She reached for it, then froze, heat flooding her cheeks.

A lean face with chiseled features and beguiling blue eyes flashed across her mind. Not again, she thought in panic. His white teeth gleamed in a wolfish smile. She stared into the closet, half expecting His Nakedness to pop out at her.

Wear something daring for me.

She shook herself and reached for the drab gray silk, suddenly realizing that the house was as quiet as a grave. This would never do.

She dressed and strode down the stairs, smiling brightly at the servants gathered in the marble-tiled hall below until she was reminded by their mournful sighs and pitying looks that a jilted fiancée would not be bouncing about the house like a firecracker.

She slowed her pace, bowed her head, and thought of the dog she had lost, attempting to look bereaved.

"Where is everyone, Bates?" she asked the tall gaunt-faced butler who stood supervising the polishing of the hall's brass fixtures.

"Your lady sisters are taking their lessons in the summerhouse," he said gravely. "His lordship had a meeting on St. James's street. Lady Belshire is puttering about in the garden, as is her pleasure."

"Thank you, Bates," she said, spinning on the heel of her slipper.

"On behalf of the staff, Lady Jane," he intoned to her back as if he were delivering a eulogy, "I would like to express my deepest sympathy for your loss."

She hesitated, ignoring the prickle of guilt that ran down her back. "That is kind of you, Bates." *Unnecessary, but kind nonetheless.*

"The same goes for me, too, Lady Jane," added the gray-haired figure at the other end of the hall.

Jane turned stiffly and smiled at the diminutive housekeeper, who was dabbing at her tearful eye with her apron string. Oh, Lord, this was an unforeseen bit of embarrassment. "Chin up, Mrs. Bee. We are the Belshires."

"We are indeed, my lady," Mrs. Bee sniffed.

Her good mood a trifle diminished, Jane wended her way outside to the lushly overgrown garden to find her mother, in a straw bonnet and bright aquamarine day gown, attacking the weeds between the wall of lupines with a pair of sewing scissors. There was something comforting about the familiar domestic scene. Life in a garden tended to go on despite the complications of the outside world.

"Hello, my poor darling." Lady Belshire scanned her daughter's face for evidence of a broken heart. "Did you manage to sleep at all? I warned everyone to be as quiet as possible."

"I slept. . . ." Jane paused, remembering the dream that had awakened her. To her private dismay, the life-like image of the naked marquess had begun to grow blurry—she certainly would never be able to admire a Roman statue again. But if she couldn't recall the unclad Sedgecroft, she couldn't titillate herself at the odd interval either.

"Dearest, are you all right?"

Jane blinked, aware her mother was waving a lupine stalk back and forth before her. "I'm fine. Did—did Sedgecroft send word by any chance? I mean, not that I want him to. . . ."

Lady Belshire heaved a sigh. "He could not manage to call this morning, Jane. I hope this is not another disappointment, although after yesterday I imagine there is not much that can damage your aching heart. Sedgecroft was detained on some family matter. He sent a message that—"

"It's all right, Mama. I really didn't expect him to keep his word. He probably already regrets making his offer, and I certainly won't hold him to it." Jane darted around the stone bench, giddy with relief. A reprieve. A chance to recover her equilibrium. Of course Sedgecroft wasn't coming. What would he want with dull jilted Lady Jane? Although for a few minutes, he *had* made her feel more desirable then she had dreamed possible. Well, it only proved she had been right about him all along.

"Are my sisters still with Madame Dumas?" she asked as she backed away.

"Yes, but—" Lady Belshire stared at her fleeing daughter in consternation. "Jane, my goodness, I haven't even finished delivering his message."

Jane restrained herself from racing into the summerhouse to deliver the welcome news to Caroline. She and Miranda were reading Molière's *Tartuffe* aloud in their dreadful French accents while Madame Dumas listened, her skinny fingers pinched to her nose as if in pain.

"May I interrupt?" Jane asked in amusement.

Madame Dumas shuddered, slamming the book shut. "By all means, please do. Your sisters are slaughtering my mother tongue."

Miranda slid to her feet and embraced Jane in a fervent hug. "Caroline told me everything," she said in an undertone. "I am bursting with admiration. And terror," she added as an afterthought. "Oh, Jane, what have you done?"

"So much for keeping a secret," Jane said, dragging both sisters down the steps into the sun. "I forbid you to tell anyone else."

"Not another soul," the two of them vowed somberly.

"And I hope you did not discuss me in front of Madame Dumas. She already thinks I'm a lost cause because I preferred studying Italian over French in protest for all the friends who've died in the war."

Caroline coaxed a butterfly away from her heavy mahogany-gold hair. "I heard Dumas telling Mrs. Bee you might have to marry a Frenchman, as it's unlikely any English aristocrat will have you."

Before Jane could react to that remark, Lady Belshire

interrupted them, breathless from hurrying across the garden.

"He's here!" With uncharacteristic aggression she wrested Jane away from her sisters. "And you're not even properly dressed."

"Properly . . . for what?" Jane glanced around the garden in confusion. Aside from the two gardeners pruning the poplars, there was not a male in sight, and certainly no reason for her mother to go all fluttery. Which gave her another one of those dreadful feelings of doom.

"Who is here, Mama?"

"Sedgecroft. Who else?" Lady Belshire put her hand to her heart at her daughter's stricken expression. "Oh, sweeting, you thought I meant Nigel, didn't you? How careless of me. How utterly stupid. Of course you are still hoping the scapegrace will appear with some perfectly understandable explanation for his appalling cruelty."

Jane stared at her mother, controlling a childish urge to yank off her beribboned straw bonnet and stomp it into the ground. "You know Sedgecroft's reputation, Mama. Aren't you the least bit concerned that he will taint me?"

Lady Belshire paused to pluck a weed from between the flagstones. "Don't be silly. All of my daughters are above temptation. Your brother is another thing entirely. I tried to tell you a few moments ago that Sedgecroft could not call this morning because he was detained on a family matter. He said he would be here this afternoon."

"This afternoon?"

"*Now,* Jane," her mother said in exasperation. "That was his carriage in the street."

"What carriage?"

"It doesn't matter now," her mother whispered urgently, turning Jane by the shoulders toward the house. "He's *here,* and, oh, look at the dress you're wearing."

Jane stared at the huge figure striding across the lawn, sunlight illuminating his hard-planed face. The expensive cut of his dark blue morning coat and buff breeches enhanced his elegant masculinity. Not that he needed enhancement in that respect. He might have been stark naked and he would still—oh, *no.* Not that image again. Not when she had to look him in the face.

He slowed and sent her a sensual smile that set off tiny shocks of panic through her system. All that virility—in broad daylight! It took a woman by storm. After she began to recover, her first reaction was to cower behind the boxwood hedge. Being well bred, however, she bravely stood her ground as he resumed his confident stride.

"There you are," he said warmly, taking her hands without the slightest hesitation. "I was afraid you had gone into hiding. We couldn't have that."

That was precisely what she had hoped to do.

Her fingertips began to tingle under the pressure of his insistent grasp. She made several subtle attempts to tug away. He took no notice. She glanced around in embarrassment at her mother and sisters, who were unconvincingly pretending not to be observing his every unrestrained move.

"Listen to me, Sedgecroft," she said in an undertone, determined to get her point into his thick head.

"Of course."

Oh, his eyes were so intense, so alive, so . . . inviting. Who cared if he was the most arrogant man on earth? His merriment was catching. "I have thought over your generous offer to use you as my ticket, as it were, back to social acceptance."

He grinned, giving her the impression she ought to be flattered by his involvement. "Good," he said with a gracious nod of his head as if that were the end of that. "And I've decided—"

Her thoughts scattered as he slid his large hand up to her wrist to steer her toward the old wooden gate concealed in the brick wall. She felt the delicious stone-hard support of his body behind hers.

"I think we can reach the street this way, can't we?" he asked, not giving her a chance to answer. "My carriage is parked there. What a tangle of traffic I fought to get here, cows and costermongers."

She raised her voice, a sense of panic overcoming her. "I believe I shall have to decline."

He marched her through the poplars, glancing up at the two gardeners, their shears suddenly frozen in midair. His mild frown set them instantly back into motion. He was a man others instinctively obeyed. "We can discuss this on the way. In private."

She stared up at him in grudging awe, wondering how a human being could plow through the world with such unfailing arrogance. "Sedgecroft, I am not ready for public exposure."

"Nonsense." He paused to examine her in detail. "You look good enough to—to take out for the afternoon, although I have to admit . . ." His deep voice faltered.

"Admit what?"

"Never mind." He glanced back thoughtfully at the three women who had trailed them at a polite distance. "I suppose it doesn't matter," he murmured, giving a small shrug. "We're too late to do anything about it now."

She dug in the heels of her silk pumps. The handsome beast had piqued her female vanity with his implication that there was something wrong with the way she looked. She ought to tell him how *he* had looked in the dream last night.

"It does matter," she said in a firm voice. "At least I'm sure it would if you'd kindly explain what in my appearance displeases you."

He tapped the side of his cleft chin in contemplation. His gaze met hers for a moment. "It's just—no, I don't want to offend you. Not after yesterday."

Her brows lifted over her narrowed green eyes. "Offend me."

"Well." He dropped his voice, sounding a little embarrassed on her behalf. "Is *that* your idea of daring dress?"

Oooh. "What is wrong with my dress?" she asked, wishing she did not care what he thought.

"Nothing shows. Nothing except ruffles and . . . gray. All those gray ruffles on your front." He made a face. Then to her horror, he puffed out his chest to pantomime her. "It puts one in mind of a pigeon. An *attractive* pigeon," he added hastily at the look she gave him.

She ground her teeth. "Nothing is meant to show, Sedgecroft."

"Why not?" the devil asked.

She folded her arms across her ruffled breasts. "I am not one of your demireps."

He cleared his throat, obviously enjoying this. "You most assuredly are not."

Jane wondered why that remark felt like an insult. A proper young lady would have been proud of her . . . pigeon appearance. "This happens to be my favorite dress."

"My grandmother had a pair of parlor curtains exactly the same color."

"Did she remind you of a pigeon, too?"

"Not exactly, but I am not going to enjoy our afternoon if every time I look at you I think of my grandmother."

"This is a modest dress, Sedgecroft. A fashionable one."

"Perhaps if you're in your eighties. Hmm." He beckoned to the figure hovering behind them. "Lady Belshire, what is your candid opinion of this dress?"

Jane rolled her eyes. The wretch, to ask her mother for a candid opinion. One might as well ask a reformer to deliver a speech before Parliament.

"It's all right, Mama," she said with ice in her voice. "We really don't need to bother you."

"Darling, I don't mind." Her mother looked flattered, eager to be included.

"Go back to your flowers, Mama," Jane said under her breath. "The garden needs you."

"The dress, Athena." Grayson gestured her closer with a languid wave of his fingers. "What do you think? Give us the benefit of your wisdom."

Her ladyship stepped forward to study her daughter in critical silence. "To be perfectly honest, I have never liked gray on the girls, except when the situation called for gravity, of course. Gray, unless in the palest hues, should be worn by governesses and housekeepers. Now, silver—"

Jane inserted herself between them. "Is this a conspiracy?"

"It is not." Grayson paused, breaking into a helpless grin at Jane's indignant expression. "It does seem to be a consensus of opinion, though. I think you ought to change, considering there will be dancing at the affair we are attending."

Jane shook her head in disbelief. She had the distinct feeling of being caught in a trap by a very clever, handsome hunter. Short of causing another unpleasant scene, there seemed to be little she could do. Not with her mother coaxing the devil on. Honestly, what a vexing man. What a muddle.

"Dancing?" Her lips thinned. "The day after I was— very well, Sedgecroft, I shall change. Would you like to select the size of my buttons? Inspect the inseams of my gloves? Do you have any particular color preference, barring the pigeon hues?"

Mischief danced in his eyes, alluring, irresistible. "I prefer pink, but of course the choice is yours."

"No, it isn't," she grumbled, pivoting toward the house, "because the plain fact is that I prefer gray."

Grayson nearly regretted his suggestion that she change when she reappeared a full half hour later. Her diaphanous pink gauze draped a curvaceous body that tempted all his latent demons. He was perfectly aware that she had made him wait on purpose, although far be it from him to complain.

Not when the end result torched his senses. Not when it was all he could do simply to breathe and remind himself that he ought to feel guilty for desiring her. He knew full well she was susceptible to seduction after having been so cruelly abandoned by his cousin. He wouldn't take advantage of her, would he?

His eyes darkened in frank male approval as he indulged his instincts in a long, hungry look. The wait had been worth it. Jane's curves made his mouth water—her full, high breasts; those rounded hips; and her lithe, tapered legs. His throat tightened as he leaned casually against the brick wall and watched her approach, his gaze returning to her face. Sultry, sweet, but not cloyingly so. She should have made mincemeat out of Nigel, not the other way around.

He had already acknowledged privately that something more than noble intentions had inspired at least part of his plan to help her. Not that he could act on these baser Boscastle motives. But there was no point in deceiving himself either. He found Jane appealing, fascinating in ways he could not fathom. It made helping her easier. It even added an element of danger to their association.

"That is a vast improvement," he said politely, no hint in his voice that he had just undressed and bedded her in his imagination. That for a moment she had cast a spell of helpless attraction over him, and he wasn't quite sure what to make of it.

"It is?"

Her annoyed frown did absolutely nothing to destroy the sexual images that paraded through his mind, the vision of their bodies joined in pleasure. His own reaction frightened him a little. Knocked him emotionally to his knees. Fortunately he had learned long ago to hide what he felt, or he might have frightened her to death.

"I never lie, Jane," he said, offering her his arm.

She stared at him before reluctantly tucking her hand into his elbow. "You might not lie, but you certainly dominate."

"That is also true," he murmured, drawing her against him to open the gate hidden in the wall.

Their bodies touched again, and Jane barely managed not to sigh in pleasure. Instead, she breathed in his scent, wool and Castile soap, the warm tang of his skin, the sheer maleness that made her feel so protected and vulnerable at the same time. Part of her wanted to lean even closer and sate her senses. The other part wanted to retreat from the attack on her judgment. Just because she had committed one enormous sin didn't mean she was destined to descend into decadence, did it? She had to wonder.

In the core of her being she felt like candle wax held against a raw flame, burned up by the heat he exuded. She lifted her gaze. His eyes ensnared hers, sultry, sensuality unhidden, before he casually flicked up the latch and guided her onto the narrow flagstone footpath to the street. She huffed out a breath. Heaven only knew what he was thinking or why she was going along with whatever plan he had in mind.

She balked, realizing she had been so enrapt in him that she wasn't paying attention to their destination.

"What is wrong with the front entrance? I thought we wanted to be seen."

"We do." He straightened his white neckcloth, giving her a conspiratorial grin. "But there happens to be a particularly vile reporter on your doorstep whom I will probably end up killing one day. You, my dear, are not about to be a baby lamb for the likes of him."

"Oh." She hadn't even thought to read the morning papers. "Is the news very ugly?" she asked in hesitation.

His hard face softened slightly. "Brutal."

"Then I refuse to do this."

He motioned with his free hand to the liveried footman waiting at the curb. His other hand firmly prevented her from pulling away. "Remount, Jane."

"Re—what?" she said in exasperation, then, "Unhand me, Sedgecroft, or I shall . . . hit you."

"I'm doing this for your own good," he said, escorting her past the growing crowd of curious onlookers who had hoped to catch a glimpse of the jilted bride and her infamous escort.

She swatted at his shoulder, whispering, "Everyone is staring at us."

"Then stop resisting me," he whispered back with a lazy smile.

"Then let me go."

"But, my little disgraced angel, what if you should fall?"

"Fall?"

"Into the street amid all those nasty cow droppings and custards."

"I suppose that's a risk I shall have to take."

"Not in my presence. I would never allow a woman I escort to come to harm."

"Would you allow her to harm you?"

His eyes twinkled with enjoyment. "It depends. What did you have in mind?"

"Presumably not what you're thinking."

He gave a low laugh and pulled her closer to him to murmur, "Smile at our audience, Jane. Remember that I have replaced Nigel in your heart. It won't do for us to be quarreling in the street the first day we are seen together."

Despite the fact that she hadn't agreed to any of this, Jane could not help responding to his confidence. He sounded as if he did this sort of thing every day. He made it sound like a marvelous adventure.

"I cannot believe my mother is letting you take me off without a chaperone," she grumbled.

"We have a chaperone." He bore her toward the elegant black carriage that had pulled up behind them, looking pleased that she obeyed him. "Your brother is waiting for us in there."

"Simon . . . a party to . . ."

He leaned into her, the playful mockery in his eyes darkening with sultry promise. She stared at his face, mesmerized, a blush burning its way up the back of her nape, her body softening in sinful anticipation.

"What are you doing?" she whispered.

"Don't look now, darling, but that press reporter is coming around the corner."

"May I faint?"

"After I get you into the coach." He brought his head to hers, speaking in a soothing voice that reminded Jane he was no stranger to scandal himself. "Ah, good, he's gone the other way. Let's just wait a moment to be sure."

His breath teased the edge of her jaw, warm, a taunt to her senses. His broad shoulders blocked her from view. In a heartbeat she was consumed in heat, in confusion, in the heady presence of him. His left arm lifted as if to protect her. His mouth grazed her skin. It was a brief contact, a casual brush of his lips against the sensitive curve of her cheekbone. One watching may not have been sure whether he had merely whispered in her ear. But Jane felt the sensual power he wielded in every erratic beat of her heart.

Her body temperature rose as she stood there, tingling in sheer pleasure, in anticipation. She half expected him to kiss her again, right there in the street.

"Er, Jane," he said, his deep voice startling her.

She blinked twice. "What is it?"

"Get into the carriage," he instructed her with a laugh. "I believe you're drawing attention to yourself."

"*I'm* drawing attention?"

He smiled into her eyes. "Yes. Perhaps you should get into the carriage."

She shook her head, trying to break the spell. "The carriage."

He looked amused. "Is something wrong?"

"Well, it's just for a moment I thought . . . I thought . . ."

He pretended to look shocked. "Don't tell me you thought I was going to *kiss* you right in front of your own house?"

She drew her breath, mortified at his perception. "I never once—"

He brushed his gloved finger under her chin. "You are a lady, Jane, and I am trying to restore your good name. If you really wish for me to kiss you, however, I shall be happy to oblige you inside the carriage."

The fact that he was making fun of her in no way weakened the quiver of pleasure that his touch sent through her system. "I don't think that will be necessary."

He made a sympathetic noise. "Shame."

"Yes, you're the shame," she retorted, finally regaining her composure. "Why are those people across the street staring at me like that?"

He crooked his finger at the footman. "I don't know. Perhaps they wish they could kiss you, too."

She made a soft choking sound as she felt his large hand nudge her impertinently up the folding step. Too embarrassed to react, she glanced at the pair of footmen who flanked her like stone statues, apparently used to their master's evil ways.

"No one has ever kissed me in public before," she whispered over her shoulder, determined to make the matter clear. "I did not wish for you to do so."

"Well, if you change your mind . . ."

She fought a horrible urge to laugh. "If Simon hears this conversation, he will certainly take you to task."

The glitter of deviltry in those blue eyes should have warned her. She climbed into the spacious carriage and stared in despair at the inert male body sprawled across the opposite seat. Some chaperone there. Her brother lay sleeping off the excesses of the evening. Utterly oblivious to her dilemma. Dead to the world except for the random snore that erupted from him like a wild boar.

"That's not a chaperone," she exclaimed. "That's . . . a corpse."

Grayson gave her a gentle shove onto the seat, his mouth quirking at the corners. "He serves his purpose."

He watched in amusement as she attempted to position herself beside her brother's sprawled body, realized it was impossible, then finally gave up, sitting down next to Grayson in flustered resignation. He was beginning to feel rather off balance himself and couldn't figure out why.

He had enjoyed his fair share of comely women and had never felt this unsettled in their company. Perhaps he was unbalanced because the role of white knight seemed unfamiliar to him. Or perhaps it was because for the first time in his life he had to contemplate every step he took. Which brought him back to the matter of Jane herself. What was he supposed to do when he knew she found him appealing? Pretend he was not flattered? Squash all his familiar male instincts?

Yes, indeed, he would have to watch his step. Not merely for public opinion. God knew he had been the object of gossip often enough in the past. It would serve the scandalmongers right if he tricked them. Malicious talk had injured his family more than once. He would be damned if he'd let Jane suffer more indignity than she already had though.

Jane wriggled against him, and the sensation brought him immediately out of the mental realm into the physical. Conspiracy or not, he suspected his aspirations to chivalry could not last forever.

Walking the sunlit path of respectability did not come naturally. . . . Dancing in the darkness was another matter altogether.

Jane was right. He had wanted to kiss her in the street, but he doubted that even her imagination could dream how far beyond a kiss he would like to go.

Chapter 7

"I have decided something," Jane remarked a moment later as the carriage set off down the street.

"What is that, Jane?" he asked pleasantly.

"I am going to pretend that conversation in the street never occurred." She cleared her throat. "And that incident between us in the Red Gallery yesterday."

He picked up the newspaper that was wedged between them, deliberately dislodging her derriere in the process. "As you like." The shadow of a smile crept across his face. "If you can."

She folded her hands demurely in her lap. "It is already forgotten."

He put down the newspaper, obviously not content to let matters rest. "Would you like me to refresh your memory?"

"Perhaps we should refresh your manners first."

She had just decided how to deal with him. Handling awkward matters could not ruffle the feathers of a Welsham swan for long. Self-control came as naturally to this daughter of an earl as flirtation did to Sedgecroft.

The situation simply required that she fight his manliness with etiquette.

"So, my lord. You look well rested this morning. Did you pass a peaceful night?"

There was a pause. She wondered suddenly if he might take her inquiry as encouragement to describe his nocturnal activities in titillating detail. She steeled herself for a recitation of naughty misadventures.

He glanced down at her, the glitter in his eyes making her catch her breath. "Let me think. A few hours after I left you, I caught Chloe sneaking out with the ladies in her social-reform society. They practically attacked me when I refused to let her go out on whatever misguided mission they had in mind. I had to lock her in her room."

"That does seem a dangerous activity for the evening," Jane agreed.

"That was only the beginning. I then proceeded to search the whole of Vauxhall Gardens for my brother."

"Which brother would that be?" she asked, envisioning the crew of handsome blue-eyed rogues in the chapel yesterday.

"I was looking for Drake, who, as it turns out, was busy selecting which pair of boots he would wear for his duel in the morning."

"He fought a duel today?" she asked in alarm.

"Fortunately not," he said with a rueful sigh. "His adversary made a public apology a few minutes before the duel was to take place."

"Good heavens, Sedgecroft."

He leaned his head back, his blond hair brushing his

collar. "It was anything but a restful night. Responsibility carries a price."

So did deception, Jane thought with a pang of unease as he settled himself into a more comfortable position, his knee pressed to hers. His powerful build heightened her awareness of how precarious their relationship was. She wondered how he could be so different from his cousin Nigel. And why she could not have met him first. Not that he would have even noticed her with a mistress on each arm, or that she would have made any attempt to make him do so.

She stared out the window, pondering the strange quirks of fate.

The carriage came to a stop, snagged in the crush of early-afternoon traffic. Oxcarts, coaches, pedestrians darting across to the pavement, crossing sweepers clearing pungent manure from the street. She gasped as Sedgecroft rose, seizing her arm, and pulled her from the seat.

She glanced helplessly at her dozing brother. "Simon, wake up this instant, you worthless excuse for a chaperone."

Simon gave a piggy snort and rolled onto his other side.

"Where are you taking me, Sedgecroft? There are people outside watching your carriage."

"I know," he said without a qualm. "That is one of my bankers and his wife on the corner. The woman happens to be a notorious gossip."

"What am I supposed to be doing?"

He helped her down onto the pavement. "Enjoying yourself." He lowered his voice. "Allowing me to spoil you. Stop frowning like an owl for one thing. Pretend to be delighted."

"Delighted? Over what?"

"Over our blossoming romance, darling." He beckoned to a pair of flower vendors on the corner, tossing a handful of coins into the baskets they held. The two older women blushed beneath their straw bonnets and thanked him by name. Before Jane could question him, she found herself smothered in masses of fragrant posies, a gift that the girl in her could not help responding to.

She bit her lip, her palms suddenly damp inside her gloves. That banker's wife recognized her, all right. She felt the woman's gaze go straight to her in scandalized recognition. Oh, how embarrassing. As if yesterday hadn't been enough, although it was fun to be spoiled in public.

"What is everyone going to think?" she whispered.

"Probably that I am enamored of you," he replied, appearing unperturbed.

"Why?" she asked, unwillingly intrigued by the thought.

"Well, you're lovely and sweet for one thing."

"No, I'm not. I'm rather ordinary and mean."

He laughed. "Well, then. You're modest."

"And the whole of London is supposed to believe you're buying me flowers to honor my remarkable modesty?"

His slow beguiling smile gave her the shivers. "Everyone will think there is something more between us."

"Something . . ."

"A serious courtship," he said with a shrug.

"Oh, really, Sedgecroft. No one would believe that you—that I—well."

"Why not?" he asked so earnestly that she almost melted.

He took her chin in his hand, and Jane felt her heart quicken in anticipation. She might not have any of the practical experience he'd had, but it wasn't hard to imagine a woman secretly wishing to be wooed by this man. And all of the pleasure and heartbreak it would entail.

"Sedgecroft, you silly thing, you're holding my face."

"I'm waiting for you to thank me."

"Oh . . . thank you."

"Not nearly convincing enough."

"No?"

He shook his head. "Try thanking me with a little more enthusiasm. I happen to be a generous suitor. The flowers are only the prelude to the pearls that will be delivered to you tonight. Let the ton talk about that."

Pearls, and what would come afterward? she wondered. She amazed herself by standing on tiptoe to press a quick kiss on his cheek. "Thank you," she whispered, blushing hotly at the contact with his warm clean skin. What on earth had she just done? Kissing *him* after all the fuss she made only minutes ago.

His eyes sparkled down at her. "That was very nice, Jane, but somehow it lacked . . . enthusiasm."

She gave him a stiff artificial smile, the posies crushed to her chest. "Oh! Oh, Sedgecroft!" she cried in a theatrical voice. "What a surprise! Pearls! And flowers! For *me*?"

He winced, giving an embarrassed cough before he

steered her back toward the carriage. "I think you need a little more practice. I've seen the ducks in my pond give a better performance."

She buried her face in the profusion of nosegays to smother a chuckle. "First a pigeon, then an owl. Now I am a duck. What bird shall I remind you of next?"

"A goose, I think." They settled back into their seats, Simon flat on his back with his arms clasped across his chest. Grayson's blue eyes traveled over her in lazy appreciation, bringing another blush to her cheeks. He really was a shameless man. "What do I remind you of?"

She spilled the posies onto the seat, filling the carriage with the delicate fragrance of gillyflowers. "A lion, I think. A lordly beast."

"A beast?" he echoed, lifting his brow. "You are brave to call me that to my face. Sit closer to me."

"Closer?" she said with a catch of laughter in her voice. "This is Brook Street, Sedgecroft, not a brothel."

"I like the feel of you next to me," he said quietly. "Besides, I am not known to be a saint, Jane."

"Does that mean you're a devil?"

He took a daisy from the seat and propped it between Simon's hands. "You shall have to find that out for yourself." He looked up slowly into her eyes. "And if I am, I shall be your devil, Jane. At least for as long as it takes to put this situation right. Good or evil, I will fight on your side."

They turned right at David Street to pull up before a Georgian mansion on Berkeley Square with row upon row of glistening sash windows. Gay strains of music wafted from the sloping gardens that lay sheltered within a grove of plane trees. Beyond rose fertile strawberry fields, clusters of red fruit ripening in the sun. The coachman veered toward the wrought-iron porte cochere.

A group of young bucks stood idly on the entrance steps, stopping their conversation to stare as the elegant black carriage and team of snowy white horses approached.

"That's Sedgecroft," one of them shouted.

"There's a woman with him," another observed, stretching his neck for a better look.

"Of course there is," said his friend, groping for his quizzing glass.

"Who is she?"

"She's wearing pink, that's all I can tell."

"My brother saw Sedgecroft's secretary on Ludgate Hill choosing pearls this morning."

"Ah, then it must be serious. I wonder if they're in negotiations."

"Didn't read about it in the papers. All the talk was of the Belshire bride left standing at the altar yesterday by Nigel Boscastle."

"Who the devil is Nigel Boscastle?"

"Sedgecroft's bore of a cousin. Do you think . . ."

The group flowed as one down the steps for a closer inspection of the mystery woman in the carriage window. The Marquess of Sedgecroft had set a standard to which many potential scoundrels aspired. It was considered a coup to be seen at a party conversing with one of his former mistresses.

As a whole, this elite circle of women remained notoriously loyal to their noble paramour, tight-lipped about their past relationships. The whys of this devotion provided a constant subject of delicious speculation.

Did Sedgecroft pay them for their silence? Was he such a skilled lover that the besotted mistresses hoped he would resume their arrangements? Or had he already done so, in secrecy? Was the man juggling three or four hot-blooded beauties at once in his bed?

His sexual successes, whether fact or fantasy, stirred the admiration of the younger set.

"Why do you think he has a passion for pink?" asked a brash gentleman. "Because it resembles a female's naked flesh?"

His brother snickered rudely. "No, because it reminds him of carnations, you idiot."

From inside the carriage Jane blushed furiously, able to pick out only a few words of this conversation. "You do realize," she said in a resigned undertone to Grayson, "that those young men are discussing me, and not in flattering terms." Although, after the scheme she and Nigel had pulled off yesterday, she supposed she had better become accustomed to such gossip. But, goodness, she had never thought herself the least bit interesting to the beau monde. Poor Nigel had absolutely bored Society silly with his love of dogs and ancient French literature.

Grayson glanced out the window, narrowing his eyes at the group of onlookers. "Leave this to me, Jane. I shall soon set them straight."

She swallowed over the knot of nervousness in her throat. "I've just decided I shall not budge from this carriage."

He smiled at her, the slow easy smile of a man who'd never had to lift a finger in his life to attract a woman, the smile of a man who did not give a damn how many scandals he ignited. "Shall I have breakfast brought to our carriage then? A string quartet to play while we eat?"

Jane's mouth curved in an answering smile; the dark amusement in his eyes sent waves of giddy heat washing through her. Anticipation prickled down her spine as he took her gloved hand in his, stroking her palm through the buttery soft kidskin. "I have never attracted a crowd in my entire life," she grumbled.

"Are you ready to attract one now?" he asked, his voice challenging her.

"Ready? Ready to face scandal and smirks of sympathy, you mean?" She turned her shoulder to the door, blowing out a sigh. "If I have to. You are a taskmaster, aren't you?"

"Come on, Jane. Let's have a bit of fun with them today. We'll drive them half mad wondering what we mean to each other."

"I've been wondering that myself."

His hand slid up to her elbow, held her fast, drawing her practically into his lap. His heart began to beat harder, and he was taken aback again at the force of his reaction. What had he gotten himself into? He probably didn't want to know. It was too late to withdraw now, even if the path to hell was paved with good intentions. "Wait," he ordered her, not certain why. Perhaps to buy time, or simply because he took pleasure in talking with her.

"But they're all watching us. They're going to think that we're . . . kissing or something even worse."

He flicked his forefinger against the mother-of-pearl button at her elbow. "That isn't a bad idea, now that you suggest it. Unfortunately I cannot indulge their prurient interests. Or yours."

"I didn't suggest it, you—you irresistible fiend."

"Irresistible fiend." He looked pleased, widening his eyes to mock her. "That sounded almost like a compliment."

She smiled reluctantly. "I suppose in your own way, you're only trying to help."

"That's right." As unbelievable as he himself found the notion. "Now do as I ask. I shall set the rascals straight on your status."

"A rake with a conscience," she went on in a thoughtful voice. "A rake with a streak of kindness running through his rotten heart."

He gave a laugh. He was not comfortable with this role. "Well, don't let it become common knowledge. I have a well-earned reputation for rottenness to resume once I have put your life back in order."

She folded her arms across her chest and sat back to examine him. "Seriously, Sedgecroft, haven't you ever considered marriage yourself?"

He gave her an exaggerated frown. "Seriously, Jane, no."

"Why not?"

"Why should I?" he asked mildly.

"One cannot remain a rogue forever. Not with your obligations."

"I can certainly try," he retorted, although the same

damning thought had haunted him lately. "In the olden days my male forebears had the good sense not to submit to wedlock until they were maimed within an inch of their lives on the battlefield, and good for nothing else."

"Their wives must have been beside themselves with gratitude," Jane said in a wry voice. "What an honor to care for an incapacitated Boscastle."

His grin was devilish. For a moment he was disconcerted by the realization that he was already revealing more about himself to Jane than he ever had to any of his mistresses or old friends. "The point, my impudent lady, was to breed another line of ill-behaved Boscastles when all other options for adventure were exhausted. My ancestors proved themselves quite capable of fulfilling this pleasant duty until their dying breaths."

"Did they indeed?" she asked faintly.

"Yes, Jane," he said, enjoying her reaction. "And their wives never complained. They performed."

"Performed?"

"Their wifely duties. Which—"

"Further explanation is not necessary."

He paused, wondering how far he dare go and why he liked provoking her so much. "Forgive me. I thought you might be curious."

She felt a telltale flush of pink warm her cheeks. The thought of breeding a Boscastle heir brought some unspeakably earthy images to her mind. How in the world had this conversation evolved?

"My brother is probably listening," she whispered admonishingly.

"In all his corpselike attentiveness."

She wiggled around to give Simon a firm shaking. Grayson watched, grinning, as she virtually pummeled her brother back to life. She had a delightfully sharp bite under all that reserve.

"Wake up, you wastrel," she said sternly. "Make yourself of use to the world."

Simon stirred, opening his bloodshot eyes to examine his surroundings in disbelief. "Sedgecroft. Jane. And all these flowers." He levered up on one elbow. "Has someone died? Was it—God, has Nigel been found? Don't tell me we're on the way to his funeral."

Jane examined his rumpled clothing in chagrin as he blinked painfully against the daylight. "No one has died, Simon," she said in a very precise voice. "You are here as my chaperone, as useless as you appear to be in that capacity."

He ran his hand through his tousled brown hair. "I wouldn't talk about appearances. That dress is rather revealing for—" The warning look Sedgecroft gave him stopped him cold. "*Has* anyone heard from Nigel?"

"Not a word," Grayson replied, his jaw hardening at the reminder. "I'm still making inquiries, of course, but it appears he's left London without a trace."

Simon released a sigh. "Where are we going anyway?"

"To the Duke of Wenderfield's breakfast party," Grayson replied.

Jane leaned forward to remove a white silk stocking from her brother's vest pocket. "Dear God, Simon, where did *you* go last night?"

He shrugged helplessly. "I don't remember. I don't even know how I got here."

"You attended a midnight masquerade," Grayson said dryly as he extended his hand to help Jane rise. "Your coachman found you half conscious between a nun and Cleopatra's handmaiden."

"Were the three of us—"

Grayson cleared his throat. The amused glitter in his eye spoke volumes. "I think we can finish this conversation in private, Simon."

Jane dropped the stocking to the floor in distaste. "And I think the answer to his question is disgracefully obvious."

Grayson did not bother to acknowledge the greetings of the young bucks who had gathered on the steps. The avid curiosity in their eyes as they spotted Jane infuriated him. One of them had finally recognized her.

"Sedgecroft," she said, her voice steady but underlaid with trepidation.

"It's all right, Jane," he said in a steely tone. "Smile but do not stop. They will take the hint soon enough."

They shouted to him, posturing like overdressed monkeys, fighting for even a crumb of his attention. Damn them, Grayson thought, his gaze completely impassive. Damn their impudence for daring to stare at her as if she had suddenly become a demirep. The muscles from his shoulders to his fingers tightened in the fierce urge to punch every last sly look from their faces.

"I told you," she said, staring straight ahead.

He glanced down at her. Despite the quiver in her voice, she looked perfectly composed. He was so accustomed to ignoring public opinion that he probably would not have minded the notoriety had he been with another woman. Mrs. Parks would have cheerfully responded to all the fuss with a crude finger gesture.

"It might do you a world of good, Jane," he murmured, "to let your reserve slip just once."

"I don't think the world is ready for the sort of slip I am capable of," she said enigmatically.

One of the bucks raised his quizzing glass to examine her, then dropped it immediately at the deadly look Grayson shot him.

For a moment he considered taking action, dragging the impudent pup down the steps to make an example of him. But another scandal would hardly help Jane, and for the first time since Grayson could remember, he forced himself to swallow his anger and consider the consequences of his behavior.

It would take effort, he thought, to guide her through these narrow straits of Society to safety. He would have to be on his guard to protect her from insults and inappropriate advances. He had understood that when he offered to help her.

What he hadn't realized was how easily he could lure her astray himself.

"What are you thinking, Jane?" he asked in an undertone.

"I shan't tell you, Sedgecroft. You would be shocked."

"Not me, darling." Ludicrous, after the life he led. As if a proper young lady like Jane had anything on his past. "Nothing *you* would do could shock me."

Chapter 8

❧❧

Their host and hostess escorted them through the gardens, introducing them to the foreign guests of distinction who graced the party. Simon found a glass of champagne and disappeared into the crowd with Lady Damaris Hill, whose whispered comment about a missing stocking explained the mystery of the nun's identity at the previous night's midnight masquerade.

An orchestra played on the grass beside a classical pavilion set at the end of the parkland's sloping lawns. A platform had been constructed for dancing; several younger people had spilled onto the east lawn. The pastel gowns of the ladies swayed like butterfly wings as they moved in graceful flutters.

"Are you hungry?" Grayson asked Jane, keeping his hand on her shoulder in a light but proprietary way.

"I am ravenous." She hesitated. "It does take nerves of steel to eat when everyone is staring at us though."

"I have forgotten them."

"How could you?"

"Perhaps because I don't care," he said with conviction.

"Well, then, neither shall I."

He stopped, studying her with a faint knowing smile. "Of course you care. All women do."

"Only those who are husband hunting," she said with a sigh.

"Which we might be."

"No, we're—" She bit the tip of her tongue, remembering how she must appear. "I am not ready to be put back on the market." Not now, and probably not ever again, she felt like adding.

"Remount, Jane," he said with an unmerciful smile. "One fall from the horse does not spinsterhood make."

She could have pinched him, reducing the complications of her life to such simple terms. "I wish you would stop equating my situation to equestrienne activity."

He gave her an apologetic look. "I keep forgetting how sensitive you are on the subject."

"Sedgecroft!" A woman's cry of delight interrupted Jane's response, not that she knew how to respond to his remark without lying through her teeth.

She and Grayson turned simultaneously to see a petite figure in brown silk bearing down on them, a flute of champagne held gracefully in hand. Jane stared. Surely that was not Mrs. Audrey Watson, the popular courtesan and former actress whose intellectual buffet suppers had made her a celebrity in the demimonde and the ton. Rumor had it that the Duke of Wenderfield desired her for his mistress.

"Audrey," Grayson said warmly, a little *too* warmly in Jane's opinion as the pair exchanged a brief embrace.

"Sedgecroft, it's been centuries since—" Audrey caught

herself and gave Jane such a genuinely friendly smile that she could not help softening toward her.

"Belshire's beautiful daughter, the eldest, isn't it?" Audrey asked in puzzlement. "What is she doing with the likes of you, Sedgecroft?"

Grayson gave Jane a long burning look that brought a blush to the ends of her hair. If she hadn't known better, she would have believed he was truly infatuated with her—oh, he excelled at this, the devil. She felt as if she ought to applaud his performance.

He drew Jane forward. "Have you ever had the honor of an introduction, Audrey?"

"No." Audrey studied the younger woman in concern; there was no pretense about her, no striving to impress. Her earthiness had earned her loyal supporters from politicians to struggling poets; her bluntness often offended. "But, my dear lady, aren't you brave to be out so soon, after yesterday? And you, Sedgecroft, you did not waste a single second before going on the pounce, did you?"

Going on the pounce? Jane thought in amused indignation. What a way to phrase it, reducing her relationship with Sedgecroft to predator and prey.

"Actually," she said when it became obvious that the aforementioned scoundrel was not about to set Audrey straight, "Lord Sedgecroft is only—"

"A man bewitched," he said under his breath, as polite and self-possessed as the next accomplished predator. Oooh. The talented wretch, making her tingle all over with his outrageous performance when she knew perfectly well not to believe him.

Jane gave him a poke in the back. "To be honest, our

association is not all that provocative. Nigel and Grayson are—"

"Rivals." He grasped her hand, squeezing the small bones of her knuckles until she glared at him. "One man's loss is another's gain, isn't it? Let us just say that I have quietly admired Jane from afar. I was not about to let anyone else take advantage."

Audrey took a deep sip of her champagne, glancing from the classically beautiful young lady to the sinfully handsome scoundrel who, she noted, was holding Jane's slender hand in a painfully possessive grip. "Whatever you say, Sedgecroft, but"—she brightened—"this means I can invite you to a supper together."

"That would be very nice, I'm sure," he replied, while Jane wondered what her parents would think of this development. Surely even her broad-minded mother would disapprove of her daughter drifting into the demimonde. Or perhaps not. This plan had taken the most unpredictable turn. Jane was beginning to think she had jumped from the proverbial frying pan into the fire.

And Sedgecroft definitely stoked the red-hot flames of hellfire in her soul.

"I think I see an old friend of mine at the table," she said, attempting to disengage her hand from his. "Would you both excuse me for a moment?"

Grayson brought her hand to his mouth to kiss her gloved fingertips, murmuring in a lovelorn voice, "Only for the shortest moment?"

It was an act. She knew it in her intellect, but all her female senses responded to the seductive timbre of his voice. "Yes," she said, flustered by the realization that he was perfectly aware of the disconcerting effect he had on her. "But I'm only going over to the tables."

He drew her forward by her fingertips, her knees touching his. A sinful flutter stirred deep in her belly. What did he think he was doing?

"Hurry back," he said, his eyes holding hers.

And then he let her go. Releasing her breath, she turned quickly to lose herself in the crowd.

Grayson watched her pensively, half aware that he himself was being watched by the other woman beside him. Acting the part of a smitten suitor was easier than he'd expected. Just being in Jane's presence made him ache for unbridled sex and reminded him he had not had a lover for longer than he cared to admit.

Perhaps her inaccessibility was what challenged him. He suspected there was more. She was intelligent, practical, his equal in conversation. She amused him with her prim dignity, and he was positive there were depths to her she had never dared reveal to anyone. He might have enjoyed plumbing those depths had his task not been to smoothly reinsert her back into Society.

His sultry gaze followed the movements of her body, her awkward dash to escape across the lawn. The fact that she strode like a soldier in no way detracted from the sway of her nicely rounded bottom beneath her pink gauze dress. Pink, he thought, his body hardening in a swelter of arousal. She'd be pink and white all over. Roses and cream. Sweet enough to enjoy in one bite. But he wouldn't devour her all at once. He would savor her in slow, tender nibbles. . . .

Dear heaven. She had his thoughts chasing one another in circles. His intention was to return her to respectability, not ruin her.

"Is it possible, Sedgecroft?" Audrey inquired softly. "Are *you* behind that wedding scandal yesterday?"

He hesitated, his lean face amused. This was a critical moment, a test of his ability to dissemble. Audrey had known him for a long time. He didn't want to lie to her, but chances were that anything he told her today would be broadcast all over London by tonight. "You know better than to ask me that. Would I admit it if I were?"

"This is very unusual behavior. I believe I am concerned. Do you know that the gossips are calling her Lady Jane Jilt?"

He felt a surge of anger. "Not to my face, they're not."

"It is the first time I have ever seen you with a decent female," she said quietly, following his lead as he merged back into the flow of traffic. "Beware, Sedgecroft."

"Beware of what?" he asked with a negligent shrug, his gaze leaving her to return again to Jane. "I am an honorable man. Have you ever known a woman to regret a friendship with me?"

She put her hand on his wrist. "It is you I worry about. That heart of yours may not easily be captured, but once it is, I suspect the loss might be fatal. Despite what happened to her yesterday, she is a woman made for marriage."

"That accursed word again. Yes, I know she is made for marriage." He frowned, noticing that quite a few of his acquaintances had crowded around the breakfast table to introduce themselves to Jane. Little boys, he thought in contempt. *They're practically licking their chops.* He couldn't see her expression, what she made of it. But was she actually going to eat while they all stood there drooling over her? "Look, we'll have to continue this lovely conversation later. The wolves are gathering, and she is in no state to defend herself."

Audrey turned to see what he was talking about. "This possessive side of you is fascinating. I don't believe I've ever seen it before. It doesn't mean—"

He brushed around her in annoyance. *Hadn't he promised to protect Jane?* "It isn't what you're thinking."

Audrey stared after his broad-shouldered body as he broke through the line of his male friends with his usual Boscastle arrogance. Her heart gave an unsettling flutter even though she had long ago resigned herself to a platonic association with the intriguing marquess. "It might not be what *you're* thinking either, darling," she said wistfully.

Several tables had been set up on the southwest lawn, draped with damask tablecloths that held silver chafing dishes, jugs of lemonade, and pots of coffee, tea, and chocolate. One of Sedgecroft's friends had brought Jane a plate of strawberries and sugared almonds.

She had just popped a strawberry into her mouth when she saw *him* cutting like a sword through the cluster of guests. Her tongue curled around the tart berry. She was conscious of the other women around her interrupting their conversations to stare. And no wonder. His masculine vitality cast a spell too potent to ignore. Who would not be swept away in his whirlwind of staggering appeal? He was a breath of fresh air to challenge the stale strictures of Society.

His male friends clapped him on the back and cast meaningful glances from him to Jane, as if awaiting a formal introduction. Which he refused to give for reasons she could not fathom. She already knew several of the young men through her brother. Sedgecroft actually looked angry at them. And at her. What an actor. What a nuisance.

"There you are," he announced across the table in a loud possessive voice that could not help but draw attention. "I have been looking for you everywhere. Do not leave me alone again."

Jane felt people staring at her, conversation arrested. Her voice caught at the back of her throat as she swallowed the strawberry whole. Color climbed into her cheeks. She wasn't as polished at this as Sedgecroft. Her natural impulse was to hide under the table. "Well, I was right here." Which of course he had known. "With your friends."

"Friends? *My* friends?" He cast a dismissive glare at the four men standing behind her. The quartet immediately began to drift away, warned by Grayson's tone of voice that they had trespassed on private territory.

"Well, who would have guessed?" one of them murmured. "Nigel's jilt and Sedgecroft?"

"Perhaps she wasn't a jilt, after all. Perhaps Nigel was given no choice in the matter."

The four men stopped and stared back at the table, sharing the same covetous thoughts. Was the Earl of Belshire's beautiful daughter about to be set up as a mistress? Who would have guessed she would be available for such a delicious arrangement? Or did the situation carry more serious implications? Was their idol about to be leg-shackled?

"That," Jane said, pursing her lips as the rogue himself came up beside her, "was a rather unnecessary act of drama for this early in the day."

"Convincing, wasn't I?" He grinned sheepishly. "Forgive me, but I had a hunch you needed to be saved."

"From eating breakfast?"

He took her elbow. "One does not accept attention from a gentleman without a certain indebtedness," he said with mock severity. "Breakfast today, bed tomorrow."

"Oh, honestly, Sedgecroft. Only a mind like yours could make such a connection. Breakfast . . . and bed sport."

"They are compatible, believe me."

"In your world, perhaps."

"Are we that different, you and I?" he teased.

"Of course we are."

"Well, far be it from me to corrupt you."

"I don't think you're all that corrupt."

He looked up suddenly, his eyes narrowing. Something had caught his attention behind her. "Don't you?" he asked distractedly. "Does that mean there's hope?"

She glanced around. She couldn't tell at what or whom he'd been staring so intently. Another woman? "I wouldn't bank on it."

"I know how men think," he said in a smug undertone, "especially those men."

"Those men," she whispered, trying to rescue another

strawberry from over his free hand before he returned her plate to the table, "are of your class and background. They admire—they *emulate* you."

He guided her off the walkway and down a cushioned slope of camomile. "Which is precisely why I know how they think. And why I was worried about you."

"That does not say very much about your character."

"No, it doesn't, does it?" He laughed suddenly. It was good fun but rather a challenge to spar with her. "Perhaps I should have left you in the gray dress."

"I tried to warn you."

They walked in silence for a few moments. Jane could not say how his hand had managed to slide down the small of her back, where it rested, provocative and proprietary, the weight of his fingers sending warm tingles down her spine. She had no idea where they were going either. All she knew was that he seemed preoccupied and that she was enjoying herself more than she should.

"I thought you wanted to place me back into the social arena as soon as possible."

"Yes. But not in the gladiator's pit. And not by yourself. Did they ask you any personal questions?"

She halted in her tracks to face him. He was starting to sound like her parents. "As a matter of fact, they did."

"Such as?" he demanded.

"Such as whether I cared for coffee or chocolate."

His eyes danced in amusement. "What was your answer?"

"I said neither."

"A woman of mystery." He feigned a disappointing

sigh. "Those rascals will take that as an invitation to intimacy."

"I told them I liked tea," she said tartly. "I do not see how that can possibly be interpreted as an invitation to *anything*, let alone to an intimate act."

"To a male on the prowl, the mere hint of a smile on a woman's lips is enough to encourage him. Trust me," he said with authority. "The fact is fixed as firmly as any scientific principle."

"My lips were engaged in eating, Sedgecroft, until you confiscated that plate from under my nose. I happen to be hungry."

He chuckled, claiming her arm again to lead her farther down the slope. "Did anyone ever tell you that your honesty will land you in trouble someday?"

Her stomach rumbled as she glanced back longingly at the breakfast tables. "Only my mother, at least a dozen times a week for my entire life. Where are we going now? People are talking about us."

"I'm sure you've made a favorable impression, Jane."

"I'm not. I told you this was too soon to make an appearance. Nigel and I never caused this kind of scene in public."

"Not until yesterday." He stopped, as if realizing what he'd said. Teasing her was one thing. Cruelty was another. "I didn't mean that as it sounded."

"Well, it's true." She paused, feeling a twinge of guilt. It was disconcerting to be treated like a fragile porcelain figure. She wished she deserved it. "I do have some inner fortitude, Sedgecroft."

"All I meant was that the ton has taken notice of us,"

he said more carefully. "That was our first aim. Give me your arm again."

Why didn't she refuse? she wondered in chagrin. If he were a pirate captain who ordered her to walk the plank, she would probably comply. She was only too happy to cling to his muscular forearm, never mind what disaster loomed ahead. This was probably why her parents had warned her to marry Nigel. To protect her from herself.

"Sedgecroft, not a step farther. This pavilion is famous for the seductions conducted within."

He guided her forward, a man on a mission if ever Jane had seen one. "I am well aware of that."

She blinked. "Then be aware that *I* am not going in."

He half turned to fix her with an imperious frown. "Stop dawdling, Jane. I need you. Come here right now."

"I beg your pardon."

"If my eyes have not deceived me, my sister Chloe just disappeared into the pavilion with a young cavalry officer who is a shade too forward for his own good. You might want to keep me from committing an act of violence."

"Are you certain it was Chloe?"

"No."

No, because he'd been too busy making sure Jane was safe from the hungry wolves to pay much attention to anything else. No, because Chloe was not supposed to be here today, and if she had gone to the pavilion, it was in brazen disregard to his orders.

"I'm not certain it was her," he said, a note of panic in his voice. "But I don't intend to take any chances either."

Jane stared at the red-brick pavilion with its four slen-

der white turrets stretching skyward, a tribute to a fairy-
tale castle of olden days. "Rumor has it that the pavilion's secret passages provide perfect trysting places for
the duke's more amorous guests."

"Yes, Jane," he said in a mildly patronizing tone. "I
doubt Chloe went inside to admire the stonework."

"Wait a moment," she said, eyeing him in open suspi-
cion. "I thought you told me you had locked her in her
room."

"A locked room to a Boscastle is not an obstacle," he
said grimly as the fragrant grass ended at a wide paved
walk. "It is a challenge, a stepping-stone to misadventure."

"She always looked like such a sensible girl," Jane
said, shaking her head. "I rather liked her the one time
we met at the foundling hospital."

"Sensible?" He snorted. "One never knows what
hides beneath the surface."

Jane bit the inside of her cheek. She could not bring
herself to look into those perceptive blue eyes, not with
the secret *she* was hiding from him. "Um, no. I suppose
not."

"That is one of the reasons I like you, Jane," he said.
"You are a very straightforward, sensible female."

Oh, dear. If he only knew how serpentine, how insensible she had proven to be in the past two days.

"I wish *you* could exert some influence on Chloe," he
added.

"I'm sure she is sensible at heart," Jane murmured,
nibbling her lower lip.

"That is because *you* are sensible."

"Stop making me sound like such a paragon." She

was going to scream if he kept heaping these undeserved compliments on her head. "It is embarrassing."

"That is exactly what I mean," he said, nodding approvingly. "I do not recall such honesty in a woman and I happen to value honesty," he went on, as if the point had not been drummed into her heart. Her dishonest, perfidious heart.

"I wasn't aware that honesty was a quality a man like you admired in the opposite sex," she said in a faint voice.

"Well, among other things." And they both knew what other things he valued by the ghost of a wicked smile that crossed his face. "Perhaps you can set an example for my sister."

"I'm not sure that's a good idea."

"She has no other female to emulate, you see. Not since our Emma went off to Scotland. I'm afraid I haven't set a very good example where morals are concerned."

"Hmm." No argument there.

"I can't simply let the family dynasty go to pot," he continued, aware he was confiding in her again. "The problem is, I thought I had a few more years of misadventure myself before I settled down."

"How cruel that your sinning must be cut short."

He laughed, the dark tones of his voice sliding pleasantly over her skin. "Isn't it though?"

The faint strains of the orchestra playing on the opposite slope drifted down toward them. A concealing row of willow trees overshadowed the walkway. A pair of white marble porpoises flanked the pavilion entrance, sending a spray of fine mist arching into the air. Grayson glanced around. No one at the party could see them now. Besides, the duke kept a parade of servants milling about outside to lend an air of propriety to the place.

"I've heard it was called the Pavilion of Pleasure," Jane murmured. "I always wondered what it was like."

"Well, wonder no more," Grayson said, unceremoniously whisking her inside the shadowed interior. "There. I don't believe we were seen."

"Sedgecroft, I'm not sure—"

"Be careful where you walk," he said, his voice absorbed in the disorienting shadows. "The floor is damp, and it's as dark as Hades in here."

Hades, she thought with a slight shiver, feeling a bit like Persephone as she followed her dark lord into the underworld. How had this happened? Yesterday she was contemplating her hard-earned freedom, and now, who could tell what twists the future held? How could she thwart his scheme without giving herself away?

"I notice that you've been here before," she commented wryly.

"Only when the pavilion was just built and the duke gave us a tour."

"Us?"

"My father and me." He turned, his handsome face looming into her vision. "Gracious, Jane, I was all of three."

"Truly?"

"Well." He coughed. "Perhaps thirteen."

"That's what I thought. What could have possessed your sister to come here today?"

"I shall give you one guess," he muttered, his brows knitting into a scowl.

"Perhaps she had a headache and needed a moment of peace."

He gave a rather insulting grunt at the suggestion. "Only an idiot would believe such an excuse. Do be quiet, Jane. Someone's coming."

He nodded distractedly to the gentleman and lady who had just emerged from the narrow corridor, both looking breathless and guilty at being spotted.

"Simon!" Jane said in shock, coming to a stop.

"Jane," he stammered, his eyes widening in recognition. "What are you doing in here?"

"I—"

"She has a headache and needs a moment of peace," Grayson said in a grave voice.

"Oh, right," Simon said, and completely missed his sister's look of indignation. "The pavilion always helps my headaches, too. Try soaking your feet in the Pool of the Pleiades. I'll meet you both back outside, shall I?"

"What a grand idea," Grayson said, glancing at Jane from the corner of his eye. "Meet us at the end of the walkway."

"Well, so much for my chaperone," Jane said archly as her brother gave Sedgecroft a friendly pat on the arm before whisking the giggling Lady Damaris Hill in the opposite direction.

"At least it shall appear we were all in here together," Grayson said, shaking his head. He motioned to a dark passageway off to the right. "Ah, that looks like a place conducive to a passionate moment, doesn't it?"

"I'm sure I wouldn't know."

"No?" he teased.

She frowned as she trailed his tall figure down a narrow corridor that gave quite unexpectedly into a series of deep scallop-shaped bubbling pools.

He turned, studying her face intently for several moments. "What are you thinking, Jane?" he asked in a low, compelling voice.

She sighed. The humid seclusion must have gone to her head, because before she could stop herself, she said, "No young man has ever lured me to such a place. Never."

He smiled slowly, his eyes meeting hers. "I do not believe you. One or two must have tried."

Her face felt warm. Her dress was clinging damply to her body from the moist vapors. She felt a flush work its way to the surface of her skin. "No, actually. No one ever tried."

"Then allow me," he said, holding out his hand, plumes of steam rising around his powerful frame. "Come here."

Her heartbeat quickened at that imperious command. To her amazement she felt herself moving toward him, obeying his dark velvety voice.

"What do you want?" she whispered, holding her breath.

"To further your education." He bent his head down to hers, his blond hair brushing her cheek. "Since there are obvious deficits, I shall take a moment to provide you with the experience lacking in your background."

"What a gentlemanly thing to do."

"There's no need to thank me," he said, his eyes flickering over her like a spark.

She felt the heat of his gaze burn to her bones. "I'm sure this isn't . . . wise."

He ran his forefinger down the side of her jaw, raising shivers on her skin. "There is a time to be wise, and a time to be wicked. Which do you suppose it is?"

His heavy-lidded blue eyes made her feel weak, made her heart quicken. "I think . . . I . . ."

A wanton flame kindled in the depths of his eyes. For the life of her she could not break away from his gaze. His silken voice lulled her. "Be a little wicked just once, Jane. Just for a moment."

He drew her quivering body into his arms. His head lowered to hers. Before his firm mouth even touched hers, she felt utterly disoriented, giddy, like a child's spinning top. He leaned into her, his breath a teasing caress at the hollow of her throat. Hellfire, she thought distantly, arching her spine. *The flames of the tempter, and I am walking willingly straight into his white-hot heart.*

His tongue traced the contours of her mouth with a sensual finesse that made her toes curl in her silk pumps. When he gently drew her bottom lip between his sharp white teeth, her legs almost gave way. A tremor of longing shuddered deep inside her. His tongue delved into her mouth, and she moaned. She could feel his heart pounding in powerful echoes through his linen shirt. The heat of his hard torso lit a fire in her belly, and spread in burning circles.

So this was what had made Nigel and his governess defy the world. This was what made sensible women turn insensible and unwise.

"Well," he murmured, his voice thick and seductive, "I had no idea how good you were at wickedness."

"As if I led the way, you demon."

He laughed helplessly, his hands tightening around her. She was too shrewd for her own good, he thought. Or for his. She would never believe that he had not meant to do this. "Say the word and I shall stop," he whispered in her ear.

"Not . . . not yet."

"Not yet?" he asked, teasing her. "Does my prim little pigeon harbor passion somewhere deep inside? Show me, Jane. Share your secrets with me."

He groaned and nudged her back against the wall, pinning her wrists to the wall with his forearms. Her mouth tasted sweetly of strawberries. Her skin burned with the sensual heat of a woman aroused, and he found himself wondering when, if ever, he had been forced to exert such restraint over the rake in him who plotted seduction, who craved release from the sexual tension that tightened his body into a coil. He was amazed at the painful ache she stirred in him.

This was embarrassing. Here he was trying to rescue her reputation while stealing kisses from her on the sly. Some hero he was turning out to be. But . . .

But she did something to him. He hadn't decided quite what it was. She wrapped his senses up in knots. He couldn't help himself.

"I want to devour you," he whispered.

"Do you, Sedgecroft?" she murmured, pressing her shoulders to the wall to steady herself against the sensation of falling into a black, heated void.

"I am lost," he said against her mouth. "Save me, Jane."

"Save you?" she whispered.

Shimmering arcs of color danced behind her eyes. She

sighed as his breath raised warm shivers along her collar-bone, skimmed the creamy rise of her cleavage until the pink tips of her breasts strained against the thin gauze gown. She stared down at his head. He looked up slowly into her desire-clouded eyes. "I am the one who needs to be saved," she said with a sigh. "I feel—"

"Better than anything I have ever touched. Dear Jane, never doubt for a moment that you are desirable."

She studied his beautiful face, the face of her down-fall, in fascination. Those blue eyes studied her back in blatant sensuality. Blue the color of a midnight sky, the color of sin.

"Close your eyes," he murmured in amusement, rubbing his forefinger across her wet lower lip.

She did, and his mouth returned to hers, greedily absorbing her gasp of excitement, his tongue seducing the very breath from her body. Heat and sensual awareness washed over her in shivery waves. Her knees bent, trapped by the iron-hard support of his thighs. She fought the urge to press herself against his body. Her back bowed slightly.

Grayson could not help responding even though he sensed that Jane was in over her head. He thrust, the movement instinctive. In his mind he was already inside her. He felt the involuntary shudder that crept down her spine. Her breasts rose and fell against his hard chest. He drew his hands down the enticing curves of her body, tracing her ribs, sculpting the ripe flesh that tempted him beyond mercy. He wanted to tear that gown off with his teeth.

He couldn't think of too many young ladies who would turn a stolen kiss into a crisis of self-control. Actually, he couldn't name a single one. Not that other ladies never engaged in pleasures behind closed doors. But Jane brought an appealing freshness to the forbidden.

"Sedgecroft," she said, taking a deep breath.

He drew back slightly, releasing a sigh of unadulterated longing into her hair. "Yes?"

"What are we doing?" she asked, her voice shaky.

The original point, he reminded himself, had been to make her feel as if she were a desirable female, to prove to her that Nigel's rejection had not rendered her unappealing to a man.

He had succeeded to a humiliating degree. His own body burned, the blood in his veins simmering with a lust he had never known. Was it possible, he wondered wistfully, that the lady did harbor a little naughtiness beneath that shell of propriety? No. He dismissed that provocative consideration. Darker motives belonged to men like him and their earthy mistresses, not to roses-and-cream-complexioned young women of impeccable breeding. Too bad for them both.

Her subdued whisper broke the spell. "I think I hear voices above us. Listen."

He angled his head to the side, his brows drawing into a frown of self-disgust. God above. In his fit of lust for Jane, he had forgotten all about Chloe. "I think you're right, and one of those voices sounds like my sister."

Jane smoothed down her disarrayed gown, feeling flushed all over. She was hardly composed enough to appear before anyone yet. Never in her life had she felt such a storm of unsettling sensations. She needed time to recover.

"Hurry up," he said, catching her hand, back to his usual arrogance. "This is a crucial moment."

"I do not hear her calling for help," she whispered in annoyance.

"That is why it is crucial," he said, dragging her down the passageway toward a small torch-lit stairwell. "Silence implies submission."

"I shall remember that in future."

He glanced back at her flushed oval face. He doubted she had a clue how badly he had wanted to take her. "It was not a criticism of *your* behavior. We both know you're sensible enough to say when to stop."

"Am I?" she muttered as they emerged at the top of the stone steps into a cozy towered chamber, so tiny that it held only a Grecian chaise and—

—a man wearing a blue military jacket and Hessian boots, and a familiar raven-haired figure sitting with her head against his shoulder.

"Excuse me," Grayson said in a low controlled voice that vibrated in the silence. "Are we interrupting something?"

The officer leaped to his feet, his face dark with fear as he surveyed the tall powerful figure that towered over him. "My lord, please, let me explain."

"I think I understand perfectly well what is happening," Grayson replied, brushing the terrified young lieutenant away with one hand as if he were a fly. His blue eyes were blazing. "I was talking to my hellion sister."

Chloe came gracefully to her feet, a slow blush spreading across her face as she noticed Jane hiding behind her brother. "What are you doing here, Grayson?"

"What are *you* doing here?"

"May we discuss this later?" she asked quietly, her voice both repentant and rebellious.

The officer tried to step between brother and sister. Chloe motioned him covertly back to the chaise a second before Grayson swung toward him. "Let me handle this, William."

"I do not wish you to be punished," he said awkwardly, swallowing at the step Grayson took in his direction.

Jane slipped around Grayson's tall rigid figure and sat down beside the other man. "Do not say another word to him," she whispered. This side of Sedgecroft was so different from what she'd seen of him. Oh, what a temper.

"But I wish to marry her," the officer said, twisting his hat in his hands. "I want to ask his permission."

Jane couldn't help smiling at this romantic courage. The poor fool didn't stand a chance in the face of Grayson's outrage. "How long have you known each other?" she asked in an undertone.

"A few days." He was gazing at Chloe with painful adoration. "I've never felt so deeply about anyone in my life. Do you understand what I mean?"

"Well . . ." Jane's gaze strayed to the marquess, her body still warm from the imprint of his well-muscled form against hers. Did she understand? she wondered, her breath hitching in her throat. Could one lose one's heart without even realizing it? Did a person have any control, or did it simply happen?

Grayson and Chloe were engaged in a bitter argument now, their emotions running rampant. Grayson was threatening to send Chloe to her aunt and uncle in the country if she did not control her behavior. Chloe retorted, "You might as well. I have no life to speak of with you breathing down my neck night and day."

Jane could not decide whom to defend, or if she dare interfere at all. Grayson was really quite effective in his protective fury, pacing around his sister as he lectured her.

Chloe was either very brave or very foolish to stand up to him. He looked capable of carrying through his threat. She leaned close to the young lieutenant, whispering, "If I were you, I would sneak out of here while I had the chance. He seems terribly upset."

The young man, studying Grayson's broad-shouldered frame and darkly furious face, was apparently having second thoughts about the situation himself.

"Do you think Chloe would understand?"

In Jane's estimation the rebellious Chloe was probably too confused to know her own mind. "I think she can handle this better by herself," she said gently. "I also think she would not wish to see you dead over . . . an unwise moment."

The man stood, gauging the safest way around the two arguing siblings. "I shall take your advice then." He glanced down at her as if truly seeing her for the first time. "How rare it is to find a woman such as you who is both beautiful and sensible. Dare I hope you will convey my apologies to Lady Chloe?"

"Go," Jane said softly. "The marquess is twice your size." And ten times as impressive.

He vanished down the stairs without further prompting. And not a second too soon. Grayson had concluded his angry tirade; Chloe stood facing the wall, her pale arms crossed over her chest, her blue eyes glittering with unshed tears of humiliation.

That the young officer had fallen in love so impulsively with the raven-haired Chloe did not surprise Jane at all. The entire Boscastle family appeared to live every moment of life with passion, and evidently inspired those who crossed their paths to do the same.

A very passionate family indeed, she thought as she glanced up appraisingly at Grayson. His angry gaze met hers, and she felt her heart jump at the raw emotion in his eyes. She didn't dare say a word for fear he might explode.

Well, she could fault him for many things, but she would have to commend him for trying to protect his sister, even if he had gone a little overboard. She supposed that his passion for life probably spilled over into every aspect of his character.

Which certainly made being close to him a challenge.

"Where did our Lothario go?" he demanded, glancing at the empty space beside Jane on the chaise. He looked disappointed that he didn't have anyone to murder.

"He remembered a previous appointment," she answered calmly.

"Well, it's a damned good thing for him, or his next appointment would be with the undertaker," he said in a thunderous tone.

Jane cleared her throat. "Calm yourself, my lord. He is gone."

Chloe whirled around, her tearful gaze suddenly focused on Jane. "What is *she* doing here anyway after yesterday? Oh, Grayson, don't tell me you have chosen her as your next victim. That is so typical of you that I can't stand it."

Jane rose, certain her face had turned several unbecoming shades of red. "There is a perfectly logical explanation."

"Which we are not about to give her," Grayson said, his tone clipped. "The fact is that you disobeyed me, Chloe, and displayed a total lack of judgment in your behavior both last night and today. No decent woman would be caught in the pavilion with a man."

Jane's mouth opened in astonishment. Had she misheard the big scoundrel?

"Find a footman and have the carriage brought around, Chloe," he said sternly, his hands planted on his lean hips. "You have had your misadventure for the month."

Chloe stepped around him, throwing Jane a sympathetic look. "I would run from him and not look back, were I you."

"The lady is here only to protect your virtue," he said in a stony voice. "Do not ever insult her again."

"Well, it's true, Grayson," Chloe rushed on, her shoulders lifting. "Jane is a decent young lady, and she has no idea what will become of her once you decide—"

"That will be enough, Chloe." His blue eyes burned like coals.

"It's true," she said stubbornly.

Jane shook her head, sorry for them both, and stared down at the floor. "Please stop this, the pair of you. You're too angry to talk in a reasonable manner."

"Run from him, Jane," Chloe whispered, wiping the back of her gloved hand across her cheek.

His face darkened. Jane had the feeling he was just as upset as his sister, but had no idea what to do. A pair of Titan tempers. "You have really pushed me to the limit this time," he muttered.

"I am sorry, Jane," Chloe said, touching Jane's hand. "Sorry that I insulted you and even more so that somehow you have fallen into my brother's clutches."

"Chloe!" he roared.

She darted around him and plunged down the narrow flight of steps, her footsteps echoing against the stone walls of the pavilion, Grayson staring after her in such bewilderment Jane would have felt sorry for him had he handled the situation better.

Chapter 9

❧❧

Grayson raked his hand through his fair hair, looking a little sheepish in the aftermath of the confrontation. "Well, what a scene that was," he said in a weak attempt at a joke. "Do you young women realize what an effort it is to keep you out of trouble?"

"As easy as it is for men like you to lead us there?"

He frowned. "What is that supposed to mean?"

"Nothing. Nothing at all."

His eyes narrowed suspiciously. "Are you actually defending the hellion?"

"I don't know." She bit her lip, aching to tell him what a bully he had been.

"You are," he said, utterly astonished. "Aren't you?"

"All right," Jane said, frowning back at him. "I suppose I am."

He looked genuinely baffled. "Why?"

She swept past him to the stairs. She was flattered that he actually cared what she thought, although she was the worst person in the world to ask for an honest opinion.

"You were rather hard on Chloe, don't you think?"

she said over her shoulder. "All that nonsense about my being here only to protect her virtue, and you with your threats to banish her. You scared the wits out of all three of us."

He stepped toward her, his large frame warm and pleasantly intimidating in the shadows. He was angry at her now, too, only this anger was controlled. "Forgive me, Jane," he said coolly, "for trying to protect my own sister from bringing disgrace upon herself."

"I still think you could have handled the matter with a trifle more tact," she said. She was determined to hold her ground, as shaky as that ground appeared to be. Then she hesitated, the lost look in his eyes touching her heart. How could one fault a man trying to be both mother and father to his siblings and failing miserably at the task?

"I'm worried about her, Jane," he admitted. "I was so close to her before our father died, and ever since then, I feel as if I don't even know who she is."

"Perhaps she feels the same way," Jane said.

"What do you mean?"

"Perhaps she does not understand herself either, Grayson. Perhaps you should allow her a little more freedom."

A frown shadowed his angular features. "Jane, I think it's you who doesn't understand." He took her chin in his hand and tilted her face back to his, his thumb stroking the underside of her jaw. "Would you have been caught on a couch kissing a man you barely knew?"

His touch sent another sparkling tremor all the way down to her toes. She inhaled slowly. "Until yesterday, I would have been able to answer that question quite convincingly. Sedgecroft, you are such a hypocrite."

He blinked, totally taken aback. "I am?"

"You are!"

He sounded embarrassed and amused at the same time. "I am not."

"You are. What do you think *we* were doing a few minutes ago? Or is such imprudent behavior so standard for you that you are not even aware of it?"

He lowered his handsome face to hers. "Of course I haven't forgotten. I don't think you have either. It was something, wasn't it?"

"Will you kindly not stray from the subject? It is a critical rule of polite conversation."

The corners of his mouth quirked in the heart-stopping grin that had brought stronger gentlewomen than Jane to their knees. "Isn't the subject kissing?"

He removed his fingers from her chin, but his sensual mouth hovered only a breath from hers. His magnetism was distracting. "This is a diversionary tactic on your part to lure me from the true topic."

"Oh? And how am I luring you, may I ask?" he said.

"The true topic," she said forcefully, praying for the strength to resist the pleasures of his enticing mouth, "is that you and I were guilty of the same sin for which you berated Chloe and her officer."

There. She had done it, made her point and resisted him at the same time, an effort that left her quite exhausted. Let him refute that logic.

"That was different," he said airily.

Her lips parted on a gasp. "How do you come to that startling conclusion?"

He was infuriatingly cool. "For one thing, my motives were not in question. I take full responsibility for my sins. Contrary to popular belief, I am not in the habit of seducing every woman I meet."

"Are you a celibate scoundrel?"

"A selective one," he replied. "I have no idea why my few indiscretions are of such interest to everyone."

"You brought two of your past mistresses to my wedding!"

"But did anyone actually see me in the arms of these women?"

"Of course not. It was a chapel, after all."

"Well, then. No one has really come forth with any evidence that I am a reprobate."

"The fact that the civilized world is afraid to confront you with your sins does not in any way absolve you of them."

"The proof, Jane?" His deep chuckle sent a shiver down her back. "The witnesses?"

"The point, Sedgecroft," she retorted, fully aware he had diverted her. "The topic of conversation. If you want Chloe to conduct herself in a seemly fashion, then it is not enough to lecture and threaten her. You must set an example."

He blinked his gorgeous blue eyes. "That is why I am making amends to you, Jane. That is why I am helping to straighten out the scandal my cousin made of your life. To show my family how a Boscastle must behave."

"And kissing me in the pavilion demonstrates this in what way?"

"All right. I admit it. That was a slight detour on the road of my decent intentions. Did it hurt anything?"

"Well."

He smiled. He meant to help her, to heal her. She was an unusual woman, possibly too much of a personality for Nigel to manage. Perhaps being betrayed had altered her perception. She had felt defenseless and delicate in his arms. But her mind was not defenseless. Oh, no. She had hidden weapons that assaulted a male before he could raise a shield. It would take a long time for her to trust again. Could she trust him? Grayson was not sure.

"I could have kissed you for days," he murmured ruefully. Shaking his head, he traced the prominent curve of her cheekbone with his thumb. "You wouldn't mind, would you?"

Sensation penetrated deep into her muscles, a pleasant shakiness that spread throughout her limbs. "For days? Isn't that a bit of an exaggeration?"

He laughed softly. His fingers slid down the pale arch of her throat to the cusp of her creamy shoulder. "Months even. Years."

Her breath caught as the buttons of his coat brushed across the aching buds of her breasts. His fingers moved over her shoulder in taunting spirals and slow touches designed to devastate, to liquefy a woman's body, and Jane discovered that when it came to resisting the Boscastle passion for life, she really was no stronger than the rest of the world.

"Soft skin," he murmured. "I do believe I have never felt such temptation before. From the moment I saw you at the altar, I have not quite been myself. Outside of my usual role, I find I've become awkward, uncertain of my lines, the expectations placed on me. I'm not even certain you should trust me, Jane."

His mouth was almost touching hers. She felt the rise and fall of his warm breath on her lips, the latent power of his lean torso against hers. Desire stirred in the secret places of her body. How easily she could be misled, she thought. How seductive it was of him to share his feelings. And awkward? Not for a heartbeat.

She swallowed. "Is this what you mean by setting an example?"

"Yes." He took a breath, his firm mouth curving at the corners.

"Excuse me?"

"If we were Chloe and her officer," he said quietly, staring into her eyes, "we would still be on that couch. You would not be questioning me. We would quite possibly be on the verge of making love."

She lowered her eyes, wondering if he actually believed this nonsense. Her body apparently did, judging by the rapid thundering of her heart. "I don't think—"

"No. I doubt you would be thinking at all, Jane. Or even talking. You would be too busy allowing me to please you."

She glanced up and gazed into his hard, angular face. Where amusement had before lent his features a look of satirical beauty, a darker mask of desire now gazed back at her. She had no idea if he was serious or merely repeating the lines from one of his famous seductions. She knew that she wanted him to kiss her so badly that every vein in her body throbbed with undercurrents of need. Her lips softened. Her breasts swelled, the pliant contours lightly pressed to the strong musculature of his chest.

"No," she said, sounding like a proper young lady desperate to retain her good sense. "You are wrong."

His nostrils flared, a male scenting female desire. "Am I?" he asked quietly.

He brought his mouth to hers, a shock of sensation that she must have experienced as intensely as he did. He felt her soften against him as her knees folded beneath her. He swore under his breath and caught her by her forearms. In the obscure part of his brain that was not aroused by her, he realized he was deviating from his purpose. And would have to stop before he did more harm than good. Yes, that was where the fault lay in his thinking. He had not foreseen that the best intentions could cause greater problems than they intended to solve.

Reluctantly he drew away from her, his voice rueful. "And therein lies the difference."

Jane struggled to achieve a semblance of normality. She felt like a ripe fruit that had been plucked from a tree and dropped. Had she wished for him to continue? No. Yes. *Yes.* "The difference?" she said in confusion. "Ah, I see. You mean between Chloe, her officer, and us?"

Her voice was uneven. Could he hear it? Her body was shaking. Could he tell? Of course he could. He had caused this embarrassing disequilibrium, and look at him standing there, as detached as a tethering post.

"The difference between us and them," he continued, sounding a little pompous, "is character."

Jane eased around him to descend the rest of the stairs, groping against the wall to steady herself in the dark. How he could talk of character when they had been moments from acting on their most basic impulses escaped her. The very stones of this pavilion must have been imbued with some passion potion. She hoped to heaven that being outside would clear her head.

"We are discreet," he added as he followed her. "Chloe disobeyed me and deceived me in order to meet that man today. I cannot imagine *you*, Jane, ever going to such lengths. I cannot imagine you involved in deception. Can you?"

She rattled off him some evasive answer and hurried from the pavilion before she could catch his response. Her ears had gone deaf to his voice. All she could hear were the bells of her own doom tolling in the future.

He could not imagine her involved in deception.

She could never let him learn the truth.

Grayson was not as unaffected by their encounter as he appeared to be. He escorted Jane from the pavilion into the afternoon warmth, studying her in guarded silence.

Well, well, who would have thought it? The respectable Lady Jane rattling him to the core. He wondered what she made of it, if she had any idea of how she had disarmed him, of how intriguing he found the situation. She had to be one of Society's best-kept secrets. What other surprises did she have in store? Certainly he had never been aroused and reprimanded so soundly all in the space of an afternoon. He shook his head, squinting at the light, keeping her pink-sheathed figure in his peripheral vision.

He thought of how sweet her lips had tasted, how soft

and yielding her curving body had felt against his. To look at her now, all prim reserve and aloof dignity, one certainly would not guess she would respond like that. He was dying to know what else he might have found if he'd prodded a little deeper. What an appalling time to learn he still had a conscience.

He glanced around, satisfied to see Simon and Damaris standing at the end of the walkway, waiting for them. This lent enough of an air of respectability to their brief disappearance that he and Jane could not be accused of a dalliance. Chloe was another matter.

He halted at the end of the path to talk to Jane. Hypocrite, was he? That stung a bit, probably because it was true. "Will you be all right for a few minutes if I leave you alone?" he asked anxiously. "I want to make sure Chloe is indeed on her way home."

Her gaze met his, and he felt another bolt of heat travel through the deepest reaches of his body. Her cheeks were stained a becoming rose, and she didn't look quite as reserved or dignified as he'd imagined. "Jane," he asked again, "are you all right?"

"Of course I'm all right. Why shouldn't I be?"

He smiled at her crisp reply. Despite her effort to appear composed, he knew he had given her something to think about. For all her intelligence, she had little knowledge of sensual affairs. What had she and Nigel been doing together all these years, for God's sake? Apparently not kissing. Absurdly enough, the thought buoyed his spirits, but really, he would have to watch himself with her in future.

"Join your brother," he ordered gently, glancing over

her head at the throngs of people on the lawn. "Have him take care of you while I'm gone."

"Since he's done such a good job as my chaperone until now, you mean?"

His gaze returned to her face. "Perhaps I should ask you to watch over him. You seem to be the more responsible one."

"Not in some matters," she murmured.

"What happened in the pavilion wasn't your fault. It was mine."

"Despite everything," Jane said in an undertone, "I find it impossible to stay angry with you. I suppose it is a waste of breath to correct a man who believes himself superior to the world in general." She paused, sighing in chagrin. "Go and make amends to your sister. I shall be fine, but do attempt not to lose your temper again."

"You try controlling the Boscastle clan in a normal temper," he said as he steered her back to the path. "On Christmas Day in our family one practically has to hang from the chandelier to get a moment's attention."

"So Nigel told me."

They were on the verge of the lawn now, the breakfast tables only a foot or so from them. Simon and Damaris were drifting away. Grayson cast a fierce look at the groups of young bucks who were pretending not to stare at Jane. This, he supposed, was what reform had done to him. Protecting desirable young women from games he'd once played only too well himself. Games he wouldn't mind playing with her now, for that matter.

"One more thing," he said carefully. "I notice how often Nigel enters our conversations, which is perfectly understandable, but I think you need to accept the fact that if he doesn't return to make things right in the next week or so, he might not return at all."

"I realize that," she said, managing to avoid his eyes. "I am . . . quite resigned."

"There's no need to resign yourself to anything yet." Perhaps he had been too blunt. "We'll find another husband for you."

"But I don't want— Oh, look. There's my friend Cecily waving to me from the last table. I'll be safe enough with her, don't you think?"

Safe from me? he wondered, his smile ironic. Had he frightened her off? Would she forgive him? It might be better all the way around if she didn't. The feelings she provoked in him were unfamiliar, more than just a challenge to his self-control.

She bustled away before he could respond, and his gaze became reflective as he watched her melt into the small crowd of young women who turned to her in welcome. For a silly moment he felt tempted to tell her to be careful. But she had stood up to him on Chloe's behalf and walked away none the worse for it. Again he marveled at Nigel's stupidity in letting her go. There were mysteries to Jane that the dimwit had obviously never detected.

Chapter 10

The old saying popped into her mind again: Out of the frying pan, into the fire. Still a little dazed from her experience with Sedgecroft, she found herself smothered in the circle of four chattering young women. She wondered if they had any idea of how warm her face felt, if they could tell her lips were still tingling from his kisses.

Of course they all knew what had happened to her yesterday. Her dearest friend, the Honorable Cecily Brunsdale, a viscount's daughter, had been one of her bridesmaids, an eyewitness to the fiasco. Jane did not know what reaction to expect from the others.

Sympathy, embarrassment, the generous courtesy of pretending the awful event had never occurred?

What she did not count on was their fleeting interest in her failed attempt at marriage. Yes, they acknowledged her loss, but only for a moment or so. That was yesterday's news, worthy of their pity, a few well-meaning if insincere smiles. Far more interesting to these four social butterflies were the details of her deliciously surprising romance with the widely adored Marquess of Sedgecroft.

"Romance?" she said blankly at their insistent barrage of questions. Now her face felt on fire. "What makes you think I am having a romance with him?"

"What else would it be?" one of them murmured.

"A woman does not walk into a room with Sedgecroft without falling prey to his charm," said Miss Priscilla Armstrong, a self-proclaimed expert on such matters after three uneventful Seasons.

Cecily, a slim ash-blonde with clear gray eyes, leapt immediately to Jane's defense. "Need I remind you, Priscilla, that Sedgecroft is Nigel's cousin. It is his duty to stand in for him as her companion until Nigel . . ."

Until Nigel did what? everyone wondered, looking at Jane in wide-eyed anticipation for a hint as to what one might expect.

But she stubbornly resisted revealing anything else, heeding Grayson's warning that a little mystery would only make her more alluring to the ton. Not that she wished to be alluring. She did wish, however, not to cross Sedgecroft. If his behavior in the past twenty-four hours was an example of his single-minded persistence, she had no desire to arouse his anger. Goodness, he was more than she could deal with as a friend, let alone as an enemy.

"I have nothing more to say on the subject," she said with a distress that was becoming more genuine by the hour.

But the four other women hardly noticed; they were listening raptly to Miss Evelyn Hutchinson's opinion on the subject of Sedgecroft, a man she had obviously been observing and analyzing with academic fervor for quite some time.

"You do know what the maid of his former mistress said?"

"Which one?" asked Lady Alice Pfeiffer, showing herself to be not exactly ignorant on the subject herself.

"Mrs. Parks," Evelyn replied.

"Tell us," Priscilla ordered. "Jane has a right to know."

"Well, I—"

"You should know the truth," Cecily said quietly.

Jane wasn't sure she wanted to know the truth. She craned her neck, unconsciously scanning the crowd for a sign of her powerful blue-eyed troublemaker. She hoped he wasn't scolding his spirited sister again. Jane felt drawn to Chloe's passion for life and sensed a wounded heart beneath the rebellion. Lord, would she herself ever be the object of his lionlike fury? Yes, if he found out what an accomplished schemestress she was.

Evelyn pressed her fan to her chin. "Mrs. Parks was overheard confiding that one night with Sedgecroft was a bacchanalian orgy to the female senses."

Jane blinked, her attention diverted. "I'm sure you misunderstood." Although she could well believe it.

Evelyn nodded slyly. "She also said that a woman had best not plan to ride in the park for at least a fortnight after."

"Oh, honestly!" Cecily exclaimed disapprovingly while the other women digested this fascinating tidbit of gossip in delight. "That is not exactly the sort of revelation I had in mind when I encouraged you. "

"And," Evelyn added, "he reads the morning paper while he carries on certain physical *activities* with his paramours."

Priscilla leaned forward, her lips parting. "He carries on these activities in the *morning*?"

"Morning, noon, and night," Evelyn said knowingly. "He indulges a woman's every whim."

Several deep sighs heralded the silence that fell until Evelyn felt compelled to continue.

"To spend time in his company is to fall under his spell. Sedgecroft is a man of deliberation. Once he makes his move, that is the end."

"The end of what?" Jane demanded, the hair on her nape prickling.

"The end of virtue. The start of vice. He has already initiated his strategy long before his victim realizes what has happened."

Cecily frowned in warning. "That is enough, Evelyn."

"Not that any woman he loves would consider herself a victim," Evelyn said as an afterthought. "A treasure is more apt."

Another silence descended.

Jane found an opening in the circle and broke away, having experienced enough of Sedgecroft's prowess for one day.

"Excuse me, won't you? I think my brother is summoning me."

Cecily hurried after her, speaking in a soft apologetic whisper. "I came to see you last night, but your parents had you under guard. How are you ever going to survive this, Jane?"

Jane stared across the green expanse of the park. Cecily was one of her oldest confidantes, almost as close to her as Caroline and Miranda. At age three Cecily had announced to an entire church congregation that she had caught the vicar in the wine pantry with her aunt. At age five Cecily had cut off all her lustrous hip-length hair to play Robin Hood with her brothers. At eleven she committed the same offense because she planned to run away in disguise and become a jockey.

No wonder Jane adored her. Cecily had backbone, and she actually loved the young duke she was about to marry. But not even her dear friend knew about Jane and Nigel's scheme to thwart the course of their untrue love.

Which was why Jane wished she could be honest when Cecily took her by the hand and whispered, "I was sick with worry over you. If I'd had a gun, I would have gone after Nigel myself and shot him dead. Believe it or not, I understand exactly how you must feel. It's so brave of you to show your face today, but Jane—is this wise?"

There is a time to be wise, and a time to be wicked.

"The ton is going to talk about me anyway, Cecily. The sooner I face that, the better."

"I'm not referring to the ton."

"Then—"

"Sedgecroft."

"Oh." Jane's gaze strayed across the lawn to the stunningly handsome figure striding toward her, every muscle moving with effortless grace. Her heart gave a leap as he looked at her. Oh, such a gorgeous monster. With regret she returned her focus to Cecily's anxious face. "I don't think you need to worry about me."

"Sedgecroft, Jane. The consummate rake."

"I am simply having breakfast with him. That's all."

"Sedgecroft doesn't simply 'have' a meal with a

woman," Cecily said. "Not unless she is the main course."

Breakfast and bed sport. Her own words echoed tauntingly in her mind.

"Nonsense," she said firmly.

Cecily glanced around, aware she did not have her friend's full attention. Her brows rose when she noticed the arresting marquess approaching. "Ah, speak of the devil," she muttered. "Jane, please, *please*, listen to me. You are in a most vulnerable state. I know how deeply Nigel hurt you, but to link up with Sedgecroft. Well, isn't it a little like walking blindfolded along the edge of a cliff?"

"Hello, Cecily," Grayson said, gazing down at Jane as he positioned himself between the two women. "How is your father these days? I haven't seen him at the club lately."

Cecily subjected him to her coolest stare. As one of Chloe's friends, she was all too aware of the lethal Boscastle charm and ever on guard against it. "He is well, thank you. And your family? They all looked hale in the chapel yesterday."

"Hale and full of hell, if I may use the word." He glanced from her to Jane, his eyes pinning her with a solicitous concern that she knew was all for show. "Would you like to dance, Jane?"

Cecily stared down pointedly at the hand he had brushed across Jane's shoulder, her lips thinning in disapproval.

Jane shook her head. "Not now, thank you. I—"

"Shall we get some champagne then?" he asked, nudging her ever so subtly away from Cecily.

"Oh, champagne would be lovely," Cecily said, deliberately refusing to take the hint. "Why don't you run off and fetch us some, Sedgecroft?"

He gave her an ingenuous grin. "But that would mean leaving Jane alone again, and I couldn't be so rude. Why don't you be a dear and find a footman for us? A duchess should practice giving orders, don't you think?"

Jane lowered her gaze, afraid she might burst into laughter, if not tears. Oh, the look of shock on Cecily's face! And Sedgecroft was the very devil, provoking her poor friend this way.

Cecily's smile was brittle. "That reminds me, Jane. Hudson and I are riding in the park Tuesday afternoon with his nieces and nephews. You will come with us?"

Grayson smiled back at her. "We'd love to, wouldn't we, Jane?"

Cecily's mouth dropped open. "I meant—"

"I haven't spent time with Hudson since we went shooting in the Highlands," he went on. "Perhaps the four of us could attend the opera later in the week."

Cecily did not know what to make of this. Sedgecroft was as arrogant as they came, and the worst thing was, Hudson *did* like the marquess. He had mentioned on countless occasions that he enjoyed Sedgecroft, a real man's man if ever there was one. But what were his intentions toward her friend? Was it possible he had an ounce of honor in him?

"On second thought, do you really think Jane should resume an active social life this soon after . . . well, after yesterday?" she asked in a strained voice.

He smiled blandly, turning Jane in the other direction as if to protect her. "I think I can take good care of Jane, although I admire your loyalty during these, let us say, awkward times. And now before we leave, the two of us will fetch that champagne for you, Cecily. You do look as if you could use some fortification."

"Couldn't we all?" Jane asked in an undertone, gazing over her shoulder at her dumbfounded friend.

A few minutes later they had made their farewells, located Simon, and Jane was whisked from the party by her handsome companion without another bite of food.

"Sedgecroft, your treatment of Cecily was so . . . so . . ."

"There's no need to keep thanking me," he murmured as he escorted her forcefully to his carriage. "Your gratitude is understood."

"Is it, Sedgecroft? I cannot tell you what a relief that is to me."

He paused, pursing his lips. "Far be it from me to criticize anyone's behavior outside my family, but I do start to wonder, Jane, whether this tendency of yours to be a little tart of tongue did not intimidate my cousin."

Jane had no idea how to react.

He looked uncomfortable. "I shouldn't have spoken. I happen to find this tendency appealing myself."

Appealing. Her standing up to him. "You what?" she said, finally managing to respond.

"To a degree. I'm sorry I brought up the subject." He gave her a penitent grin. "I'm also sorry if I seemed inattentive today."

Jane turned away, again thunderstruck. Any more of his attention, and she would have melted in her slippers.

His deep voice over her shoulder gave her another jolt. "It's all this rebellion of Chloe's," he confessed, revealing what was obviously weighing on his mind. "I cannot control her every action, and I fear she is bent on some course of self-destruction. The truth is, I do not generally attend these insipid day affairs. I'm better at night."

"That isn't what I've heard."

"Pardon?"

She felt his large body behind her, remembering in embarrassment what Evelyn had said. "It was only gossip," she said hurriedly. "They said that in the morning— goodness, forget I mentioned it." Was it true? Did Sedgecroft read the newspaper while he made love?

He followed her closely up the steps into the carriage, his expression mocking. "Don't listen to the gossips, darling."

She glanced around at her brother standing outside. She was starting to understand how much more there was to this man than met the eye. "What do you mean?"

"Find out the truth for yourself." He waited for her to sit before he lounged back, his brazen gaze studying her. "If you're curious about my personal habits, all you have to do is ask."

"I hardly think I would dare."

"Then you shall never know for yourself."

"Perhaps in some instances, one is better off remaining blissfully ignorant."

"But not you, Jane." He nudged his shoulder playfully against hers. "I have a feeling your curiosity has not begun to be sated."

Chapter 11

❧❧

Jane locked herself in her room as soon as she arrived home, ignoring her sisters' barrage of curious questions. She needed to ponder. Of course all she could ponder was Grayson. In leisurely detail. When they were together, her brain ceased all but its most basic functions.

She would have thought less of him today had she not been so strangely touched by all the emotions he revealed when he had shouted at his sister. The love and sheer panic of a man who was finally realizing that he could not control the world.

Pompous Grayson. He meant well, even if his heavy-handed methods left something to be desired. She did not understand why she felt so at ease with him. Perhaps because he was not easily shocked by the things she said, and she had done a very shocking thing.

Would her secret shock him?

Probably—if his treatment of Chloe were any indication. Even his liberal standards apparently extended only to the male prerogative for misbehavior.

But no matter what happened in the end, for this moment he made her feel valued, and no one, except her dogs, had ever seemed to value Jane for herself.

Except that Grayson *didn't* know who she really was. Or what she had done. What would he think if the truth were revealed?

As surprisingly enjoyable as the day spent with Jane had proven, Grayson did not look forward to the inevitable confrontation with Chloe that same evening. Of all his siblings his younger sister was the one he worried about and collided with the most. Possibly because in too many ways they were alike.

Arrogant. Adventurous. Always taking up lost causes.

Attracted to trouble. Determined to have their own way and damn the consequences.

He paused outside her bedroom door, bracing himself for another battle. At times like this he wished their spine-of-steel sister Emma were here to do the honors. Or even Heath, whose gentle intensity seemed to disarm women quite effectively. Having Jane at his side would help, even if she scolded him afterward. Grayson realized that in personal matters he possessed all the tact of a battering ram. But there were certain issues on which one must stand firm. He was the head of the family whether he liked it or not. He would be obeyed.

Why did Chloe defy him at every turn?

What was he going to do about her?

He opened the door. He had no inkling of what to say.

She was seated at her desk, her wavy black hair spread across her shoulders like a raven's wing. She looked young and vulnerable but grown up at the same time. She stiffened her back as he entered the room, but did not turn around. "Ah, my gaoler appears," she said. "Please leave the bread and water by the door."

"Chloe."

"Grayson."

He started to speak, then paused as he noticed a sketch of Brandon sitting on her desk. Brandon had been the baby of the family and Chloe's fervent champion as well as partner in childhood mischief. His death, on top of their father's, had devastated her at a time when she should have been preparing herself for marriage.

Once again he blamed himself for not being with his father and Chloe when they received word that Brandon had been killed. For months Royden Boscastle had been begging his eldest son to come to their country home for a week of hunting and entertaining old friends. Grayson had put him off and promised to come at a later date, not realizing that time was running out for their reunion.

Had Royden Boscastle had a premonition of his death? Grayson could not help wondering whether his father would have survived if he'd been at his side to soften the blow of Brandon's murder. Chloe and their father had been alone when the letter came, and she'd held him in her arms, helpless and afraid, as he died. The shock and sadness had changed her.

"What did you think you were doing today?" he asked her quietly.

"I do not want to discuss it."

He sat on the edge of her chaise. "Chloe, turn around and talk to me. We *will* discuss this."

She hesitated, then turned, her blue eyes cold . . . and wounded. He sighed, his heart aching for her.

"What did you expect me to do?" he asked in chagrin. "He was a soldier, for the love of God."

Her pen tapped the desk. "So, if I had been kissing a duke, you would have granted your approval?"

"Of course not," he retorted. "But at least someone of your own class, well, if you really were in love, marriage would have been an option. I'd never even seen him before."

Her white teeth worried the edge of her bottom lip. "And what did you intend to gain by bringing Jane along to witness my disgrace?"

"Jane defended you, actually."

"Someone ought to defend her against you," she burst out, the blue eyes so like his full of fire.

He drew a breath, allowing the insult to die unchallenged. "Chloe, you can't tell me that you really love that young man."

"I might."

He shook his head in chagrin. "I don't like this wild turn you have taken. Nor do I approve of your work at the Foundling Hospital and the Female Penitentiary for that matter, with ruined young women and whores."

"Nobody cares about them, Grayson," she said, her voice underscored with passion. "They have no parents to watch over them."

No parents. Was her sense of loss so acute, so pervasive, that she felt more at home with these anguished beings than her own family?

"I care about you, Chloe," he said in bewilderment. "All of us do."

"Then allow me to live my life as I please."

"Not until what pleases you meets my approval." He rose, his large hands buried in his pockets as he began to pace behind her. "Perhaps we should find you a husband. I don't know. Someone Papa would have chosen."

A flicker of pain darkened her blue eyes and was masked before he could decipher it. "Papa would have let me choose for myself."

"We both know that's a lie," he said quickly. "He was a tyrant, Chloe, as much as we loved him. He could be quite hurtful at times."

She came to her feet, her cheeks flushed, her voice distressed. "Don't say that."

"Well, it's true. It doesn't mean I didn't love him. Or that I don't miss him as much as you."

"I want to go to Nepal," she said unexpectedly.

"What?" he said in astonishment.

"I want to find Brandon's body."

He vented a deep sigh. He wasn't about to tell her that animal scavengers had probably left no remains to be brought home. That Brandon and his companions had died in a ravine after being ambushed by rebels. As far as he knew, no one had revealed the grim details to her. In fact, no one really knew for certain what had happened, despite Heath and Drake's efforts to uncover the truth.

"It's out of the question, Chloe," he said, shaking his head for emphasis.

"It was Papa's idea."

"Perhaps for him to go."

"Devon said he would take me."

"Then I shall wring the young devil's neck when he

comes home," he said, his deep voice rising at the very thought of the danger involved.

She stared at him, clearly fighting tears, of defiance, of grief. "One day I shall do exactly what I like."

"Not if I have a say in it." He put his hands firmly on her shoulders. She stiffened and refused to meet his gaze. "Don't see that soldier again," he said, sounding so much like their father that he winced.

"You've probably frightened him away forever anyway," she muttered.

"I hope so."

She lifted her gaze to his, a glint of amusement in her eyes. "You might have frightened Jane away, too."

Grayson struggled against the urge to laugh as he remembered the setdown Jane had dealt him in his sister's defense. Had everyone underestimated her? "She took your side, if you must know."

"I like her, Grayson," she admitted, expelling a deep sigh. "There's something appealing about Jane. Please don't do anything to make her situation worse."

He looked surprised. "Chloe, it's partly because of you that I have become her friend. You convinced me in the chapel that helping her was the right thing to do, and it made me think. And, you know, it's really odd, I like her, too. It's so easy to talk to her."

"Just don't take being her friend too far," she said quietly.

He exhaled in relief, tempted to take her in his arms like the little sister she would always be to him. So Jane was to be their common ground, the link to reestablish their damaged relationship. Jane, his sensible peacemaker and unwitting seductress.

"I think Jane is able to take care of herself," he said. "Especially if we remain loyal to her."

"I hope so." Chloe gave him a tentative smile. "Perhaps she will bring out the best in you."

"Not the beast?"

She laughed reluctantly, unable to resist his charm. "For her sake, I hope not."

Chapter 12

For the next five days Grayson played the part of an attentive suitor, escorting Jane to soirées, to lectures, and even to a late-night supper with a few close friends at the Clarendon. He introduced her to the sophisticated pleasures of his world, a glittering realm into which she had only peeped before. Instead of slipping into the peaceful obscurity she'd hoped for, she was toasted by rakes and radicals; she made friends with actresses and gamblers and deposed artists from Paris. She visited the docks to see Grayson's latest ship unloaded from China, and with every passing moment she knew that this illegitimate enjoyment would soon come to an end.

She did not want it to end.

She had begun to live for every moment of his wicked company. She had never laughed so much in her entire life. He was arrogant. He was thoughtful. She was so attracted to him she feared she could not hide it.

Today they had watched a balloon ascension in Green Park, and on the way home she had come perilously close to admitting everything. The strain of keeping her secret from a man of his experience was more than she could bear. Especially when he was confiding his own hopes and fears to her. To think that he trusted her with family secrets while she continued to mislead him. Wasn't it usually the other way around? Wasn't the scoundrel supposed to trick the young lady?

If he had not become so personally involved with her, taking the uncharacteristic role of hero, she suspected he might actually be the sort of man to appreciate what she and Nigel had done.

Ironically, under different circumstances, Grayson Boscastle would be the very person to turn to for advice. He would be the most loyal and understanding friend one could wish for. And she wished with all her heart to deserve him.

Caroline and Miranda crept into their sister's darkened bedchamber, peering down through the gloom at the slender figure stretched out flat on the four-poster. Jane lay like a stone effigy with a cold cloth clapped to her forehead, her hair streaming over her pillows. She pretended to be asleep until her nerves could not take another second of their intrusive silence. She could not continue in this manner. Her conscience would not allow it.

"Go away, both of you," she said between her teeth.

"Oh, Jane," Miranda said in breathless sympathy, "you look . . . you look positively wrung out."

"Quite possibly because I am."

Caroline plopped down on the bed, her voice ruefully assured. "I was right. Sedgecroft is horrible."

"No." Jane yanked off her cloth and opened her eyes in protest. "He's wonderful. The most wonderful thing I have ever had the misfortune to experience in my life."

Her sisters exchanged startled looks. "Do tell," Miranda said, sinking down beside Caroline.

"I am telling you nothing."

"If you are trying to say that he seduced you," Miranda whispered, "on your very first week—"

"Of course he didn't seduce me," Jane said in irritation. "He might have kissed me. Once or twice."

Caroline's brow furrowed in a frown. "And that is why you are lying here in the dark?"

"If you had ever been kissed by Sedgecroft, you would not ask such a stupid question. You might even be incapable of coherent speech."

"I think we might have misjudged him," Miranda said after a long silence. "He can be quite charming when given the chance."

"Was there ever any doubt of that?" Jane gave a sigh as she vividly recalled just how potent his powers could be. "That is what makes him a successful scoundrel."

"Then how," Caroline asked, "do you intend to resist him?"

"With the greatest of difficulty, I assure you. Apparently I am not as immune to his charm as I had hoped. I have yet to recover from our outing today."   •

"Well, you'd better start making a recovery." Miranda glanced at the clock on the nightstand. "His footman Weed left a message that the marquess would be calling on you within the hour."

Jane sat up in alarm. "Why?"

"The annual ball at Southwick House," Caroline said. "It's one of the biggest affairs of the Season. Only a favored few are invited early. Honestly, Jane, we do attend every year."

Jane stared past them in mild panic to her wardrobe. Never had her flair for fashion been quite so challenged as in the past five days. She hadn't minded looking like a pigeon until Sedgecroft had cast the gauntlet, challenging her in his devilish way. "It might have been nice if he had told me. What am I supposed to wear?"

"The pale rose gauze with the fringed shawl," Caroline replied. "The one in your trousseau made for the wedding reception."

"Wedding reception?" Jane said vaguely, wondering if rose could be considered pink, thereby pleasing to Sedgecroft's reprobate tastes. "What reception?"

"The reception you were to have with Nigel," Miranda said archly. "The man you went to Machiavellian lengths to avoid marrying."

Jane frowned and slid off the bed in her stocking feet. "I am perfectly aware of his name, thank you."

"The rose gown isn't in your wardrobe," Caroline called after her, sharing an amused look with her other sister. "Miranda and I sneaked in while you were recovering to have it aired and pressed."

Jane spun on her heel. "Does anyone consider that I might have a mind of my own?"

"Of course you do," Miranda murmured in a sly

voice. "That's what's gotten you into all this trouble with Sedgecroft."

"She isn't in trouble with Sedgecroft." Caroline studied Jane in concern. "Yet."

"You really ought to ring for Amelia to do your hair and face," Miranda said, her eyes dark with worry. "You've gone all pale and thin on us."

"I have not eaten a thing all week except for a strawberry!" Jane exclaimed, feeling any control she wielded over her life slipping away. "I need sustenance to deal with that man. Did that occur to His Wickedness?"

Caroline bit her lip to suppress a smile. "Actually, it did. He said there will be supper before the dancing. He suggested you eat an apple to hold you. The Austrian chef at Southwick is divine, an absolute genius in the kitchen. Sedgecroft said we must come with an appetite."

Jane stared grumpily at her reflection in the mirror. Supper and dancing. An apple. And another round of resisting Sedgecroft. The memory of the arrogant blue-eyed Adonis kissing her made her feel breathless, unsteady on her feet. He was relentless in his pursuit of pleasure, and her own sense of guilty doom would ruin what could have been an enchanted evening. Why couldn't her parents have pursued Grayson as a son-in-law in the first place?

"What if I don't wish to go?" she said to no one in particular. "I'm sure no one will find my absence remarkable under the circumstances."

At that precise moment footsteps rang outside in the hall, and Lady Belshire popped her head into the room.

Her silver-brown hair was elegantly upswept and studded with diamond pins. The gold taffeta gown that displayed her youthful figure sparkled like stardust in the false twilight.

"Not ready yet, darling? Goodness, why are the three of you whispering in the dark? It makes me think of naughty little mice in a nursery."

"Miranda and I are ready, Mama," Caroline said.

"Well, do hurry, Jane," Lady Belshire said breathlessly, adjusting her fichu. "Sedgecroft just arrived, dressed to the teeth. I must admit he cuts a fine figure. I daresay the pair of you will cause a stir."

"Lovely," Jane muttered. "Just what I need, to cause another stir."

Lady Belshire gave a deep sigh of despair, looking like a crestfallen elfin queen at her eldest's mutinous remark. Of course Jane's morose spirits had absolutely nothing to do with the adorable marquess, whom Athena had obviously misjudged. The sad truth was that Jane would not forget her beloved Nigel in only a few days, and the best her family could do was distract her and prove that her young life was not over.

"When you talk in such an inappropriate manner, I could murder Nigel for what he has done. But you must remember the Belshire name, my dear." Her ladyship took a deep breath, pleased at how she had decided to handle this. "And now you have Sedgecroft on your side."

"Sedgecroft," Jane said, subsiding on the bed with a groan.

"A young lady could not ask for a better champion,"

Lady Belshire added, forgetting that she herself had thought him an irresponsible rake only a short time ago. But then what did it matter if he applied all that . . . overwhelming maleness to helping her daughter out of this disgrace? "In fact," she thought aloud, "I shudder to think what he will do when he finds Nigel."

"Don't we all," Miranda said under her breath as her mother disappeared from the doorway.

Chapter 13

❧❧

By that evening the papers had posed a provocative twist to the Boscastle wedding scandal: Had Sir N jilted Lady J, or had he been threatened off by the dominant branch of the family? Had a certain marquess been waiting in the wings to make a move? Or had this handsome plotter set the stage to begin with?

It posed a mystery as to when this drama had actually started. Or how it would all end. Why were Lady J's parents so outwardly accepting of this affair? Had Sir N vanished from the face of the earth entirely? And, the most provocative question of all, Was another marriage between these two illustrious families in the offing?

Within hours the ton could talk of nothing else. Conversation stopped at Southwick House when the crowd spotted Grayson and Jane together, although she wasn't convinced it was her audacity to appear in public repeatedly after her failed wedding as much as Sedgecroft's popularity that created a reaction.

The ladies definitely had their eye on her attractive escort. His lean elegance and unhurried stride as they crossed the reception hall turned heads and had fans fluttering all over the place.

Grayson had a different perspective on the furor their appearance caused.

Yes, he noticed that people were watching them. Especially the men, and the barely veiled desire in their eyes confirmed his fear that Lady Jane Jilt would be targeted as an easy female.

But the heated looks sent her way died out the moment Grayson turned his crushing glare upon the men who dared to demean her. Then there were averted glances, whispered questions, shrugs of resignation. No one had the courage to challenge Sedgecroft, neither in word nor action. His easygoing temperament had earned him few enemies, but his loyalty to those he loved was well known.

He'd seen the papers naturally. He was not at all bothered by the speculation that he was courting Jane as a potential bride. As Lady Belshire had predicted, this seemed to be raising Jane's social value, and Grayson was glad to be of service. In fact, he'd instructed his secretary to neither deny nor confirm when questions were asked.

An enigmatic smile would suffice.

Weary of his status as a scoundrel, Grayson did not care if the ton believed he was considering Jane as his wife. They were a plausible match. What did it matter if anyone thought he was behind the wedding scandal?

Let them label him the devil.

In fact, if he'd met Jane a few months earlier, he . . . he what? A thoughtful frown overshadowed his face. They probably had attended several affairs at the same time before.

Yet their paths had never crossed. Why not? In the mists of memory he saw Nigel huddled around her, protecting her from rogues like Grayson so that he could hurt her later himself. Which reminded him that he had received word from Heath only two hours ago about Nigel's disappearance and needed a private moment to deliver it to Jane. He hated to spoil a pleasant evening, but she had a right to know the truth about his cousin.

"The damn idiot," he muttered.

Jane glanced up at him, her face startled. "What did you say?"

"Nothing. Have a good time."

"How?" she whispered, gazing around at the crush of guests crowding the candlelit room. "This is absolute torture for me."

"No one will bother you with me here. Ignore them."

"Are you always so blindly arrogant?"

"I believe so," he said, moving instinctively closer to her. It would remain a mystery to him until his dying day how bright young women like Jane and Chloe could be so easily damaged by the opinions of virtual strangers.

He drew a breath as a passing guest inadvertently bumped them into each other. His body ignited with desire at the all-too-brief feel of the side of her breast, the arch of her elbow against him. He ached to know then and there what she looked like beneath that pale rose gown, what color her skin was in all the secret places. He wanted her in his bed so badly he had to clench his jaw to stop from pulling her into his arms.

He glanced away, perplexed that he could entertain such potent thoughts of seducing a woman he claimed to befriend. But the hidden shadows of her sexuality unsettled him a little more every time he saw her. Or was it her character that drew him to her? How peculiar he could not tell. One trait only enhanced the other, he supposed.

He glanced back at her. She looked so utterly miserable that he had to laugh. "Are you always this resistant to enjoying yourself?"

"How am I supposed to enjoy myself?"

"You dance a little. You drink a little." He motioned to a footman to bring Jane a glass of champagne. "You talk to me. And," he added lightly, his large body shielding hers, "since we're here, we may as well try to make the best of it."

She smiled up at him, and he felt another reckless urge to grasp her hand and carry her out of this place to have her to himself. Just riding in the carriage with her tonight had put him in the mood for a night of lovemaking. Of course, she was the one female in the world he couldn't own, which might have something to do with the fact he wanted to debauch her up and down.

And now he was going to distress her further by revealing what Heath's brief message had said. He was going to make her cry by explaining that it appeared Nigel had planned his escape in advance. Ah, well, let her have an hour of enjoyment before he broke the news and ruined the evening.

As it turned out, he rather liked making Jane laugh. He liked irritating her, too, only a little, just enough to watch those green eyes of hers ignite with so many interesting emotions. It probably wasn't nice to do, but those demons of his couldn't seem to resist her. His demons were drawn to Jane in a very mystifying way.

* * *

Jane searched the crowds of elegantly dressed guests for sign of her sisters until she felt Grayson gently turn her back toward him.

"Are you looking for Nigel?" he asked her.

"For—oh, no." Her throat closed on the words.

"Don't worry." His mouth flattened. "I'm sure in due time he will answer to us both. I shall derive personal satisfaction from meeting my cousin again."

Her eyes darkened at the merciless determination on his face. Pray God *she* wasn't going to answer to Grayson any time soon. "I'm not so sure of that," she murmured.

"Unless he's dead," he added, sounding rather wishful.

"I—I hope he isn't dead."

"Ah, yes." There was a trace of disapproval in his low voice. "You love him, as incredible as I begin to find the notion."

In a manner of speaking, she did love Nigel. In the same fond way she loved Simon or Uncle Giles, or the family dogs. "I have known Nigel forever. He put a frog in my cradle four days after I was born, or so the story goes. We were inseparable as children."

"Do you have any idea where he might have gone?"

"Gone? Well, he mentioned Scotland once or twice." As in the last barbarous place on earth he would visit. Nigel was the type to sit in an armchair in front of a fire for the rest of his life. Oh, Jane absolutely despised being so dishonest.

"Scotland?" Grayson frowned. "Strange. But I shall pass that information on to Heath."

She felt an icy chill slide down her spine. "Why?"

"Because Heath has the tracking instincts of a wolf,

my dear. He was well-suited to his work in secret intelligence."

Wolves. Secret intelligence. The mesmerizing sensuality that glittered in Sedgecroft's eyes. It was enough to send a lesser woman to the couch. Jane felt the web of her own deceit drawing more tightly around her at every turn, strangling her good sense, thwarting her escape.

The ball was a grand affair. The master of ceremonies handed a red rose to every lady in attendance. A band of Italian musicians gave a concert during supper, and three card rooms hosted gambling afterward. Despite the elegant atmosphere, Jane could not relax for a single moment, pretending not to notice that people were stealing curious looks at her all night.

No one had ever noticed her to this degree before. The truth was, without Sedgecroft at her side, she was not considered an interesting enough person to continue to stir rumors. Not that she didn't have friends. She did. But the scandal surrounding her would have passed soon enough. She would have happily slipped into oblivion before the season ended.

But no one overlooked the marquess.

Jane found it impossible for even a second not to be aware of him, and having him hover over her hardly eased her anxiety. She felt as if she were accompanied by a big golden lion that might turn feral at any moment. Who knew what he really thought of all this? Those heavy-lidded blue eyes gave nothing away, and the nagging feeling that she would pay dearly for deceiving him persisted.

He danced with her twice. Then, with practiced ease, he waltzed her through the French doors and out into the gardens, where a group of younger guests were playing an impromptu game of blindman's buff.

"What are we doing?" she asked in amusement, resisting as he pulled her down the terrace steps onto the lantern-lit lawn.

"Do you really want to dance with all those pretentious people watching us?" he teased her. "I know now where that owlish scowl of yours comes from. Your brother looked as if he might swoop down on me any minute."

Jane smiled. "The Belshire Scowl can't be as dangerous as the Boscastle Blues."

He stopped at the bottom of the stone stairs, blinking innocently. "The Boscastle Blues? Is that some sort of military regiment?"

She stared up at his angular, teasing face. He was still holding her hand, well, only her gloved fingers, but the warm pressure was enough to send a frisson of forbidden excitement deep down into her belly. It was so tempting to press herself against that strong, hard body and pretend the rest of the world didn't exist.

"The curse of the Boscastle Blues," she said. "And don't act as if you don't know what it is."

He shrugged his shoulders in bafflement. "But I don't. Is it something horrible?"

"Only if you're a victim—one of the unfortunate souls who falls under the bewitchment of those blue eyes."

"Well, I apologize that my family has claimed you as a victim."

"You don't look all that sorry."

He stared at her in curiosity. "I didn't mean as *my* victim, sweetheart. I meant as Nigel's."

"Oh." Could her cheeks blush any hotter? How could she forget she was supposed to be wallowing in heartbreak over Nigel, not fighting an attraction to his sinfully desirable cousin?

"He had green eyes, anyway," she murmured.

"Then perhaps the curse can be broken," he said, leaning toward her to brush a stray curl off her shoulder.

She caught a whiff of his shaving soap and shivered involuntarily. "Umm. Perhaps."

"Hey, you two, are you playing?" a friendly voice shouted, and a young man yanked his blindfold off seconds before he bumped them back into the steps. "Oh, hello, Sedgecroft. Have I caught you?"

"Not yet." Grayson steered Jane firmly down the flagstone path, into the garden twinkling with beguiling fairy lanterns. "Give us a chance."

"But I don't want to play," Jane protested.

"Well, neither do I, but I have no desire to be accused of luring you outside for a tryst either. Have you ever toured the gardens here by moonlight?"

She subjected him to a suspicious look. "Are they anything like the Pavilion of Pleasure?"

"I need to talk to you."

"That sounds rather ominous, Sedgecroft. Why this secrecy all of a sudden?"

"I don't want us to be overheard. Let's separate and meet in the middle of the maze."

"But the maze isn't lit."

"I know. Don't be frightened. I shall be with you."

"Do we really need to skulk about like spies?"

"Only if I mean to protect your name. Go."

He watched with a grin as she turned into the labyrinth

of privet hedge, only to take a wrong turn and summon him for help.

"You might have common sense, Jane, but you show absolutely no sense of direction," he said through the hedge. "No, go to the right. I'll meet you on the other side."

"Everyone saw us arrive together," she whispered in his direction. "What do you suppose they're thinking?"

He didn't answer, and she decided she was talking to herself, until a strong pair of hands clamped down upon her shoulders and spun her around. She suppressed a gasp as she stared up into his grinning face.

"Perhaps they're thinking that we are caught up in a love greater than the world has ever known," he replied, looking so attractive in the shadows that Jane half wished it could be true. "That you are a femme fatale no man can resist."

"Really? Have you thought about writing for the scandal sheets? Wait. I have a bit of gravel in my shoe."

"Here. Sit on that bench. I'll help you. I don't think we were seen."

She sat obediently on the carved stone seat as he knelt to remove her dancing pump, running his long fingers across the sole of her stockinged foot until she sighed.

"Better?"

"Much." A treacherous warmth was stealing up into her leg. "May I have my foot back now?"

"I don't know." He turned it this way and that. "It's a very nice foot. Perhaps I'll add it to my collection. There are men like that, you know. No, you probably don't know. No one has ever gotten into your slippers before, I can tell."

She smiled ruefully down at him. "Is that your secret pleasure, Sedgecroft? Feet?"

He straightened with a deep chuckle. "Not me. I prefer the whole thing rather than the few odd parts."

"How very democratic of you."

He rose to sit down beside her, his voice deepening to a tone that raised shivery impulses on her skin. "In your case, a man would have a difficult time deciding which part is most desirable."

"Is that what you wanted to tell me?"

"No." His amusement fading, he took her hand, stroking his forefinger across her gloved fingertips. "Not many people know that my brother Heath was involved in espionage for the Crown some time ago."

"I had no idea." What was he trying to tell her? Jane sat very still, lulled by his touch.

"Heath is a very clever young man."

And rather a lady-killer himself, she thought, or so her sisters claimed. "What are you saying?"

"I set him on Nigel's trail," he said slowly. "I discussed this with your father in private, Jane, and we both agreed it was preferable to hiring a Bow Street man."

The muscles of her stomach tightened into a knot of nervous tension. "Oh, but you didn't need—"

"It wasn't just for you. Nigel's behavior has put an irreparable dent in the Boscastle name." He put his thumb to her lips before she could speak. "Yes, I know the rest of us haven't exactly set a shining example, but we are usually a little more discreet than shaming a woman in public."

She exhaled as he removed his thumb from her lips. "Has Heath found him then?"

"No. But he has learned that Nigel was seen boarding a coach in Brighton. To where, we have not learned yet, but it won't be long before we find him." His voice grew more determined, angry. "Heath is persistent if nothing else."

Brighton. Jane schooled her face into an impassive expression to hide her alarm. Nigel had an aunt in Brighton, the wife of a retired barrister, so it was entirely possible he and Esther had made a detour there before proceeding to the quaint Hampshire village they had chosen to set up house.

But Sedgecroft certainly didn't know that. After all, he was only human, not some omniscient deity for all his lordly airs. He could not possibly trace Nigel to an almost invisible country village.

He rose from the bench, his broad shoulders straining the tailored lines of his black evening coat. His longish blond hair shone in the moonlight as he delivered the next blow. "I think you ought to know that Nigel has an aunt in Brighton, the wife of a retired barrister."

She stood abruptly, the blood rushing to her head as he continued.

"It is entirely possible he passed a night there before proceeding to—" He stopped, taking her by the shoulders. "Jane, my gracious, are you going to swoon on me?"

"I am not sure," she said in a weak voice. What would he do next? Produce Nigel from his vest pocket? "Proceeding to . . . where?"

"God only knows. But trust me, I will find out." He gave her a gentle squeeze, his face sympathetic but resolved. "I know this does not solve your problem, but I hope it at least makes you feel a little better."

"Words escape me. I cannot begin to describe what I feel."

"Then sit down again. I'm afraid you look a little faint."

She sank down onto the bench, swallowing hard. "I shall be fine."

"Of course you—"

The sound of furtive footsteps on the path outside the maze interrupted their conversation. Whispers and laughter erupted from behind the hedge, another man and woman clearly engaging in stolen pleasures.

Jane stared at Grayson in consternation, rising as if to escape. In her opinion it was almost as embarrassing to be eavesdropping on a tryst as to be caught in one, but the truth was, she embraced the interruption with relief.

"What do we do now?" she whispered.

"Wait," he murmured, frowning at the hedge in vexation.

Reluctant, she obeyed, only to understand a moment later what had caused the frown on his face.

"So tell me now, Helene, before I expire of suspense, it is over between you and Sedgecroft?"

Jane swallowed a gasp of surprise. Helene Renard. The beautiful young French widow whose English husband had died less than three months ago. The woman Sedgecroft allegedly had been courting as his next mistress. Of course it was a scandal for her to appear in public this soon in her mourning period, not even in gray or black. But pink.

Yes. Jane caught a glimpse of Helene's dark pink satin

gown through the hedge. Pink the color of a woman's flesh. The color that pleased a certain reprobate's tastes.

On behalf of womanhood in general, she directed a scowl at the man sitting beside her.

"Is it over between me and Sedgecroft?" Helene mused in a bitter voice. "That is impossible to say as 'it' never properly began. And now he is here with that mousy little jilt, Janet."

"Jane," murmured her male companion, whom she vaguely identified as the rather florid-faced Lord Buckley, heir to a vast fortune that he would soon squander on gambling and women. Jane disliked him, picturing his pudding cheeks.

"I did not find her at all mousy, Helene," he said in a hesitant voice. "In fact, I found her rather appealing. In an aloof sort of way, of course," he added hastily.

Well, perhaps Jane would have to revise her opinion of him. As soon as she recovered from hearing herself referred to as "that mousy little jilt." Did she really resemble a mouse? Could it have anything to do with her penchant for gray?

She glanced up at Sedgecroft, all thoughts for herself dissipating at his brooding silence. If Helene was indeed the woman he was rumored to desire as his next mistress, this must be painful for him to overhear. Jane had no idea whether he cared enough for Helene to call Buckley out. What a scandal that would make if she were accused of igniting a duel. Of course the possibility of a duel would depend on her escort's reaction to this revealing conversation.

Detached, uncaring, heartbroken? One could not draw any conclusions from those half-closed blue eyes, nor from the faint smile on his chiseled lips. He might have been listening to a poetry recital for all the emotion he displayed. Most men would be absolutely livid at over-hearing themselves betrayed by their love interest.

"Will you consider my offer?" Buckley asked after a breathless pause during which Jane could only conclude he and Helene had been kissing. "I have already had the contract drawn, and you shall want for nothing."

"Ask me in the morning. I am in a foul mood tonight."

"And what about Sedgecroft?"

"What about him?" Helene retorted in a snippy voice.

"Well, I mean, he has a certain reputation—not only as a lover, but as a fighter."

"He loves himself well enough."

"But I've heard—"

"I think he's boring," Helene said in a burst of emotion. "Yes, he bores me to tears."

"Even in bed?" Buckley inquired in an incredulous voice.

Helene gave such a wistful sigh that Jane had to raise her eyebrows at the man beside her. Sedgecroft gave a helpless shrug, having the grace to actually look sheepish.

"What I meant," Buckley said quietly, "is that perhaps you ought to ask him for permission to take up with me. I don't relish the thought of facing him in a duel."

"If you want his opinion, then you ask him, Buckley." Helene's voice faded away as she returned to the central path. "That is, if you can pry him away from the paws of his pathetic little mouse. I cannot imagine what he sees in her."

"That Belshire elegance is quite impressive," her companion said unhelpfully.

"Oh, shut up, Buckley," Helene tossed back at him. "You British are so unbearably obsessed with your bloodlines. I say she is Lady Mouse. The Princess of Mice. She'll probably squeak when Sedgecroft beds her."

Jane drew a breath of indignation, half rising again from the bench before Grayson drew her back down beside him. Scandal or not, for two shillings she would shake that woman senseless—

"Don't squeak, my adorable little mouse," he said in an amused whisper. "Wait."

Jane folded her arms across her bodice and stared up at the starlit sky, startled when, after a minute of silence passed, he burst into quiet laughter.

She looked down her nose at him. "Have you gone quite mad?"

He pointed his forefinger at her. "Your face—it was priceless—and when she said—"

"You don't need to repeat anything," she said indignantly. "I heard every insulting word." He was making fun of her, not even trying to hide his amusement. What sort of man was he? Heat flared into her face. What sort of woman had she become?

"Well." He gave a deep wicked chuckle, blowing out his cheeks in a ridiculous effort to appear under control.

"Well, what?" she demanded.

"You have to admit it was an interesting conversation," he murmured, his blue eyes dancing.

"That's easy for you to say." She pulled her feet away from his. "No one accused you of looking like a rodent."

"Well, those certainly weren't my words." He shook his head to underscore his denial. "Or my thoughts."

"Then why are you laughing?"

"You're laughing, too," he pointed out.

"Now I am," she admitted, "but I wasn't at first, you cruel man. I was too offended." Offended by the almost-mistress of the rogue who was protecting Jane from the aftereffects of her own devious act. She despaired of ever digging herself out of the mess she'd made.

He smiled. "Don't be angry with me. I would never accuse you of being a mouse."

"Oh, no. Only a pigeon. Or an owl."

He stared deeply into her eyes in what she assumed was an attempt to look sincere.

"Jane, it is only laughable because it is so absurd. You are a desirable female, as I've told you before."

"I'm not feeling very desirable, thank you. I feel . . . like nibbling on a wedge of cheese. Do you think the Austrian chef has any of that Cheshire left?"

He took her chin in his hand and turned her face back to his. He wasn't laughing now. He looked a little too serious, in fact. "I said you were desirable. Do you think I say that only to make you feel better?"

"No, because if you wanted to make me feel better, you'd be fetching me that cheese. And a big sticky bun to—"

The dark gleam of unmasked desire in his eyes sent the thought from her brain. No man had ever looked at her with such naked yearning before. Certainly she had never allowed herself to be placed in a situation that left her vulnerable to seduction. With a master of the art.

Was it possible that he saw something in her that no one else could see? When he looked at her like that, she was tempted to believe him. Even if he wasn't sincere, it gave her a lovely feeling. The two of them could have sat alone in this darkened maze, and that would have been enough stimulation to fill her entire evening.

The sensible Jane told herself she ought to ask him to take her back inside, but she was riveted to the spot. It seemed that the wedding scandal had not satisfied her need for trouble. It had unleashed it.

"Perhaps we are both to be unlucky at love this season," he said reflectively, his head dipping closer to hers.

She caught her breath, waiting in an agony of suspense. This unleashed Jane had absolutely no sense of shame. "It would appear so," she murmured.

His lids lowered over his piercing blue eyes. Jane sighed in pleasure, only to sabotage a potentially perfect moment by asking, "You didn't even mind that she said you bored her to tears?"

His lips lifted in a smile. "Do I bore you?"

"Oh, no."

"Well."

She could practically feel the heat that radiated from his body. It penetrated her skin, spread into her blood and bones, sapping her strength.

"Aren't you going to do anything about Buckley?" she asked, watching his face in fascination.

He leaned a little closer. Jane's pulse points took off at a reckless gallop. "Why should I? He appears to have good taste in women."

"Helene is beautiful," she murmured, even though privately she thought the woman deserved to fall into a rabbit hole and never be seen again.

"I meant his taste in women as in *you*, Jane. That Belshire elegance *is* impressive."

"Well—"

He cupped her face in his hands and kissed her deeply, drank from her lips as if his very life depended on reducing her to breathless acquiescence. She brought her hand to his chest. Her fingers met a wall of granite muscle beneath which his heart beat in the heavy cadence of desire. Hard. Warm. Devastating male to the last inch.

"Yes," he whispered. "Touch me, Jane. Allow me the same favor." He stroked his fingertips from her shoulder down into the valley between her breasts, brushing back and forth across the distended peaks until she gasped. "We shall make our own luck, you and I," he murmured as he set his teeth to the edge of her ear.

His mouth moved down the arch of her throat. She had no idea what he meant by luck—it was all she could do to control the quivers of arousal that rocked her body. Within moments his capable hands were traveling up and down her slender frame in patent possession, caressing the indentation of her waist, the slope of her belly, the warm hollow between her thighs. Incredible. In a heartbeat he already knew her body better than she.

She flexed her spine, felt the excitement coursing through her blood. When he touched her, she became her unleashed self, different, lush and alive, so ripe for his seduction, burning with the most outrageous urges she could imagine. Every brush of his chiseled mouth, every foray of his fingers sensitized her skin.

"Come closer," he said in a husky voice, drawing her against him until she was practically straddling his thigh, his hand hooked around her bottom. "That's better, isn't it?"

"Better for what?" she whispered, the hunger inside her so deep it actually hurt.

He had realized in the chapel that she had a sensual body, a man's private fantasy. Now he indulged that fantasy by exploring those luscious curves, the soft globes of her breasts, the shapely backside that sat so plushly between his thighs.

"I wanted to do this on your wedding day," he admitted, burying his face in the white mounds of her breasts. His hands tightened around her rib cage. "I was entranced by you even while you waited at the altar."

She arched her back and gave a breathless laugh of shock and pleasure. "Well, considering the scandal I caused myself, it's a good thing you didn't act on your impulses."

He tugged down her sleeves, giving him access to her tempting breasts. His mouth closed tightly around a dusky nipple, drawing the pebbled crest between his teeth to tease with his tongue. He resented even the dress of hers that came between them, the fact they weren't exactly in a spot conducive to uninterrupted exploration. This was reckless, impetuous, insane, and he loved every moment of it. Of course he would not allow anything to go too far. But for now he was aroused past the point of reason.

He moved his left hand down to her ankle, stealing up her skirt until his fingers closed around her knee, tickling the silky underside. Seconds later he was touching the creamy skin above her stockings, drawn to the warm delta of dewy flesh between her legs. He imagined the pleasure of tasting her there, being inside her, and desire knifed through his body.

She shivered as he tangled his forefinger in her nest of curls, but her shock was soon replaced by a longing so intense she could not move. She had wanted her freedom from Nigel, the chance to find her own love, but was this what she had bargained for? Her blood sizzled at this intimacy, and even though she was afraid, anticipation electrified her nerve endings. Being with Grayson was beyond anything in her experience or personal fantasies.

He groaned against her mouth. "Oh, my God, Jane, you're trembling all over. Just relax and let me give you pleasure."

"Relax? I feel as though I'm going to die."

"You're not going to die. Well, perhaps in a way, but trust me, it will be very nice."

"Trust you?" she whispered unevenly. "Just look where trusting you has taken me."

Then stop me, he thought, because he couldn't find the willpower to end this exercise in self-torture. She had never been touched like this before, and the last thing he would do was deflower her on a garden bench. Yet he wanted to. He wanted to bury himself inside all that sultry heat and unawakened fire. The scent of her filled his mind with black selfish passion. His whole body shook with it.

Jane buried her face in his neck, trying to fight the glorious sensual haze that hung over her. When he parted the damp folds of her sex and pressed his finger inside, she was too surprised to resist, too distracted by the unbearable rush of pleasure to mount a defense. It was enough to cling to sanity as the friction of his petting took her to the edge and released her to the waves of sensation that inundated her. Oh, the wonder of it. The dizzying pleasure. Her head swam with a blur of colors.

He held her so tightly that she found it hard to draw a breath, to return with reluctance to earth. In the distance she heard a swell of laughter, voices growing louder like the buzzing of bees as a group of guests approached the maze. She turned her head in apprehension.

"I think—"

"I hear them," he murmured hoarsely, his face buried in her hair. "It's all right. Let's put you back together, darling. No harm done."

She covertly straightened her dress, her voice unsteady. "Perhaps not to you. I do not think I will ever be the same. Dear heaven, my hands are shaking, Sedgecroft. Am I putting all the pieces back in their proper place?"

He examined her over from head to toe, his perceptive gaze lingering on her face. The white knight had failed miserably in his attempt at chivalry again. What had he done to her tonight? What folly had possessed him? "Lovely pieces they were, too," he said softly. "It does seem a shame to hide them." He lifted her from the bench, holding her against him for a moment, wondering whether she would run from him after this and never return. How was seducing her supposed to fit into their scheme?

"You look even better than you did before," he added in a quiet voice. "I'm the one returning to the party with his rhubarb at full rise."

"Your—"

"Hurry, Jane, before we are missed. We must not be seen leaving the maze together." Teasing aside, he was not about to chance involving her in another scandal. "We'll find that cheese you are craving, shall we?"

Chapter 14

They strolled back across the garden and allowed the night air to cool their passion, blending into the cluster of guests outside as if they had never left. He held her hand only until they reached the revealing lantern light. In truth, he did not feel like letting her go. It had been wrong of him to take advantage of her vulnerability. Yet for the life of him he found it impossible to resist her.

He wondered what it was about Jane that undid him when he had encountered every sort of feminine wile under the sun. And then he knew. Jane was simply herself. She did not put on airs. She wasn't out to entrap or impress him. She was Jane and that was more than enough.

No one had missed them, thankfully. They might have been chatting on the lawn for all anyone knew. But still this had to stop. Grayson had to stop himself, or Jane was going to end up worse than before.

"Are you going to render me insensible every time we're together?" she asked without looking at him.

He glanced down at her with a rueful smile. "I suppose I deserve that."

"It wasn't part of your plan for my social redemption, was it?"

"I never plan in that much detail, at least not when it comes to women," he said. "Being unpredictable creatures, they require a certain freedom of expression from a partner if peace is to be had."

"That is not an answer, Sedgecroft."

"Would you feel better if we scheduled these 'renderings' ahead of time?"

She sighed. "I suppose I'm as much to blame as you, but I think I'd feel better if we could control the urge to commit them at all."

"Commit them? As if they were mortal sins or murders." He came to a dead stop in the middle of the parterre, his face half shadowed in the lantern light. "It's Nigel, isn't it?"

"Nigel has nothing to do with this," she said, managing to sound quite convincing.

"Yes, he does. I understand something of women, Jane. In your heart of hearts, you hope he will return. As a loyal woman, a woman of integrity, you intend to show him that you did not yield to temptation while he was off on his—his bachelor's pilgrimage."

"What bachelor's pilgrimage?"

"It does not appear that there was any foul play involved in Nigel's disappearance. I'm sorry that he appears to be alive."

"You're sorry that your cousin isn't dead?"

"It would have saved me the trouble—do you wish me to find the truth or not?"

A flush of foreboding swept through Jane like wildfire. How close to the truth would he come? Nigel had promised to cover his tracks until such a time that he and Jane deemed it safe for the fact of his marriage to come out.

Neither of them had counted on Sedgecroft's, and now Heath's, interference. What a complicated game this had become.

She drew a slow breath, summoning all her courage. "Speaking of the truth, I think you ought to know how I feel about Nigel."

He frowned. "I do."

"You couldn't possibly."

"You are an intelligent, unusual woman, Jane, but you aren't as adept at hiding your feelings as you may think."

"What about you, Sedgecroft?" she asked in hesitation.

He regarded her with a puzzled smile. "What do you mean?"

"No regrets over Helene?" she asked gently.

"You must be joking."

"No, I'm not. She must have wounded your feelings."

"Not in the least."

"Are you being honest with me, or is this pride?"

"I find the situation altogether too amusing and enlightening."

"Hmm. Someone is putting on a good front."

"Now who would that be?"

She gave him a skeptical smile. "Let's just say one of us is a brave little soldier, and it isn't me. The woman who was supposed to be your next mistress is parading around with another man."

"Darling Jane, if Helene had meant anything at all to me, do you think you and I would have been alone together in that maze?"

She wavered, rescued from a reply by the sight of her

brother walking toward them. She had not even begun herself to make sense of that magical interlude in the maze. One complication seemed to lead to another until her life had become a veritable Gordian knot. "Ah," she said. "Simon finally appears, and only twenty minutes too late to investigate what we were doing in the dark."

Grayson laughed. "Oh, Jane, that sensible side is showing again."

"Yes," she said, moving past him at a brisk walk. "And only twenty minutes too late to do me any good."

Jane felt awash in misery, dancing with young men who were either too stupid to realize she was a scandal, or too socially disconnected to care. How could she concentrate on a proper conversation when her heart was still racing from that encounter with Sedgecroft? How could she engage in a game that there was no hope at all of winning? The more she knew of Grayson, the more she was enthralled by him. And the way he had touched her. Oh, her body still quaked from it.

"Oh, just look at him," she muttered. "Standing there like a lion."

"I beg your pardon," her dance partner said as the final steps brought them back together. "What did you say?"

She snapped open her fan. "I said that I was tired of standing in line."

"Oh, yes. Silly dance, isn't it? Would you care for a lemonade?"

"If you don't mind. I'm parched."

She wended her way across the dance floor to talk to Cecily, who held court before a cluster of aristocratic friends. Jane could hardly ignore Sedgecroft, so she gave him a covert wave. The smile he gave her in return was positively smug and infuriating, a reminder that he would never let her forget what had just happened between them.

She wondered why *she* had been so accepting of what they had done. Why she wasn't more shocked and repentant instead of basking in the afterglow of her glorious sin. She knew all about his reputation with women. But then no one had explained how wonderful it was to be the object of his notorious attention either. No one had explained that while she could deviously plot out her life, what happened to her heart was another matter altogether.

Grayson watched as Jane danced with two or three young gallants, all of whom were undoubtedly drawn to her radiant pink glow. Well, he thought cynically, leaning his shoulder against one of the ballroom's four enormous pillars, he could claim responsibility for putting that blush on her cheeks. He ought to have apologized to her instead of teasing. But he was more sorry at the moment that he hadn't been in a position to take their encounter a little further. The truth was, he had probably done enough damage for one night, and he could not possibly continue their relationship. Damn it, what had he been thinking? Away from her, his ability to reason had returned.

He would dearly love to lure her to his bed. He wanted to take Jane in every way known to man. Yet that pleasure would never be his. Family obligations, he reminded himself, were his priority. Which also reminded him that Chloe had been openly scornful of his threat to pack her off to the country should she give him one more reason to mistrust her. Her unhappiness, her rebellion, troubled him deeply. It was only a matter of time before her defiance would force his hand.

His thoughts returned to Jane. The scent of her, the creamy texture of her skin. The shy-aggressive exploration of her hands over his body. That awkward touch of hers had brought him to the boiling point. He didn't know what to do with himself except stand here, shaking inside, like an adolescent.

"Coming to play cards?" a friend called behind him.

He shrugged, welcoming the reprieve from this exercise in self-torture. "Why not?" And as he turned, he noticed a tall dark-haired young man break from Cecily's group to gaze at Jane with a look Grayson recognized only too well.

"Denville, who is that man there, the one watching Jane like a hawk?"

"Oh. Baron Brentford, isn't he?"

"He looks rather intense."

"Intense is the word. I heard he tried to kill himself last year when Portia Hunt left him for his brother. Are you coming or not?"

"In a minute."

Grayson narrowed his gaze. Jane was staring the brooding young baron in the eye, nodding gravely at whatever he had said. Suddenly her focus shifted, and she met Grayson's stony regard as if she sensed his disapproval.

She sent him an uncertain smile. He did not smile back. God knew the baron was probably considered a catch, but a cheerful spirit like Jane didn't need an emotionally unstable suitor to add to her woes. Considering how well she had accepted Nigel's desertion, Grayson had to commend her inner fortitude.

He gave her a firm, admonishing shake of his head. She could do better. Yet who, he mused, would be a worthy man for Jane?

He was at a loss. This was odd. He and Jane had come closer to making love on a garden bench than he would have dreamed, and still he lingered, guilt-ridden and lurking in the shadows, while she danced and did her best to ignore him. Was this an act to show the world she would survive Nigel's desertion? Well, he couldn't fault her for taking his advice.

"Abandoned by your latest conquest already, Sedgecroft?" a woman's cool voice said at his shoulder.

He recognized the provocative French accent as Helene's, the voice of the woman he had briefly considered taking as his next lover. In recent weeks her charms had taken on a decided tarnish, and he turned reluctantly to face her. "I don't see Buckley at your side. Loosened his chain, have we?"

"He's fetching me a drink." She studied his handsome profile in silence, experienced enough to know that his ardor had cooled. "Actually, he's afraid of you."

"Why?"

"Because you and I . . ."

He smiled at her with the polite disinterest of a stranger. He wasn't a cruel man, but he did wish she would disappear. "Yes?"

She flushed at his dismissive coolness. "Your conquest is having quite a conversation with Brentford, isn't she?"

He glanced back at Jane, his face dark with irony.

"Well, you know what they say, Helene. 'While the cat's away, the mice play.' And speaking of rodents, isn't that Buckley hiding behind that potted fern in the corner?"

He chuckled at the obscenity she muttered in French before she excused herself to rejoin her new protector. Grayson bore her no ill feeling; in fact, he was grateful that he hadn't gotten deeply involved with her before realizing how incompatible they were. Of course, in the past, before his father died, he would have plunged in head first and damned the consequences.

Which did not mean he had foresworn wicked fun forever. Only until the clan was back in control, and this mess with the unlucky Jane had been tidied up to everyone's satisfaction.

Now, where had she gone? Her morose baron had also disappeared.

"Excuse me, Lord Sedgecroft. May I have a word with you?"

Grayson glanced around into the sharp assessing gaze of Baron Brentford. In the background he caught a glimpse of Jane standing with her two sisters, neither of whom lacked their share of admirers. "This concerns Lady Jane, I assume?"

Brentford nodded his dark head. "Is she spoken for?"

"That depends," Grayson said guardedly.

"On what, my lord?"

"On what you have in mind—and whether Nigel . . ." He faltered. He and Jane hadn't thought this far ahead. What the blazes was he supposed to say? Half the ton believed that he and Jane would marry. Perhaps it was to her advantage to encourage this illusion. "Isn't this a question you should be asking her father or brother?"

"The viscount directed me to you, my lord. He was involved in a political debate."

"I hardly know you well enough to speak of my personal affairs," he said at last.

"I see."

They stood in silence, each trying unsuccessfully not to look at Jane. Grayson had felt comfortable with her from the start, as if she'd been an old friend, but after tonight, he was afraid there might be more to it than that. What he could not guess. The baron was the first to speak again.

"I understand the pain of unrequited love," he said unexpectedly. "I know the humiliation of betrayal that she has suffered."

Grayson stared. Had he suddenly become someone's maiden aunt who dispensed advice to the lovelorn?

"I did not think I would live through it," Brentford added.

"Yes, well, let's not go turning maudlin at a party, Brentford. Jane is here to distract herself."

"Then you are forbidding me to approach her?"

Grayson glanced away from Jane. God knew he didn't own her by default. To forbid a man from courting her was not his right, especially not when he hoped to restore her availability in the marriage mart. Yet neither could he blithely hand her off to the first undesirable who came along either. He owed her at least that degree of protection.

"Yes," he said, at a loss. "I suppose I am." And let Brentford make of that what he would.

There was a pause. Both men watched as Jane went out on the dance floor with one of her brother's close friends. She was actually laughing, apparently enjoying herself, until in the middle of a turn she glanced over at the two dissimilar males studying her with brooding intensity. Her face clouded over, and she faltered a step.

"That is what I mean," Grayson said, shifting his shoulder from the pillar. "She is *not* going to wallow in heartbreak over my cousin if I can help it."

"I don't know how she can appear so carefree when he abandoned her only a week or so ago," Brentford said thoughtfully. "I applaud her acting ability. It is uncanny."

Grayson, only half listening to this melancholy nonsense, gave Brentford a piercing look. "What are you saying?"

The baron hesitated. "Far be it from me to believe gossip. It's just that some of her friends suspect she never really loved Nigel to begin with. A few have even speculated that she wasn't that unhappy to—"

The contempt on Grayson's face cut him dead.

"Gossip, my lord," Brentford said quickly. "Only low gossip."

"Then do not repeat it. Ever."

Brentford lifted his brow. "My grandmama always said gossip is a seed that bears ill fruit."

"Then do listen to her," Grayson said in a cold voice. "Do not plant ill-begotten seeds."

Brentford nodded. "I shall leave you to your duty as her guard."

"Do that," Grayson said curtly, hoping that whatever other malicious rumors about Jane were circulating through the ton would die stillborn.

Chapter 15

❦❦

The following morning a small box arrived for Jane from Rundell, Bridge, and Rundell, the jewelers on Ludgate Hill, containing a diamond mouse brooch with onyx eyes. There was no card attached. No message to hint at that passionate encounter in the maze, just this very costly reminder of a moment she could never forget had she so desired. While Caroline and Miranda admired the unusual gift, wondering aloud at its significance, Jane sneaked downstairs to the kitchen to see Cook.

"A rhubarb, you say, my lady?" Cook wiped her damp hands on her apron. "Well, I haven't seen one in ages, but there is an apothecary my aunt visits who sells imported Chinese potions. Dried rhubarb roots and such."

"Rhubarb roots." A pleased grin spread across Jane's face as she pictured repaying Sedgecroft in kind. "Oh, splendid. Have a nice big one wrapped in a pretty box and sent to the marquess at Park Lane. With my best wishes. And tie a pink ribbon around the rhubarb."

"To the marquess. A rhubarb root. With a pink ribbon."

"In a fancy box, mind you," Jane added, before turning away.

Cook stared at the scullery maid frozen at the sink, her face perplexed. "Rhubarb root," she whispered. "Lord help us. What would a young lady be wanting with a root unless it was one of those hocus-pocus love potions the gypsies sell? Resorting to magic to get herself a man," she answered herself. "Poor thing."

The scullery maid threw down her spoon. "I'd like to buy some arsenic to slip into Sir Nigel's tea, I would."

"Wouldn't we both?" Cook said. "But arsenic is too kind, dear, for what that miserable sod has done. I'd like to get my hands around his neck and wring it like a pullet."

The maid glanced down at the towel Cook was squeezing in her powerful hands. "Calm yourself, Mrs. Hartley. The young lady has the marquess to take care of those matters for her."

Cook frowned. "And sending him a rhubarb, as if I'm too thick to know what *that* signifies. No subtlety there, my girl. Not that even an old woman like me cannot see the attraction."

Grayson approached the Earl of Belshire's Grosvenor Square mansion on his horse later that same afternoon.

He had thought about Jane all night long, at turns perplexed, amused, and terrified by his attraction to her. He'd thought about her as he revisited Nigel's club and favorite haunts, none of which rendered any helpful clues to his disappearance. He was beginning to wonder if he wouldn't be better off joining Heath on his search, but then he had promised to stay here and defend Jane from social cruelty. Defending her from himself was yet another matter entirely.

He wanted her more every time he saw her.

He knew he shouldn't have her.

He wanted her anyway.

Yet a promise was a promise, even if it had caused a problem he hadn't anticipated when he had thrown himself into the unlikely role of maiden rescuer. Yes, he regretted the impulse, but not for the reasons he might have foreseen. Although his treacherous body hungered for her with a persistence that challenged his moral views of courtship, far more disturbing was the fact that he enjoyed her company and conversation. He certainly liked her too much to foist her off on the first suicidal baron who desired her.

If he couldn't pursue her in a normal fashion, he would simply have to think up another way that was acceptable to them both.

His mood lifted as she appeared on the front steps, her brother in tow. Simon looked green about the gills, nursing a headache from the previous night's indulgences. He probably did not even remember that Grayson had brought him home last night to deposit him on the exact spot he now stood.

He grinned at Jane and dismounted to help her onto her mare, covertly waving away the groom who had appeared for that same purpose. If the truth be told, he didn't particularly want anyone touching her but himself.

"I see you're wearing my brooch," he said in an undertone.

"Oh, yes. Everyone admires it, even if no one quite understands the significance. I might even start a fashion for mice and diamonds in the morning." She gave him an arch smile. "How thoughtful of you to commemorate our evening."

"My pleasure entirely." He eyed the tight cut of her burgundy velvet riding costume, the thrust of her full breasts, his body tensing in response. His pleasure indeed. "Is Simon coming?"

They glanced around in unison to see Simon sagging forward on his horse, one hand clapped to his eyes.

Jane laughed. "I wonder if he'll make it to the park."

"Don't worry." Grayson guided her horse into the flow of traffic. "If he falls, the crossing sweepers will find him."

They rode the short distance in silence, Grayson dodging children rolling hoops and barking dogs while studying the way Jane's backside bounced in rhythm with her horse. The sensual jostling of her body made him think of a different sort of ride, which explained the smoldering look on his face when on Upper Brook Street she glanced around to look at him. Unfortunately he could not mask his lustful thoughts in time to escape her detection.

"Grayson Boscastle," she said in soft tones of despair, "don't you dare look at me like that in public!"

He gave her a lazy smile. "I was simply admiring your seat."

"What is one to do with you?"

"I cannot help it if I think like a man." And if he remembered how soft and wet she'd been last night, open and receptive in her sensuality. The memory burned deep into his bones.

"Yes, it's that appalling manliness of yours showing again," she said.

He didn't know what to make of her. She seemed at times sophisticated. At others she was vulnerable. She was a contradiction at every turn. Yet so was he.

She did little to make herself attractive to another potential husband. She attracted him without the smallest effort when other women had plotted to gain his notice.

She saw through him whenever he slipped. She dared to call him names when he wanted to help her. This was a different sort of friendship than he had ever known, and he liked it.

"By the way," he said, drawing his horse close to hers as they reached the corner of the park, "it was thoughtful of you to send the rhubarb root this morning. You'll pardon me for not wearing it."

She pretended to look crushed. "You didn't like it?"

"Oh, I did. I almost fell off the bed laughing."

The pale sunlight caught the golden highlights in her hair, drawn back into loose waves on her neck. He studied the delicate bones of her face and felt a strange emotion stir in the depths of his heart.

An unfamiliar, frightening emotion.

He didn't want to put a name to it.

He hoped against hope that whatever it was would go away all by itself.

He had an awful feeling he wouldn't be that fortunate.

"I think the world is deceived by you, Jane."

She hesitated, the sparkle in her eye fading. "How so?" she asked in a subdued voice.

"There is a vixen's mind at work beneath all those lady-like airs. A true devil you are."

"Oh, look who's talking."

He grinned, tightening his powerful thighs to urge the stallion toward her. "One devil recognizes another, I suppose. Shall we try to lose your brother?"

At her nod they took their horses onto the bridal path for a brief ride before Grayson slowed and suggested a walk. Several other couples waved at him, studying Jane covertly, as if unsure whether to pretend they knew about the wedding scandal or not.

She ignored their glances and stared fixedly at the water of the lake, embarrassed by all the attention. To think that the beau monde might assume the pair of them were destined for marriage. She and Grayson. Man and wife.

"I wonder if Simon is looking for us," she said suddenly, more to divert her imagination from that provocative possibility than any concern over her errant sibling.

Grayson caught her by the hand as she dismounted, the press of his hard body against hers a pleasant shock. "You can let go of me now," she whispered in a shaky voice.

"Why?" he murmured, his lips grazing her hair. "You feel divine, that riding habit fits you like a glove, and I fit against you even better. As to Simon," he added, slowly releasing her, "he appears to be heading toward the Serpentine with a group of young ladies."

"Well, I hope he doesn't fall in," Jane said. "He was

wobbling on his horse like Humpty Dumpty the entire way here. I wish he would find a decent young woman to marry."

They fell into step together, skirting nursemaids chasing after children and dogs, an elderly duke and his servants taking the air. Grayson noticed Baron Brentford's appearance on Rotten Row; heads turned at the two spirited bays drawing the elegant phaeton along the track. Deliberately, Grayson guided Jane rather forcefully in the opposite direction. Brentford brought out a very aggressive streak of possessiveness in him.

"What are you doing?" she asked with an uneasy laugh.

"Protecting you from the ill wind about to blow our way. And back to the subject of Simon. Why is it you females always think marriage is the cure-all for our woes?"

"Marriage is the cornerstone of our civilization," she said distractedly, peeking around Grayson's shoulder.

He glanced back, his face darkening in anger when he saw the baron slow his well-sprung phaeton to look at her, making a show of bringing his bays under control. Hadn't he made his point clear to Brentford at the ball?

"You are staring at him, Jane," he said in a cool displeased voice.

She started. "I'm sorry. I was, wasn't I?"

"Yes. Why?"

"I don't know. He was staring at me first. One is compelled to stare back."

"Jane." His smile was strained, his manner uncompromising. "One of us might be compelled to stop his staring once and for all."

"Not here?" she said in horror, afraid he was rash enough to do exactly what he threatened.

"Why not?" he asked lightly. "Blood has been shed on these grounds before. I do, after all, come from a family that follows tradition."

This time she captured his muscular forearm and dragged him to a peaceful patch of grass, abandoning the groom who had been trailing at a discreet distance. "A tradition apparently steeped in violence and the pursuit of pleasure. Instead of picking on Brentford, why don't you do a good deed and introduce my brother to some sweet young lady who might exert some influence on his errant ways?"

He was rather amused at her efforts to shepherd him; not that she would influence his mind one way or another, of course. If the baron became a serious problem, Grayson would deal with him, not in a public place, but he would deal with him nonetheless.

"I sense another talk coming on the virtues of holy matrimony." He collapsed on the grass and closed his eyes, releasing a loud theatrical snore. "Am I dead yet?"

"Get up, Sedgecroft. The papers are already full of gossip about us."

He opened one eye. "Ah, more gossip. What have we been doing now?"

She folded her arms and glared down at him. "We're getting married next month."

"Well, what's wrong with that?" he said mischievously. "I thought you approved of marriage."

"Except that our engagement is a lie, Sedgecroft," she said, making a face. "We can't fool everyone forever.

Now please disengage yourself from that undignified position this instant."

He rolled onto his elbow, reminding her again of a gorgeous lion as he stretched in the sun-dappled grass, his morning coat falling open at the waist. "What exactly did you and Nigel do when you were together?" he asked in a lazy voice as his gaze traveled over her. "Sketch still life?"

"We talked, if you must know. We had what is known in polite circles as conversation."

He plucked a blade of grass, his face cynically amused. "What did you discuss?"

She sighed. "Life. Books. Love." Specifically, in the last year or so, Nigel's growing passion for the family's governess.

"Nigel's love for you?" he asked curiously.

She met his gaze, a shiver sliding down her back. "Umm, not exactly."

A frown darkened his face as he rose, engulfing her in his shadow. "Sometimes I think he could not have been a Boscastle at all."

"What do you mean?" she asked in hesitation.

"Well, to put it bluntly, a Boscastle would not have spent all those years in your company without progressing further than a conversation, if you take my meaning."

"I'm afraid I do—" she said in despair, then exclaimed in a deliberately overloud voice to distract him, "Oh, look, isn't that Cecily walking by the water?"

"Jane." He tugged at the tail of her riding jacket, drawing her back into the broad support of his body. With an indulgent smile, he lowered his face to her neck to murmur, "Does it make you uncomfortable to talk about desire? No one can hear us this far away."

Her body tingled alarmingly where it came in contact with his, her shoulder blades, the curve of her buttocks and calves. "You're the only man who ever dared broach the subject," she answered, turning abruptly at the sound of her name being called. "That's Cecily asking us to join them. Shall we go? I think Simon's with her."

"You're so obvious, sweetheart."

"So are you, Sedgecroft."

"Am I?"

"Absolutely transparent."

"Then tell me what I'm thinking."

"I'm sure my tongue could not form the words."

"I was thinking about what happened last night," he said softly, lifting a strand of hair from her neck.

He saw her pulse flutter at the base of her throat before she moved away. "Then try to think about something else for at least the next few moments," she said, her breath catching. "We don't want you walking into the water."

Grayson sauntered behind her, his angular face reflective. For all her evasive tactics, he couldn't stop thinking about her unguarded openness in the maze last night and how it had changed his feelings for her. He'd never met a woman quite as disarming before. Demure one moment, a temptress the next. Pliant, delicious. Dignified. A bit of a shrew.

A woman who made a man hunger for sex. And commitment.

He stopped, took a breath, shaking his head in denial. Where had that last thought come from?

But it was true. Someone would come to treasure her. There was in Jane, he had discovered, a wealth of qualities to be treasured. And the obvious itself was not uninviting. Why should Nigel's stupidity label her undesirable for life?

His own desire for her rendered the ton's standards ridiculous. His cunning mouse was leading him on quite a chase, and he didn't mind anywhere as much as he should.

Some of her friends suspect she never really loved Nigel to begin with.

Oh, Jane, he thought, smiling to himself. *You do need a lesson or two in love. Perhaps we both do.*

Her friends stood together at the shoreline, lamenting the loss of Simon's silk top hat, which a cheeky lord had tossed impulsively into the lake. There was a chorus of cheers as the hat made a false drift back toward the shore, then a collective groan when it began to sink, never to be seen by the haut ton again.

"This is so unlike you, Jane," Cecily said from the corner of her mouth, pretending to ignore the devastatingly handsome marquess who stood a distance from the others. She was dressed in a chocolate-brown silk riding habit, her small face overshadowed by a matching cap jauntily adorned with swan feathers. "Have you seen the papers?"

Jane stared at the water, conscious in every particle of her being that Sedgecroft hovered behind her, apart and yet so present she could think of no one else. She could still feel the brand of his warm, muscular body against her. Apparently she was not alone in her attraction to him; most of her female acquaintances were sending him winsome smiles and pleas to save the sunken hat. The fact of his universal attraction made her feel inexplicably irritated, that on top of her edgy guilt over the secret she harbored from him.

"Yes," she said after several moments. "I saw them. You know half of what is written is untrue."

Cecily's eyes narrowed in speculation. "So the other half is? No. Don't answer."

"I don't intend to."

"Everyone is saying that he's going to propose to you, Jane. If he hasn't already."

Jane sighed. This morning, when she had seen their personalities linked in print, when she had read that a certain marquess had fallen in love with her, she'd experienced the most unjustified burst of joy that had deflated as soon as she put down the paper.

"A part of me actually admires you for this, Jane," Cecily added after a long hesitation.

From the corner of her eye, Jane noticed Grayson glancing back into the park—Helene was strolling on the arm of Lord Buckley, her pale yellow hair reflecting the sunlight. The Frenchwoman stopped when she caught sight of the tall marquess, covertly giving her escort a tiny nudge away.

Sedgecroft put his gloved hand to his sensual mouth and yawned.

"Admire me for what?" Jane asked absently, engrossed in the nonverbal drama she had just witnessed. What on earth did it mean? Why were people's emotions so hopelessly complicated? She wondered if in a few months that would be her on another man's arm, desperate to attract Grayson's interest. She wondered if Grayson had ever taken Helene into a maze and pleasured her senseless. Or if he would one day look at her and yawn.

"For taking Sedgecroft as your lover," Cecily whispered in her ear.

That certainly grabbed Jane's attention. She felt a blush begin at the soles of her slippers and rise to her face in a tidal wave of embarrassment. Worse, to judge by that devilish glitter in his eye, Sedgecroft had heard it, too.

"He is *not* my lover," she whispered back, sounding less convincing than she should have. "He is a companion, a . . . a family friend."

"Such friendship," Cecily said in a tart but more subdued voice, "is known as fattening the lamb for the kill. Yes, the entire world sees that enormous diamond brooch on your bosom. We all know exactly where it came from and that if this friendship ends in marriage, everything will be forgiven. But what if he follows in Nigel's footsteps? What if Nigel returns?"

"Kindly change the subject, Cecily," she whispered, positive she heard Grayson chuckle.

Cecily pulled her to the water's edge. "You must break off with him. At least until you are calm enough to think this through."

"You try breaking off with Sedgecroft."

"I am truly worried about you, Jane. It looks for all the world as if you're enjoying his company."

"Perhaps I am."

"And perhaps you are too heartbroken to know what you are doing."

"I might be doing what I want to for the first time in my life."

Jane was surprised at how strongly she felt about defending the rogue. Her friends saw only his facade. They did not perceive the kindness and love of family that quite stole Jane's heart. He might be a wretch at times, but he did take care of his own. If Grayson ever did fall in love, she thought wistfully, the woman he chose would not only be pleasured senseless but also cherished.

"It—" Cecily subsided into a deep silence as a shadow fell between them.

"Do you want to ride now, Jane?" Grayson asked in a pleasant voice, as if he weren't aware he was the topic of this whispered conversation.

Jane looked up at him, a thrill of pleasure going through her. Devil he might be, but the way he made her feel defied description. Cecily gave a moue of disapproval and faced toward the lake, where a handful of flowers had been tossed as a memorial to Simon's sunken hat.

"If you like," Jane said, afraid that her two friends would start a fight over her at any moment. Cecily and Sedgecroft were both her friends, she realized, a pair of dissimilar people who were only trying to protect her in their own opinionated way. How was she possibly to keep peace between them?

"Yes," she said, sending Cecily an apologetic smile. "I think a ride is a good idea."

*   *   *

"Now Cecily is angry at me," Jane remarked in distress to Grayson two hours later as they strolled in the humid shadows of her Grosvenor Square garden. "She's predicting all manner of misery will be heaped upon my head, and she might not be wrong."

"Well, she's wrong about me," Grayson said, obviously assuming he was the accused source of impending misery. "I hope you came to my defense."

"I did, but . . ."

She stopped at the potting shed, glancing up at the house just to see a bedroom curtain fall quietly into place.

"The spying network has spotted us," she said with a grim smile.

"Who is it this time?" he asked in a stage whisper. "Caroline or Miranda?"

"I think it was both. In fact, I think Caroline had a spying glass in her hand."

He studied her with a slow smile. "Shall we give them something to worry about?"

"Oh, Sedgecroft, what a scapegrace you are. What are we going to do? We shall have to stop this silliness before the ton demands to know our 'wedding' date."

"Are you breaking off our engagement, Jane?"

"Would you be serious for a moment?"

He glanced up, distracted by the distinctive creak of a window opening. His face dark with amusement, he grasped Jane's hand and led her around the potting shed. "Now they can't see us at all, which should really alarm them. So, what will it be tonight, a soirée or a private supper for two?"

Jane resisted the temptation to melt against his hard

torso. "Did it ever occur to you that normal people simply stay home at times to read . . . or rest?"

"There's no rest unto the wicked, my dear, or so the Bible says."

"As if you had ever read it."

"Oh, I did." His blue eyes danced at the memory. "With a governess who was practically my own age holding a rod to my backside. I've had some difficulty studying Scripture since then though. Sometimes I wonder what ever happened to that woman and whom she's torturing now."

Jane forced a smile to hide her reaction. She could believe what a handful he had been as a boy. But heaven help her! By governess he could only mean Esther Chasteberry, or Lady Boscastle, as she would now be called, mother to another generation of misbehaved Boscastle schoolboys. The Governess of the Iron Glove. It set off all of Jane's anxieties to discover he remembered the woman so well. He certainly wouldn't be joking if he knew Esther had married his missing cousin.

"I don't know what to say. You probably deserved whatever punishment she dealt. I—"

She blinked as he caught her chin in his hand and gave her a quick hard kiss. In an instant a dangerous surge of warmth flooded her senses, then disappeared as he drew away, leaving her feeling a little unbalanced and annoyed. "That will have to hold you for a few hours," he said with regret. "The gardeners are coming."

"Hold me for a few hours. Honestly, Sedgecroft, as if a woman cannot live and breathe between your kisses. That is arrogance."

He laughed, casually steering her off the path to avoid

the wheelbarrow being pushed their way. "I've been told that more than once," he said, and kept his hand on her shoulder. "Anyway, it's just insurance to make sure you don't fall into the clutches of any brooding young barons who fancy you."

"I feel sorry for him," Jane replied. "You shouldn't make fun."

"A male on the prowl can use such sympathy to his own advantage." His voice was cynical.

"Spoken as one who knows all the tricks of his trade."

"But you can do better than Brentford, Jane. We have only begun our quest."

"Has your heart ever been broken?" she asked him softly.

He took a step away from her, drawing his hand to his side. Caroline and Miranda had just appeared in the garden, making an embarrassing show of pretending to admire the hollyhocks.

"Only once. Horrible feeling." He grimaced, escaping in the direction of the garden gate. "We'll have a good time tonight. Bring your Bible or a rod. Whatever pleases you."

Chapter 16

❧

Her Bible or a rod.

Jane felt a glacial chill go through her as his tall frame disappeared from sight. She was going to need all the prayers in her Bible and a rod for self-protection when Grayson found out the fate of his iron-gloved governess. And what part Jane and Nigel had played in her life. How long could she maintain this charade before she broke down? How long would it take him to realize that she had been deceiving him?

She folded her arms across her chest as her two sisters crept up behind her. "What happened?" Caroline demanded, one eye on the garden gate.

"We hurried outside as fast as we could when we saw you," Miranda said, pausing to take a breath. "We would have been faster, but Caroline couldn't find one of her shoes."

"Nothing happened," Jane said unconvincingly.

Caroline gave her a cool tiger-eyed stare. "He took you behind the potting shed."

"And I was going to show him the bulbs Aunt Matilde sent from Brussels."

"Is that why the top three buttons of your riding jacket are unfastened?" Miranda asked with an innocent look. "Because you were showing him your bulbs?"

"I had gone riding in the park," she said indignantly. "It was warm this afternoon."

Caroline sighed. "I'm sure it was. Oh, Jane, my sensible, respectable, scandal-free sister, how *could* you let this happen?"

She nudged a stone with the tip of her shoe. "I ask myself that every hour."

They flanked her on the flagstone walkway. "It's all so unlike you, Jane," Miranda said, staring at her eldest sister's profile. "You know what he is."

"I'm not exactly sure what he is," Jane said in a pensive voice. But whatever it was, she liked it very, very much. "I only know that he does not deserve my deception."

"Are you going to tell him?" Caroline asked hesitantly.

"I have to, don't I?" Jane replied in distress. "Although I keep hoping that by some miracle he'll decide he's done his duty, and he'll never have to find out the truth."

Caroline frowned. "Not unless Nigel vanishes from England and never returns. And certainly not as long as you . . . show him your bulbs."

"Would you like us to tell him for you?" Miranda asked after a moment of reflection.

"No," Jane said forcefully. "That would be the coward's way out." She paused, biting her lower lip. "I shall tell him on Friday."

"Think this through very carefully," Caroline said. "If Sedgecroft decides to betray your confidence out of anger, another scandal on the heels of the first will be the end of you. We are not entirely sure we can trust him to keep your secret."

"I cannot see him merely shrugging off the whole thing without a grudge," Miranda added ominously. "A Boscastle might make an excellent friend, but I would not wish for one as an enemy."

The same thought had crossed Jane's mind more than once. She stared back at the potting shed, feeling another chill of foreboding go through her. What an unbearable prospect. All that charm and male energy turned to anger, to retaliation. All the delicious fun they shared cast under a shadow of deceit.

"I shall have to take that risk, won't I?" she said firmly.

And another scandal would not be the end of her at all. Losing Grayson's trust would.

Grayson realized he was heading into treacherous, uncharted territory with Jane. More than once he even considered calling off their arrangement, but he could not bring himself to it, making up a dozen excuses to continue seeing her. At the very least he decided he should make an attempt to put her out of his mind when they were not together. He'd been neglecting his own affairs anyway. He had never felt comfortable wallowing in the idle affairs of the aristocracy.

Business matters at the wharves awaited him. He'd vowed to investigate a rumor that Drake intended to follow in Brandon's ill-fated path and serve in the East India Company's ranks. Grayson could not afford to think about a woman all day long, no matter how appealing she was.

Yet he thought of little else, and found himself constantly looking forward to seeing Jane again. He felt eager to share some amusing event with her, or to discuss his concerns about the family, to seek her advice.

What had their arrangement become?

He did not dare speculate.

Another five days sped by, and Jane still could not dredge up the courage to make her confession. Five days of Sedgecroft occupying her time, seducing her spirit, five of the happiest and most terrifying days in her life. Happy because he made her laugh with his good-natured audacity and honesty, terrifying because she realized she was more than a little in love with a man whose courtship of her was a generous charade.

Terrifying because of the secret that stood between them.

The handful of hopeful suitors who actually dared to call on her were turned away with polite excuses. She even refused to go shopping with Cecily on their weekly excursion to Bond Street, not wishing to be lectured again. Instead, she and Grayson went boating in Chelsea with Simon and Chloe, racing against Drake's boisterous crowd. Naturally Grayson's boat won.

The next evening they attended a ball, and on the Thursday night before Doomsday, the date designated for her confession, the two of them went to a play with her parents and returned home alone when Lord and Lady Belshire decided to play cards with an elderly friend in Piccadilly.

"See her safely home, Sedgecroft," Lord Belshire said, approving of this arrangement only because Jane seemed happier than she had been—well, since before she started planning that ill-fated wedding, actually. And no one had heard a word from that cruel wretch Nigel. So Belshire felt heart-sorry for his eldest daughter, sorry enough to encourage her to spend time with a purported rogue who was proving himself to be more reliable than his cousin.

"Simon and the two girls will be home," he added as a precaution. "So the pair of you will not be alone."

But Jane and Grayson did end up alone, except for the servants who shuffled about in the shadows of the house. Lord Belshire had forgotten that Simon was taking Caroline and Miranda to a birthday ball.

So she and Grayson stood in the black-and-white marble entrance hall like figures on a chessboard, with undercurrents of tension and temptation in the air. Who would make the first move?

He plucked one of Lady Belshire's peacock feathers from the brass urn and tickled Jane's nose with a theatrical waggle of his eyebrows.

"Alone with you at last," he whispered, his mouth brushing her hair. "What do you think we should do first?"

"Stop being silly for one thing." She pulled off her plum silk pelisse, her voice catching at the dark look he gave her. Not since that night in the maze had they given in to temptation again. "And now you've made me sneeze—"

"God bless you." He tapped her on the head with the

feather. "And I'm serious. Shall I seduce you in the rose damask drawing room or in the gold?"

She started to laugh, more to cover how his question aroused her than anything. "Well, we have neither, so it looks as if seduction isn't in the cards. But . . . it is late. I suppose the proper thing is for you to go."

"Why?" He pulled her gently against him, wrapping his powerful arms around her waist. Jane caught a glimpse of their reflection in the hall-stand mirror, his tall form in black evening clothes overshadowing her, her body bent to his. For a moment the mirror's illusion made them become one, joined in shadow. She swallowed, her heart pounding erratically at the thought. The feather dropped from his fingers and drifted to the floor.

"I'm not going to leave you all by yourself," he said, tilting her face up to his.

"The servants are here. I'm safe." Safer than with him in one way. But in others—well, she knew in her heart Sedgecroft would never let anyone harm her. If only he could have saved her from herself.

"We can stay up late and play cards," he said casually, leading her down the hall to the drawing room. "I'm sure you can wager something I want."

"I—oh, no, I forgot. I'm supposed to have breakfast with Cecily and Armhurst tomorrow."

"Beg off until next week," he said firmly.

"I can't. I have to see her before her family leaves for Kent to ready the estate for her wedding."

He closed the door quietly behind them, his gaze focused on her. The room lay in darkness, and he watched her as she went to the sideboard. He'd been dying all night to touch her, even with Lord and Lady Belshire sitting beside them in the box. Every brush of her soft shoulder against his had sent a shiver of lust down his spine. Temptation quickened his heartbeat to a dangerous tattoo as she came toward him. His blood thickened, hot waves of desire washing through him.

She took a tiny sip of his whiskey before handing him the glass. "Oh." She grimaced. "If that doesn't light a fire in your belly, nothing will."

Except you.

His long fingers curled briefly around hers as he took the glass, loosening his cravat with his free hand.

Make me leave, Jane, before I forget this cannot go further.

She turned toward the enormous sofa in the center of the room, sinking in a rustle of silk. "What did you think of the play?"

"I didn't watch it." He sprawled out beside her. "I was a little distracted."

She studied him in wonder. His eyes looked silver in the shadowy dark, heated, sparkling with sin. "I don't think I'm going to ask what distracted you."

Of course it had been her. While pretending to watch the play, he had been wracking his brain to remember all the gossipy things he'd heard about Jane over the years. Everyone had assumed she belonged to Nigel, and Grayson hadn't paid much attention. Well bred. Beautiful. A bluestocking. Yes, all right, a bluestocking with a body that belonged in a royal brothel. No one had mentioned her wicked humor and those bewitching green eyes, or that attractive touch of insecurity. Or that with her all his devils would meet their match.

"Who is Armhurst?" he asked, taking a sip of his drink.

"A friend of Cecily's."

"A young man?"

"I think so."

"There was an Armhurst involved in a duel last year over a broken romance."

She took a breath. There was ice in his voice and heat in his gaze as he slowly leaned toward her, his golden mane of hair brushing the lapels of his black evening coat. The scent of whiskey on his breath tantalized her. The scorching heat in his eyes seared her.

"Don't go," he said, his tone deceptively light.

Her heart skipped a beat. They hovered on the verge of something, a fall into the unknown. She sensed it and could not decide whether she should be afraid or not. "What?"

"You're not meeting this Armhurst. I forbid it."

"And if I do?" she asked, teasing him a little.

"Then I'll be there, and Armhurst won't dare even look at you."

"Don't tell me you've never been involved in any duels," she said, her heart quickening at this display of possessive autocracy. What had changed between them?

"My morals are not in question right now, Jane." Which, he reflected wryly, was a damned good thing, considering the immoral things he wanted to do to her.

She laid her head back on the sofa. "Tell me something, Sedgecroft. Would you marry a woman if you didn't love her? If your family insisted, or she had pots and pots of money and was a great beauty?"

He reached back to put his glass on the table behind

him. This was dangerous ground, being able to talk so openly to a woman. "Jane, to be completely honest, I have never been sure I would marry a woman I loved, pots of money or not."

"You wouldn't?"

"Well, a month or so ago I would rather have been boiled in oil than submit to being leg-shackled. But lately, I've been looking at life in a different way."

She felt him shift forward, a move on the chessboard. Her mouth went dry. In another moment she would slide into his lap. She would pull that warm, powerful body against her and disgrace them both. "Since your father died, you mean? The Boscastle burden of responsibility you told me about?"

He brushed his knuckles across her plush lower lip, responsibility the last thing on his mind. He wanted her so badly that his very bones ached. "That, and other things. Has anyone ever told you that your mouth is highly erotic?"

"Of course not," she said quickly. "Nigel probably doesn't even know what the word means."

Suddenly she could not remember what they had been discussing. Not with his decadent mouth a whiskey-scented breath from hers. Not when those blue-silver eyes speared her with sensual possession, and her body thrummed, tightened in response to his unspoken demands. She wanted to give him whatever he desired, however wild, however dangerous that might be.

"I shouldn't have stayed," he said, his voice thick.

"I know."

And she closed her eyes as his hands slid up the sides

of her gown, gently enfolding the globes of her breasts in his large palms.

"Do you know how much I wanted to do this in the theater?" he asked huskily, kissing her neck, the underside of her chin, pulling the bronze silk bodice down to bare the top of her plump breasts. "What a beautiful body you have. I want it, Jane."

She shivered in a surge of desire and disbelief. "I thought we were going to play cards."

"Let's play something else instead."

He pulled her by her shoulders onto his lap, pushing her skirts up as he kissed her, her breasts wantonly pressed in his face. She felt light-headed with the flood of sensations this position unleashed, her bottom trapped between his solidly muscled thighs, his deep, wet kiss wringing a whimper from her. Her head reeled as his hand trailed up the side of her leg, and then he was touching her with an intimacy that set her nerves on fire.

"Oh, my God," he whispered, his fingers tangling in her damp patch of hair. "You're already wet. I could drown in you. I have thought about you every hour since that night in the maze."

His deep voice came from so far away, barely penetrating the haze of desire that enshrouded her. She was overwhelmed by his strength and gentleness. She clung to his shoulders and felt his muscles ripple like hot steel beneath her fingers. Below, the most intimate recesses of her body opened to him, an erotic response beyond her control, a surrender to the elemental male who had captured his prey and now would play with her at his pleasure.

The house was so quiet. The soft intimate sounds of a

man pleasuring his woman seemed amplified in the silence, absorbed by the heavy layers of damask curtains, the tapestries on the walls. The cry she gave when he pressed his forefinger deep inside her. The ormolu clock behind them that marked the passage of time. His groan of satisfaction to be touching her like this.

His eyes almost black with remorse and desire, he said roughly, "I shouldn't be here. You tempt me beyond reason. I have to leave—"

"No." She could not believe the desperate note in her voice. She touched his cheek, fingers caressing the chiseled bone structure, and looked into his eyes. "I don't want you to leave."

"Oh, Jane," he whispered, turning his face into the soft palm of her hand. "Do not encourage me. I am already on the edge. I know all too well what this could lead to."

She felt her pulse pounding in her throat. He looked like temptation incarnate with his disheveled golden mane of hair and warlord's body disguised in the elegance of his evening clothes. And he desired her, this man who had befriended her at a time when she was a social disgrace. What *would* this lead to?

"I don't care," she whispered, leaning forward to kiss his firm mouth. "I want you to stay."

His voice was anguished. "You don't know what you're saying." He couldn't resist her. No other woman could calm this turmoil deep inside him. And she felt the same. Or thought she did. "You haven't done this before. I have an unfair advantage."

"Then who better to instruct me?" she whispered, twining her arms around the strong column of his neck. She heard him draw a breath. She refused to look away. His mouth glistened from her kiss. He was everything she had ever wanted. Let him do his worst.

He went as still as death, his gaze hooded and unfathomable, looking down at her lovely face. His nostrils flared, and a tingle of foreboding raced across her nerve endings. For an unbearable moment she thought she had shocked him with her question, as she had shocked herself. Shame brought color to her neck. What sort of woman asked a scoundrel to seduce her?

Then suddenly he came to life, his big body stirring beneath hers. His eyes held her a helpless captive with their intensity. Mesmerized, she did not move. There wasn't time to wonder if she'd made a mistake. His left hand worked free the bindings of her gown with such competence that she was naked to the waist before she quite realized what he'd done. Well, this was what she had wanted.

His gaze flickered down, and his wide mouth curved in a smile of sensual anticipation. Her invitation had shredded the last of his restraint. "Who better indeed?" he muttered, as he pressed another finger deep inside her damp sheath. "The answer is no one, Jane. I claim this privilege for myself, with your permission."

She arched her spine; his skillful invasion into the most sensitive core of her body rendered her utterly powerless even as pleasure inundated her senses. He stretched and stroked her with a finesse that bordered on torture, his long fingers cool as they penetrated her warm flesh; the intensity of her arousal made her feel as if she were dissolving, going up in steam.

Grayson inhaled sharply as the spicy musk of her

wrapped around his senses. The family drawing room was hardly the place to make love to her for the first time, but all he could think of was burying himself in her tight passage. She was drenching his hand in her wetness, moving against him with an unconscious sensuality that unchained the devilish side of his nature. This was what he wanted, too, had been afraid would happen. Why had he ever imagined he would be good for her?

"Grayson." She groaned, her gaze unfocused. She was open and willing, the most desirable woman he'd ever met.

"It's nice, isn't it?" he whispered, "and I'm going to make it even nicer for you in a few moments."

He pulled off his coat with his free hand, craving the feel of her against his chest. With her beautiful body half naked, the basic male in him threatened to throw aside what scant control he could muster. Pleasuring her would not slake the fever raging in his blood. He needed total possession. The muscles in his back and shoulders corded with the restraint it took to subdue the lust that pounded through him.

His thumb teased the tender bud of her sex until she grasped the crisp fabric of his evening shirt, her body bowed with tension. His silver-blue eyes studied her face the entire time, and his heart hammered in the hollow of his throat as she neared her peak. He glanced at the door, reassuring himself he had remembered to lock it. She was all his in that moment, and nothing was going to ruin it for him or her.

She came against his hand in a rush of sensation, struggling to breathe as he moved his fingers even deeper inside to heighten her pleasure. She felt fragmented and relieved and mortified all at once by the spasms that shook her body. And yet in the aftermath, it seemed natural to sit there with him in a comfortable tangle of arms and legs, her gown wantonly bunched up at the waist. She wanted to remain like this forever. To not think.

She stole a glance at his sculpted profile, heard his ragged intake of breath. They lay side by side, his leg hooked around the delicate arch of her foot, one arm crossed behind his head. He looked indecently tidy, and he was frowning up at the ceiling with a dark absorption that made her shiver. Where had her playful scoundrel gone? Was he upset that he had not found his own satisfaction? She could not bring herself to ask, but he did look . . . unfulfilled. Or was he lamenting the loss of his imaginary paragon? The thought brought her crashing back to earth.

"Grayson?"

"Just give me a moment, Jane. I need time."

Time? She glanced around the darkened room. "We really ought to make an effort not to be caught wallowing in sensual guilt like Anthony and Cleopatra," she whispered after waiting for what seemed like ages for him to move again. "All we lack is a slave fanning us with a palm frond and feeding us grapes."

Her effort to restore his good spirits did not work. He sighed heavily. He would not sleep the rest of the night, although pleasuring her had been worth it. He and Jane had crossed a line tonight. This bore serious thought as to their future. "All right. Get up and find some cards while I light the candles. We'll look properly behaved when your family comes home."

"Why were you frowning like that?" she asked in concern as they rose together from the sofa.

"What?" He looked away from the candelabra on the sideboard. "I was trying to control myself. And thinking. Oh, my sweet Jane, there is quite a lot to think about."

She pulled her gown back in place, her hands not quite steady. "About—"

Candlelight framed the carved symmetry of his strong features. Frowning, he reached forward to help her settle the folds of her gown. "Heath sent word earlier today that he's coming back to meet with me. I suppose he might have news."

She turned to the card table. A coldness settled over her, banishing all the energizing warmth she had felt only a moment before. "What sort of news?" Not that she wanted to know. To let anything ruin her illicit happiness. Her mouth went dry.

He shrugged and took the pack of cards from her hands as she returned. "I have no idea."

They sat back together on the sofa, a discreet distance apart. Jane watched him shuffle the cards with the same casual expertise with which he had reduced her to raw pleasure on the same spot. She stared at his strong, well-manicured hands, entranced and filled with anxiety at the same time.

"He must have given you a hint," she said.

He shook his head, his mouth firming. "His message was all very ominous and mysterious, not a hint of what, if anything, he's learned. But that comes from his intelligence background, I suppose. Of course Drake was involved in some shady business, too, or so I suspect. Yet they are entirely different." He glanced up, grinning at her. "All I know is that I wouldn't want to be the enemy of either."

"No," she murmured, catching her breath as their eyes met. She glanced down at the cards he had dealt her. Red and black blurred together. He trusts me, she thought. He doesn't know yet. "What if I confessed to you that I didn't care whether Nigel ever returned?"

He couldn't hide his approval. "I wouldn't blame you one bit."

Her throat tightened. This was even harder than she'd expected. "And what if I said that I never really wanted to marry him?"

His cool eyes searched her face. What did he see? "Hindsight always imparts the wisdom we might wish for."

"Not hindsight," she said quickly. "I am being truthful. I don't think I ever loved him. Except as a dear friend."

Grayson mulled over her words as he dealt. His tight smile might be the only outward sign that her admission had pleased him, but deep inside he felt an absurd burst of relief. Imagine having to compete with Nigel. "Well, it makes things easier all around, doesn't it?" he said in an even voice.

"Things?"

"Other loves. Not mourning what we lost. I feel the same way about Helene, if you must know. I look at her now and wonder what on earth attracted me to her. Anyway, the only real question is, what will you do if Nigel comes back with his heart in his hand?"

"I don't know." She stared down at the cards on the table. "Nothing. What—"

"Are you prepared to forgive him?" he asked, his smile fading.

She searched for the strength to clear her conscience. "We don't know yet if there's anything to forgive," she said after hesitating.

"Oh, you are a coolheaded one, Jane, my love," he said with a deep laugh. "And, as I noted before, exceptionally honest."

"Please stop making me out to be a paragon," she said in a burst of irritation. "I am a remarkably flawed person if you must know. As you *have* to know by now."

"Well, so am I."

"No." She swallowed over the knot that constricted her throat. "You aren't awful at all. Not in the manner which counts."

He grinned in an attempt to sweep aside her concerns. "I can be when I'm crossed, an event you are unlikely to personally experience unless I catch you cheating at cards."

She picked up her hand, her mood utterly miserable. She knew she had to tell him, not merely flirt with the truth, but she was afraid. Afraid that the playful affection on his face would turn to contempt. Afraid he would walk out of this room and never return. Or that they had passed the point in this relationship when telling him what she had done could be forgiven.

"Grayson, I'm sorry. I cannot concentrate on a game of cards right now."

"I'm sorry, Jane. I knew I should have left."

"No, it isn't that."

"Then what is it?" His blue eyes scanned her face. "Do you feel you have betrayed Nigel?"

"You really make me out to be far nicer than I am. Please. I don't feel like playing cards."

"Then we can—"

The sound of voices in the entrance hall interrupted him. Grayson rose swiftly to unlock the door, sat back down, and rested his arm casually over the sofa. When the drawing room door opened, he and Jane presented a picture of innocent activity to the three people who stared at them in surprise.

"Sedgecroft." Simon cast an experienced glance at his sister, satisfied that all was in order except for the satin pumps she had kicked under the table. "I thought the pair of you went to a play with my parents."

"So we did." Grayson had risen in deference to Caroline and Miranda. "And I offered to keep your sister company when we discovered you weren't home."

Caroline stared pointedly at Grayson, as if she knew in humiliating detail what had been going on a few minutes earlier. "What a gentleman you are to protect her."

"Isn't he, though?" Jane's cool voice cautioned her not to pursue the subject.

Simon cleared his throat. "Would you like a drink, Sedgecroft?"

Grayson glanced down at Jane. "Thank you, but I'm meeting my brother early tomorrow anyway. I should be on my way. Ladies, I wish you pleasant dreams."

Jane stared down at the cards that had fallen across the sofa. Pleasant dreams were unlikely—she wouldn't sleep a second until she heard what else Heath had learned about Nigel.

"I shall walk you out," Simon said. "I understand you are something of an expert on shooting, and I have been invited—"

Caroline closed the door the moment the two men made their exit. "You didn't tell him, did you?" she whispered. "It was the perfect time, the two of you alone in the house."

Jane moistened her lips. "I *almost* told him. I might even have gotten to the worst part if the three of you hadn't barged in here like the Trojan army. Anyway, tomorrow is Friday. I said I would tell him then."

"Are you frightened of him?" Miranda asked, sitting down on the sofa amid all the fallen cards.

"Terrified," she admitted.

"We could hide behind the desk during your confession in case he takes a violent turn," Caroline said thoughtfully.

"Don't be silly. Sedgecroft isn't going to hurt me." She bent at the waist and picked up the King of Hearts, her voice low with emotion. "At least not in a way either of you can prevent."

Chapter 17

❦

Grayson paused outside his bedroom door as he perceived the faint creaking of bedsprings. He smiled grimly. If his nocturnal visitor was a certain Frenchwoman, he trusted he could evict her with a minimum of hysterics.

It wasn't that he didn't crave a night of uninhibited sex; it was just that his current tastes ran to a more sophisticated green-eyed lady who challenged his emotions as well as turned his body into a smoldering hotbed of suppressed frustration.

And if Helene hoped she had the slightest chance of reviving their relationship, well, there was no hope. None at all. He wasn't the same man he'd been when they met.

Everything had changed tonight anyway. He and Jane had reached a point where their arrangement had become either a beginning or an end. And since he had no intention of giving her up, he realized he was up to his neck in trouble.

Not that trouble bothered him in the least. It appeared to be a Boscastle way of life. But as he was the eldest of the brood, and the first male officially to lose his heart, he supposed he should consider carefully his next step as family pathfinder.

Marriage?

Why not?

He'd realized long ago a wife was a necessity, but he'd privately abandoned hope of finding her among his circle of close friends. He had even formed a vague picture of her in his mind. What color hair, the sound of her voice.

Then Jane had come along, and the image had slowly altered. Reshaped itself into the most contrary female who kept him awake at night, who was nothing at all like what he'd been looking for.

But was everything he needed.

He wasn't stupid. He'd watched enough of his friends drop like flies when the fatal illness struck.

Now he was himself stricken; he showed all the Six Deadly Symptoms of a Man in Love:

1) Inability to think straight.
2) An alarming propensity to smile at the oddest moments.
3) Constant thoughts of the object of one's desire.
4) Absolutely no interest in other members of the opposite sex.
5) A startling sense of goodwill toward the world in general.
6) A perpetual state of sexual arousal.

This was it then. Their beginning. He *needed* her. She had worked her way into his heart and could never be replaced. A sense of rightness stole over him.

He opened his bedroom door, unaware his tidy summary of the situation was about to go up in flames.

He entered his room, his mind resolved. He refused even to glance at the figure reclining on the bed to save them both embarrassment. "If you are not dressed, kindly cover yourself before I turn around. I am not in the mood for a casual toss tonight."

"Neither am I," Heath said, swinging his booted feet to the floor. "At least not with you."

Grayson started to laugh, his left hand frozen on the spotless white cravat he had loosened. "I understand that espionage is in your blood, but is all this sneaking about necessary with Napoleon safely tucked away on his little isle?"

Heath picked up a pair of gloves from the nightstand and made a show of examining them. Grayson stared at him for several seconds before he resumed taking off his cravat and evening coat.

"One never knows."

"I see. Well, I trust you don't expect to encounter any problems of *that* nature in this house."

Heath glanced up, grinning boyishly. "It's Mrs. Cleary, if you must know. Ever since your housekeeper caught me posing as a Roman soldier for Miss Summers to paint last month, I have not been able to look her in the face."

Grayson unbuttoned his waistcoat. In spite of Heath's joking, something was wrong. He sensed it and hoped it would not hurt Jane. "I thought we were meeting tomorrow at the club."

Heath settled in one of two armchairs by the window,

his face toward the door. "I've other business in town. I hope you don't mind."

"No." Grayson sat down opposite him, a little baffled by this change in plans. What revelation could possibly require this degree of secrecy? "I don't mind. Do you want a drink?"

Heath rarely drank; it was simply a courtesy to ask, and Grayson's premonition of trouble was confirmed when his brother's grin slowly gave way to a concerned frown.

"You might need one after I'm finished, Grayson."

Grayson stroked his chin. "Then you have found him. How was he?"

"Under a sheet when I left him."

Heath's blue eyes glinted. In the darkness the two men looked more alike than by daylight, when Grayson's golden male beauty contrasted with his younger brother's dark aura of dangerous composure.

It took Grayson a few seconds to react. "Under a— oh, my God, Heath—don't tell me you've gone and killed the moron. Not that I don't understand your motives. But I had hoped to at least make Nigel apologize publicly to Jane before I throttled the life out of him."

"He's alive. Very much so."

Grayson was surprised at the relief he felt. Nigel probably did deserve to die, but he was family. "You did actually see him then?"

"In the flesh." Heath blew out a sigh. "Quite literally, I'm afraid to admit. I have now seen much more of Nigel than one would ever wish."

Grayson leaned forward, fascinated. "You caught

him in the act—under a bedsheet—dear God. Don't tell me it was with another man."

"It wasn't."

"Then not—not with an animal, or anything so perverse I cannot explain it to Jane?"

Heath removed a cigar from his vest pocket. "Do you remember Miss Chasteberry?"

"How odd you should mention her. I was explaining that piece of our boyhood history only yesterday to Jane. The Governess of the Iron Glove, who turned her students to jelly. And let us not forget her infernal rod. Why—"

"Apparently, she is still raising rods."

Grayson sat back in amusement. What an unexpected development. "Nigel was thumping the family governess?"

"To be more accurate, he was thumping his wife. Or rather, she was thumping him. I did not make the distinction."

Grayson laughed uneasily. "I don't believe you."

"Believe me. I did see the wedding register in Hampshire."

"He *married* Chasteberry?"

Heath smiled slowly, staring at his unlit cigar. "She of our youthful fears and fantasies. Perhaps Nigel is one of those men who harbors a penchant for dominant women. There are men who pay for such dubious pleasure."

There was a long pause. Then Grayson shook his head. "I have no idea how I will break this to Jane."

"That bit of drama will be unnecessary."

"The devil," Grayson said in vexation. "You told *her* before you told me?"

"Grayson, are you completely besotted? Do I have to explain every detail? My God, you do not make this easy. Jane did not need to be told. She knew all along. She and Nigel sabotaged their own wedding. Most young women will go to any lengths to leg-shackle a man. Your Jane did the opposite. You and your noble intentions interrupted an artful plot."

"A plot?"

"I'm afraid so. Jane and Nigel never wanted to marry each other."

Grayson looked away from the window, utterly stunned, struck speechless by what his brother had revealed. A plot. A sabotaged wedding. God above, a conspiracy between Jane and his own cousin. He could not believe it. Yet at the same time so many little mysteries now made sense. Of course Jane had not been jilted. The minx had been manipulating her own life, *him,* all along.

He drew a sharp breath as if to dampen the anger burning in his breast. He couldn't trust himself to speak. How noble he'd imagined himself. How arrogantly stupid to believe his sacrifice would matter. Damnation, who had he been to label Nigel a nitwit? *He* was the one who had proven to be the fool, who had let the wool be pulled over his eyes. A plot, and he had been a pawn. No, an obstacle.

He tried to clear the red mist swimming in his mind. Why hadn't he seen the signs? he asked himself savagely. From the start he had suspected the whole situation was amiss. Why hadn't he put two and two together? Why hadn't he guessed?

Because no proper young lady would sabotage her own marriage. No young lady of Jane's background would dare. His darling paragon had thumbed her nose at Society. At him.

When, if ever, had she intended to tell him the truth? he wondered, his outrage growing by the moment.

How long, how far, would she have carried on this charade?

Had she been too afraid of him to admit what she had done? Good. She ought to be. He was a little afraid himself of what he would do to her. She would pay dearly for this. Oh, how he would enjoy making her pay.

He looked across the room and gave a low humorless laugh. Puzzled by Grayson's apparent lack of reaction, Heath took the flint and tinder box from the table and carefully lit his cigar.

A cloud of fragrant blue-gray smoke drifted between them as he spoke again. "Perhaps you have misunderstood me," he said cautiously.

Grayson regarded him with a chilling smile. "Why do you say that?"

Heath shifted uncomfortably in his chair. "You would *not* be smiling like a satyr if you understood what I had said. She has been deceiving you, Gray, playing you for a fool while the world has watched in wonder."

A flame flickered in the depths of Grayson eyes. A flame of anger. Of hellfire unleashed.

"It is you who misunderstands," he replied evenly.

"Oh?"

"This is not the smile of a noble fool you see." He paused, his tapered fingers gripping the arms of his chair. "It is one of a man plotting a punishment."

"Now wait a minute," Heath said in alarm. "This is more of a reaction than I anticipated. Is punishing Jane the right thing to do?"

Grayson's smile thinned. He would not allow a sense of guilt to manipulate him again. He'd done his duty and look where it had brought him. Practically to his knees. "It was doing the right thing that got me into this situation. Jane needs to be shown that I can give as good as I get."

"This sounds ominous, Gray. All that biblical eye-for-an-eye nonsense."

Grayson's gaze mirrored little mercy. Jane had hurt him in a way he had not dreamed possible. "'He maketh rain on the just and the unjust.'"

"Yes, but this sounds more like a thunderstorm than a little shower," Heath said worriedly. "What exactly are you going to do?"

"Marry her."

"Marry her?" Heath said in shock.

Grayson laughed at his brother's incredulous expression. "After I make her pay."

"And how do you do that?" Heath asked in a guarded voice.

"I am going to play with her, Heath, exactly as she has played with me. The simple fact is that I love Jane."

A glimmer of good-natured admiration replaced the anxiety in Heath's dark blue eyes. He could not hide his relief. "I take it this revenge will be sweet? For you, I mean?"

Grayson folded his muscular arms behind his head, closing his eyes in contemplation. "Seduction is always sweet, isn't it? Revenge will merely add a pinch of spice to the pot."

Grayson sent Weed for his secretary the instant Heath left the room. The hour was late. It did not matter. The best plots were hatched in the dead of night.

Was that when his clever little mouse had laid her daring scheme?

Why? His initial fury had subsided enough to allow him to think more clearly. Why had she done it?

He mulled the most obvious answer. She and Nigel, being brave young fools, still believed in the concept of a happily-ever-after love. If she had refused her parents outright, they would either have forced her hand, found another match, or disowned her.

And Jane, for all her human foibles, adored her family. So in a rather brilliant but desperate way, she had schemed to have her cake and eat it, too. But her plan had failed, as such desperate schemes are apt to do.

Grayson would be far more devious in constructing his counterplan. He would use all means at his disposal: legal, spiritual, financial. And, yes, sexual, too. Her deception had given him carte blanche to fulfill his deepest fantasies even if he had come perilously close to acting on them more than once.

At last. At last. The rake in him was back in charge. The hero had had his day. He no longer felt unbalanced. Never mind the emotional maze Jane had led him through to reach familiar ground. He was finally back on his feet.

More the pity for Jane.

The irony of it did not escape him. He was plotting to

marry a woman who had executed a brash plan to avoid the parson's mousetrap, a fate he had avoided all his adult life.

Grayson wasn't stupid. He loved the damned woman not only despite her deception—perhaps even in part *because* of it. Yes, he was furious at her for playing a game with him. But now the tables had turned. The game was no longer to be played in black and white but rather in the more nebulous shades of gray in between.

A game of revenge?

Perhaps a little. But more than anything it was a game of love.

For somehow he sensed that if Jane were capable of sabotaging her own wedding, she would not respect him if he did not respond in kind. A woman of her passion for life, of her capability to plot her fate, would expect the same of her mate. And who else but Jane could match him misdeed for misdeed, word for word? Who else could bring that hunger to live, that gambler's daring to a marriage?

He wanted her, and there was absolutely nothing left for him to do but submit, even if he refused to do so gracefully.

He had found his mate, his match, but before he applauded her wiliness, he would have a little fun taking his revenge on her for deceiving him. Let her earn his forgiveness.

Lord Belshire awoke in the darkness of the carriage to feel himself being roughly prodded by an unfamiliar hand. "What? Home already? I was not snoring, Athena. I was not even—" He blinked, staring around the unmoving vehicle in astonishment. "Sedgecroft. Where—What have you done with my wife?"

Grayson rapped on the roof, and the carriage lurched forward into the maze of London streets. "She is safely at home with the rest of your family." His mouth tightened. "Including your eldest daughter."

"Jane." The older man fumbled to pull his gold pocket watch from his embroidered waistcoat. "Where . . . where the blazes are we going at this time of night?"

Grayson settled back against the squabs. "To my house, in order to conduct our business in peace. My solicitors and banker are already awaiting our arrival."

"Banker—what sort of business is conducted in such a clandestine manner at this hour of night?" Belshire demanded in a thunderous voice. "My God, you scoundrel, if you have brought dishonor on my daughter . . ."

Forty minutes later Lord Belshire understood exactly the nature of Sedgecroft's "business" and had reluctantly agreed to the terms listed in the marriage contract he signed. The conditions set forth for the betrothal were bizarre to say the least, but then so was Jane and Nigel's underhanded deception of all those who had loved and trusted them.

"I cannot believe she would do this," he muttered. "All the same, I insist that she will not suffer as a result of this agreement. Before God you must swear to honor our contract."

"Make no mistake, Belshire," Grayson said, his eyes glittering like ice. "I love your daughter."

"At the moment I cannot say I share the sentiment. That does not mean I will see her misused in any way."

"Trust me. Jane will be well treated. In a year or less I hope she will present you with a grandchild."

A glint of hope lit the older man's face. A grandchild. A future marquess. "I question your methods—"

"You will not question the results," Grayson said without hesitation.

"I assume that Jane is ready to become your wife."

"I assure you, she is."

"It does solve several problems at once, Sedgecroft."

"I thought so, too."

As he brooded over Jane's underhanded plotting, Belshire decided on the ride back home that his willful daughter probably deserved to marry a man like Sedgecroft, who had the same sort of duplicitous mind as she. Or so he tried to explain to his wife when he returned to her.

Athena was reading in bed when he rather dramatically paused in the door to their room. "I am in shock," he announced. "Complete and utter shock. My entire body is numb."

She put down her book. "That's the price you pay for going out drinking with a man practically half your age. Not that you ever had Sedgecroft's stamina to begin with. What was it he wished to discuss with you anyway?"

He closed the door and strode into the room to explain. When he had finished, she was pacing angrily around the bed upon which he had collapsed.

"And you agreed to this? You put your name to this contract?"

"You are missing the crux of the matter, my dear. Jane

deceived us. She never wanted to marry Nigel in the first place."

"How dare she do this!" she exclaimed. "I am going to her room right now."

"No. You're going to pack so that tomorrow morning when she arises she will discover us all gone. Except for Simon and Uncle Giles, whom I will ask to stay with her while Sedgecroft carries out his . . . courtship."

Athena came to the foot of the bed, her face distressed. "I know it is a wicked thing she has done, but she did beg us to call off the wedding to Nigel. And to leave her alone at the mercy of a man like Sedgecroft—"

Howard scowled. "A man who will be her husband, my dear. Sedgecroft loves her despite her deceptions, and I believe she loves him. Besides, do you think there is a decent male in the whole of England who will have her after her plotting is revealed?"

"Well," Athena said coolly, "there is always Scotland, or Wales. And don't forget the displaced aristocrats from France."

"I tell you, it is a young Medea we have raised," he said. "It's a wonder she has not turned us all to stone."

"You are thinking of Medusa. Medea murdered her own children."

"Medea. Medusa. Only you would know the difference. That's what I get for marrying a bluestocking and producing a daughter with a devious intellect. Jane will be damned lucky if she has any children of her own to murder."

Athena sat down at her dressing table, already resigning herself to her fate. "With Sedgecroft she will most certainly have children, and handsome ones, too, with a brood of uncles to spoil them after we are gone," she thought aloud. "Things could be worse."

Howard stared across the room. "I do not see how, but it does not matter. She is marrying Grayson Boscastle, and that is the end of it. How he will handle her I cannot imagine, but I can only wish him well."

"Does Jane know any of this?" she asked suddenly.

"No. And Sedgecroft wants to be the one to tell her. Alone."

"How romantic of him. I hope Jane shows sense this time."

Lord Belshire frowned. Romantic was hardly the word he would have used to describe Grayson's air of ruthless determination in drawing up the marriage contract.

"He's nothing like Nigel, Athena. Jane will not find a way out of this situation unless she chooses to become a spinster."

"Can't we at least say good-bye to her before sending her into battle?"

"It is a courtship," he said, "not a battle, although in this case one cannot be sure. And, no, we will thankfully be gone before she arises. If Jane possessed the cunning to trick us, she is more than capable of standing up to Sedgecroft on her own."

Chapter 18

※

Jane woke up later than usual the next day, aware that an unnatural silence pervaded the house. Nine mornings out of ten Miranda awakened her with her pitiful practicing on the pianoforte, or Mama and Caroline would be arguing in the hall about the inappropriate state of Caroline's attire.

"They have all gone to Belshire Hall in the country, Lady Jane," the head parlormaid informed her after Jane had hastily dressed to investigate. "Except for Lord Tarleton, who left early for a horse race with your uncle, Sir Giles. The two gentlemen said they would be home in time for supper."

"My own family left me here without asking if I wished to go?" Jane said in disbelief.

"Lady Belshire's cousin has apparently taken sick, and she thought it was unnecessary for you to come along," the maid replied, her eyes lowered as if she didn't believe the story any more than Jane did.

"I don't suppose any of them bothered to leave me a personal message," Jane said in irritation as she turned away.

It seemed all very mysterious and suspicious, and her sense of unease was only confirmed when, on instinct, she ran into Caroline's room and found a hastily scribbled note stuffed under the ink blotter on the desk.

Jane,
     Have been taken against our will, practically bound and gagged. Beware—the lion has chosen his mate—

And then there was a huge, ugly smear on the paper as if Caroline had been forced to hide it from whoever had entered the room.

"How peculiar," she said to herself, gooseflesh rising on her forearms. "'The lion has chosen his mate.' Who—?"

She jumped as the footman knocked loudly at the door. "The marquess is here, Lady Jane. He has insisted I summon you without delay."

"Summon me? Summon me for what?"

"I didn't think to ask, my lady."

"I wonder—you don't think anything was wrong?"

Without waiting for an answer she hurried downstairs to the drawing room to find Grayson standing at the window, dressed in an elegantly tailored royal blue morning coat and snug nankeen trousers, his riding crop tapping against one iron-hard thigh. Tapping, she thought fleetingly, like the tail of an animal about to strike in anger.

"Well," she said, so glad to see him that she started to laugh, "at least you haven't abandoned me. My entire family has gone a little mad. It seems some cousin of mine has taken ill and my parents are gone on a mission of mercy to the country—"

Then he turned, and her breath caught in her throat. No man had the right to look so sinfully handsome this early in the day.

Her laughter faded as their eyes met, and for the second time that morning a prickle of foreboding raised goosebumps on her arms. She didn't remember ever seeing that dark regard on his face before.

"Did you meet with Heath?" she asked, her heart thumping in her breast.

"Yes."

"Oh." Her legs felt unsteady as she searched his face for a clue to her fate.

"I'm afraid it is not good news, Jane," he said heavily.

"No?"

"It seems your hopes of marrying Nigel must be forsaken. He does indeed appear to have run away."

"To where?"

"Does it matter?"

She wondered if he could hear the erratic pounding of her heart. "I suppose not."

"I say good riddance to him."

How aloof his gaze had become. Or was she imagining things? "Yes."

"You will not forgive him."

"I—"

"It would be best to forget him, Jane."

"But—" How much did he know? She was confused by his behavior. Did it embarrass him to break this news?

"He does not matter anymore." He held out his hand, beckoning her. "Does he?"

A disconcerting flush of heat went through her. "No," she said, staring at him, wondering if it could possibly be this easy. Was there the wildest chance he would not uncover the truth, or that he knew and they could continue to pretend that he didn't? That he was content to say Nigel is gone, life must go on, and you, Jane, are part of my life?

"Now," he said in a low, even tone, "fetch your pelisse. We have an appointment."

Whatever shadowy emotion had darkened his gaze was gone before she could interpret it. There was a subtle difference in his manner toward her. Had Heath learned more than Grayson would tell? No. Nobody knew of Esther's Hampshire home. And if Grayson knew, he would not be able to control his anger. Did he feel guilty about what they had done last night? Her blood quickened at the memory even as she wondered if his opinion of her had been lowered.

Tell him everything. Tell him the entire truth.

He does not matter anymore. . . .

She shook her head. "What appointment? I told you I was supposed to meet Cecily—"

"Your carriage is waiting, my lord," the footman said from the door.

"Thank you," Grayson murmured. "Bring Lady Jane a light cloak and meet us outside."

A few moments later Jane found herself suddenly ushered rather ungently into the hall and out the front door. "Grayson, kindly explain what you are doing."

"Get in the carriage, Jane. I will explain in due time."

But he remained infuriatingly silent as the vehicle set off through the busy thoroughfares toward the shopping district of Bond Street. She was afraid to speculate on his intentions, or what this brooding mood of his meant. Clearly he had something on his mind. Perhaps it had nothing to do with her at all.

She knew it did.

"At least tell me where we are going."

His gaze traveled over her briefly, bringing a blush of heat to her face. "To the modiste Madame Devine."

"Devine—but she is the dressmaker for the demimonde, for Cyprians and dancers."

He closed his eyes, his relaxed pose not deceiving her at all. "Her gowns are exquisite."

Jane frowned. "I know. Cecily's fiancé requested a few scandalous pieces for her trousseau, which reminds me. I should at least inform her we aren't meeting today."

The carriage passed an art gallery and pulled up before a fashionable Georgian-style brown brick shop, where a pair of footmen waited to escort customers inside the tiny candlelit interior. The small crowd of shoppers on the pavement watched them in curious silence. Wherever he went, Sedgecroft was certain to spark interest.

"Cecily will not be missing you," Grayson said as he guided her past the front counter toward a concealed side staircase. "I took the liberty of notifying her you would be unavailable. Today and in the near future."

"You did what?" She was certain she had misunderstood what he'd said.

He pulled her up the stairs. "Cecily's friend, this Armhurst character, is not a suitable companion for you.

And, Jane, I meant to ask you something last night," he added as if it were an afterthought. "I suppose this is as private a place as any."

Her temples began to throb. What was wrong? Something. Something different. Her family had deserted her, leaving her with this outrageous rogue, who might on the surface act like his usual arrogant self, but there was a change, and she still had to tell him—

"Ask me what?" she whispered, aware of movement in the hall above them.

"To be my mistress." He glanced around in anticipation. "Ah, there is Madame Devine now. I have requested our own private fitting room."

Her throat went dry, and her ability to think faltered for several moments. His mistress. The two words chilled her. This time there was no misunderstanding what he'd said. So this was what he had been leading up to all along. How stupid, how blind she had been to believe his pretense of kindness and responsibility. While she was falling in love with him, he had been planning the whole time to do what he did so well.

The ultimate seduction.

Well, had he ever claimed to be a saint?

She had blithely followed the same path as his other women. Step by step. No one had forced her.

He smiled down at her, obviously uncaring that he was breaking her heart with his indecent offer. "Darling, don't look so surprised. It's unlikely that a proper marriage proposal will ever come your way again. At least as my mistress your financial needs, as well as those of whatever children you give me, will be taken care of for life."

"Children?" she said numbly.

He shrugged. "Mating as often as we will do, children are an inevitable part of a sexual relationship. I have always wanted a large family."

"Have you?"

"A dozen or so of little Boscastle brats, the start of my own dynasty."

"Far be it from me to stand in the way of your breeding ambitions."

"Let's discuss it in comfort, shall we?"

She stared up at him as if he had just revealed he was the devil, and before she could reply to his incredible gall, he had turned to climb the remaining stairs, whistling as if he did not have a worry in the world.

"Well, come along," he added cheerfully over his shoulder. "I won't keep you in my bed every night. There will be times when you'll need to be well dressed to entertain. No more pigeon gray for my little dove."

Her limbs leaden, she followed him into a small chamber furnished with a dressing screen, two comfortable armchairs, a looking glass, and a rosewood table on which sat a crystal decanter of sherry and two glasses alongside a stack of pattern books.

His mistress.

One of the outrageous women who had attended her sabotaged wedding.

He meant for her to become another Helene or Mrs. Parks. A woman he visited for sexual pleasure. A woman he paid to see in private. A partner he would discard when his interest in her waned.

Jane wanted to push him down the stairs and jump on his offer.

A pair of seamstresses bustled her behind the screen and efficiently stripped her to take her measurements while Grayson poured their sherry and explained to the trim, bespectacled Madame Devine and her assistant exactly what he wanted from the samples she brought him.

"Not that." His low, arrogant laugh made Jane's blood boil. "Too many buttons. I'm a man who prefers to have a woman in bed with a minimum of fuss."

Madame Devine gave a girlish giggle. "*Mais oui,* my lord. I understand. These undergarments, perhaps . . . ?"

"No. The lady doesn't need her bosom enhanced. Nature has endowed her with all I can handle."

"Ah. Well, then, this pink satin?"

"Oh, yes. And that black lace, too."

Madame Devine's assistant sighed. "Very, very nice together, under a ball dress."

"What dress?" he murmured. "I thought she could wear them alone."

The woman blushed. "These stays with the ribbon knots, my lord?"

"Why bother? I prefer the natural feel of a female's flesh."

At that the assistant rose to open a window; the atmosphere had grown so steamy that Madame's glasses had fogged over. This was a man on a very wicked mission indeed.

Jane stuck her head around the screen to glare at him. "I think that will be quite enough of your nonsense, Sedgecroft."

"Jane, you are surely not going to refuse me the indulgence of spending a fortune on you?" he said placidly.

She was aware that the ears of the seamstresses

pricked to attention at this question. She replied, "Grayson, I am not a complete idiot. You may indulge me until you are bankrupt." She paused. "But I am *not* promising anything in return."

He fixed her with an infuriating smile. "Famous last words, my dear. I shall have as much fun taking those things off you as I will buying them. Now let me see what you have in the sheerest silk," he instructed the modiste, settling back in his chair. "Something I can see through. Yes, those drawers with the slit are nice."

Jane's cheeks flamed, and her embarrassed gaze met the envious eyes of the two seamstresses in the mirror. He was a rogue to the marrow.

She told him as much when the four flustered women finally left them alone to discuss the details of her wardrobe. "Are you quite mad?" she demanded, taking the sherry he handed her with an innocent smile.

"I intend to lavish gifts on my mistress," he said in an injured voice. "Is anything wrong with that?"

"Only that I have not agreed to any of this," she said between her teeth. "My father will be livid."

He examined the glass in his hand. "Sweetheart," he said gently, "your father is a man of the world. He understands."

"Why in heaven's name would you say such a thing?"

"Because he and I talked at length last night about your future," he replied with a shake of his head. "Yes, at first he resisted, but logic won out."

"I do not believe you. My father would die of shame if he thought I—"

"Your family is dying of shame, darling. One must face facts. Your marriageable days are over."

"They are not."

"They most certainly are," he insisted. "No one is marrying my mistress."

"I will not agree."

"Of course you will." He gave her a knowing look. "Remember last night? I carried you halfway to heaven already. A person in your position must be practical. This is the most sensible solution to your dilemma."

She took another burning swallow of the sherry, tempted to hit him over the head with the whole bottle. Coughing, she sputtered, "I don't want to be a kept woman."

He reacted with an indulgent smile. "What do you want?"

"I want . . . well, I suppose I want love."

"Love?" He *tsk*ed in amusement. "Ask me for a chest of diamonds. Or a palatial manor. A shipload of silk."

"You needn't make it sound like an obscenity." She came to her feet, the potent sherry, his offer, making her feel light-headed. "Some people do fall in love, Grayson."

"Do they?" He stood to tower over her, his eyes sparkling. "Ah, I had forgotten how deeply you loved Nigel. I trust your attachment to him will dwindle over time."

She took an involuntary step back. "I told you last night that I never loved him."

"Then that leaves room for me in your affection, doesn't it?" he asked without hesitating.

She stared at him, her stomach clenching at the cool mockery in his voice. "I feel unwell all of a sudden. Would you please take me home?"

His blue eyes reminded her of storm clouds, darkness brewing in their depths. "Of course, Jane. Pleasing and protecting you are part of our bargain."

Heath raised his brow when Grayson recounted the details of his day in the privacy of his study. "All in all, I'd say it went rather well."

"I cannot believe you took her to Devine's. In broad daylight. What of her reputation?"

Grayson stared at him, shrugging off a faint sense of guilt. "What of it? It was my original goal to protect Jane from the damage Nigel's fictitious desertion had done. But she did not care a fig about her name when she constructed her scheme."

"But the ton—"

"I have never cared what the ton thought," Grayson interjected. "Anyway, all's well that ends well. Once we are married, the gossip will stop. It's amazing how holy wedlock can restore honor."

Heath managed a grim smile. "Did it ever occur to you that something might go amiss with this line of reasoning?"

Grayson glanced through the stack of letters on his desk, dismissing his brother's warning. "I have a legal contract with her father's signature to marry her. Will Jane be angry? Perhaps. But in the end she will realize that she has no choice. I do believe she loves me."

Heath gave a worried sigh. "Well, I certainly hope you know what you're doing. And that nothing goes wrong in this game."

"It won't." Grayson looked up, meeting his brother's concerned look. "As you said, it is a game, and I will not take it too far. A few days at the most. What could possibly go wrong?"

"Tell him I've taken desperately ill," Jane whispered in her bedroom to Simon three hours later. "Tell him I have a raging fever. The plague. Malaria. Cholera. Smallpox."

Simon felt her forehead in concern. "I did tell him. He sent Weed to his physician for advice. He's been waiting here all evening."

"All evening?" A note of panic crept into her voice. "Grayson has been in our house that long?"

"He was playing billiards with Uncle Giles. The man is determined to have you." He hesitated, looking completely at a loss. "What have you done, Jane? I know you're in dire trouble somehow."

She covered her face in her hands. "Don't ask me. I can't tell you. I cannot explain. It's such a hideous mess, and I caused it all myself."

"Then you can hardly expect me to help," he said in bewilderment.

"There's nothing you can do anyway," she muttered.

"Are you certain? Jane, you—you aren't with child?"

"Oh, *Simon*."

"Well. It's not that bad then, is it?" he asked in a hopeful voice.

"I have dug my own grave," she said. "It is beyond bad."

"Sedgecroft is a powerful man. Perhaps he has a solution."

"Don't you understand anything? It is Sedgecroft who

is my problem. He wants me to be his mistress. Yes, Simon, he asked me this afternoon."

He glanced down at the floor, a flush of anger suffusing his face. "I suppose this is all Nigel's fault," he said awkwardly. "I could kill the fool for this. What are we going to do?"

What Jane wanted to do was hide under the covers and pretend she had never started this whole debacle. "You're my brother," she said in desperation. "You know what Papa would do in your place. *Make* him leave."

For a moment Simon looked so appalled at the prospect of confronting a personage like Sedgecroft that Jane might have laughed. Had she not wanted to die.

Then Simon's gaze slid away from hers, and she knew she had lost her last defender. "That's the problem," he said, swallowing hard. "As much as I'd like to plant the marquess a facer, Papa left me explicit instructions that I was not to interfere in this courtship. Strange, now that I think of it."

"Courtship?" Jane cried. "This is not a courtship. It is Wellington taking Toulouse, the French peasants storming the Bastille, the . . ." The color drained from her face. "Do you mean to say that Papa has no objection to my becoming Sedgecroft's mistress?"

"Ah," said a deep voice from the doorway. "Our patient is well enough to argue. There is hope for her then."

Jane shrank beneath the covers even as that velvet baritone seemed to penetrate into her bones. "Grayson, this is most unseemly. What are you doing in my room?"

He came up to the side of the bed, his masculine face

a mask of oversolicitous concern. "Simon had been gone so long, I began to fear you'd taken a turn for the worse. I must say you look better than I expected, Jane."

"I thought so, too," Simon said, throwing another clod of dirt on Jane's self-dug grave. "In fact, I never would have believed there was a thing wrong—" His voice cracked at the frown she shot him. "Except for the fever, of course."

"Let me check." Grayson leaned down and pressed his cool hand to Jane's forehead, his blue eyes boring into hers. "Oh, dear."

She felt a traitorous glow of pleasure at his familiar touch. "'Oh, dear' what?" she asked suspiciously.

"You are rather warm." He leaned down a little lower, his voice a teasing murmur. "Is it really the fever, or are you thinking about what we did last night?"

"Go away," she whispered. "My brother is watching."

"Shall I ask him to leave?" he whispered back.

"You're the one who should leave," she managed to choke out. "Simon?"

Simon cleared his throat. "What did your physician say about her condition, Sedgecroft?"

"Well, without a complete examination, his best advice was either a bloodletting or a holiday by the sea."

"I am not submitting to a bloodletting," Jane said with a shiver of repugnance.

Grayson straightened, his gaze moving over her huddled form. "And so I told him. Which is why I have made arrangements for a stay at my villa in Brighton. We leave first thing in the morning."

"Well," Simon said, missing his sister's frantic looks. "There's nothing like the sea air to revive one's spirits."

"Except that we are going to meet the family at Belshire Hall," Jane said in a shrill voice. "An unplanned holiday really is tempting but impractical."

Grayson stared down at her, his eyes glittering with unholy determination. "Where your health is concerned, Jane," he said in dulcet tones underlaid with iron, "we will not take risks. I insist you stay at the seaside. I refuse to allow you to go to the country."

"Good for you," Simon said; he was obviously of the mind that peace should be had at any price. "She never listens to my advice."

Jane sat up slowly, her gaze locked with Grayson's. "Are you going to force me?"

His lips curled into a thin smile. "If it comes to that. I have promised your father that I would protect you in his place. I would be remiss in my duty if I did not take this illness of yours seriously."

"I suddenly feel much better," she said with enforced heartiness.

He shook his head. "The strain of what you have suffered recently has finally come home, Jane. Perhaps it is not good to stay in London."

"Do you suggest I go into hiding?"

"We cannot have you languishing in bed to grow plump, my little pigeon."

"I do not want to go," she said, biting off each word.

"You need a holiday, Jane. I shall push you along the promenade in a bath chair with all the other hypochondriacs."

"Talk about a tempting offer."

"A donkey ride then."

"I know who the donkey will be."

He smiled. "You might enjoy a scrubbing down with the local seaweed."

"I might enjoy strangling you with it."

"I shall have a maid help you pack," Grayson said in a quiet voice, his stare challenging.

She stared back at him and wondered whether the first woman who had fallen victim to the Boscastle Blues felt as she did now. For while she was in shock over what he had proposed, in her heart of hearts she wished to go wherever the gorgeous devil beckoned. She wanted to be in his arms, to give herself to him, to be the woman he desired. Foolishly she had fallen in love with the illusion of a protector.

"Your offer is more then generous, Grayson," she said in one last attempt to resist him. "But I can hardly go off on a holiday with you alone."

He raised his heavy eyebrows in surprise. "Of course not. Uncle Giles and Simon will be there for the sake of decency."

There was a pause, his diabolical smile informing her that decency was the last thing on his mind.

So, everything *had* changed between them. He had planned this down to the last disgraceful detail. A calculated coolness had come over him, a detachment that signaled danger. Yes, he was as charming and attentive as ever, but beneath those virtues he displayed the cunning of a . . . a jungle animal waiting for just the right moment to attack.

Had she imagined all that gentleness, the good-natured instincts that made him so irresistible to a woman? Or was her own guilty conscience muddling her ability to see? Never in her wildest imaginings had Jane envisioned herself the mistress of a rogue. Her life had taken an appalling detour off the road of decency, and it would be a dark, hard journey back. Perhaps an impossible one. Perhaps she would even enjoy it.

"Really," she said, with more courage this time, "it isn't possible, or proper. A woman alone with three men, even if two of them are her family."

His smile patronized her, made her suspect he'd moved two steps ahead in their game. "Jane, you know me better than that. Naturally I have asked Chloe to accompany us."

"And she agreed?"

"Yes," he said.

But, he thought cynically, only after two hours of threatening and tears, followed by Chloe concluding that her presence at Brighton might be the only consolation in Jane's devastating fate: a Boscastle seduction. Not that Chloe or anyone else would interfere in the lesson he intended to teach his darling deceiver. Grayson was merely setting the stage with the appropriate props. Oh, how he was looking forward to this holiday.

"Of course Chloe agreed," he said. "She will come to enjoy your company as I do." He turned back to the door, the matter clearly settled in his mind. "It works out quite well, really," he added offhandedly. "This way I can keep my eye on both of you."

"You mean keep us both under your thumb, don't you?" Jane called out to his retreating figure.

Chapter 19

❧❧

Spending an entire day trapped inside a traveling coach with Grayson, Simon, Uncle Giles, and Chloe did not resemble Jane's idea of a relaxing experience. The men talked of steeplechasing and parliamentary reform. Chloe refused to talk to or even look at her brother, using Jane as a medium of communication as the well-sprung vehicle lumbered along the coast road.

By the time they stopped for a luncheon at Cuckfield, no one was speaking at all, and it was a silent and stiff-limbed little party that tumbled out of the carriage that same evening at Grayson's Georgian-style villa on a terrace overlooking the sea. Jane examined the graceful three-storied house in wary silence. The elegant red-brick facade impressed the eye as did its owner. Yet who knew what surprises lay within? She wondered what she'd learn about the man she loved behind those closed doors. What would she learn about herself?

They dispersed in the entrance hall with its marble pillars and a soaring plaster ceiling of Baroque design. Chloe locked herself in her suite, murmuring that she craved a sea bath and a glass of claret. Simon and Uncle

Giles disappeared for a late-night stroll on the promenade, hoping to meet up with old friends.

Jane and Grayson stood alone. As he had undoubtedly planned. As she had secretly hoped, if she were to be honest with herself.

"Well," she said, admiring a Ming vase on the corner pedestal in an attempt to pretend she were not on pins and needles. "Here we are. Is Heath joining us?"

"I'm really not sure." Grayson watched her from the shadows, amused by her attempts to evade the inevitable. "Would you feel better if he were here?"

Her heart was beating furiously. "Why should I?"

He took her into his arms, murmuring, "My brother has a strange effect on women. Some are attracted to him. Others find him rather intimidating. Jane, my dear, is it possible that you are afraid of me?"

Afraid? Only of losing him, of ruining her own life.

"I begin to think I don't know you, Grayson," she said in a subdued tone.

"Have I not proven myself your friend?" he asked, his hand sliding up her nape, his thumb stroking the tender spot behind her ear.

His caress brought heat to the surface of her skin. "I suppose that depends on one's definition of friendship."

"Oh, Jane," he said in a deep, sardonic voice. "Always so on guard." He blew softly against her ear.

Her voice faltered. "Apparently my guard has failed me."

"Then perhaps the wisest . . . the wickedest course is to surrender."

"And then?" she asked, her breath catching.

"I don't know." He asked lightly, "Why spoil the surprise? I suppose we shall have to follow our instincts and let the dice fall where they may."

She swallowed over the knot in her throat. "There is a little more at stake than you realize. At least for me."

"But there is so much pleasure to be gained."

"Stop," she whispered.

"I cannot stop." He shrugged helplessly. "I won't stop. Not until you are mine in every way."

She shivered in reaction, despite herself. "This isn't the way I wanted it to be."

"Do we always have a choice in our lives, Jane?"

"I would hope so," she said, her voice almost inaudible. "Yet perhaps not always."

"Will you accept my offer?" he whispered, his other hand already unfastening the back of her gown, stroking, stealing down her spine. His charade had almost come to its end. He would not tease his scheming love much longer, using what remained of his time to full advantage. His lesson could go only so far. Every time he looked into her beautiful green eyes, he felt his anger melt a little more. Soon it would be gone. They would make amends to each other.

"Do you not love me at all, Jane?" he murmured.

She met his gaze, her voice clear, her eyes clouded with emotion. "You know I do, or I would not be here."

In this, at least, Grayson knew she had given him an honest answer. He knew Jane now. Her secret fears, her cunning. The key to her desires. And for an instant, he questioned the benefits of continuing this charade. Perhaps she had misled him, but she, too, had fallen in love with a fraud.

He was not the rescuer he had presented himself to be.

He was not a hero, but he loved her. He loved her with a desperation that brought both his strengths and weaknesses into play.

And in the end, they would belong to each other. Their game would soon be over. Their future as man and wife would begin. She would understand she could never deceive him again. Nor would she need to.

She would realize she could trust him not only with her secrets, but with her life. All their passion and capacity for love would be centered on each other.

"Come to my bed, Jane," he coaxed her. His impatience was not part of his plan. But he could not wait any longer. He wanted her so badly, had dreamed of this so often that he intended to savor every moment.

He ran his fingers down her throat into the deep cleft of her breasts. "Come. Leave your dignity at the door."

"What dignity do I have left?" she whispered.

"Be undignified with me," he taunted her.

She closed her eyes. How it had come to this, she could not say. She had made a mistake, taken a wrong turn in her longing for a love of her own choosing. She had branded herself an outcast. What, if anything, in his pretended courtship of her had been real? Only their desire for each other? Surely there was more—

His voice broke into her thoughts. "Be your wildest, Jane. I have not seen every side of you, have I?"

"What—what are you saying?"

"There is another Jane deep inside you, isn't there?"

"You are certainly showing your true colors," she retorted. "As in black, blacker. And blackest."

He backed her into the staircase, his laughter low and alluring. Soon she would be laughing with him. They would laugh at each other—after a huge passionate argument, perhaps. It would feel good to be himself with her again.

"Yes or no, Jane? Kiss me and give your answer. I have been dreaming of how I will take you. I will surely die if you say no."

She felt as if the room had suddenly gone up in flames. Fire. There was fire everywhere. In the sting of his lips on her throat, in the air they breathed, fire running up the backs of her legs, leaping in her belly, to her fingertips. How frightening it was to love like this. How thrilling. What would be left of her after tonight?

"Yes," she whispered, wrapping her arms around his neck to kiss her fill of him. There was no other answer. "Yes."

They were both burning with need.

His bedchamber was cavernous, the plaster ceiling adorned with Baroque ornamentation. A pair of beeswax candles in scrolled silver sconces on the wall threw mysterious shadows across the thick Persian carpet, and a moist sea breeze blew in from the open windows. The curtains fluttered. The silk coverlet had been turned down enticingly to reveal lavender-scented sheets.

She was breathless with desire before he deposited her on the bed and undressed her with a leisurely expertise that should have offended her but instead only heightened her arousal. She was eager for pleasures she could not even name. She fell back against his other arm, opening herself to him, inviting him.

Her heart raced as she gazed up into his lean face. Never had she felt more vulnerable or more beautiful as she did in that moment when he studied her body without bothering to hide his lust for her. When he was finished, Jane felt as if every inch of her flesh had been examined and found desirable.

"You are perfection, Jane," he said, his voice deep and unnerving. He stroked the curve of her cheek. "Trust me."

She was spellbound by his voice, aching for him to touch her. As he shifted on the bed, her pulses leaped, and she felt moisture pooling between her thighs. He kissed her once, slowly, deeply, until she was writhing beneath him. The ache inside her grew unbearably.

"Trust me, Jane," he said again, and only later would she remember the faint hurt in his voice when he spoke.

"I do trust you," she said, realizing it was true. "I have never trusted anyone as much before."

He leaned even lower. His eyes smoldering, intense, he feathered kisses on her face, her throat, her breasts and belly, the delta of her sex. She tangled her fingers in his silky mane of hair. He groaned in pleasure and pushed her thighs apart, breathing deeply of her scent, rubbing his jaw against her nest of curls. He was a lion, her lover.

Her spine curved at the potency of this forbidden act. His tongue parted her swollen folds and found the hidden bud he sought. "Grayson, you can't—"

"You cannot deny me this, Jane."

In the shadows he was a stranger, her seducer, not the man she had come to trust, but a rake whose sole purpose in life was pleasure, who made seduction an unhurried ritual. Yet even as a stranger, she could not resist him. Her heart knew his name. Her body answered to his skill.

Perhaps his voice seemed deeper, different. But Jane had desired him since the day of her wedding. She had been drawn to his potent masculinity even then, and look where her desire had led her. Discovering the gentleness beneath his sensual allure had doomed her. Now she could not resist his cruelty.

"I cannot believe we are doing this," she whispered as her body began to respond, hips moving, her hands stroking the ridged muscles of his shoulders.

"I think it is a natural progression of a relationship between a man and a woman," he said in a low voice.

Whatever she might have said was forgotten as the pulsing tension in her belly neared its peak. She moaned, awash in pleasure as he took full advantage of her helpless sensuality to drive his tongue deeply inside her.

It was bliss. It was humiliating and uplifting and not enough for either of them. She smothered another moan as her body came apart, pinned where she lay between his arms. For a full minute she could not bring herself to open her eyes, knowing he had proved his power over her in the most elemental of ways.

"Natural progression, my foot," she whispered into the dark. "I could almost be convinced you planned it from the start."

"How devious that would make me," he said with a deep laugh. "We have always been honest with each other, haven't we?"

No answer for that. She opened her eyes, her heart still pounding, as he slowly unbuttoned his shirt and trousers. His nude silhouette warmed her blood, as if she had fallen asleep too long in the sun. Her gaze traveled the length of his muscular torso to the swollen member between his legs. She looked up slowly into his face, not certain what she had gotten into, knowing only that she wanted him, that she wished this could be forever, her fate.

His silver-blue eyes gleamed in the shadows. She craved what she saw in their smoky depths, the fulfillment of her secret desires. He held her heart in his wicked hands. Whatever happened between them tonight would involve her whole being. Jane would never be a woman who could separate her sexuality from her deepest self.

"Grayson," she whispered. "One day someone will tame that arrogance."

"Perhaps it will be you," he said, taunting her.

"Perhaps."

"I think I might enjoy that, Jane."

"I long for the day."

"Practice is required."

She stared at him, wondering how he could captivate and infuriate her at the same time. "Is it?"

"Months and months of it," he answered in amusement. "Unless of course you show a natural talent, as I suspect you might."

Heat suffused her neck and shoulders.

"Shall I show you how it's done?" he asked in a deep whisper.

She suppressed a shiver, her body more than ready for what he promised. "Please do."

He lowered himself to her. Instinctively she pressed her breasts against the hard plane of his chest. He shuddered at the contact and ran his hands down her back to knead the rise of her bottom. His fingers followed the arch of her spine, teased the heart-shaped indentation below. His large hands moved over her, taking possession.

"Give me everything," he whispered. "I want it all."

Turning onto his side, he took her in his arms. The feel of his muscular body against hers flooded her with longing. She lifted into him, craving closer contact. With a shiver of anticipation, she felt his erect penis pulsing against her belly. Before she could stop the instinct, she brought her hands down to touch him. Her fingertips closed around hard silken muscle. He groaned and pushed himself against her, muttering, "Touch me like that, and I will be tamed."

"I wish that were true," she whispered. "I think you'll always be wild at heart. I shall have a devil of a time taming you."

She was wrong, he thought. She did not know what he felt, how she had changed his life, how empty and shallow his world had been before her. How only in her hands, at her touch, could he be gentled. He was entranced with her, as hard as iron, hurting so badly he had almost forgotten the part he was supposed to play. No. No playacting right now. Loving her was too real.

"I am wild for you, Jane," he muttered.

She was beyond answering, surrendering to instinct. He swept his right hand up over her hipbone to her breasts. His thumbs massaged the rosy tips until dizzying pleasure stole over her and she pushed herself against him. Slowly he stroked the silky inner skin of her thighs with his other hand until she was spread open to him, her cleft glistening with pearlets of moisture.

"Grayson," she said, her voice catching. "I'm not ready—"

"Oh, you are," he said as he tangled his fingers in the damp curls of her sex and caressed her creamy flesh with a magic that set off wild shivers inside her. Jane closed her eyes, drugged with pleasure, too in love with him to question her instincts, to stop. His finger pushed inside her, and she felt the heated sensation all the way to the base of her spine.

Seduction. The merest brush of his fingertips scorched her skin like a brand. She was falling apart while he remained strong, sure of himself, a man who reveled in the art of sensuality. She buried her face in his shoulder; the carnal promise in his smile had brought a blush to her very soul.

"It feels good, doesn't it?" he murmured. He slipped another finger inside her snug passage, his jaw muscles tightening. She moaned and moved against his hand, answering him without words.

"I knew you were a devil," she said softly.

"You have no idea how demonical I can be." A rich laugh rumbled in his chest. "But you'll find out. We'll do some very, very wicked things to each other tonight."

She peered up at his chiseled profile. "Do you really think I'm bad?"

"Of course, Jane. Every woman is, if given the chance."

She couldn't help laughing at that. "Listen to you, making decadence out to be a virtue."

"Well, from my position, it is."

"I hate that you sound so experienced," she murmured.

"I love that you don't."

But the truth was that he might have been making

love for the first time. He could barely remember all the techniques he had mastered, the lovers who had taught him, and yet somehow his instincts felt sharper than ever, focused on pleasing this woman. His heart beat like a war drum in his chest with his desire to possess her.

Everything had gone as he had planned except for the unexpected erosion of his restraint, his emotional involvement. But Jane would be Jane, even at the moment of her moral downfall, practically turning the tables on him until he wondered who indeed would emerge the victor in their game. The possibility of defeat, however remote, only stimulated him.

But he would win this battle. He would master her body, mark her his own, make her beg him for more. He quickened the movements of his fingers and felt her delicate muscles contract as he brought her to a climax. She twined her arms around his neck and molded herself to his body, a seductress in her own right as the aftershocks of pleasure inundated her. He watched her in shameless enjoyment. The fierce tenderness he felt for her humbled him. Making love had never involved his heart before.

Then he was positioning the tip of his penis to enter her, his ballocks nestled below her cleft. The invasion into her body made her tighten all over, and he reacted by slowing his penetration, whispering soft reassurances and sliding his large hands under her hips to steady her.

"Jane," he said hoarsely, "give in to me."

Her hands tightened around his neck. His shaft felt huge inside her, pressing into her moist passage, stretching her in a ritual of pleasure and pain. "I'm trying," she whispered.

"I want you." He pushed a little deeper inside her, relentless in his need. "I want you so much."

She wanted him, too. She wanted to know him this way, to take him completely into her body. She wanted to drown in him, to feel his power in every part of her. Her eyes widening, she stared up in unabashed fascination at his shadowed face. He was beautiful, her seductor. The erotic intensity in his blue eyes sent little shocks of lightning up and down her back. His muscular biceps strained as he held his body motionless above hers. Her blood thrumming in suspense, she whispered, "Yes. Oh, yes."

He threw back his head, and she felt herself splintered by his initial thrust. Uncertain what would follow this sensual onslaught, she dug her fingers into his shoulders and anchored herself for the next stroke. Even then she was taken by storm when his hips surged forward, embedding himself inside her to the hilt. She felt the strength forced from her body.

"I—can't—"

He grazed her trembling mouth with a kiss, murmuring, "I'm sorry. I'll make it up to you."

His voice mesmerized her, breaking through the misty haze of her mind. Her inner muscles quivered and gripped him, adjusting to the rhythm he had set. The way he rolled his hips, the gentle slamming into her, and the raw sexuality on his face stole her breath.

"Oh, God, woman," he muttered. "You feel good."

"So do . . . you."

"Like nothing—like no one I have ever known."

His words thrilled her. "Truly?"

His eyes glinted. His voice was a low purr. "Truly,

Jane," he answered softly. "I have never opened my heart to another as I have to you."

She was too lost in his seduction to acknowledge the prickle of guilt his confession awakened. Surrendering her maidenhead might have been a lot more uncomfortable than she had anticipated, but there was no denying how exciting the basic crudity of it all was. Just to follow the mysterious instincts of their bodies. Bumping. Shoving at each other. Moonlight silvering the corded muscles of his chest. She shook with the violent beauty of their mating.

Grayson had kept his entire body wound taut to stop himself from coming at the first thrust. The unbreached walls of her passage closed around him like a silken fist. The pressure in his loins had him gritting his teeth. If she gave another one of those sexy little shivers again, he would explode inside her. Only when he felt her coming apart beneath him did he allow himself to let go, driving into her so deeply he was afraid he had hurt her.

His climax reduced him to basic sensation, gripping him from head to toe. He heard her breathing his name as he buckled, wrapping his arms around her slender white shoulders. She was so small compared to him, and yet she had proved his equal in passion. They lay together like two warriors who had declared a truce after a battle, exhausted, drained, exultant.

He had planned her seduction—and succeeded—with the same unyielding resolve he applied to the rest of his life. But he had not anticipated the feelings that accompanied his pleasurable victory. Holding her warm body next to his, their hearts beating in unison, he was overcome by emotions he could not quite reconcile with his intended revenge. Tenderness ravaged his heart and laid it bare. Never had he loved anyone so completely.

He wanted to resent her for deceiving him; he did. He wanted to regain the upper hand in their relationship; physically this was a fait accompli, but otherwise . . . the balance remained uncertain. Revenge *had* been sweet, especially in the elemental form it had taken. She belonged to him now; he couldn't let her go. Neither could he let her get away with deceiving him even if there would be hell to pay when she discovered he knew her secret.

She stirred and opened her eyes, her heavy honey-colored hair wrapped around his wrist. Her voice was low with emotion. "Oh, Grayson, don't look at me like that."

"Like what?" he whispered, his large hand splayed on her belly.

"Like a big satisfied beast who's just eaten a—"

"Mouse?" he teased gently, wedging his knee between her legs. He couldn't stop touching her now. He felt a stab of jealousy to think she might have ended up with his cousin.

"Perhaps you ought to go back to your room."

"This is my room," he reminded her good-humoredly. "They are all my rooms."

"I meant—listen, Grayson, despite all appearances to the contrary, I am *not* mistress material. We cannot indefinitely behave like pagans."

He knew that, of course. She had marriage and motherhood etched into every bone of her delightful body. And her distress roused a great deal of guilt inside him. But he couldn't pardon her quite so easily. Let him finish the game before he granted mercy.

He pretended to give the matter thought. "Well, we certainly cannot let you become a spinster."

She sat up slowly, the afterglow of their lovemaking apparently fading in the face of reality's complications. "I cannot become a courtesan either."

"Lie back down, Jane," he soothed. "You have a few things left to learn before you attain that status."

"There is no alternative, Grayson. We have to get married."

"Married?" he said, lifting his hand to his heart in mock horror. "Heavens above, somebody put a gun to my mouth."

She narrowed her eyes at him. "Continue in this manner, and it is not outside the realm of possibility."

"You know how I feel about the parson's mousetrap." He smiled slowly. "Even if you are a delicious little mouse."

She drew a deep breath. "I am a decent woman, or at least I was, you overbearing ox. It was you who presented yourself as respectable to my parents."

"Are you proposing to me, Jane?" he asked in amusement.

"I'm afraid I am," she said, sounding none too pleased at the admission.

He released a rueful sigh. "I thought we had come to a suitable arrangement."

"Being a harlot does not suit me," she said with an indignant scowl.

"No? I think you have a natural talent for it, though."

"Where is that gun you mentioned?"

He traced his fingertip across her belly, watching her muscles quiver in response. "Marriage? Let me think about this for a day or two. Perhaps I can be persuaded. In the meantime, darling, turn onto your stomach."

"On my—" She swallowed a gasp. "What are you going to do?"

"There's a looking glass to your left if you'd like to watch," he said in a silken voice. "Otherwise, I suggest you simply close your eyes to enjoy the experience."

He spent the entire night awakening her body. He took no precautions to prevent a pregnancy, for the first time in his life. He was completely ready to claim the children she would give him, to protect her and those she cherished. Friend, mistress, wife. He would seduce his lovely schemer all the way to the altar. He would love her for the rest of his life.

●

Chapter 20

ℰℰ

Jane lifted the sinewy male arm that imprisoned her midriff like an anchor and let it drop onto the bed. The owner, a great naked, blond beast who had ravished her, gave a grunt of contentment and rolled onto his side. This reaction afforded her an eye-popping view of the long torso that tapered into lean buttocks, then iron-hard thighs. As she admired the sight, he wrapped his arm around the bolster she had vainly attempted to shove between them throughout the night.

Not, she reflected wryly, that such an insubstantial barrier had deterred him one bit. He had not made poetic love to her. He had gleefully debauched her, and she, just as gleefully, had encouraged him to new heights of decadence.

She stared in wonder at the devastation of the bed-chamber. It had been a night to remember. Chairs over turned, champagne glasses on the floor, her chemise hanging like an emblem of surrender from the bedpost.

Surrender? Good heavens, she had been the one on the attack toward the end, making the most of her glorious fall from grace. Had she really let him bind her to the bed with her stockings? And those little love bites all over their bodies . . .

How had this happened? She had been such a decent young lady until recently, so well behaved, so virtuous. Yes, rebellion had always simmered under the surface, but the acts in which she and Sedgecroft had participated were unspeakably naughty by any standards. Loving him had turned her entire world upside down. The thought he might resist returning her affection was unbearable.

A hesitant footfall sounded outside the door. A soft knock followed, and she held her breath as the knob did not turn. That could only be Simon, she thought, aghast, sliding off the bed where her partner in decadence slumbered on.

She dressed in her robin's-egg blue muslin traveling gown and fished her half boots from the tangle of bedding on the floor. At the door she stopped to stare back with reproach at the reflection in the looking glass of the ruined woman she had become. Obviously she had made a muddle of her life and needed pots of tea and days of solitude to think it through.

"You could at least look as if you were sorry," she whispered to her disgraced reflection. "The best of the beau monde tried to warn you, but did you listen? No, you became a mistress."

Halfway down the stairs she remembered that Nigel's aunt lived in Brighton with her retired barrister husband. Since to stay in this house would only encourage her own latent indecency, she supposed she could ask for refuge until she convinced Simon to take her home.

If anyone in her family ever spoke to her again, she thought, sighing at what she had done.

As she tiptoed between the marble pillars of the entrance hall, she spotted her pelisse and reticule on the hall stand where a servant had left them while their owner shamelessly revealed the wanton side of her nature in the bedchamber above.

She pulled on her pelisse and eyed the front door with its fanlight allowing pale shivers of sun to penetrate the villa's peaceful gloom. She would look like a Cyprian strolling the promenade alone at this hour of day, but if Sedgecroft had his way that would probably be her fate.

A deep voice reached out to her from the shadows. "My brother would never forgive me if I let you escape." A tall broad-shouldered figure detached itself from one of the pillars and stepped in front of her. "Neither would I forgive myself, for that matter. Why don't you join me for breakfast in the green drawing room? That way, I can acquaint myself with the lady who has the head of the family behaving in such an odd manner."

There was an air of command behind the invitation. In fact, he had taken her arm and was guiding her toward the east wing of the villa. This, she thought, sneaking a glance up at him, would be Heath, a darker, quieter, more intense representation of the Boscastle male. His straight black hair was brushed back from an angular face with chiseled features and a square jaw that denoted strength. He was practically as tall as his brother, perhaps a little leaner, with the coiled, dangerous control of a panther. The arrogance was there, but more subdued. She could sense him examining her as they walked the length of the marble-tiled floor.

"It is early to be up." He hesitated. "Especially after a day of travel. I'm Heath, Jane, as you probably have guessed. I believe we have never been properly introduced."

She smiled ruefully. "I don't know that one would call these circumstances proper, either."

"No?" His deep blue eyes glittered with guarded amusement.

"You know what Grayson is like."

"Yes." His tone was low, inviting trust. "But I don't know you, Jane."

"I am hardly at my best," she said, her voice breaking.

She moistened her lips, aware that his dark blue gaze flickered over her, assessing every detail of her appearance from the shadows under her eyes to the reticule she clutched nervously in her right hand. Of course he knew she was not exhausted from traveling, but from a night spent in intimacy with his older sibling. The realization brought a hot stain to her cheeks.

She shook her head. "I don't want breakfast."

He raised his eyebrow. "Perhaps I can change your mind."

"I know what you must think of me," she said in a soft, halting voice.

"I doubt it."

She swallowed, wondering what it was about him that so immediately put her at ease. "It was you at the bedroom door, wasn't it?"

"Yes," he admitted with an apologetic smile.

"Then I am caught."

He led her into a large room in which a cheerful fire burned and a linen-draped table tempted the appetite with a hearty breakfast for two. "Yes. I caught you going out for a walk before you had eaten. What a terrible sin that is. Come, Jane. Sit down and eat."

"You don't understand," she said in chagrin. "My life is unraveling thread by thread."

"And there is no way to piece it back together?" he asked cautiously.

She thought of the rogue asleep upstairs and smiled a little sadly. "I don't see how."

Her stomach contracted in hunger as he lifted the lid of a silver dish to entice her with a dish of crispy fried bacon and poached eggs. She sat, her hands folded in her lap, and sighed. "I could not eat after . . ."

His perceptive gaze rendered the end of the thought superfluous. She fell silent as he mused aloud, "Do you really love the monster all that much?"

"I would not be in this house if I didn't."

"Ah." He glanced down, holding back a grin. "Then I am sorry." Although for which one of them, he had not yet decided. Obviously Grayson had gone ahead with his plan for revenge, which a few days ago had seemed amusing. But now that Heath sat face-to-face with Jane and formed his own personal opinion, he did not perceive her to be the shallow, duplicitous female he had imagined. Instead, he admired her spirit of initiative in escaping an undesirable marriage—his grin broke free as he remembered Nigel in bed with the Iron Glove.

"Do you find my situation amusing, Heath?"

He shook his head. "Life is what amuses me, Jane." Rising from his chair, he retrieved the silver teapot on the sideboard to pour cups of steaming black tea for them both. "The servants in this house are remarkably well trained. They do not appear unless they are summoned."

She wrapped her fingers around the porcelain cup. "I imagine that suits your brother's needs quite well."

He returned to his chair. "Actually, I do not believe Grayson has ever brought a woman here before, although I know it is the fashion to maintain a mistress at one's seaside resort. The villa has been reserved for family. And do not repeat that I told you this."

Jane put down her cup. She tried to recall what Grayson had told her about Heath. A spy and soldier, wasn't he? And he had ferreted out information about Nigel. She glanced up covertly and searched his handsome features. He seemed very patient, pleasant, but she realized it would be dangerous to underestimate him. Had he guessed her secret? Not to judge by the mask of masculine angles and shadows that were arranged into a very beguiling face. Or else he was a master of masquerading his thoughts, a valuable skill for an intelligence officer. She was afraid to ask him what new discoveries he might have made, but she really had to know.

"Grayson said—"

Heath turned his dark head a split second before his older brother appeared in the doorway. Jane wondered if he had been there all along, listening. He strode straight toward her, looking lithe and elegant in a pewter gray long-tailed morning coat over a white linen shirt and buff breeches. His wheat blond hair had been brushed back, revealing the bones of his face. A bolt of heat went through her as his gaze caught hers.

Despite her confusion, her uncertainty over their future together, she felt herself softening at the sight of him. Last night had tipped the balance between them even more, but she wasn't sure what it would mean. He had stolen her heart. She had shared his bed. What would be hers in return?

Everything, she thought. She wanted every single wicked inch of him for herself. She wanted him for life. What a scandalous pair they made. How Society would be shocked by their behavior. She blushed suddenly, feeling Heath's gaze upon her. Who knew what he made of this?

"I heard my name." Grayson bent and boldly kissed the back of her neck before taking the chair beside her at the head of the table. "Was I mentioned in a flattering way?"

She wanted to slide under the table at the pleased grin on his face, even if his kiss had sent a shiver dancing down her spine. "What do you think?"

His eyes sparkled as his gaze held her immobile. "I think that after last night a little flattery is in order."

Heath coughed and set down his cup. "As modest as ever, aren't we?"

"I'm in too good a mood to bother with modesty," Grayson said, sending Jane a sensual smile that flooded her with warmth. "Why aren't you eating, sweetheart?" he asked in concern, putting his hand over hers. "Has my brother been intimidating you?"

He was so male, so possessive and open about what was happening between them that Jane had no idea how to react. Obviously he didn't intend to hide anything from his brother, who looked a bit at a loss himself over

Grayson's behavior. "I'm not hungry," she said, trying to wrest her hand from his.

"How could you not be hungry after we—" He glanced at Heath, his manner suddenly sober and disapproving. "Did you tell her about Nigel? Is that what has killed her appetite?"

Heath leaned back in his chair, regarding his brother with a resigned smile. "Why don't you tell her, Grayson? I do so hate to be the messenger of bad news."

"Bad news?" Jane said, her heart missing a beat. "About Nigel?"

"All right." Grayson's hand tightened protectively over hers. "Heath has confronted him, Jane. I don't know of any easy way to say this, so I will be blunt and tell you everything. My cousin has married another woman. She is carrying his child."

The room seemed still and stifling, the two men watching her so closely that she could barely swallow. Jane had never considered herself a good actress or liar. Her natural instinct was to confess her guilt. "I see. Then that is that."

"How accepting you are," Grayson murmured. "I would not be so in your place. Jane, really, this must be settled."

"I cannot say it is a complete surprise." She raised her head, forcing herself to meet the curious regard of both men. "I told you that Nigel and I never loved each other in that way."

Grayson released her hand, running his tapered forefinger along the sharp blade of a knife. "Still," he mused, "he must be made to pay. Your parents will insist upon it. *I* insist upon it. Perhaps I shall even call him out."

She caught her breath. "Except that he's your cousin. It would cause the worst scandal, not to mention the chance he would probably be hurt or die. I didn't want to marry him. I . . ."

He stared steadily at her, turning the knife over in his hands. "It is a question of honor, Jane. I shall do what I must to maintain my family's honor."

Heath cleared his throat. "I'm not certain I agree."

Grayson speared him with a quelling look. "Agree? Of course you do. There are legal ramifications, after all. Jane could sue Nigel for breach of promise, although personally I prefer to shoot him in the heart and be done with it."

Heath arched his brow in reproach. "Leaving his wife a widow and their child with no papa? What are you thinking?"

Grayson gave a careless shrug. "Jane must be avenged."

"Not necessarily," she said, finding her voice, which emerged as an unflattering squeak. "In time the whole scandal will die down—"

"Never." Grayson's voice resounded across the room like a clap of thunder. "His behavior was deplorable. I refuse to let the matter rest, and *that* is the end of it."

"The Lord has spoken," Heath said, with an ironic smile in Jane's direction.

She rose from her chair. At this point a coward's retreat seemed her best option. "I think I should leave the two of you alone to discuss this."

Grayson frowned at her. "Don't feel you must leave, sweetheart. You have a perfect right to know exactly how I plan to avenge your honor."

"Quite frankly," she said, her eyes darkening. "I

would prefer to pretend the whole affair never happened."

I'm sure you would, Grayson thought wryly as he glanced down at the knife in his hand. *But, don't worry, my darling, I promise you the happy ending you deserve. We both owe Nigel a debt of gratitude for bringing us together. The tale of our romance shall entertain our descendants for years to come.*

"Would you like Nigel to make a public apology to you before the duel?" he asked, his expression solicitous.

She paled at the thought. "That will not be necessary. Grayson, you must understand that I do not care whether he is married. He could have seven wives for all it mattered to me."

He shook his head in dismissal. "Women are far too forgiving. Besides, he is a Boscastle, and I have taken it upon myself to be your protector. What would people think of me if I failed to make a stand? What would my father think if he knew I had let my own family down?"

She closed her eyes briefly. "Heath, please try to talk some sense into your brother. I am apparently unable to dissuade him from this course of male idiocy."

Heath lowered his gaze, seeming quite at sea himself. "I shall do my best, but my brother rarely takes advice."

She cast a dark look at Grayson as she stepped around her chair. "Yes, I know. But try anyway. I am going back up to my room."

Grayson caught her hand before she took another step. "We've been invited to Plumpton for the races tomorrow, if you are up to it. And there's a puppet show on the promenade this afternoon. I thought we might watch it before the ball tonight." He smiled up into her eyes, his voice deliberately provocative. "Unless you would rather stay home alone with me again. That thought appeals to me, Jane."

To Jane's horror she felt his large hand sliding around her backside, and instead of resisting the outrageous wretch, she caught herself leaning into him, eager to be held against that warm hard body. While his brother watched in utter, fascinated silence. "Stop it right now," she said firmly.

"Kiss me before you go."

"Take your hand off my bum, you silly beast," she whispered, twisting at the waist.

His hand caressed the curve of her bottom. "Not until you kiss me."

"Your brother is watching."

"It wouldn't be the first time."

"Grayson, you are—"

"A kiss," he demanded. "Heath, turn your head."

She bent to brush her mouth primly across his freshly shaven cheek. A second later she found herself sitting in his lap, her arms wrapped around his neck as he kissed her with a flagrant sensuality that left him breathing as unevenly as she. His eyes glittered with raw desire when he finally, reluctantly, set her back on her feet.

She marched toward the door. The flare of passion between Grayson and her had charged the room like the stillness before a thunderstorm. The imprint of his powerful body seeped deep into her bones. She could not bring herself to glance back at Heath as she hurried into the hall, but if she had stayed she might have intercepted the meaningful look that passed between the two men. She might have seen the love and hunger for her that Grayson tried so hard to hide.

"Whew," Heath said, pressing the heels of his hands against the table, "after that little display, I am feeling rather deprived myself. Congratulations. I understand everything now. One doesn't need a fire in the room when you two are together."

"Don't congratulate me yet." Grayson's voice was husky as he exerted a conscious effort not to follow her from the room. The woman weakened him without even trying. "I haven't gotten her to the altar yet. She might find a way to dispose of me."

Heath stared at him in disbelief for several seconds before throwing back his head to laugh. Grayson, worried he would lose the woman he desired? Grayson, insecure in the role of seducer? His eyes shone with appreciation. "A first in the Boscastle family history—one of our men plotting to capture a bride."

"Your legendary memory is failing, Heath," Grayson said dryly. "Our predecessors kidnapped their brides as a matter of course. And don't forget the shame of our recent history—Nigel himself went to quite desperate measures indeed to marry his heart's desire."

Heath grinned in delight at the reminder of their boisterous past. "But we never really considered him one of us, did we? As I recall he failed our rite of initiation in the castle when he turned thirteen."

"That's right." Grayson broke into a grin. "I'd forgotten that one myself. Do you remember his face when our milkmaid began to disrobe in front of him?"

"And then he was rescued by—"

"The Iron Glove." Heath looked stunned. "Oh, my

God. That must have been the start of their infamous love affair. Esther rescued him from our corruption only to corrupt him years later herself."

"Did she actually beat us with a rod or her bare hands?"

"I'm not altogether sure," Heath said. "Whatever it was hurt like the devil."

"Whose idea was it to sabotage the wedding?" Grayson asked curiously. "Jane's or Nigel's?"

"Nigel refused to say, which was either remarkably brave or stupid, considering that I had two pistols trained on him."

"It was Jane's," Grayson decided with absolute certainty. "Nigel would never have the courage or wits to dare. I suppose they might even have gotten away with it had I not come charging in to save the day. No wonder Jane was so appalled by my offer to help."

The two brothers lapsed into silence. Heath stirred first, glancing up with a concerned frown. "Just remember that schemes can backfire, Grayson. Jane is a delight for all her faults. Neither of you is exactly what one would call of meek character. It isn't fair to toy with her heart when she clearly adores you."

Grayson's voice was quiet. "I adore her, too. Right now in my desk sits the special license I obtained before leaving London. Jane and I are a day away from respectability."

"Then tell her you know what she did. You'll have to sooner or later."

"And I will," Grayson said. "When the proper moment arrives."

He was more convinced than ever that if Jane were capable of sabotaging her own marriage ceremony she would not respect him if he allowed himself to be duped. Jane's cunning called for the same devious subterfuge from her partner.

"I don't want to disappoint her, you see," he added in a thoughtful voice. "I cannot let myself be outwitted by my future wife."

"It is a gamble to play with her. You might not be as clever as you think."

"Our game will end soon enough."

"Are you certain you will win?"

"How can I lose?"

Heath shook his head. The unguarded love on Jane's face for his older brother touched something deep in Heath's heart. Jane and Grayson were perfect together, a dynamic match for a family on the verge of falling apart. Until he had met Jane himself, he had not fully understood Grayson's attraction to her. Now he did. Where would his brother find a woman with the backbone Jane had shown, a mate to challenge his headstrong nature? They complemented each other so well.

"Tell her, Grayson. Trust my instincts. Tell her tonight after the ball or there might be more trouble than you bargained for." He chuckled softly. "I shall quite enjoy seeing how this all ends."

Chapter 21

Jane leaned against the bedchamber door, her heart beating in panic. If Heath had found Nigel and Esther, it would only be a matter of time before one of them broke down and revealed her role in their scandalous marriage.

Nigel was a friend. He would defend her to a certain degree, but she could not expect him to stand up to the likes of Grayson. Especially not if Grayson went ahead with this pigheaded notion of a duel. Nigel fainted at the sight of a pricked finger. His wife was more likely to be the one to meet Grayson on the dueling field. The way Jane's life was headed, she might end up serving as Nigel's second herself.

There was only one thing left to do. Confess everything. Apologize to all parties involved. Then throw what was left of herself upon the mercy of Cecily and her duke while the world decried her. Perhaps she would become a governess to their children and spank wicked young boys for a living. The worst of it would be Grayson's reaction. He would hardly show that her deceit had hurt him. He would simply cut her dead.

She wasn't fool enough to think she could confess to his face and live to tell of it. He would never forgive her. He would probably laugh if she tried to explain how desperately she had wanted to avoid an arranged marriage. And, frankly, she was too much of a coward even to dare. She would write him a letter and leave it under his pillow.

As she turned to the rosewood escritoire by the window, she noticed that the room had been efficiently tidied by one of his discreet staff. A hip bath sat beside the screen, filled with steaming water. Thick clean towels lay plumped up on the bed, and a bowl of fragrant musk roses occupied the nightstand.

And on the dressing table next to her treasured mouse brooch sat a new blue velvet jeweler's box with a card tucked beneath it. She read it twice, tears blurring her eyes.

Something to commemorate our first of many nights together.

G

Inside the box she found a large marquis-cut diamond pendant on a gold chain. Costly. Elegant. The gift a generous man would give a mistress to mark a night of passion.

"Do you like it?" Grayson asked quietly from the door.

She let the necklace slither through her fingers. "It's absolutely extravagant. I wish I could accept it."

"Of course you can. Why don't you undress and model it for me?"

"I beg your pardon. At this time of day?"

He gave her a long sultry look. "Morning or midnight. I am obsessed with you, Jane." He closed the door behind him. "It is my pleasure to give you jewels."

How was a woman supposed to rally a defense when a man made remarks like that? How was she expected to think when he locked his arms around her waist and pulled her down with him into the chair? Her heart was aching as he sank his fingers in her hair and silenced her protests with the most tender of kisses. She had shared his bed and did not regret it.

"Jane," he whispered. "Thank you for last night."

She closed her eyes, envisioning his face when he found her letter, cringing at the very thought of how disgusted, how angry he would be. He was so unforgiving of Chloe's rebellions, so convinced of the male duty to dominate a woman's life. He would never understand what she had done.

"Is something wrong, Jane?" he asked gently. "Those aren't tears in your eyes, are they?"

"Promise me something, Grayson."

"Anything," he said, brushing her cheek with his knuckle.

"Promise me you won't hurt Nigel."

He went still. "It really is intolerable that you mention his name to me while you are in my arms."

"Will you promise me that?"

His blue eyes bored into her. "People deserve to be punished when they hurt others. Don't you agree?"

"I'm not sure." His gaze pinned her unmercifully with its piercing intensity. As much as she loved him, there were moments when she could have cheerfully hit him into oblivion. "There are times to forgive."

"Not in my book. Shall we discuss something else?"

"Please, Grayson. I ask only this one thing of you."

"What will you give me in return?"

She might have agreed to give him whatever his wicked heart wanted had heavy footsteps not come echoing up the stairs, pounding down the hall to their room.

"Grayson!" an irreverent male voice shouted outside the door. "Where the deuce are you hiding? I just left Helene in London, and the woman is cursing you to the heavens. Are you in there?"

"God almighty," Grayson muttered, throwing an irate look at the door. "It's Drake. Stay here while I get rid of him."

She eased herself out from his arms. "Promise me you will not do anything to Nigel."

His face reflective, he rose to his feet and straightened the long tails of his coat. "I shall have to think about this, Jane. Remember that Nigel and his parents have depended on the largesse of my family for years. His behavior is an insult to both me and you."

The male voices outside the door gradually faded away. Jane undressed and lowered herself into the copper-lined bath, contemplating her future as a fallen woman. As soon as she had completed her toilette, she would compose two letters. One to Grayson, another to her family, although after the way her father had practically thrown her to the lion, she did not hold hope that he would forgive her for the shame she had caused the family.

She sighed, thinking of her sisters, of the pleasant life she had taken for granted, of the way Papa had bullied and protected her, of the marriage he'd arranged because he believed that Nigel would be good to her.

She sank deeper into the scented water, her brow furrowed in troubled concentration.

Papa's behavior seemed so irrational. And had her mother actually supported his moral about-face, this shove of their socially disgraced daughter into her sybaritic lifestyle? It was so out of character for her parents. After all, their reasons for selecting Nigel had been his good-natured gentleness, his puppylike loyalty, his apparent lack of interest in rakish pursuits.

In short, they had chosen Nigel because he was the exact opposite of Grayson. Which only made their betrayal all the more mysterious. Unless—

She dropped her sponge into the water.

Unless they knew. Unless one of her sisters had blurted out her secret about her pact with Nigel. Making Jane in their eyes to be the betrayer, not the betrayed.

And if her entire family knew her secret, chances were that Grayson knew, and this whole humiliating situation smacked of Boscastle arrogance through and through.

He knew everything.

Their session at the modiste's. The change that had come over him. The heartless gleam in his eye. His sudden desire to bring her to Brighton.

He knew.

She had been the unwitting pawn in his diabolical scheme. But for how long? For what purpose?

He knew.

She surged out of the tub, Venus on the warpath as scented water sloshed all over his plush Axminster carpet.

"Oh, the fiend," she muttered, standing stark naked and dripping in front of the dressing table. "That scheming son of Satan! Playing with me like a lion would"—her eyes lit on the diamond brooch—"a mouse!"

The fact it was her scheming that had caused this imbroglio did surface in her thoughts, but she promptly buried it under a blanket of righteous indignation. Turn her into a high-class courtesan, would he? Parade her in diamonds and pink silk, eh? Never in a thousand years with her strait-laced Papa have agreed to such a thing without a compelling reason.

Well, it would take a Boscastle to best a Boscastle, and Jane had no doubt where to find the weakest link in the family line.

She dressed and marched barefooted straight down the hall to Chloe's room, chasing out the maid who was trying to return the room to a semblance of order. Chloe apparently had plunged back into her passion for social reform after learning that her cavalry officer William had been sent to a new barracks in Devon. Now she lay curled up on the chaise, her lap heaped with letters to friends in Parliament, a box of half-nibbled chocolates, and a list of works she intended to tackle. The blinds were closed to emphasize the aura of solemnity, and Chloe merely raised her brow when Jane stormed into the room.

"Ah." She tossed back her thick black hair, her voice sympathetic. "Your first fight with my beastly brother, is

it? I don't know what you see in him anyway. Chocolates for the lovelorn?"

"I want the truth, Chloe."

"Truth?" Chloe put down her pen, her attention
caught. "He's a tyrant, a destroyer of all one holds dear.
That is the truth. He went over William's head and had
him sent to Devon to deal with smugglers. My brother
ruined any chance that I would ever see him again. Not
that I should have, mind you, but it would have been
nice to say good-bye."

"I am sorry for your loss, Chloe, but I must know
something. Why did Grayson bring me here?"

"I should think that was obvious," Chloe said, not
unkindly. "Poor Jane. I held such high hopes that you
would resist him."

"Answer me."

Chloe appraised her in silence, her blue eyes bright
with conflicting emotions. "I have never, never, ever in
my life betrayed a Boscastle secret, but as you are practically a Boscastle and a member of my sex, I am honor
bound to do so."

Jane sank down on the chaise, her skin tingling at the
vengeful note in Chloe's voice. "What are you saying?"

"Grayson and Heath don't know that I know," Chloe
said in hesitation.

"That you know what?"

"They didn't tell me."

"Didn't tell you what?"

"I eavesdropped, you see. I was hiding in the library
when Grayson sent for the solicitors."

"Chloe, if you do not give me a straight answer this

instant, I shall dangle you out the window by your hair until you do."

Chloe's soft pink mouth pursed in disapproval. "You already sound like a Boscastle."

"Why did Grayson send for his solicitors?"

Chloe leaned forward. "Will you protect me from his wrath when he finds out I was the one to peach on him?"

Jane straightened in alarm. What horrendous thing had Grayson done behind her back? "I shall do my best."

"Nigel told Heath everything, *everything*, Jane, about how the pair of you conspired to thwart your parents so that he could marry Esther, about the generous wedding gift you gave them, about the months of plotting."

"Nigel, who swore to me he would never reveal our pact even if he were put to torture," Jane cried in outrage, although she really ought not to be surprised. "Oh, the spineless coward. I shall throttle him for this. If Esther has not already done so."

"Heath can be very intimidating when he wants to," Chloe said.

"So can Grayson."

"It appears to be a family trait."

"Kindly return to the subject, Chloe."

"Oh, well, as you have probably already guessed, Heath told Grayson, who reacted in typical high-handed fashion. Did he confront you and give you a chance to explain? No, he summoned his solicitors in the middle of the night and met in secret with your father."

"To sue me for sabotaging my own wedding?"

"No. To arrange one. Yours and his."

Jane's heart skipped several beats. She could not picture her father involved in this midnight intrigue. What was that devil lover of hers doing? "I believe I have misunderstood you. Grayson intends to—"

"Marry you."

"Not that I should become his mistress?"

"Oh, good heavens, no. That was part of his plan to teach you a lesson." Chloe popped a chocolate into her mouth while Jane stared at her in wordless shock. "Are you sure you don't want one of these?"

"The scoundrel," Jane said, exhaling slowly, a smile of delight spreading across her face. So, he *had* been toying with her, had he? Planning a naughty game to punish her for deceiving him. Perhaps she deserved it. But he hadn't won yet. Jane's fighting spirit rose to the challenge. Her next move must be thought out carefully. She had played right into his hand last night by demanding he marry her. How he must have enjoyed watching her panic.

"I should have known the unprincipled rogue was up to something," she muttered.

"Don't you just hate him?" Chloe asked in sympathy.

Jane's smile tightened. "Of course I don't hate him. I love the blackguard, or I would not have allowed myself to be placed in this unspeakable position."

"I wish I could be placed in an unspeakable position with a man I loved," Chloe said, her eyes glinting with wistful mischief. "Every time I come even close, one of my odious brothers makes an appearance to ruin everything. Ever since my father's death, Grayson and Heath have protected me to the point that I may as well live in a cage. I think I'm a lot like you, Jane."

Jane was quiet, reflecting on Grayson's comment about how Chloe had taken to wild behavior since their father's death. What kind of man would make a good husband for Chloe? A suitor very strong yet kind. Marrying into the Boscastle brood was not for the faint of heart. Still, unless someone intervened, it appeared that brother and sister would soon come to a clash of wills.

And Jane herself was about to come to blows with Grayson, who thought himself so clever planning their betrothal in secret. Only a devilish mind would go to such lengths to ensnare her so completely. She might have been furious at him for having fun with her if she hadn't started this whole thing.

"What am I going to do, Chloe?"

"I say you should teach him a lesson right back."

"Do you?" Oh, Jane liked that idea. To keep the devil she loved on his toes.

"Perhaps we could ask Mrs. Watson for advice," Chloe suggested, brightening at the thought of stirring trouble in her brother's life. "The woman is an expert on the English male."

"Mrs. Watson—the courtesan par excellence in London?"

"The courtesan par excellence in Brighton—she arrived yesterday afternoon. The coaches run every half hour from London."

"Would you mind taking me to see Mrs. Watson today? I could use the advice of an experienced female."

"Why should I mind? It's not as if I have anything else

to do with my day except languish under Grayson's guard."

"Do you think she would mind helping me?"

"Mind?" Chloe said. "I think she'd be honored. Audrey has always had a soft spot for my brother. And she thrives on this sort of fun."

Jane rose decisively. "I'll fetch my shoes and gloves while you finish dressing. And please do not let your brothers know where we are going."

"I shall tell them we are going to the library," Chloe said, bubbling over with glee. "To further our education."

Mrs. Watson had been on her way back from taking the sea air on the promenade with an escort of gentlemen when the two young women arrived. Their carriage slowed at her charming little house with its bow windows and wrought-iron fence. Audrey was stylishly attired in a high-waisted yellow poplin dress and straw hat with ostrich feathers, looking more like a respectable matron than a notorious courtesan.

She clapped her gloved hands in delight when she recognized her visitors. "Oh, darlings, how good of you to call. And just in time for cake and brandy." She hugged Chloe warmly, whispering, "You silly girl. Falling in love with a soldier with all those foreign princes about to visit for our victory. I thought you had more sense. And you, Lady Jane, well, you and Sedgecroft are certainly giving my small scandals some competition. Come inside and enlighten me. I am starved for gossip."

Audrey ordered refreshments before leading them to a drawing room furnished with a blue-and-cream-white theme that carried over into the damask draperies and Persian carpet. She presided like an empress from her ivory-inlaid chaise while Chloe explained what had brought them to her.

"I am *so* flattered," Audrey said, one hand to her heart, her third glass of brandy in the other. "I am also a little drunk, but so much the better for scheming."

Chloe stretched out comfortably on the sofa, explaining Jane's secret and the unexpected results. "My horrible brother is allowing Jane to think that he desires her as his mistress when behind her back he has contracted with her father to marry her."

"Then a mistress she shall be," Audrey said, her eyes sparkling with anticipation. "Speak up, Jane, do you want to have some fun? I say it is your calling to stand up to this wicked boy."

"I'm not quite sure I have the courage."

Audrey looked at her. "Any woman who can jilt herself has courage in spades, believe me. The question is: Are you prepared to best Sedgecroft at his game?"

"How?" Jane asked, suddenly wondering if such a task were possible.

"By becoming a courtesan to end all courtesans!" Audrey cried, her cheeks flushed becomingly. "We will teach you to seduce Sedgecroft right down to his socks."

"Well, I'm not sure—"

"We'll do it," Chloe said, setting her glass down on the table. "But we'll have to start this very afternoon because Heath is watching me like a hawk, and he'll think I'm meeting a lover here. Not that I shall ever have a lover at this rate."

"Chloe, my dear," Audrey said, gently reprimanding,

"that I teach Sedgecroft's future wife to be a seductress is an act for which he will only come to thank me. Profusely. Instructing his unmarried sister in the sexual arts is another matter entirely. Come back when you are affianced."

"The sexual arts?" Jane said with a nervous laugh. "It's, um, rather straightforward, isn't it? I mean, what does a woman really need to know?"

Audrey rose and went to her escritoire, her voice as crisp as a schoolmistress. "There is so much more to the 'ins and outs' of lovemaking, as it were, than the typical English wife ever realizes." She untied the blue silk ribbon from a bulging portfolio and brandished a detailed sketch. "Regard this illustration."

Jane gasped, sputtering for breath. Was *this* what she had in mind? "Oh, my."

"You do know what it is?" Audrey asked matter-of-factly.

Chloe finished her brandy in a gulp. "It's not one of those new Congreve rockets, is it? Drake showed me a sketch of one in the newspaper, but I have to admit, I wasn't really paying much attention."

"Chloe," Audrey said in a firm voice, "you may leave the room and entertain yourself in my library. Although for want of a more delicate term, we shall indeed refer to this drawing as a rocket, the proper handling of which a well-informed wife must understand lest it fire before its time."

"Do I really need to know this?" Jane asked, taking a deep sip of her brandy.

"Would you want a rocket to explode in your hands before you have guided it home?" Audrey demanded.

Chloe turned halfway to the door. "It isn't fair. I brought her here, Audrey. I should be allowed to hear what is said."

"Your turn will come," Audrey replied, waving her away to reveal another illustration in her portfolio. "Now, Jane, study this if you will."

Jane leaned forward, her lips parting on a gasp. "Good heavens! That is a physical impossibility."

"It is not only possible," Audrey retorted, "it is highly pleasurable to the male."

Chloe popped her head around the door. "Where did the rocket go?"

Jane closed her eyes, her voice quivering in amusement. "You do not want to know."

Chapter 22

❦

Jane and Chloe arrived back at the villa late that same afternoon. For all appearances they were two well-bred young ladies who had spent a few benign hours at the library. Fortified with brandy and a treasure trove of sensual knowledge that had shaken her aristocratic sensibilities, Jane lingered in the entrance hall. From abovestairs drifted the sound of male voices. One of them belonged to the man she was going to seduce. Right down to his socks.

"What do I do now?" she whispered in a low voice.

Chloe removed her bonnet. "Implement while that brandy is still in your bloodstream."

"I can't do this."

Chloe gave her a push toward the staircase. "Take charge, Belshire."

Drawing a breath, Jane unfastened the frogs of her pelisse, handed it to Chloe, and proceeded toward the stairs. A few moments later she found Grayson emerging from his room, with Heath and Drake engaged in conversation at the other end of the hallway.

That conversation stopped at her appearance, and she

felt a frisson of uncertainty at experimenting with Audrey's ideas. Perhaps every woman secretly wondered how she would fare as a courtesan if given the chance; beneath her anxiety she was aware that it was rather a challenge to seduce the man who had made an art of seduction.

"Jane." He gave her a rather stern frown. "There you are. I was getting worried. Uncle Giles and Simon have gone out to look for you. I searched the library twice. Where did you go?"

"Oh. Just here and there." She glided toward him, taking the slow undulating steps that Audrey had demonstrated, which at first made her feel rather silly, then gratified when she noticed Grayson's eyes widen.

"Did you hurt your foot, Jane?" he demanded.

She stood on tiptoe to wind her hands around his neck. "How sweet of you to ask. No kiss hello for your lover?"

He peeled her hands off his neck and smiled in embarrassment over her shoulder. "Heath and Drake are watching."

"Are they? Well, good for them."

"It isn't good," he said in a puzzled undertone.

She walked her fingers down the muscular wall of his chest. "But it was good at breakfast."

"Yes, but—did you just touch me where I think you touched me?"

"It is my function as a mistress, isn't it?"

"Not in front of my family, darling," he answered, a deep flush mounting on his cheekbones. "Jane, are you certain you are feeling well? Perhaps I did not take that fever seriously enough. Perhaps I overexerted you last night."

"What a fusspot you are." She nudged him back into the drawing room he had just exited, giving the door a kick shut with her foot. "Now we are alone. Lie down on the sofa."

"I think you are the one who needs to lie down. Do they serve brandy in that library, Jane?"

"I have been reconsidering your offer."

"Have you?"

She led him toward the curved-back sofa in the corner. "Perhaps it is not such a bad idea after all."

"Well—"

She pulled him down beside her by the lapels of his long-tailed coat. "I will need practice, mind you."

"Practice?" He raised his brow, looking intrigued. "In—"

She began to unbutton his coat, then the black embroidered vest beneath. "In pleasing you."

"You please me well enough."

She ran her hand over his chest. "But one can always do better."

He caught her hand in his, a muscle ticking in his cheek. "You do better than anyone I've ever known. What is this about?"

"Desire."

"Desire?"

"Lust, Grayson. Passion. Setting off rockets."

He cleared his throat. "This is all very arousing and unexpected. But—" He raised his thighs to draw her against him only to freeze at Drake's voice outside the door.

"Are you coming downstairs or is our meeting canceled?"

"What meeting?" Jane asked, grateful for the interruption. She was more uncertain by the moment that she could actually put Audrey's plan to work without giving herself away. She was not dealing with a nincompoop but with a hot-blooded, sneaky opponent.

"The meeting about my family's future." He sighed, giving her a long, deep kiss before he released her. "My brothers and I are hoping to find a suitable husband for Chloe before she ruins herself completely."

"How good of you, Grayson, to make such a decision for her. Heaven knows we women are incapable of choosing even a pair of shoes for ourselves."

He came to his feet, studying her with a strange smile. "I never said anything like that. Start to dress for the evening, won't you? I mean to show you off."

"As your latest mistress?"

He hesitated, his hands on the buttons of his vest, his voice neutral. "Of course, darling. What else?"

They arrived late to the race ball, the coachman parking in the crush of carriages lining the hilly lane. Drake had begged off at the last moment, presumably to call on a certain young lady who had just arrived from London. Simon and Heath set off with Uncle Giles for the card room, where bets were being laid on tomorrow's race. Grayson herded Jane and his sister toward the candlelit ballroom of Viscount Lawson's house.

He had been mulling over Heath's warning and decided that perhaps his brother's intuition should be heeded. The time had come for revelations. And Jane was definitely up to something.

Again.

He thought of the two Janes he had learned to love. One was the pragmatic, sensible young lady he had been squiring about London supposedly to heal her broken heart. He adored this side of her. Her respectable image dovetailed perfectly with the sort of woman his parents would have chosen for him. This Jane was the ideal bride for a marquess.

Polite, refined, a jewel in the crown of the aristocracy.

But the other Jane. Ah, yes. The mysterious beauty in a wedding veil standing at an empty altar. That enigmatic woman and her shadowy motives beckoned to his darker side. The side of him that scorned convention. The side of him that would strip off her final veil and behold her bare soul in all its sinful glory.

Which Jane did he prefer?

Not one over the over. It was the merging of these two incongruent beings that held him in thrall. It was the woman in her conflicting entirety that he loved and wanted to outwit at the same time.

It was almost the midnight of their masquerade.

As they separated outside the cloakroom, Grayson touched Jane's face with the back of his gloved hand. "Look how flushed you are, all bundled up in your wrap. No one would ever guess what a temptress you have become. I cannot wait to see what you have in store for me later in the evening."

She lowered her eyes demurely, answering in amused silence: *Just wait, my arrogant darling. Do I have an-*

other surprise for you. "It really is rather overwhelming, Grayson—this public exposure as your mistress."

He stared at her. "Nonsense," he said, glancing past her to Chloe, whose dark head was suspiciously down-bent. "You shall cause a sensation."

I certainly intend to.

He frowned. "Did you say something, Jane? I cannot hear for the harpist playing in the gallery."

"I didn't say a thing."

He glanced back toward her, his eyes narrowing. "Take off your wrap before you faint. We are packed in here like pickled herrings."

"As you wish, Grayson. I exist only to please you." Jane's voice sounded cool, but her heart had begun to thump. Was she about to let the lion out of his cage? How would she handle him then?

He swung around. "What did you say?"

"That I hope never to displease you," she answered meekly.

Chloe nudged him away. "Meet us outside the cloak-room after we beautify ourselves, Gray. We didn't come here to chatter the evening away in the hall."

A few moments later Jane shed her silk-lined pelisse in the cloakroom, whispering, "I can't go out there in front of all those people, those strangers, looking like a . . . an East End strumpet."

"You look positively gorgeous," Chloe whispered back as she examined the high-waisted sheer peach gauze evening gown that she had lent Jane from her pri-vate unworn wardrobe. "I think we ought to dampen it again once more for good measure. Do you want more rouge for your—"

"No!" Jane's mortified shriek caught the attention of the young maid at the door. "I'm showing enough of my pinker parts as it is. I may as well be wearing a lace doily."

Chloe smothered a giggle of amusement. "You have a body that a goddess would envy."

"Envy, Chloe. Not luridly expose."

"I would not miss the look on Grayson's face when he sees you for anything."

"He'll be beside himself," Jane muttered.

"Isn't that the point?"

It took Jane a minute or so to pick out the tall golden-haired figure in the throng of guests that encircled him. Stylishly dressed ladies who hoped to renew his acquaintance, aristocrats from old families who moved in the same exclusive social circles. Grayson looked so at ease, so comfortable in this world of wealth and elegance, that Jane wondered if it was even possible to unsettle him. Her cheeks burned as she moved toward him, the young men around her falling completely silent in deference to this new star in their glittering galaxy.

One of them gave a low appreciative whistle. A second slipped a bank note to the master of ceremonies to learn her identity. Another clapped his hand over his heart and professed his undying love. Grayson half turned, in the middle of conversation, his expression amused until he recognized who had caused this consternation. His gaze met hers, then traveled in frosty disbelief down her alluringly revealed body before returning to her face. The furious shock in his eyes, controlled but eloquent, almost undid her.

In the dampened peach gauze, she felt . . . like a naked peach, flesh-colored with only the sheerest layer of cloth to shield her uncorseted body from prurient eyes. Her breasts pressed upward against the flimsy bodice so precariously it seemed a risk to breathe.

"Jane." His smile did not reveal his displeasure, but the crushing grip of his fingers around hers did. "That was not one of the gowns I selected. Where did it come from?"

"I borrowed it from a friend, Grayson. Do you like it?"

"Every male in the room does," he said in a clipped undertone. "Do not do this again in public."

"Do what?" she asked in a cool voice.

"Share what is mine alone."

"I really thought this dress was appropriate for my debut as a courtesan-in-training."

He glowered at her. "Did you indeed?"

"Well, darling, a mistress can't afford to look like . . . a mouse."

He pulled her away from the circle of guests, throwing his host an apologetic look over his shoulder. "Perhaps we ought to dance," he said curtly.

"As you desire, darling."

"I wish you would stop talking like that," he snapped.

She pretended to look hurt. "I can stop talking altogether if you prefer. Except for the matter of my allowance. I do think we should discuss that before we proceed."

"With our dance?" he said darkly.

"Shall we publish our negotiations in the paper?" she asked at the edge of the dance floor.

"I hardly think that's necessary."

She bit her lip, wondering just how far she could tease him before his temper broke. Now that she had started, she couldn't seem to stop. "But if I'm to carve a name in Society . . ." She hesitated as he took his position on the floor. "I don't suppose you brought a pen and paper?"

"Pen and paper?" He looked incredulous. "To use during a dance?"

"No, silly. For my memoirs. It is highly unlikely that you will be my only protector, Grayson. I shall need another source of income in the future. A woman must be practical."

"Excuse me," a hesitant male voice said behind them. "Might I interrupt this conversation to ask the lovely lady for a dance?"

"Might I interrupt your face with my fist if you do?" Grayson retorted, his expression fierce.

"My face . . ." The young man blinked, then backed up in horror several steps before disappearing into the crowd.

Grayson and Jane assumed their positions on the dance floor. The orchestra struck up a quadrille. He bowed; she curtsied. But neither of them had their minds on the movements of the dance. Grayson was preoccupied with glaring into oblivion all the male guests who dared to ogle her. Jane attempted to appear graceful while covering her body with her arms until Chloe, moving past her whispered, "I have never seen a woman who looked more like a windmill than you. Hold out your skirts, for heaven's sake."

"I can't," Jane whispered back.

"Why not?"

"Because you can see right through them."

Grayson walked around the floor with wooden strides, his gaze black and menacing. Then, as the dance ended, he guided her with chilling determination into the darkest corner of the room where the elderly guests congregated in chairs.

"Why are we standing here like a pair of wallflowers?" she inquired in an innocent voice. "Shouldn't we be more sociable?"

"I am not in a sociable mood," he bit out.

"Well, no one can see us standing here."

"Which was my objective, Jane." His face darkened as he glanced down at her. "There is a little too much of you to be seen tonight."

"Perhaps you would like to play cards," she suggested.

"Perhaps I would," he drawled. "If I were not busy guarding you from all the lascivious aristocrats in Brighton."

She peered around him, refusing to meet his angry stare. "Oh, look. Isn't that your old friend, Mrs. Watson?"

"So it is."

"Would it not be polite to acknowledge her?"

"I am not in the mood for that either," he said, clenching his teeth.

"Well, what are you in the mood for?"

He refused to reply, but the answer was infuriatingly simple: her. Along with most of the eligible men in the room, he was imagining her without the dress, Jane on the altar of their lust with her luscious body and honey-gold hair spilling loose over her soft white shoulders. Like an unattainable goddess, she had challenged the mortals around her to prove themselves worthy of her attention. Well, Heath had warned him. The dark Jane was having her day.

On impulse he took her by the elbow and led her toward the side door. "Is this the way to the refreshment room?" she asked, an edge of panic in her voice.

"No." He gave her a meaningful look. "We're going home."

"Why?"

"To have that discussion you mentioned."

"What about Chloe and Simon? And Uncle Giles? We cannot just leave them here."

"I'll send the carriage back for them later."

She glanced back into the crowded, candlelit ballroom. Audrey gave her a tiny nod of approval; their objective had been to disarm a certain scoundrel, but suddenly Jane had her doubts—doubts that escalated as she found herself captured against a steel chest in an unlit corridor, Grayson's firm mouth inches from hers.

"Are you trying to drive me insane?" he asked quietly. "If so, it has worked."

Held in his muscular arms, she could easily forget that the man had arranged her entire future without asking her consent. Or that she would have to deal with this sort of behavior for the rest of her life. She knew only that she already belonged to him, her fate sealed by a single look across a crowded wedding chapel a short time ago. On the day she had been meant to pledge herself to another. And Sedgecroft had appeared in his place, proving himself to be the best ally and worst threat a woman could ever face.

"What has happened?" Chloe demanded behind them.

"Jane is feeling rather"—Grayson's gaze swept her willowy form—"chilled."

Chloe's blue eyes danced with devilish amusement as she approached Jane. "Oh, dear. Then you will have to take her home, Grayson. Audrey shall keep me in her guard."

If the remark seemed strange to Grayson, he was too distracted by the events of the evening to question it. Jane, of course, knew exactly what Chloe meant, and she did not appreciate the reminder—that the second part of her plan had to be implemented as soon as possible.

She could still hear Audrey's voice in her mind. *Take him off guard, darling. A man is never more vulnerable than in the boudoir.*

But was a woman any less vulnerable? Jane wondered suddenly, wishing she could bring Audrey along to give her moment-to-moment advice. It was one thing to discuss seducing a marquess in the safety of a drawing room. It was quite another to put proposed seduction into action when facing that marquess in the flesh. When exposing his flesh. When breaking past his anger to arouse him.

Yes, Audrey was an expert in such matters, having revealed to her student techniques that would have made a brothel master blush. But Grayson was an expert, too. And Jane was not.

She looked at him, feeling the floor tilting beneath her.

Would it be possible for anyone to render such a man helpless?

"Stay out of trouble," he told his sister curtly, his arm firmly guiding Jane away. "I appear to have enough of a problem on my hands for a night."

"Wait," Chloe cried. "She's forgotten her wrap."

"Then hurry and fetch it for her."

And as he turned, she whispered in Jane's ear: "I shall be thinking of Congreve rockets the entire night. Be brave. And tell me everything in the morning."

If she lived to tell of it, Jane thought, shuddering in anticipation of the seduction she would undertake.

Chapter 23

❦

Jane was spared the full brunt of Grayson's displeasure during the short ride back to the villa by her uncle's sudden decision to leave the ball with the two of them. Never before had she felt such icy disapproval in Grayson's manner toward her. Never had she tested the depths of his feelings to this degree before. She could only hope Uncle Giles would provide a buffer between her and a very angry marquess.

"At my age," the older man explained as he followed them to the carriage, "I am more of an embarrassment than an entertainment at these affairs. My eyesight isn't what it used to be. Here I was playing cards with a charming young viscount, or so I thought, until a footman kindly took me aside to tell me my opponent was a viscountess. Wouldn't know it from that costume. Epaulets and military buttons on the Hussar jacket. You always look like a lady, Jane. Don't you agree, Sedgecroft?"

Grayson turned his gaze from the window, his voice laden with irony. "No one would argue that."

Jane shivered inside the safety of her pelisse. Had she ever heard that razor-sharp edge in his tone before?

"You are catching a chill, my dear," Uncle Giles said in concern. "Go right to your bed when we get in."

Jane was only too glad to take his advice, grateful for her brief respite when her uncle trapped Grayson in the entrance hall to discuss the following day's race. A true gentleman, Grayson stayed to politely answer the man's questions. But there was nothing polite in his heavy-lidded gaze as he watched Jane escape upstairs to her room. His expression warned her she would not evade his anger for long.

Audrey's voice mocked her cowardly retreat.

Take him off guard, darling. A man is never more vulnerable than in the boudoir.

"I cannot do this," she muttered. "I cannot, cannot, cannot. . . . I'm not proving a point. I am making a spectacle of myself."

What had she done tonight? Taught him a lesson or unleashed a beast? One would think she had learned from her wedding scandal that schemes did not play out without unexpected repercussions.

She heard him less than twenty minutes later in the room that adjoined hers. Her heart pounding in anxiety, she sat down at her dressing table in her rose silk robe and began to brush her hair. The door to the room opened. She saw his tall figure in the mirror. Her fingers gripped the handle of her silver-backed hair brush. The chilliness in his eyes seemed to lower the temperature in the room several degrees.

"You haven't changed out of your evening clothes," she said, her breathing suspended as he took a step toward her.

He stood behind her, his shoulders as rigid as a soldier's. "Shall we discuss that dress?"

"It—it was only a dress."

"On another woman perhaps." His voice curled around her like the soft warning stroke of a whip. "On you it is a scandal."

"I was under the impression that you liked me in . . . what were your words at the modiste's? 'A minimum of fuss.'"

His lips tightened at the corners. "That does not mean I wish you to flaunt your charms to the world."

"We can hardly keep our relationship a secret, Grayson."

"Perhaps not. But I am a private man, and I do not intend to share you either."

She pulled the brush down the length of her hair. Their eyes met in the mirror, and she swallowed at what she saw. Why had she dared to challenge a master at his game?

"What did you really hope to gain?" he asked, taking the brush from her hand, continuing its downward strokes with a slow, steady hand. "What . . ."

She stood and removed her dressing robe, utterly naked except for his diamond pendant as the garment slithered to her feet in a sibilant whisper of silk. "The dress offended you. I took it off. Is this better?"

Grayson paused, not quite certain he could believe his eyes. His dark Jane had made another dramatic appearance.

He tossed the brush onto the dressing table, his gaze moving slowly down her body, her rouged nipples, her rounded belly and the triangle of fluff beneath. His heart pounded against his chest. Another step ahead of him, was she? Well, he was a good sport and a man who liked to gamble. If the lady desired him, no matter her motives, who was he to deny her? In fact, he could not refuse.

"The matter of your behavior tonight is not closed." He began to untie his cravat, his eyes darkening with desire. "A discussion can, however, wait until later."

She slid her hands up around his neck. "Undressing you is my job as a mistress. Let me."

"As you like, but—heavens above, Jane, slow down a moment. You're ripping my shirt."

Her lips formed a pout. "Can I help it if I'm eager to worship my wonderful protector?"

He looked down at the floor in mild astonishment. "That was a button. You tore a button off my shirt."

"Do you mind?"

"Not personally, but my tailor might."

She clasped his face in her hands and kissed him for all she was worth, her tongue thrusting against his until his arms went around her waist and crushed her to him. At that point Grayson took the initiative and walked her backward to the bed. She fell against him, her nude body trapped securely between his thighs.

He lay back, still a little puzzled but receptive to what she was doing as she balanced on her knees to undress him. "Not that I'm objecting, but I am curious," he murmured. "What *is* this about?"

She threw his shirt over her shoulder and went to work unbuttoning his breeches. "Seduction."

"What did you and Chloe do today?"

"Let's not bring your sister into the boudoir, Grayson."

"Did you say boudoir?"

"It's more of a mistress word than bedchamber, don't you think? Do you mind if I tie you to the bed?"

With his sensual mouth curling into a grin, his muscular body bare to the hips, he looked like sin incarnate. "What brought this on?"

"Just something I saw in a book."

"Ah. A book." He ran his hands up her rib cage to her breasts, cupping their weight in his palms. "Not a book from the circulating library, I take it?"

She gave him a taunting smile, reaching over him to the nightstand. "No."

"Then—" He stopped, narrowing his eyes as she took his hands, her stockings in her mouth, and deftly bound his wrists to the bedposts. "Interesting reversal of fortune," he murmured. "Tying me up in a pretty package, eh?"

"Those are not mere bows, Grayson. Those are the Belshire Knots of Annihilation. My sisters and I perfected them on Simon during our childhood. They work particularly well on the male who prides himself on subjugating others."

He strained experimentally, shoulders and biceps flexing to test the bonds. "Very nice. Please continue."

To her surprise Jane found she enjoyed the sense of power over him. She could feel all the pulse points of her body quickening as she remembered Audrey's instructions. With a decadent smile she slowly removed his breeches and ran her fingers up the insides of his thighs to the dense triangle of hair that cradled his thick male organ.

"Now don't move a muscle."

"I wouldn't dream of it," he muttered, his hips coming off the bed as her fingers closed around the base of his engorged penis.

"Darling, do hold still," she murmured wickedly.

Somewhere in the swelter of sensations that assailed him, he realized there was more to her aggressive sensuality than met the eye. As always she surprised him, challenged him to plan several moves ahead, but for this . . . well, whatever she was up to, there really was no strategy but to submit. He didn't give a damn what she had planned as long as she did not stop.

Her fingertips stroked his pulsing shaft, in light, tantalizing flutters. "Don't try to get away. Those knots are very secure. I wouldn't want you to hurt yourself."

Gentleman that he was, he didn't bother to point out he could have freed himself and tossed her onto her back with a minimum of effort. In this case, turnabout was definitely fair play, and when she bent with her soft hair brushing his groin, when her moist pink tongue traced the root of his organ to the tip, he nearly exploded, his body straining in a sweet agony of restraint and sexual excitement.

"How does that feel?" she whispered.

"I—"

Her mouth closed over the bulbous knob of his sex, and he jerked upward, a groan bursting from him. "Get on top of me," he muttered, flexing his spine.

"But I haven't finished—"

He tore his wrists free of her bonds, surging upward to catch her under the arms and settle her on top of him. "Show me what else you learned today at Audrey's."

She stared down into his face, stricken. "How did you know?"

"Do you think I would allow you to trick me again, Jane?"

"Perhaps I ought to leave."

"You must be joking. You're finally right where I have wanted you."

Several awful moments passed before Jane could manage to move, captured by her tormentor with his large hands clamped around her hips. Unfortunately, learning that her beloved was a sneakier scoundrel than she had guessed did not dampen her helpless attraction to him.

To the contrary. Her body was already acutely sensitive to his touch. When he pulled her gently downward to suckle her breasts, she weakened and felt herself grow wet in anticipation.

"I'm a better reference than any book, Jane," he whispered, turning her onto her back. "There are some things that really have to be experienced firsthand."

She could hardly argue that. Not when he hooked her legs over his strong shoulders and buried his face between her legs. Not when she climaxed within seconds, awash in shame and sensual enjoyment, her heart beating wildly.

"What else did you learn today?" he asked, his eyes burning into her, challenging her.

"Let me show you," she said softly, disentangling herself.

"I'm all yours."

She straddled him, easing herself onto his swollen rod, taking his full length inside her. For a moment she actually believed she would be able to control him. He gave a low growl and shifted, caressing her breasts with his hands and mouth. Arching her back, her hair falling to her belly, she began to move. To experiment with pleasing him. He allowed this for a while then gripped her hips and flexed upward, penetrating deeper than she had dreamed possible.

She thought she would dissolve on the spot. "Grayson . . . oh, my God."

He arched, his voice uneven. "You're doing a good job. Don't stop now."

"I'm going—"

"More, Jane."

"It's . . . I—"

"More."

She moaned, moving in the rhythm he set, riding him up and down, her inner muscles stretching to absorb him until the moment came when she could not move at all. His hands steadied her by the hips as her body buckled in the throes of another powerful climax.

"Grayson . . . have mercy."

Even then he kept up the tempo, kneading her breasts and buttocks, pounding at her until the very moment his own release came, his muscular frame shaking in pleasure.

"I have never had sex like that before," he admitted in a husky voice when he could finally speak.

Jane could not find words herself, thinking she must remember to send Audrey a thank-you note in the morning. Not that this was the sort of thing one could easily put into words. She closed her eyes and slid bonelessly to his side, a beguiling blackness beckoning her. Until his sardonic voice penetrated her daze and she realized that her hour of reckoning had finally come.

"Now, Jane, do you think it is time for our confessional?"

She sighed and opened her eyes to stare up at his hard candlelit face, both of them finally unmasked, the last of their secrets revealed. She gave a sigh of surrender. "I'd say it was well past time."

Chapter 24

❦

She sat at the dressing table, wrapped again in her robe, the glass of burgundy he had given her in her hand. Her prosecutor paced before her chair, dressed only in his black evening breeches. He pushed his rumpled blond hair back from his face. His expression was intense, yet absent of the anger she had anticipated.

"You did not love Nigel," he said slowly, as if struggling to piece together a puzzle. "He did not love you, harder still to understand. But countless other couples are forced by their families into arranged marriages. The two of you might have carried on affairs after your wedding."

She shot him a chastising look. "Your way, perhaps. But Nigel loved Esther, and she was carrying his child. I did not expect you to understand sacrifice. Or what it feels like to be a woman forced to share her life with a man she does not love."

"It is true," he said, stopping to stare at her, "that I do not understand what it feels like to be a woman. I do understand, however, your reluctance to commit yourself to a marriage without passion."

"Oh, Grayson," she said with a soft sigh. "It really does not make me feel better that you have decided to be so reasonable."

He hesitated, looking vulnerable and hurt.

"What I really do find hard to understand," he said, balancing his hands on the table to brace her between his arms, "is why you deceived me."

"I'm not sure exactly how it happened," she said quickly. "The situation between you and me just somehow evolved, and before I knew it, things had gotten beyond explaining. It's not as if I deliberately misled you. One thing led to another, and then, all of a sudden, I . . . I had fallen in love with you."

He stared at her, steely-eyed, the vulnerability hidden again.

"And," she continued, "you kept making me out to be such a paragon, playing up my virtues until I was dying inside with shame."

"A paragon did not tie me to that bed, Jane," he pointed out.

"No," she said with a rueful nod, "a very wicked woman did."

"I have told you I admire your wickedness. What were you hoping to prove by seducing me anyway?"

"I found out about the marriage contract. That this mistress nonsense was all a sham to discipline me."

He almost smiled. "Ah."

"'Ah.' That is all you have to say for yourself?"

The familiar arrogance returned to his face. "We will be married, Jane. What more is there to say?"

"I refuse to be bullied into another wedding," she said.

"What do you want?" he asked curiously, not doubting for one moment that the matter had already been settled and his will would prevail. He hadn't come this far, hadn't countered her strategy to admit defeat.

She took a breath. "I want to be courted."

Courted. Was that what she had said? he wondered in amazement. Dear heaven, how enigmatic were the workings of the female mind. Especially this female. Courted.

"What the blazes do you think I've been doing these past two weeks or so?"

"Grayson, if you do not see the difference between a courtship and a seduction, then I do not know what to say."

He threw up his hands, laughing helplessly. "I have never spent so much effort on a woman before."

She shook her head. "You make courting me sound like—like an ordeal."

"Well, there were times."

"Will anyone ever let me decide whom and when I am to marry?"

His smile smoldered with confidence. "You are marrying me, Jane. That part has been decided. As I recall, you have already proposed to me. You can go ahead and buy me a wedding ring if you like."

"It is the manner in which you went about this that has upset me. You and Papa plotting my life in candlelight behind closed doors."

"How did you—" Of course. There was only one possible person who could have found out. He made a mental note to have Chloe incarcerated in the Tower of London. "Plotting your life. Put that way it does sound a little unsavory. Not that *your* conduct hasn't taken its own devious little detours."

"I know. I have apologized. . . ."

He took the glass from her hands. His smile was faintly sardonic. "There is no need to apologize. Your devious nature is one of the things I find oddly attractive about you."

She rose and turned away from him, staring at his reflection in the mirror. "Then you understand my desire to be courted?"

"I did court you," he said, his shrug dismissive.

"No, you didn't." Jane pressed her hands down on the dressing table. "You conquered me like a citadel. I hunger for the romantic, Grayson, for flowers and billets doux and intimate rides in the park."

"We went riding in the park, and I bought you an entire flower cart," he said in amusement, brushing a lock of hair from her shoulder. "Do you require your own meadow?"

"No one has ever courted me," she said softly.

He watched her candlelit reflection, drinking in the details of her face.

"Stop feeling sorry for yourself. It's not as if you have lacked for male attention. Nigel might be a nodcock, but he did take you to social affairs."

She gave a little sniff of uncharacteristic self-pity. "All Nigel talked about at those affairs was Esther. Esther this and Esther that. Esther's beauteous bosoms and shivery voice."

He chuckled. "Esther has a voice like a Prussian general."

"I thought so, too, but Nigel certainly responded to

it." She paused, her own voice wistful. "All I ever wanted deep in my heart was for someone to love me like that."

"Well, give me a chance," he said, his tone seductive. "I think I can do as well as Nigel, don't you?"

"Yet this all started as a charade," she said, wanting him to deny her fears. "How do I know I shall not become another Helene?"

"There is no comparison between you."

"You always hinted you would never marry at all."

"And then I met you," he said, as if that explained everything.

Jane's throat closed at the emotion in his eyes. "I thought I had lost everything until you saved me."

"You took a risk few women would dare."

"You wretch, making me believe you wanted me only as your mistress."

"And courting you will excuse the cruel trick I played?" Grayson was hopeful he could find a straightforward way to allay her anxiety. Heaven forbid Jane should decide to put him to the test by more devious means.

Before she could reply, there was a quiet knock at the door. "I say, Jane," Uncle Giles whispered, "how is that chill now?"

"What chill?" she asked, distracted as Grayson set down the glass to gather her gently back into the provocative warmth of his body.

"The chill you contracted at the dance when you appeared half naked to teach me a lesson, darling," Grayson said in an undertone, running his hands lightly down her shoulders.

His lips brushed the back of her neck, and she shivered involuntarily. "It seems to be getting worse, Uncle Giles. It's moving down into my neck now. At a rather alarming rate."

"Sounds like it's taken a good hold of you," her uncle said in sympathy through the door. "Don't want it settling on your chest."

"Indeed, we do not," Jane retorted, blushing in reaction as Grayson's large hands slipped inside her robe to her breasts.

"The best remedy is a good night in bed," Uncle Giles said.

"I couldn't agree more," Grayson murmured as he drew one tender pink nipple into a point between his fingertips.

"I'm sure I shall feel better in the morning," Jane said, then whispered breathlessly, "Stop doing that. He might be old, but he's not incompetent."

"I didn't catch that, Jane," Giles replied. "Did you ask for a hot compress? Excellent idea. I shall bring one up with a glass of warm milk posthaste."

As his heavy footsteps died away, Jane disentangled herself from Grayson's arms. "Will you court me?" she asked, placing her heart in his hands, her request not pleading but more a condition of her terms.

"Jane, I would take on all of Napoleon's armies single-handedly to have you." Having confessed that, he felt compelled to add, "But it does go against the grain." He tugged her robe open. "Wooing one's own wife."

"Oh," she said in exasperation as he caught both ends of the robe's sash. "The objective is to woo me into becoming your wife."

"What is the point of wooing a woman you have already won?" he teased, pulling her toward him by the sash.

"Grayson," she said, "that remark is another example of your astounding arrogance. Go away."

He breathed a sigh of pleasure at the contact of her body against his. "May I remind you that this is my house?"

"You may call on me at a later date when I am not indisposed."

"I may call on you any damn time I please." He gave the ends of the sash another firm pull to show her who was in control. At least for the moment. "Dash it all, Jane, we have gone about all this backward. Meeting at the altar first, becoming friends, having a love affair. And now a courtship at the end."

"I suppose it's all right if it ends well."

"I owe you your heart's desire," he said gently. "If that is what it takes to prove my love, then I will."

"Really, Grayson?" she asked, placing her hands against his bare chest.

"For you and our families. We shall do it properly this time."

She bit her lip, laughing up at him. "Properly? You and I?"

"Well, as close to properly as the pair of us shall ever come."

Grayson stared pensively across the candlelit library at his brother Heath, his arms folded behind his head. "Go on and have your laugh. She turned me down."

"Who would believe it?" Heath said in a droll voice. "A woman rejecting my irresistible sibling."

"This is a serious matter, Heath. She has refused to marry me unless I meet certain conditions."

"Well, no one makes *you* do anything, so that's the end of it then."

Grayson's eyes glistened in amusement. "The hell it is. The devious lady is probably carrying the family heir. Do you think there is the slightest chance that we won't be married?"

Heath set aside the book he'd been reading, rather enjoying the situation. He had never expected to like Jane as much as he did. Secretly he admired her for standing up to his brother. "That presents an intriguing problem. What are you going to do? Abduct her?"

"Don't think the idea hasn't crossed my mind," Grayson said darkly.

"Scotland is rather pleasant this time of year. I assume her parents wouldn't raise a fuss if you eloped?"

Grayson snorted. "Belshire is so infuriated with her, he'd probably push her out the window into a waiting coach. But my Jane wishes to make the choice herself, and I don't fancy a bride who won't speak to me on our honeymoon."

"Nor would I."

"You?" Grayson looked closely at his brother, a man whose actions and emotions had for years seemed cloaked in shadows. Heath had always been subtle in his affairs. "You don't fancy anyone for a bride at all. Do you?"

Heath gave an evasive smile. "I have other obligations to fulfill."

"Then your work for British Intelligence isn't over."

"I don't know. I have yet to be officially contacted."

"There is danger involved?"

"Obviously to some," Heath answered, choosing his next words with care. "Napoleon in exile can only hope for discord between the world powers. Europe is unsettled. The unemployed are massing to our borders."

"And treasuries are drained."

"Why are we even talking of politics when you have woman troubles, Grayson?" This was Heath's way of saying he would not discuss the subject further. "Truthfully, between war and courtship, I am not sure which is easier to win."

Grayson grinned. The truth was he looked forward to this uncertain future with Jane. "You may be right, although there is more pleasure in my battling. I promise you that."

"Then I can only wish—"

Heath was out of his chair, a pistol drawn from the desk, before Grayson had even reached the sideboard. A commotion had erupted in the entrance vestibule, footsteps echoing, a woman shouting, horses snorting in the street.

"Who in God's name is that at this hour?" Grayson demanded, following his brother to the door.

The wall sconces in the vestibule had already been extinguished for the evening. At first the two brothers had difficulty recognizing the unlikely arrivals who stood before them, one a rather nondescript young man in a brown greatcoat, the other a woman in a fur-lined mantle, her body in the full blossom of a healthy pregnancy.

"There is the scoundrel, Nigel, skulking about in the

dark as scoundrels are wont to do," she announced in a crisp voice as she removed her gloves and tossed them to the stunned butler, who was well trained enough to hold his tongue.

"Oh, my God," Grayson said to Heath. "That is the voice of my nightmares."

"And mine," Heath said, amused and appalled at this development. "What do you suppose she wants?"

"I . . ." Grayson hesitated, raising his gaze to the top of the stairs where Jane stood peeking down in her lawn nightdress. "Well, that might be our answer there."

Esther Chasteberry, now Lady Boscastle, whose keen eyes had never missed a social aberration once in her career as a governess, gave a gasp. "In her nightrail, Nigel! He isn't even subtle about it. The world has gone to Hades, I tell you. She is absolutely ruined!"

Nigel looked up at Jane in slack-mouthed astonishment. In all their years of friendship he had never expected to see his kind, generous Jane come to this. Worse, he knew he was responsible. If he had married her, they might have been miserable together, but at least they would have been respectable. To be sure, she would not have become a rake's mistress who greeted people on the stairs in her nightwear.

"Oh, Jane," he said quietly, shaking his head in despair. "How could you? And with my own cousin."

"It is *not* her fault," Esther said indignantly, moving down the hall like a royal barge on the Thames. "She has been taken advantage of by that"—she pointed accusingly at Grayson—"naughty boy."

Heath started to laugh.

"I think," Grayson said, finally recovering from his surprise, "that there has been a misunderstanding."

Don't let him intimidate you, Nigel," his wife said. "Do something."

Nigel swallowed, rousing himself into action. Truth was, he was intimidated by his dear wife, but Grayson had always scared him a little, too, with his Boscastle temperament backed by physical prowess. He had seen Grayson knock out an opponent with the first blow. He steeled himself as Esther reached back and grabbed his arm.

"Are you going to do something or am I?" she demanded.

Heath's eyes glistened with humor. "Watch out, Gray," he said, "she might have brought her rod."

Nigel stepped forward. He was at least a head shorter than his cousins, with thick, wavy brown hair, the start of a double chin, and a pleasant if not handsome face. Even now he looked more like the humble baronet he was than a valiant defender of despoiled young ladies.

Except, blast it all, Jane wasn't just a ruined woman. She was his best friend, a courageous spirit who had sacrificed so much for him. Anger surged through his cowardly hesitation. When he found his voice, it sounded so gruff and manly that he almost frightened himself.

"You ought to be ashamed of yourself, Sedgecroft. What is the meaning of this? Answer me this instant."

Grayson was having a hard time keeping a straight face. Only out of a residual fear of the family governess did he manage to respond without laughing. "I should be asking *you* that question, Nigel, don't you think?"

"Well, I—"

"Unbelievably selfish of you to leave your betrothed to the wolves, dear cousin," Grayson said with a little frown at Jane before she vanished back up the stairs, presumably to don presentable attire. "It was a bit of a scandal you left me to clean up for the family. Not that I minded. Not that it hasn't been a highly entertaining scandal. But, well, it was a scandal."

Nigel hung his head, easily defeated by his cousin's logic. "Well . . ."

"It wouldn't have been quite so scandalous if you hadn't interfered," Esther said when it became obvious Nigel's bravado was deflated. "Not surprising, though. Your branch of the Boscastle line always did take the initiative."

"Why, thank you, Esther," Heath said, grinning at his older brother. "I think that's the first time you have ever complimented us."

"I might not have," she said in a strained voice, "except for the fact we are family now. I shall not tolerate anyone outside criticizing those who are mine."

"What precisely are you doing here?" Grayson asked again, his arms folded in resignation across his chest.

Esther raised her chin, not in the least cowed by a man whose bottom she had spanked. "We have come to salvage what is left of Jane's name."

"Then lower your voice," Grayson said mildly. "Her brother and uncle are asleep upstairs."

Nigel glanced around. Jane, dressed in a muslin gown and at least seeming decent for a fallen woman, had just descended the stairs to join the fray. He felt guilty for his own happily married state in contrast to her disgrace, although—good gracious, what was that look that passed between her and Sedgecroft?

Electrifying. White hot, like an arc of lightning on a summer night. The very air sizzled with its sultry undertones, and here Nigel stood in the middle, a helpless bystander who suddenly wondered how he could possibly persuade a man like Sedgecroft to do the honorable thing.

Grayson cleared his throat, looking bigger, taller, stronger than Nigel had remembered. "Why don't we gentlemen retire to the drawing room to discuss this?"

Nigel straightened his narrow shoulders. A discussion he could handle. "Stay here, Esther," he said with authority, then added softly as he turned to follow Grayson, "Please."

Chapter 25

❧❧

"I should never have agreed to any of this had I known what a tangle it would become," Esther confided in Jane as they stood abandoned in the vestibule.

"Nor would I," Jane said. Which, on reflection, was totally untrue. She had enjoyed every minute with her Boscastle male as Esther had enjoyed hers. "No one could have foreseen any of this." That part was at least true.

"I hope Nigel stands up for himself," Esther said with a worried frown.

Jane could only respond with a halfhearted nod. Against Grayson and Heath, what chance did Nigel have?

"The talk of you two is all over town," Esther said, the governess in her evident as she shook her head. "At least Nigel and I were discreet."

"Because I covered for you," Jane pointed out.

"Yes. Yes, you did. And don't think we're not grateful. Of course Nigel's father will cut him off without tuppence now that our marriage is public knowledge. But it's you who are the immediate concern. When Nigel and I rushed to London to rescue you, your ruination was all everyone could talk about. What on earth possessed you to do this, my dear?"

"The same thing that possessed you and Nigel, I imagine."

"Nigel and I were shocked to the teeth when we found that your parents had washed their hands of you and retreated to the country."

"Well—"

"Never fear. We shall not abandon you in your hour of shame and notoriety as your family has," Esther said consolingly.

"That's very kind of you," Jane replied, not quite ready to be taken into custody yet. "But I'm bearing up well, and I do have Uncle Giles."

"You are not bearing up well at all," Esther insisted. "You are deluded by your passion for Sedgecroft."

"How can you tell?"

"Because I have battled similar temptations in the course of my career as a governess." Esther's light brown eyes misted over with memories. "There was a duke once . . . oh, never mind. The problem is, what to do with *you*."

"I am perfectly capable of managing my own affairs."

"The fact that you are in this house contradicts that statement." Esther released a sigh. "Perhaps we shall think up a solution on the way back to London."

"London?"

"Yes, Jane. Nigel and I must face his parents together and place you under our protection. Unless of course Nigel can persuade Sedgecroft to do right by you."

Jane smiled. "Grayson has already asked for my hand."

"Oh. Well, then. You must stay with us anyway, Jane, until the talk dies down."

"For once, Esther, just for once, I really would like a say in my life. Just a word here and there, mind you. A chance to offer an opinion."

Esther gave her a level look. "You should not have fallen in love with a Boscastle."

"I hardly had a choice in that matter," Jane replied, remembering her first encounter with Grayson, and how her life had taken so many intriguing turns after that. "In fact, I do not understand even now how I lost my heart to him."

"None of us ever do, Jane. For all my wisdom and experience with handling wayward young males, even I could not resist my sweet Nigel, and every day I thank heaven that his cousins did not manage to corrupt him."

Nigel had downed two glasses of port before scraping up the nerve to come to the point. The knowledge that Esther was probably listening at the door emboldened him. It also terrified him. He would rather face Grayson blindfolded in a duel than return to the wrath of his pregnant wife.

"There is only one solution, as I see it," he announced, covertly fanning away the cloud of cigar smoke that Heath had blown toward him.

"Solution to what?" Grayson asked. He was stretched out on the sofa with his eyes half closed.

"To this . . . this mistress mess that Jane has fallen into." There. He'd said it without actually accusing

Grayson again of being the villain who had pushed her into the aforementioned fall.

"I think he ought to marry her," Heath said.

Grayson sat up. "Really?"

"It would tie up a few loose threads," Nigel said, hiding his relief.

"Then you think it is an acceptable answer?" Grayson asked, as if the idea had never entered his mind before this very moment. "I could count on you to convince Jane to accept the proposal? Being her best friend, and all."

"Why, yes." Nigel was so flattered at being in on a conspiracy with his two cousins he completely lost sight of his original objective. "I will do my utmost to persuade her, providing . . ."

"Providing what?" Heath said, his eyes narrowing.

"I shall have to ask Esther's advice first, of course. As a mere courtesy to her condition."

"Does she still wield that rod of hers?" Grayson asked, turning his head.

Nigel flushed; it still stung to remember all the times he had been excluded from the boisterous Boscastle clan. "I hardly know how to react to such a question," he said in embarrassment.

"I think she still has it," Grayson said.

Heath grinned devilishly. "I think you're right."

Chapter 26

❧❧

So it had come to this, Grayson mused as he stood in his bedroom window to watch the loading of his traveling coach below. Back to London with the woman he loved. He and Jane would retrace the steps of their scandalous affair in a socially acceptable manner.

Only to end up where they had started. At a wedding altar. Neither one would escape this time either. The two of them would be married to each other if they had to complete the ceremony in chains. Grayson had no intention of letting Jane get the better of him again.

He glanced back into the room where they had become so intimate that his skin burned at the memory. Heaven only knew how many silly dances and picnics he would attend with her before he enjoyed her in his bed again. He felt a bit like the devil chasing after his own tail, but there had never been any doubt that he would catch her.

He wondered whether this balance they had found would last or would fluctuate throughout their marriage. They understood each other now. He had a feeling the days of deceiving each other had ended. Yet he was certain there was not another woman who could unsettle him as Jane did. He was certain she would challenge him mightily in the years to come.

He would not have it any other way.

Jane stared from the coach window at the elegant seaside villa. She felt a pang of regret at leaving the house where she and Grayson had ended their masquerade. Still, it was gratifying to know he had never brought another woman here before. If he had, she might have been forced to insist he sell the place. Now they could return throughout the years for nostalgic holidays.

She sat back against the squabs with a sigh. She missed him, even though he was following in his own vehicle right behind her. She wished she were at his side rather than in the smothering care of Nigel and Esther. They treated her like an abandoned child they had just rescued from an orphanage.

"We shall all travel the road back to respectability together," Esther said heartily.

And Jane had to smile. It was good to have the comfort of friends when one had almost ruined one's life.

She was relieved to find her family back in residence at their Grosvenor Square home when she and her entourage of protectors arrived in London. Her father embraced her in a crushing hug, his face pinched with emotion. She had not expected this, had not realized how she had missed her parents. Their heartfelt anxiety forced her to forgive them for the trick they had played on her.

In fact, forgiveness seemed to be in order all the way around. They forgave her. She forgave them. They were even polite to Nigel and Esther, acting like true aristocrats, as if the sabotaged wedding had never happened.

"Well, then," Lord Belshire said as he served brandy and biscuits to his guests, "all we lack is Sedgecroft for our little reunion. Where is your fiancé, Jane?"

Jane paused, a petit four halfway to her mouth. "We aren't officially engaged yet, Papa."

Her father looked as if he might faint. He glanced helplessly at his wife, who had managed to decode this mystery from what Simon had told her. "There is to be a period of courtship, Howard."

He turned a ghastly shade of gray. "Why? I mean, the contract is signed. They courted. Yes, they did. In this very town, in this house. I saw them with my own eyes. I—" The cool smile on his wife's face told him to expect no help from that quarter. "I thought it was a courtship," he finished lamely. "Was I wrong?"

Athena's mouth tightened in warning. She had been so guilt-ridden, so worried about her daring eldest daughter during Jane's stay in Brighton that she was determined to mend the breach. Even if it meant naysaying Howard for the first time in their relatively peaceful marriage. "It wasn't a proper courtship, Howard."

"Proper?" He blinked, once, twice, like an owl exposed to a burst of bright light. "As if anything in this household has been proper of late. Pregnant governesses. Sabotaged weddings. Conspiracies in every corner."

Nigel looked down at his plate. Jane nibbled her petit four with a pensive expression. Caroline and Miranda sat on the sofa like a pair of statues with their heads bend over a scrapbook. Esther took a third pastry.

"A courtship," Athena said, drawing a breath, "will put an end to the gossip once and for all."

"Only if it ends in a marriage," Howard said, staring at his wife in frozen horror as another possibility struck him. "This *is* all going to end in a marriage between them, isn't it? Jane isn't going to change her *mind again*?"

"Honestly, dear," his wife said with an impatient shake of her head, "one simply cannot answer that question without spoiling all the romance."

It was a question that had clearly been answered to the satisfaction of Jane's two younger sisters. By candle-light in Caroline's bedchamber the pair poured over fashion plates and menus in preparation for the grand event.

"We'll have to start completely from scratch," Caroline said, stretched out across the bed. "Jane cannot wear the same gown."

"Should we invite Nigel?" Miranda asked.

"Yes, but we will have to reserve an entire pew for the Chasteberry. The woman must be carrying triplets."

"Do you think Grayson will invite his past mistresses this time?"

Caroline's eyes glimmered with mischief. "I think he at least ought to ask Jane first, although they do bring a certain flavor with them."

"I'll say."

Caroline rolled onto her back, sending lists and sketches fluttering to the floor. "Can we get that French chef from Gunter's again?"

"We'll want new dresses, too," Miranda murmured.

"I wonder if Drake and Devon will show up this time," Caroline said absently.

"I should think so. They seem to be a close family."

"A scandalous one."

"And passionate."

"So are we."

Miranda perked up. "What? Passionate or scandalous?"

"I think the potential is there for both."

Caroline gazed up at the plump *amorini* romping on the plasterwork ceiling. "We should have known that Jane had something devilish in mind when she balked at the fitting for her trousseau. She never wanted to entice Nigel."

"How could we have known?" Miranda drew a bride holding a bouquet of weeds and droopy roses in her sketchbook. "Would you ever consider sabotaging your own wedding?"

"I'm going to elope," Caroline said. "If I ever meet the man of my dreams, I shall carry him right to the altar myself."

Chapter 27

๛

Patience was one of the few virtues Grayson had cultivated between his vices. If Jane desired courtship, he would oblige her. In their game of love, he had no doubt who would emerge triumphant. She might tease him to death, but in the end the male would dominate. He would gladly wear his heart on his sleeve to prove to her and the world that he adored her.

Yet if he was confident of his ability to win, he did not take much else in life for granted. Jane had challenged him emotionally and intellectually from the moment they'd met. Until they stood before man and God at the altar, he would continue to pursue her. Even if only to prove his devotion. To prove that while seducing her had been sublimely pleasurable, it had not been his sole aim.

He was utterly serious when he told her he needed her help to handle his family. What a wildling bunch they had become. He sensed in Chloe a revolution brewing, a deep unhappiness that, if not thwarted, could only lead to disaster. Heath also appeared to be headed for some enigmatic, undoubtedly dangerous course.

The worry did not end there. His prim and proper sister Emma had lost her husband, and, as a widowed viscountess, stood in a vulnerable position in society, even if she refused to see herself that way. Drake and Devon had always been restless souls, drawn to trouble time and time again. And brave young Brandon would never be coming home to bedevil them again.

The Boscastle line needed Jane's strength and cunning to survive the perils of another century. Grayson needed her for his own survival.

He called formally that same evening at her house to escort her family to the opera. The two of them stood alone together in the drawing room for several minutes. Grayson, in elegant black evening wear and gleaming boots. Jane, in an off-white satin gown draped across her soft shoulders like the petals of an exotic lily.

They went so well together. What other woman in the world aroused and tamed his demons at the same time?

He circled her slowly, a lion examining his prey. "That dress," he said in a low voice, "looks a little too nice on you."

"Do you like it? You should. It is one you picked out for me, the only selection from the mistress wardrobe that I could wear in public."

He stopped, leaning down to rub his chin on the enticing curve of her shoulder. "I think I had a private affair in mind when I chose it. Did the drive back from Brighton give that devious mind of yours a rest?"

"Indeed, my lord. And your devious mind?"

He pressed a kiss on the arch of her throat, murmuring, "Plotting all over the place to have you to myself again. I miss you, Jane." She shivered lightly as he placed his hands on her shoulders. "How long do we have to wait?"

"We can't get married until after Cecily is married, and one simply can't throw a wedding together in a week."

"Elope?"

"Except, Grayson, I *do* have my heart set on a proper ceremony, a wedding to remember. . . ."

"You had one as I recall."

"Well, I thought this time I might invite the groom."

He sighed. "When is Cecily's wedding?"

"A fortnight from now, in Kent, at her father's manor. Are you coming?"

"Why not? The last wedding you and I attended was certainly entertaining."

"My family will be there," Jane said, warming at the thought of showing her rogue off to the rest of her relations. "You can frighten my sisters with your appalling manliness."

"I suppose I shall have to get used to these family affairs," he said quietly. He turned her around to face him, drinking in the sight of her satin-draped curves. Was she carrying his child? Had that delicate waist begun to expand the tiniest bit? They had certainly made love enough in Brighton to make it a possibility. He ran a finger beneath her throat. He felt very protective of her all of a sudden. "I want to set a date."

"A date for what?" she asked with a smile.

His fingertip teased the underside of her breast. He watched in satisfaction as her breathing quickened. "For baking Christmas pudding. What do you think?"

Jane lifted her face to his. "Wasn't that part written into the clandestine contract?"

"Despot that I am, I neglected that important detail."

"I'm surprised the other despot who is my father allowed the omission."

"I believe he was in shock," he said, and stole a kiss a few seconds before the father under discussion appeared in the doorway with his wife.

"Are you two going to stand here all night or accompany us to the opera?" Lord Belshire demanded, his gruff tone hiding his pleasure that his Jane had found a man like Sedgecroft to take care of her. "Nothing worse than arriving right in the middle of a damned aria."

"We shall cause a scene no matter when we arrive," Athena said behind him, slim and elegant in a white satin shawl and an ice blue moire taffeta gown. "People are dying to know what sort of arrangement Grayson has made with Jane. I shall be delivering snubs all night long."

The social uproar Athena had predicted came true only seconds after they took their box in the opera house.

Even those in the audience in the know could not quite decide what to make of this. Lord Belshire, his family, and his vibrant eldest daughter poised on the arm of a handsome scamp, the notorious lady looking radiant for someone who was allegedly ruined. Hadn't the papers reported only two weeks or so ago that a certain marquess was shopping for a wardrobe with his *mistress*? And an indiscreet shopgirl had reported the naughtiest conversation in the upstairs chamber of a well-known Bond Street establishment. . . .

Wives and daughters borrowed quizzing glasses to take a look at Jane's ivory satin gown, recognizing the work of the demimonde's darling modiste Madame Devine. No one remembered that particular dress on Jane before and then . . . oh, the ever-delicious Sedgecroft had just kissed her ear! Trust him to please the crowd. Yes, he had kissed his love in public. At the very moment the scandalous couple bent heads simultaneously to pick up the program Jane had dropped.

"Everyone saw that," she whispered with a hot blush as he glanced up, grinning into her face.

"Your father didn't," he whispered back. "That's all I have to worry about."

"The scandalmongers will say they were right all along, and the papers will keep printing horrible things about us."

"Gossip will not kill us, Jane, or I would have been dead long ago."

She pretended to scan her program, tempted to throw her arms around his strong neck and kiss him back. "You're probably right."

He settled his large frame back in his seat. "The truth, my darling, is that anybody who is anybody will hope to be invited to all the social affairs hosted by the new Lady Sedgecroft. That would be you."

"Would it?" she whispered, smiling as she pictured the pair of them presiding over the ton in the ballroom of his Park Lane house.

"I am the head of the family," he added. "As such, it will be my privilege to enjoy watching the other eligible Boscastles be cornered at the supper parties my wife will give." He leaned down to whisper, "That would be you again."

She glanced up at his handsome face and felt her heart overflow with an almost fearful happiness. Yes, this Boscastle was hers. His wonderful, wicked brood would become her children's heritage. The prospect should have sent her straight to the sofa with a vinaigrette, but Jane had always been the type to challenge fate.

She said, "Which of your siblings do you think will marry next? Drake?"

His blue eyes darkened. "At the moment, I am focused on achieving that status for myself. Perhaps I shall have to make you want me more."

"How?" she whispered, unable to imagine how such a thing could be possible.

"I shall not touch you again, Jane, after tonight. Not so much as a kiss until our wedding day."

"You, Sedgecroft, showing self-control?"

"We shall see who weakens first," he said smugly.

"Did you just issue me a challenge?" she whispered.

"I believe I did."

"What shall we bet?"

"What do you have to offer?"

"Excuse me." Jane's father, seated behind them, stretched forward to tap them on the shoulder. "Is the opera interrupting your conversation? Shall I ask Signora Nicola to take her solo into the alley?"

"My apologies, sir," Grayson replied with a straight face. "Pay attention to the performance, Jane, dear," he added in a voice loud enough to carry.

"Oh, I am," she replied, giving him a scowl that might

have had more effect if behind her Caroline and Miranda had not suddenly burst into giggles.

Grayson glanced around to flash them a charming grin. "All right, you two. You're going on the list along with the other family members who need to be married off for the benefit of Society."

"Which is all very well and good," Lord Belshire said grumpily, leaning forward a final time to speak. "But let us see *you* married first, hmm?"

Chapter 28

For the next week Grayson behaved as quite the perfect gentleman, the perfect suitor. He squired Jane and her sisters to the museum, to the amphitheater, to lectures and soirées. He bought her flowers. And he did not lay a finger on her, aware that he was teasing her, torturing them both with his promise to show self-control.

Proper she wanted. Proper he would give her, if only on the surface. There would be plenty of time for private improprieties during the course of their marriage.

Two weeks later Cecily exchanged vows with the Duke of Hedleigh in an ancient Gothic church only minutes away from her father's family seat in Kent. Jane served as a bridesmaid, and Grayson caused another small scandal when he sat in one of the front pews with her father, who kept commenting on how happy the bride and groom looked, and how he hoped to see his own daughter at the altar soon.

A few minutes after the wedding procession drove through the wrought-iron gates of the estate, a cloud of white doves was released from the tower of the east wing. Wedding bells pealed from the village church into the mellow blue skies as the birds fluttered free.

"How lovely," Jane exclaimed, shielding her eyes to look up.

"Not if they decide to fly over the wedding breakfast," her father grumbled as they took their seats at the tables where ham, grouse, jellies, and roast beef tempted the guests. "Why can't these affairs be held inside?"

Jane took a sip of champagne. Where had Grayson gone? Ah, there. Strolling down an avenue of high evergreens with two young ladies in tow. She frowned as the trio turned around a corner. True to his word, he had not touched her since that night at the opera, and she was burning, positively on fire to be in his arms again. He was playing with her, proving another of his wicked points.

His tall figure disappeared. A moment later a burst of gleeful feminine laughter drifted from the direction of the evergreens. The sound tore years and years of Jane's good breeding to pieces.

"What are they doing?" she asked, putting down her fork.

Her father speared a slice of ham. "What is who doing?"

"Grayson and those girls."

Lord Belshire glanced around the table. "I don't see Grayson with any girls."

"Precisely. They are hidden from view, making their behavior all the more suspicious."

"I daresay Grayson would be a trifle more discreet if you were to announce your engagement."

Jane rose from her chair. "Do you think he's trying to make me jealous?"

"My dear child, it is beyond me to fathom what either of you is doing. All I really care about at this point is that you set a date." He refused a second glass of champagne offered by a hovering footman. "Once you are married, the pair of you can behave in whatever manner you please."

She tossed down her napkin and hurried off toward the trees where she had last seen her rogue. It was rude of him, really, to be openly flirting in the midst of the wedding breakfast. With everyone watching. And him making such a beastly point of not touching her for two weeks.

She came to the corner where he had disappeared. A stone Cupid stood in the center of the pathway, pointing an arrow at her heart.

"Shoot if you like," she muttered, "but you're a little too late."

A deep mocking voice spoke behind her. "Too late for what?"

She spun around, bumping against Grayson's muscular body. A rush of blood warmed her all the way to her toes. It was the closest they had come to physical contact in over a fortnight, but even then he did not touch her. No, he just stood there in all his virile power, letting her smolder. "I was talking to Eros. Where are your giggling girls?"

"Ah, the Misses Darlington. Well, we rescued the dove, and they took off to find their mama."

"What dove?"

"One of the wedding doves got itself entangled in a

tree. The gardener and I staged a heroic rescue." He stared down into her face, his eyes searching hers. "Were you jealous, Jane?"

She pressed her hand against his chest. "Horribly. Insanely. Grayson, you are never to go off in the trees with any other female but me. Were you *trying* to make me jealous?"

He grinned. "Me? Capable of such a juvenile act? Of course I was, darling, and obviously my ploy worked."

He reached down and took her hand, breaking his vow. "We're announcing our engagement at the ball tonight."

"Do you think—"

"I do."

"So do I," she whispered, winding her hands around his neck to kiss him. "I cannot bear to be away from you. I am ruined, Grayson, inside and out, thinking of you."

A discreet cough interrupted Jane's long-awaited passionate moment.

Grayson glanced around first, irritated that anyone would intrude on their privacy.

"What the—"

"Forgive me. I was looking for Chloe." Heath held up his hands, trying not to laugh.

Grayson caught Jane by the hand. "Since it's only you, you're forgiven, although I can't imagine why you couldn't wait a minute. We were finally celebrating our engagement."

Heath glanced around the avenue. "Congratulations."

"Is something wrong?" Jane asked quietly.

"I don't know," Heath replied, his gaze returning to hers. "Chloe disappeared during breakfast."

Grayson shrugged. "I'm sure she's somewhere on the estate."

"But with whom?" Heath asked in a low voice. "Baron Brentford disappeared the same time as she did."

"He was staring at her during the wedding ceremony," Jane said in concern. "He's such an intense young man."

Grayson frowned. "I thought he was staring at you."

"Only until Chloe caught his eye. She really is unhappy about losing her officer. I think she was talking with Brentford this morning."

A blur of movement at the end of the avenue attracted their attention. Jane gestured at the two figures on horseback riding back toward the park gates. A gentleman in black from head to toe. A young woman in royal blue, her head of dark curls thrown back in laughter. No groom. Jane sighed, wondering who she was to pass judgment. These Boscastles wielded their charms like a weapon.

Grayson swore, a Boscastle not at his charming best. "We're too late now. Whenever mischief passed between them is already done."

"Which doesn't mean we will allow this to happen again," Heath said with a grim look. "I wondered why Brentford took that bottle of wine off the table."

"Now we know," Grayson said, his jaw taut.

Heath pivoted on his heel. "I think it's time I introduced myself. I assume you have a few choice words for him, too, Gray. Shall we include Drake?"

Grayson looked at Jane before backing away to join

his brother. "No. One of us will have to stay here to guard the queen. Jane, please give our excuses to our hosts."

"Queen, am I? Well, listen to me, both of you, I am ordering you not to embarrass your sister again—"

"I am subtlety incarnate," Heath said, laughing.

"And that word is not in your brother's vocabulary," she said in exasperation.

She watched them hurry off to harass their sister and thought, This will be my life, my fate. All her actions subject to Grayson's approval, the concerns of his family her concerns. She turned to the statue of Cupid, picturing the stormy days ahead. There was no help for it once that winged-tip arrow struck home, and all she could hope was that one day Chloe would find the love she desperately sought and that he would love her in return.

Grayson and Jane announced their engagement at the end of the bridal ball held in the oval salon that same night. Lord Belshire was so relieved that he led a toast and celebrated by drinking an entire bottle of champagne. In the peculiar standards of Society, the betrothal instantly canceled out all the scandals of the previous weeks. The roguish implications of Grayson's conduct suddenly took on the rosy glow of a romantic courtship. It was quite the thing to pretend one approved of the couple's antics.

"The rogue must have planned this all along," whispered a dowager to her niece. "Go and talk to Heath, darling. He'll be looking for a bride next."

"Don't they make a perfect match?" cooed the same people who had predicted disaster only a few days ago.

"So it's to be a Boscastle-Welsham connection, after all."

"Except that Jane's traded in an ordinary baronet for a marquess."

"He hasn't taken his eyes off her all evening," sighed one happily married matron. "He makes no secret of his love for her."

Jane found herself surrounded by a crowd of female well-wishers, with Cecily at the front of the crush.

"It seems I was wrong about him after all," Cecily whispered sheepishly. "He isn't the scoundrel everyone thought he was."

Jane hugged her friend in a celebration of their mutual happiness. Cecily's bridal wreath was a little lopsided from dancing, and her beautiful white satin gown lacked a silk knot here and there. "Well, he certainly is no saint, although heaven knows, neither am I."

Cecily did not even pretend to disagree. "At least your papa looked very happy about the engagement. He was acting as if he had arranged the match himself."

"Speaking of arranging matches," Jane said, lowering her tone, "I don't suppose you know what happened between Chloe, her brothers, and Brentford earlier today?"

Cecily frowned. "My maid said Brentford left the house shortly after their meeting, looking shaken but still alive. Chloe is playing cards with Drake."

"Grayson probably scared everyone to death again." Jane glanced around the cluster of elegant figures in the candlelit room. "Where did he and my father go anyway?"

The two men had slipped away to the billiard room, where Lord Belshire puffed away on a cigar and congratulated his future son-in-law on his engagement.

"Well, you did it, Sedgecroft." He practically had to restrain himself from dancing a little jig around the table.

Grayson positioned his queue stick. "I still have to get her to the altar."

"She'll be there, believe me, or I'll marry you myself. *You'll* be there, won't you? History will not repeat itself. . . ."

Grayson glanced up, grinning, before he took a shot. "I was there the first time, sir, remember?"

Chapter 29

There was such a flurry of activity in the days preceding the wedding that Grayson and Jane barely found time to exchange a few words, let alone succumb to temptation. For one thing Grayson's widowed sister, Emma Boscastle, the Viscountess Lyons, had arrived from Scotland. An energetic sprite of a woman, Emma took charge of the arrangements with a snap of her graceful fingers.

Known for her flawless deportment, her genius at hosting a party, she also served as a veritable fountain of advice for the socially unaware. Which, in her educated opinion, unfortunately included her own undisciplined family.

As Drake said on the day of her arrival, "Well, there goes the end of uncivilized life as we know it. The Dainty Dictator has arrived. Fall in everyone. She's liable to inspect behind our ears."

With the Boscastle reputation for scandal, the crème de la crème of the nobility waited in anticipation for the ceremony. Which, judging by the bride's last attempt at matrimony, promised to provide an unforgettable entertainment if nothing else.

And then the day arrived. Jane awoke with her heart pounding all through her body and wondered if Grayson felt the same way. Goodness, what if he decided to trick her and not show up at his own chapel for the wedding?

Except that Emma would be there to keep Grayson in line. Beautiful blue-eyed Emma, in whom the Boscastle penchant for wildness seemed to have gotten itself reversed into a penchant for propriety.

In his Park Lane residence, the marquess's valet cheerfully sharpened his razor on the leather strop and lathered the handsome face of his master. "Well, today's the day, my lord, and if I may be so bold as to say, I never thought I'd live to see it."

Grayson nodded, his square jaw smothered in shaving soap. "Nor did I. In fact, I can hardly believe it will happen."

It did happen, though, exactly three hours later. In a poignant echo of the previous ceremony, Grayson Boscastle, the fifth Marquess of Sedgecroft, turned to openly admire the bride walking the nave of his private chapel. He knew for a fact that she had a beautiful derriere. And the rest of her was something else altogether.

Not that he made a point of lusting after young women in wedding dresses, but this particular bride happened to belong to him.

Or shortly would. After all, both of them had managed to put in an appearance. He straightened his shoulders as her father bore her to the altar, his arm securing hers in an until-death-do-us-part grip.

"Done," Belshire said in a terse voice.

Grayson stared down at her veiled face, took her hand, and said, "Thank you, from the depths of my heart. I will cherish her forever."

A buzz of appreciation rose from the guests seated in the pews. The bride, everyone agreed, could not have been more beautiful. She wore a cap of embroidered silk with seed pearls threaded through her honey-colored hair. A cream white satin dress, with a fitted bodice in the palest pink and a sash of pink rosettes that dropped to the flounced hem, draped her graceful curves beneath a long train of Valenciennes lace.

Grayson felt his throat tighten. This was it. No ending here. A beginning. So he would stand beside her for the rest of their lives. At births, at baptisms, at balls, until his dying breath. He stared down at her in adoration. He did not regret his past, except the times he had neglected his family and taken their existence for granted. He wouldn't repeat that mistake as he embraced the future. Perhaps he wasn't as good as he should be, but he'd learned he wasn't all bad either.

He glanced up from his wife's face at his brothers and sisters, those handsome, heartbreaking siblings of his. Unbelievable as it was, he loved the whole aggravating lot of them. . . .

Dear God. Not the mistresses again. His gaze lit on a pew occupied by two of his former mistresses and the products of their previous relationships.

Mrs. Parker blew him a friendly kiss. Her pair of gangly sons from her first affair grinned and gestured at Jane, elbowing each other in approval. Tomorrow Grayson would have to see about securing the two oafs military commissions.

He returned his attention to his bride, his shoulders lifted in a shrug. "I swear I didn't invite them. . . ."

"I did," she whispered, biting her lip to hold back a mischievous laugh.

He blinked. "Oh."

"Aren't you glad?"

"Should I be?"

"I wanted everything to be the same as the day we met."

"The same?"

"Well," she whispered, "this time I thought I'd invite the groom."

He laughed low, thinking of how many times they would look back in private amusement at this moment.

The minister cleared his throat, and silence settled over the chapel. The rich perfume of roses mingled with the fragrance of melted beeswax. Jane's eyes misted with tears of happiness as Grayson gave her hand a possessive squeeze. Same place, same guests, but a very different groom and an entirely different feeling. This time her heart was on the altar. She stood, accepting his in return, committing herself to a lifetime of his leonine arrogance, his devotion, repeating her vows in a clear steady voice.

The guests waited, craning their heads for a view of the groom kissing the bride. Jane whispered against his cool lips, "Everyone was waiting for a scandal."

His heavy eyebrows lifted as he gathered her against him for their first married kiss. "Give the people what they want."

"Which means—" And she broke off, gasping with

laughter as her scandalous love chucked her up in his arms and over his shoulder.

"I wanted to do this before," he said above the whoops of the well-wishers, who rose from their seats to watch them, "on the day you were to marry Nigel."

She pushed her bridal cap back off her forehead and hit him on the shoulders with her bouquet. "I wanted you, too," she said breathlessly. "But I never dreamed we—"

"Grayson Boscastle," said a woman's low cultured voice behind them. "Kindly remember a sense of time and place. Unhand the marchioness this instant."

Even in her upside-down position Jane could feel the automatic response in her husband's body, her slow slide to the floor as he settled her back on her feet. "Was that Esther?" she whispered, her cheeks flushed with delight. Oh, to be a woman who wielded such power over this family of naughty boys.

"Ah, no." He rubbed the side of his nose, his eyes crinkling in an unholy smile. "It was your sister-in-law Emma. Mrs. Killjoy."

Emma, a beguiling woman with apricot gold hair and soft blue eyes, gave Jane a sympathetic look. "Remind the almighty there's the breakfast to get through before . . . other things."

Other things being taking his bride to bed. Grayson traced a possessive hand down the curve of his wife's spine to the rise of her bottom. An aristocrat to the bone, he would make his social appearance at the wedding breakfast. He would graciously accept the toasts and blessings given them. And then heaven help anyone who interrupted him and Jane afterward.

For the second time that year a wedding breakfast was held in the banqueting hall of the Park Lane house. This time the newlywed couple, both bride and groom, actually sat together with the bride's parents at the head table.

Cut-glass chandeliers sparkled like stars above the guests who chattered and devoured lobster salad and champagne. Emma politely reminded everyone to leave room to sample the hothouse pineapples and huge multi-tiered wedding cake from Gunter's.

Then, in the middle of the toast, Nigel's mother looked at Jane and burst into tears. "For almost a decade, I have thought of her as my daughter-in-law."

"There, there, Mother," Nigel said comfortingly. "You have your first grandchild coming to console you."

"Yes." She sniffed, eyeing Esther's gargantuan belly over the top of her handkerchief. "A grandchild who might be as large as a gorilla by the looks of him . . ."

At the adjacent table Emma set down her silver fork in alarm. "Oh, no. Nigel's mother is going off like a waterworks. I knew it was gauche to have a huge wedding after that last debacle."

Caroline smiled at her. "I don't think we need to worry about appearing gauche. Grayson and Jane have risen to the top of the scandal broth like cream."

"I suppose you're right," Emma said with a resigned smile. "It's your turn next, isn't it?"

Miranda leaned toward them, whispering, "Actually, we heard a rumor about *you*, Emma, and a certain man—"

"This," Drake Boscastle announced to the guests seated around him, who, as a group, were a little less well behaved than those at the bridesmaids' table, "is exactly why I hate weddings."

Mrs. Parks arranged the pearls on her bosom and gave her sons a scowl against stuffing too much cake in their mouths. "Why is that?"

"All the emotion. I mean, look at Nigel's mother bawling into her champagne. All the potential for disaster."

"Except," Mrs. Parks said in a wistful voice, "your brother really does love his bride."

And Grayson did, openly, prompting a consensus of opinion among his acquaintances that the wedding was proof a Boscastle could be domesticated. A few of his more astute friends, however, interpreted the blazing possession in his eyes whenever he glanced at his wife to mean his wildness had not been quite strangled by the bonds of holy matrimony.

Two hours later he proved the point.

"Champagne in bed, and in the middle of the day," Jane whispered, admiring the powerful lines of her husband's chest as he removed his blue frock coat. "This is decadence."

"Isn't decadence under the pretense of decency what you wanted?" he asked, and took the half-empty glass from her hands.

She stretched up to kiss him, short teasing flicks of her tongue against his, heat rising between them like steam. "I think you know me a little too well."

"I think you're right," he said in a husky voice.

He slid his large hands up her ribs to the lush contours of her breasts. She drew away, teasing him, to remove the petticoats he had untied.

His gaze traveled over her in burning anticipation. Her languid movements as she undressed, her back to the bed, taunted him. He lounged across the pillows, watching her through narrowed eyes, and felt his body heat, felt the potent rush of blood through his veins.

"Go ahead, tease me," he murmured, pulling off his neckcloth. "In a few minutes I'll have you begging for it."

Her unbound hair swirled around her hips as she spun to the bed. There was not an inch of his wife that did not excite him.

"I have no idea what you're talking about," she said with a mischievous smile.

"I think you do."

She raised her leg on the bed for him to remove her white lace garters and stockings. The duty, his first as the lady's husband, made him painfully hard. His heart thundered in his chest as he eased his hand around the curve of her calf to comply. Small intimacies such as this brought him deep pleasure.

The female scent that was hers alone heightened his animal instincts. Her gentle smile uplifted him. From the depths of his soul he was drawn to her. Slowly he peeled off the lace garters and stockings, one leg at a time. His eyes glistened with love and erotic intentions as she waited nude before him.

He rose and unfastened his breeches, his face dark with desire. She reached down to help him, sliding her hand inside his waistband. "Touch me like that, temptress, at your own peril," he said, with a soft growl of approval.

"Like this?" she whispered, sliding her fingers down the silken length of him.

"You're really asking for trouble."

"Don't I always?"

He pulled her against his hard, aroused body. "And don't I always give it to you?"

"Yes, but not nearly often enough."

He gave a low appreciative laugh. "That's easily remedied."

"Then remedy it, Grayson." With a suggestive smile she began to unbutton his embroidered waistcoat and white linen shirt. "Or may I do the honors?"

"We'll take turns, shall we?" he murmured, loving the way she responded to him, the passion in her nature. With her he was at peace, his best, the future a beacon of hope and happiness. The forever commitment they had made today only sweetened their sexual pleasure.

He finished undressing, then drew her into his arms.

His hands drifted over her creamy flesh, sculpting her curves like an artist; he needed to feel her against him. His entire body pulsed with pleasure at the thought of bedding her whenever he liked.

"We did it," she whispered, her breasts swaying like opulent pearls against his warm chest. "An entire wedding, and no scandal to speak of."

He bent his head to kiss her moist pink mouth. "Imagine that," he murmured. "Both the bride and groom showed up at the same time."

"A shame they didn't stay for their own wedding breakfast."

"Shocking," he said, reaching down to clasp her hand. "I thought the bride looked a little wild," he added. "I know it was bad of me, but during the entire ceremony, all I could think of was getting her in my bed."

"I had my eye on the groom myself."

"Did you?" He led her toward the bed, his manhood flagrantly erect. "Why was that?"

"I burn for him," she whispered, her eyes lifting to his face.

"Is that right?"

"Don't tell anyone though," she said. "A decent woman probably shouldn't burn for a man during breakfast."

He sat down on the side of the bed and pulled her snugly into his lap with her legs straddling him. The head of his shaft pressed against her belly, and his hard thighs supported her bare bottom. "I'm rather drawn to indecency myself."

"Do you mind explaining that remark?"

He rolled her across his chest and spilled her down onto the blue silk coverlet. "Perhaps I ought to show you. This sort of thing calls for a detailed explanation."

She laughed, hiding her face in the crook of his arm. She thought of the days and afternoons and nights they would share. Of the wedding vows they'd exchanged before God and family. And, yes, she had done it properly, perfectly, this time.

"Grayson—"

"Don't interrupt me, darling. Demonstrating indecency is serious work."

His fingers brushed feathery strokes over her full breasts, down to the dip of her navel, before disappearing into the damp curls of her sex. With unerring finesse his thumb found her hidden nub of flesh, arousing the sensitive nerves with slow, exquisite strokes.

"Oh," she breathed, rising up on her elbows only to subside as he spread her open, exposing her to him. She felt moisture seeping from the depths of her body. She shifted her hips, locking one leg around his thigh.

With his silky blond hair lying upon his broad shoulders, his smoky blue eyes full of seductive promise, he was the wicked lover of a woman's dreams. And he was her husband.

She strained upward. "Grayson, please—"

"Patience is a virtue."

"Don't tell me about virtue at a time like this. I *want* you."

He slid backward onto the floor, clamping his hands around her waist to position her on the edge of the bed. Standing, his legs planted wide apart, he parted her thighs to open her fully to him. Her flesh glistened, pink and swollen.

The tip of his shaft slid between her damp folds and sank into her sheath. Bliss. Heat. Wet female flesh pulsing against him until the blood in his groin began to boil and his body tightened. He ground his hips against her, positioning each thrust to intensify her pleasure. Deep plunges into her fertile core, slow withdrawals in a steady rhythm that left her gritting her teeth with frustration.

"More," she whispered. "Harder."

Moving on pure instinct, he brought her tantalizingly close to the peak only to pull back at the very last second. A minute later she arched, trembling in climax, and he followed, savoring the fulfillment he knew only in her love.

A half hour later they still had not moved from where they had collapsed, the late afternoon sun casting its warmth from the window onto their bridal bed. Jane lay snuggled against his muscular torso, listening to the interesting echoes that drifted from below.

"Oh, dear," she said, trying to sit up and disentangle herself from bare limbs and bedsheets, "those voices are rather disturbing. I cannot tell if they're coming from the doorstep or the street. Do you think—"

"Ssh." He gathered her back against his chest. "Emma and Heath can take care of whatever it is. Celebrate with me, my love. Let us concentrate on each other."

She closed her eyes, her head resting comfortably on his shoulder. A glow of gratitude warmed her heart and stole over her. This was what she had yearned for, this closeness and acceptance, the prize for which she had sacrificed her reputation. How well worth it had been the risk, her unwillingness to accept what others believed was best for her. Perhaps her methods could have been more refined, but no one dared question the reward, all her fears of an empty life replaced with Grayson's love.

How could she have known that her scheming would end in such undeserved sweetness? Who would have guessed that a rogue would be the most devoted of mates, the man to teach her the true meaning of love?

"What I wish," she murmured, "is that every one of them could find the contentment that we have. I couldn't help thinking that Emma and Chloe looked a trifle sad today. And Drake with those women, well, what can I say?"

Grayson gave a deep chuckle. "Scarcely is she done with one scheme than she hatches another. My marchioness is already matchmaking. Do you suppose we could put off plotting for a few hours at least?"

"Do you have something else in mind?"

"Now that you ask . . ."

She half turned, touching his face, the proud bones, with her fingertips. "It *was* the perfect wedding."

He held her and felt his heart brim over with happiness and tender possession. His wife, mistress, and clever strategist. His partner in devious pleasures, the woman who had helped him find his place when he was floundering. "I do love you, Jane."

"I have always loved you, scoundrel."

There was laughter from below, doors slamming, a shout that might have been a challenge or a cheer. The sounds of family and friends joined together to celebrate two hearts brought home.

Read on for a sneak peek at

The Love Affair of an English Lord

**the second novel in
Jillian Hunter's Boscastle Trilogy!**

England
1814

The late Dominic Breckland, Viscount Stratfield, was returning to life in a sea of women's underwear. From ear to ankle he fought a sensual undertow of lacy shifts and white silk stockings, his muscular arms tangled in the ties and tapes of lavender-scented buckram stays, his heavy thighs wrapped in a pair of dainty French percale pantalettes. Like a wounded beast of the night he had eluded capture and taken refuge in the last place his pursuer would think to look.

Summoning a primitive instinct for survival, he had climbed the sturdy oak tree outside the manor house and hauled his bruised and bleeding six-foot frame over the windowsill. Hopeful he had outwitted the man who chased him, he had then collapsed—into an open trunk stuffed with personal female attire and frivolous accessories. He was not too exhausted to appreciate the irony of the situation.

For now, at least, he had managed to escape the man who was hunting for him. Yet moment by moment his life blood was saturating an unknown woman's muslin petticoats and blush-pink stockings. Pain seared his upper body. Gritting his teeth, he unraveled from his elbow a flimsy lawn chemise embroidered with blue silk forget-me-nots. His gaze unfocused and brimming with deviltry, he examined it in the moonlight.

If he was going to die, for the second time in a month, he might as well go out on a rousing sexual fantasy. "Well," he murmured, "what sort of woman are you anyway? Fast or merely fashionable? Do I have a choice? Then give me fast."

Unfortunately the maidenly garment failed to inspire a potent sexual image in his mind. The owner did appear to possess a decent pair of breasts, although Dominic was admittedly not capable of objective appraisal in his current condition.

God help them both—the poor woman would suffer a heart seizure when she found his carcass buried in her drawers. It seemed to him that he had once owned this creaky old manor house, at some time in the murky past, and he tried to remember who had bought it from him. To his frustration his brain refused to focus, images flitting elusively behind his eyes like moths in the shadows.

A retired sea captain, wasn't it? Sir Hickory or Humpty Something, his wife and daughter. Their names escaped Dominic at the moment. Bleeding to death, he hoped he would be forgiven the lapse in manners.

"Humpty Dumpty had a great fall," he muttered. "But who the devil was his wife?" If he was wallowing in the woman's underclothes, he ought to at least know her name.

Many would remark that Dominic being found dead in a trunk of petticoats was not surprising for a former

English scoundrel who had thumbed his nose at Society. His closest friends might even have chosen to bury him in a shroud of female underclothing as a loving tribute to their past sins.

Except that Dominic had been officially "buried" a month ago, mourned by a few, cursed by many. Aside from the persistent rumors of his ghost popping up in the oddest places and doing the naughtiest things, no one really expected to see him again.

Not his servants or scattered acquaintances.

He trusted only one person. The man who had helped him arrange his own funeral.

The late evening silence of the country estate was marred by thumping footsteps, the sound of a bucket being kicked over, and an irate male voice from the front of the house.

"Somebody open the bloody gate!" the gardener shouted from the driveway below. "The carriage is coming over the bridge!"

"The bloody gate has been open for an hour!" the groom shouted back.

"Company," Dominic said with a mordant sigh, tossing the embroidered chemise over his shoulder. "I suppose I ought to tidy myself up—if I'm expected to entertain."

He looked like a nightmare cast up from hell, and he knew it. His lanky frame had lost flesh. The hollows of his cheekbones gave his masculine face a dangerous gauntness. The lugubrious pattern of surgeon's stitches that crisscrossed his chest and left shoulder had been torn during his tree-climbing escapade. Taking a breath that burrowed into his lungs like talons, he felt with his uninjured arm for the windowsill and hoisted himself upright for a few moments of enlightening agony.

His gray eyes widened in approval as he took stock of his surroundings.

"Well, isn't this convenient?" he said, clenching his teeth against a wave of pain. "A room with a view."

His own estate lay across the swathe of moonlit road on a wooded rise. Warm beams of candlelight glowed from the bedroom window, where he had been brutally stabbed to "death" three weeks ago. His uncle, Colonel Sir Edgar Williams, had already taken possession of the house, and if Dominic had access to a spyglass, he could have identified the shadowy figure behind the curtains.

The taunting silhouette belonged to a woman, he thought in cynical detachment. Of that he had no doubt. But whether she was the same lady who had shared his bed while he was callously being stabbed, he could not say. Nor did it matter now. That love affair belonged to a past life and had died along with his previous identity. He feelings for his former mistress were as dead as she believed him to be.

The clip-clop of approaching horses, the churning of carriage wheels on the road, interrupted his troubled reflections. Pray God whoever owned this trunk would not decide to explore her dressing closet tonight. For if he was any judge of women's underwear, and it so happened that he was, then the delicately proportioned owner of these garments would quite indelicately scream her head off when she discovered a ghost in her intimate garments.

Pillow Talk